CW00420887

09/17

www.edlc.co.uk

776 3021
956 2776
943 0780
777 3141

THE
FLOODING

DEATH IS JUST THE BEGINNING...

SEAN HANCOCK

You didn't come into this world.
You came out of it like a wave in the ocean.
You are not a stranger here.

—*Alan Watts*

For Simone and the family I know we'll have.

EAST DUNBARTONSHIRE LIBRARIES SERVICE

Class _F_

Barcode

Location _KIR_ Received _9·17_

Supplier _Amz_ Price _£7·99_

DYNIX BIB NO.

ONE

I'm about to open the front door of the Clark family home and walk into the night, to disappear, to start running, when something inside me asks, *What about them?* A crippling sadness and guilt accompanies the question, stopping me dead.

The less they know the better, I reply silently, reminding myself to keep focused. It's been only three days since the harrowing ordeal that was my Flooding, so it's no surprise I'm feeling so vulnerable and exposed. It will get easier, and I will grow stronger, but I have to be patient. I know because I have run this gauntlet many times before. I also know there is a great deal more pain and suffering to come, but that is a price I am willing to pay for the truth. The side effects of "Awakening" include paralyzing headaches and strength-sapping seizures, but it's the emotional instability I fear the most. After all, there is a hormonal teenage girl fighting for survival inside of me. Until she accepts the inevitable, my behavior and mood swings will be erratic and unpredictable.

While there is so much I remember, I don't have the complete picture yet. Indeed, I recall nothing of my life before this one—how I died, where I lived, who I was—it's just a huge black hole, and it's not the only one. I'm not overly concerned, though, as memory gaps are common during the early stages of transitioning, a phase notable for the intensity and frequency of side effects. Thankfully, it lasts only a few weeks, and eventually, answers will come in my dreams. But I can't sit around waiting for that to happen. And I am nothing if not resourceful. For millennia, I have been burying survival kits all over the world, each filled with valuables (precious metals where possible) and information. First and foremost, I try to list the people I have been (those I can recall), the men and women I have loved, and the enemies I have made, including those who hunt me now.

Toward the end of the nineteenth century, three cycles ago (if my calculations are correct) I lived in London. Again, it's patchy, but there's one thing I remember clearly: being outside at night during a powerful storm, on my knees, sobbing, digging . . . thrusting a small container into the ground, covering it with earth. Then being startled by a fork of lightning, seeing a gravestone in the sudden glare, reading the familiar name.

Getting my hands on whatever's inside that box should be all that matters. So why is the voice in my head saying, *But it will crush them. You know how much they love you.*

They love Rosa, and Rosa is a fantasy.

Rosa lives inside of you, I think. *They all do . . .*

"Not if they catch me," I whisper, but instead of leaving the house I grew up in—that Rosa grew up in, I mean—I put my backpack on the floor, turn to the hallway table, and grab the pen beside the notepad, pausing for a moment, thinking what a stupid idea this is, how it won't make a tiny bit of difference anyway, before writing:

> *Mum, Dad, Joe—when you read this I will be gone, and you will never see me again. I can't explain why but wanted you to know I'm alive and okay and there's nothing you did wrong. I realize you will never understand, and that this will cause you pain, but there really was no other way. I love you, and I am deeply sorry. Rosa xxx*

They will think this has something to do with the fact they adopted me as a one-year-old. Rosa's birth mother, who was second-generation Chinese, was a drug addict and a prostitute. It's a miracle the Clarks were willing to take me on, but I guess they were desperate, having failed to conceive a child of their own. But a few years later, they did exactly that. The result was my little brother, Joe.

At least they've got him. Their flesh and blood.

I put the pen down and glance up, catching myself in the hallway mirror, annoyed, but not surprised to see tears streaming down my latest face. My heart is pounding, my chest tightening. I remind myself that this is normal, that I've been here many times before. This isn't the me who has lived so many lives. This is just eighteen-year-old Rosa Clark from Exeter, desperately trying to work out what the hell is going on.

Half-Asian, half-white, Rosa has long, black hair and a small birthmark on her left cheek (a physical blemish that follows me from life to life). She's pretty, with hazel eyes, showing an epicanthic fold and a light dusting of freckles.

Right now, Rosa is having a panic attack. And who could blame her? She's slowly realizing she'll never see her mum, dad, or little brother ever again. More terrifying than that, she's wrestling with the idea that she doesn't really exist, that her whole life was just someone else's dream.

I want to tell her everything will be okay, that things will get better, but that would be a lie, and she'd know it. The truth is, it's all downhill from here for Rosa Clark. As with her family, she'll never see any friends again, including her ex-boyfriend Mike, whom she was thinking about taking back.

I have already thrown away her precious mobile, and soon I will shave her hair off. Clothes, makeup, the food she eats, all of it is going to change. Even her weak, skinny body will be pushed to its limits and transformed so that it can match and handle the skills of my consciousness, skills it has taken four thousand years to amass and hone.

My soul is female, and as such, I have always reincarnated as a woman. For the first part of each new life, I am ignorant of the truth. Then one day, without warning, the Flooding comes, and I remember so much. Like how deeply I love Ashkai, my master and soul mate of four thousand years. With each new cycle of life, we endeavor to find each other. Sometimes we succeed, but not always.

We have sworn enemies. Flooders who hunt us across the ages. They claim we have broken sacred laws and have sentenced us to annihilation, from which there is no coming back. That's why I can't let them find me. That's why I have to run.

Wherever you are, Ashkai, be safe and know that I am coming.

Across my many lives, I have witnessed civilizations rise and fall, fought in wars, and explored every inch of this majestic blue planet. I have been poor and rich, ugly and beautiful, weak and strong. I have died of old age, disease, and tragic accidents. I have been physically and sexually abused and even murdered. All of that is but a tiny fraction of what I have seen and experienced, and yet what have I amounted to? A scared, pathetic little girl who can't stop crying.

The ridiculousness of that makes me laugh, and almost instantly, I feel stronger and more focused. Seizing the moment, I grab my backpack, pull my hood up, and reach for the door. This time, no voice halts me, so I step outside, the cool October breeze sharp against my wet face. After using the sleeves of my jacket to wipe the tears away, I check my watch and immediately break into a jog.

The night bus to London leaves soon.

I need to be on it.

***

Ten minutes later, at 1:02 a.m., with just three minutes to spare, I arrive at Exeter's outdoor coach station with my hood down, huffing and puffing because I ran all the way, reflecting on how I need to get this body into shape as quickly as possible. There are some local red buses parked for the night and a few guys wearing fluorescent vests milling around. One of them is telling a group of alcoholics to move on, but only gets a "go fuck yourself" as a response.

There are a handful of people at the other end of the depot with bags at their feet. I figure they must be waiting for the bus to London, so I head that way. As well as being out of breath, I can feel a dull ache in my head, which could be a seizure brewing, and I am considering what I'll do if that's the case when I hear, "Oi, you . . . you over there . . . hey, lassie, I wanna ask you somethin', lassie, just a quick question, won't take a second . . ."

I glance left and see it's one of the alcoholics, special brew in hand, trying to get my attention. He's a disheveled, dark-haired

4

Scot with a shaggy beard and hunched shoulders, fortyish. I ignore him and keep going. I even veer right, detouring behind the parked buses, to avoid getting too close. It's not that I'm scared; I just want to stay out of trouble and blend in as much as possible. That's easier said than done as a pretty eighteen-year-old girl walking the streets late at night, but I do what I can.

"Hey, missy!" he shouts, even though there are vehicles between us now. There's venom creeping into his tone. "Hey . . . oi . . . you deaf or what . . . rude bitch, think yer better than me, do yer? All I wanted was ta ask ye a question . . ."

He gives up after that, and a few seconds later, I reach the small group waiting to leave town, and my breathing is pretty much back to normal. Closest to me is a guy about Rosa's age with messy, dark hair, which he's running his fingers through, revealing a shaved undercut. His eyes are blue and piercing, and he's wearing jeans and an old, black jumper that has seen better days. The next thing I notice is the birthmark on his neck. It's about three inches long and a centimeter thick. Blemishes of this kind are often the physical echoes of a violent death that concluded a previous incarnation. The one on my left cheek, which looks like a dark-red flame, has been with me since the first life I remember, and I have no idea why.

"Do you know what's happening with the bus?" I ask.

We make eye contact, and for a split second, I feel like we've met before. I wonder if he goes to my college as he gestures toward a raised screen, saying, "Running ten minutes late, according to that." He sounds like he went to private school.

"Oh yeah," I reply, glancing at the monitor that I'd missed. "Thanks."

"You're welcome," he says with a smile that makes me feel good. "Ten quid a ticket means they don't care what we think."

"We haven't met, have we?" I ask.

After a pause, he says, "I don't think so."

"You from Exeter?"

"No, London. Been visiting family."

"My mistake," I say, letting go of the notion.

"Guess I have one of those faces." He says it with that smile I like.

The ache in my skull is intensifying, so I decide to head for the station toilets, which are down the stairs over to my left. I don't want anyone to see me freaking out if it comes to that.

"Just gonna use the bathroom," I say, smiling back, noticing he's wearing a touch of eyeliner, wondering if that means he's being himself or still trying to find himself, and guessing it's probably a bit of both. "Will you let me know if the bus arrives?"

He turns to his right as if he heard or saw something unnerving, then looks back at me. "Sure, yeah, no problem."

I glance to where he'd been looking to see what distracted him, but there's nothing.

Still carrying my backpack, I hurry to the toilet, which is all white tiles, bright lights, and bad smells. After making sure there's nobody else in here, I position myself over the middle of three chrome sinks and place my bag on the floor. I run the cold tap and splash water on my face. I also close my eyes and breathe deeply. If things go bad, I'll lock myself in one of the cubicles, bite down on the wooden spoon I packed before leaving the house, and pray the seizure runs its course before the bus leaves.

After another minute or so of meditative breathing, eyes still closed, I start feeling a little better. Relieved, I lean forward for one last splash of water and then straighten, opening my eyes at the same time, facing the mirror. I nearly jump out of my skin when I see a bearded man standing directly behind me, his back to the cubicles. I go to spin, but he's on me in a flash, his left arm across the top part of my chest and shoulders, pulling me in; his right is holding a knife to my throat. The guy is a few inches taller than me, and he says in a gravelly Scottish accent, "Scream, 'n I'll slit your throat."

His breath stinks of halitosis mixed with alcohol and cigarettes. His dirty black beard, thick, matted, and coarse, feels like a Brillo Pad against my left cheek.

"I was only gonna ask if ye fancied a drink, but ye were too good for that, walkin' round me like I was a dog shite or somethin'. Well now I've got another question for ye: which hole do ye want my cock in first?"

While this situation is not without jeopardy, now that the initial shock has passed, I'm relatively calm and focused; after all, in terms of remembered life experience, I'm dealing with a child. This is not the first time I've had a knife to my throat or had someone try to rape me. I think about pretending to be scared to give him a false sense of security, but then I decide on another tactic that will achieve the same effect with a little more cruelty. I get a sexy look going as I say, "You don't have to be so mean; I was counting on you following me in here . . ." Slowly reaching for his penis with my right hand, I continue with, "And in answer to your question"—I pause to lick my lips—"definitely mouth."

He looks at me in the mirror as if I've just turned into a mermaid. My eyes are conveying the false message that I want nothing more than to be screwed senseless, giving him what I know deep down he yearns for, to be wanted. Desperate to believe I'm for real—that after years of rejection and self-loathing, he might not be totally repellent—his body softens just slightly, the knife edging away from my throat by an inch.

That's when I explode into action, bringing both hands up to grab his knife arm, jerking it away from my throat as I simultaneously roll my upper body left and downward, my head squeezing under his shoulder, taking his arm with me, twisting it around until he drops the blade. I keep the move going, as I manipulate his wrist, until I hear a satisfying snapping sound, his hand going floppy as I release my grip. The maneuver has put me behind my attacker, so I kick the back of his right knee out, stepping forward as he falls, using the momentum to smash his head into one of the chrome sinks with an encouraging swing of my left hand. This knocks him out cold before he has a chance to make any noise.

This new body I'm wearing may be weak and untested, but combat is principally technique, and I've had a lot of practice. I also despise souls who seek to impose themselves on others, whatever their story.

I step over the unconscious Scot and grab my bag. Before leaving, I check the mirror to make sure I don't look like I've been in a fight. Unsurprisingly, my face is flushed and sweaty, and my hair is a mess. While sorting it all out, I notice my heart is pounding like crazy, and I realize I must have been more scared than I thought. Then I realize it was more likely Rosa Clark having another of her moments, and I wonder if that's the reason my headache is back in a big way.

I dry off with some paper towels and hurry out, bumping into Eyeliner at the bottom of the stairs. He's smiling at me. "Hard as it is to believe, our chariot awaits."

I try my best to look relaxed. "Great," I say, feeling a sudden and excruciating shooting pain in my right temple as I lead the way back, aware that no amount of breathing is going to help this time. I need to get on the bus quickly.

Rudely distancing myself from Eyeliner so he doesn't think he's got a travel buddy, I show the driver my ticket, which I bought yesterday, and head straight to the back, huddling in the far left corner, relieved there's nobody within a few rows and that it's dark. As calmly as possible—my head throbbing, flecks of white light moving in—I unzip my bag and pull out the wooden spoon. Dizzy now, hands trembling, I get on the floor and wedge my knees against the back of the chair in front. Knowing I've only got seconds, I place the handle between my teeth, and in that moment as I bite down, the world goes a searing, blinding white.

TWO

I'm lying on my side, leaning on an elbow, totally naked, skin glistening with a mixture of oil, sweat, and sex. I'm smiling and happy, wondering how many other slaves are as blessed as I am, knowing the answer is none. The hard stone floor beneath me has been made soft and comfortable by thick layers of animal skins and aromatic rushes. The distant ceiling is so far away I can barely make it out in the flickering candlelight.

The balcony doors, ten paces to my left, are wide open, letting in the sounds of the night, which, as always, are dominated by the relentless and strident hum of cicadas. Coming in with the warm breeze are the fragrances of worship: hints of frankincense, myrrh, and other offerings to Anuket, goddess of the Nile, and Khonsu, god of the moon, who right now is riding the sky in all his glory, rivaling his brother Aten's magnificence.

During the day, the veranda offers breathtaking views across the Nile and of Thebes, a city owned and ruled by my benevolent and wise master Ashkai, who sits opposite me, his legs crossed in that strange way he favors, back upright but leaning forward slightly. He pours the pungent blue lotus tea he has been preparing, something usually only imbibed by priests and sorcerers. He is neither, although he is able to do things nobody else can.

Ashkai, like me, is naked, his long locks (dark except for one thick strand of gray starting in the center of his forehead) hanging freely, tickling his broad, muscular, battle-scarred shoulders. My hair has been cut short, save for a few long tufts of curls, as is the fashion for Nubian women, especially if they are slaves and their duty is to look beautiful and give pleasure to their owners, as mine is.

My master, who hates it when I call him such, who treats me as an equal, ignoring the protestations of those who serve and advise him, fills a second clay chalice—there is nothing grand or glamorous about this ritual—and asks me to sit upright, which I do, pulling one of the animal skins over my small, delicate shoulders. I'm mimicking his posture now, one he has trained me in during the many hours we have rested in silent contemplation these past months.

I know what's about to happen. We have been building to this ceremony for a very long time, preparing my mind for the journey ahead. I remember the night when I had absorbed the idea that he would "awaken" me.

Unsurprisingly, I had a lot of questions.

"How long have I been sleeping?" I asked.

"You have been sleeping all of your seventeen years, and many more." That was exactly a year ago.

"What if I am enjoying the dream?"

"The dream imprisons you."

"Of all the people in the world, why have you chosen to set me free?"

"Because you are special."

"But I am just a slave."

"That is nothing more than a label. Don't identify with it."

"Who am I then?"

"That is what we will find out."

Now he picks up one of the cups and offers it to me. I peer down at the brown liquid and realize something.

"I am afraid."

"Of what?"

"Letting you down."

Ashkai smiles, his kind and perceptive eyes giving me all the reassurance I need.

As I'm readying to drink, there's a bright flash, then darkness, followed by a violent and disorienting propulsion through space, as if I'm attached to a shooting star. And just like that, I am somewhere else, distilled to my very essence now, an ethereal ball of consciousness floating down a long, dark hallway, gliding past a door with a number on it: 4320.

What's in there? I think, but then my attention is drawn to the awe-inspiring beauty in the far distance, knowing where I am

10

now: the world between worlds.

I'm trying to remember how I died and came to be here, in this majestic theater of energy and color, but at the same time, I'm acutely aware of my need to focus and prepare for the ordeal ahead.

Thank you, master, for showing me the true path, I think, but then it dawns on me something is not quite right, and almost immediately, I hear a voice say, in a language I don't recognize but somehow understand, "Hey, time to wake up, we're almost there . . ."

Things slow down and I open my eyes. Everything is muggy and dim, and I'm not sure where, or what I am . . .

"Master, is that you?"

I hear laughter. "I've been called a lot of things in my time, but that's a first."

I begin to come to my senses, finding myself in a human body . . . the material realm, then . . . lying on . . . ah yes, the back seat of the National Express bus, bunched up on my side, face nuzzled into the corner. I roll over, noticing I have been covered with a blanket, and see Eyeliner looking down on me from the next row of seats.

Did he witness me having a fit?

"Had me worried," he says. "Thought you were dead at one point until you started speaking. What language was that?"

"Where are we?" I ask. I look at my watch: 5:53 a.m. Over four hours since we left Exeter.

"Victoria, close to the station. Thought I'd better wake you, hope that's okay?"

I sit up and tidy my hair, saying, "thanks," following up with, "this yours?" as I lift the blanket. It's still dark outside, the only light coming from a few weak bulbs above the seats.

"I do this journey a lot, so it comes in handy."

I give it back. "That was kind of you."

"It was nothing. Looked like you needed it more than me, so glad to be of help."

"How'd you mean?"

He throws the blanket on top of his bag, which is on the adjacent seat across the aisle.

11

"I got up to use the toilet about an hour in and saw your feet sticking out on the floor"—he points down—"just there. Thought maybe you'd been drinking. You were really cold as well."

"How'd I get up here?"

"I lifted you." He smiles. "You're heavier than you look."

"Or you're not as strong as you think," I say, and watch as his handsome face lights up. That's when it occurs to me he's flirting.

"That's no way to speak to your master," he says, which I have to admit is pretty funny. Eyeliner is coming across as a guy who doesn't take life too seriously. While I know it's just the top, protective layer of his personality, a mask for the vulnerability below, it's exactly the kind of energy I need right now.

The bus pulls into Victoria Station, and as we stand, he says, nodding toward the seat beside me, "Not sure if that's yours, found it on the floor when I picked you up."

I look down and see my wooden spoon. Out of nowhere, the number 4320 flashes in front of my eyes. It reminds me of the hallway and door I saw in my dream, both of which were strangely familiar, although I can't put my finger on why.

"Thanks," I say, shoving it in a side pocket of my bag.

"What's it for?"

Because I don't have any energy to expend on lies, I say, "For biting on when I have an epileptic fit, stops me chewing my tongue off."

"You're messing with me, right?"

I swing my bag over a shoulder. "Mind stepping aside? I'd like to get off this bus before it takes me back to Exeter."

"Shit, sorry," he says, grabbing his bag and blanket, letting me pass. He follows behind, asking if I'm heading to the tube, and he says that he can carry my bag if I need a hand.

As we step off the bus, I glance at my watch and remember that Rosa's parents will be up soon, and they'll start phoning friends and raising the alarm. The thought of how desolate and scared they'll feel makes me deeply sad, and for a moment, I'm on the verge of tears. Well, Rosa is. I realize what I need to do can wait a few hours; the last thing I want is to be alone right now, especially as I'm tired, hungry, and cold.

That's why I turn to Eyeliner and say, "What's your name?"

His eyes go shifty for a split second. "George."

I'm about to challenge him and ask why he'd lie about something so silly, but decide against it. "Who cuts your hair?"

After a confused narrowing of the eyes, he says, "I do . . . obviously, have you seen the state of it?"

I keep a straight face. "What with?"

He sweeps his hair back. "Um . . . scissors . . ."

"What about the shaved bit?"

His hand goes to his undercut. "Use clippers for that."

"Where are they?"

"My place."

"Where's that?"

"Archway, North London."

That's very close to where I'm heading, and experience has taught me there's no such thing as coincidence.

"Who d'ya live with?" I ask.

"Few mates."

"Have a girlfriend?"

"Not at the moment."

"What does that mean?"

"Recently split with someone."

"She live with you?"

"No way, was only seeing her for a couple months. This conversation's a bit intense for six in the morning, don't you think?"

Ignoring his question, I say, "The last thing I need is an angry girl screaming at me when we get to yours."

He raises an eyebrow. "You coming to mine?"

"Considering it."

A knowing, goofy smile takes over his face.

"Never gonna happen," I say, my eyes emphasizing the truth of the statement. "I just want to borrow your clippers, maybe get a bite to eat. You try anything, I'm gone, understood?"

He comes over, all innocent and jokey. "The same goes for you. It may seem unlikely right now, but the more you get to know me, the more irresistible I get. So when the urge comes, I need you to keep your hands to yourself. Deal?"

I try to suppress my smile but only partially succeed. "Which way we heading?"

"Follow me," Eyeliner says, already walking when he adds, "What's your name?"

The answer I give sounds cocky. "I haven't decided yet."

But it's also the truth.

THREE

"That's extreme," Eyeliner says as I enter his bedroom holding the clippers he lent me when we arrived at his student house half an hour ago. After washing some toast down with a cup of tea, I headed to the bathroom to give myself a very short haircut. I'm wearing just a T-shirt and jeans now. My jacket, hoodie, and bag are on the floor by the chest of drawers. Eyeliner continues, "You lose a bet or something?"

Feeling drained and not at all in the mood for this guy's seemingly never-ending banter, I hold the clippers up and say, "Where do these go?"

Still awed by my new, army-inspired look, he replies, "Just leave them on the desk," which is easier said than done, as the desk is a mess of papers, books, empty Red Bull cans, plates, an iMac computer, a scooter helmet, keys, and an "I Love London" mug. The rest of the room is slightly less shambolic, but that's only because he did a quick tidy while I was in the bathroom.

Seeing me about to lose patience, he steps across and clears a space, nervously pocketing a container of pills that had previously been concealed behind a stack of books.

What's he trying to hide? I wonder.

"Had a deadline on an essay," Eyeliner says, "so haven't had a chance to tidy up. Grades first and all that." Then, still captivated by my new appearance, he adds, "I'm not just saying this, but it actually suits you. Don't get me wrong, you looked good with long hair, like really good, but this is . . . well, sort of crazy, yeah, but I dunno . . . unique . . . brings out your freckles, which are super cute by the way. You mind if I touch it . . . your head, I mean?"

I let out a loud, tired sigh. "George, I appreciate everything you've done for me; you're obviously a nice guy, but could we try coexisting in silence for a while? Actually, I should just go . . ."

By the time I've grabbed my stuff, he's standing in front

of the door, palms raised, saying, "I'm sorry . . . weird, shaved-head girl . . . I talk a lot when I'm nervous and make lame jokes, it's like a tic, that's why I'm being such an idiot . . . You look knackered . . . not in a bad way, you just . . ." He pauses, obviously getting frustrated with himself. "How about I leave you alone so you can rest? I've got stuff I can do downstairs, how's that sound?"

Awesome. I'm too tired to go anywhere, and some alone time, without actually being alone, is exactly what I need. Besides, Eyeliner's not so bad; he's just struggling with what has been a very strange morning.

Deciding to cut him some slack and stop being a bitch, I relax a little and say, "It's Sam."

"Huh?"

"My name. It's Sam. As much as I like 'weird, shaved-head girl,' it's a bit of a mouthful."

He smiles, and there's genuine kindness in it. I wonder for a moment about his previous lives and if our paths might have crossed at any point, if that's why I thought I recognized him at the bus station. I've been around a long time, and souls, especially ones with interconnected karmas, often reincarnate together, so it's possible.

"Good to meet you, Sam. You need anything, more food, a cup of tea, a wooden spoon . . . ?"

I roll my eyes, just messing, though, and he says, "I'm doing it again, aren't I? Wow, you must think I'm special needs."

By the time the door closes, I'm smiling, and my smile holds as I put my belongings on the floor, pull my boots off, and curl up on the bed, noticing how weightless and textured my head feels against the white cotton sheets and how the pillow smells of Eyeliner. I find both things strangely comforting as I drift off, ready for the dream I know is coming, hoping to find answers in it.

Before long, trails of luminous, pulsating color begin taking shape in my mind's eye, their paths crossing in the darkness like comets, another glimpse of the world between worlds, the place from which my Flooding came.

Amid this cosmic spectacle of energy and light, I hear a deep male voice saying, "Samsara, they have found us. We must go."

16

There's a white flash, hot as the sun, followed by the familiar and irresistible pull of a human body. I open my eyes, gasping for breath, and see Ashkai standing over me, no longer the ruler of Thebes but instead a broad-shouldered African American wearing shorts and a T-shirt. The only physical constant, as my birthmark is to me, is that thick wedge of gray in the center of his hairline.

The sky is clear, save for a few wisps of cloud, and I can feel dry, haylike grass underneath my bare, sweaty arms and legs. I realize where we are now: Central Park, New York. We've been staying in my master's nearby apartment and coming here every morning, pushing our latest bodies to their limits, sharpening senses, honing skills, getting ready.

Even though I'm pretty certain of the answer, I ask, "Shadow or Chamber?"

"Chamber," Ashkai replies, confirming my suspicion.

The Chamber of Infinites (what a self-important and arrogant name they have given themselves) has been chasing us across the ages and will stop at nothing. Their leader is a female entity known as Meta, and she regards us as outlaws. If captured, we would be taken to a secret location, where we would be heavily drugged until we are comatose. They keep prisoners alive in this state (known as "Long Sleep") for hundreds of years, damaging the souls inside so badly they forget the art of reincarnation, which is, of course, the point.

"Could have been worse," I mutter, referring to The Shadow, an ancient cult of pure, unadulterated evil. As practitioners of the dark arts, they dispatch their enemies in the most heinous of ways, feeding their souls to dark and malevolent scavenger entities. Known as the *Decimatio*—or True Death—those scavengers end a person's story once and for all.

I have never encountered any members of The Shadow and know them only by reputation. For obvious reasons, I'd like to keep it that way.

I get no reply from my master, so I ask, "Where are they?" prompting him to lower his head and close his eyes.

After two slow, deep breaths, he says, "Close, and they are many."

I am twenty-one years old (in this life at least), and so is Ashkai.

If he dies first in any given cycle, I kill myself so that we can always be together. He does the same when the tables are turned. I had a lot of trouble with this the first few times—bodies have an annoying tendency to cling to life, even when the soul knows there's another one coming—but I got used to it. Although, I must say, it's never easy being reborn in a new place with new parents being a helpless, oblivious infant. And some parents are not as loving as one might wish . . .

"We can forget about the Natural History Museum," I say. It's on the other side of the park and just happens to be Ashkai's favorite place in the city. After our workout, the plan was to head over there, grab lunch, and check out the new exhibition on human origins. It would have been our third visit this month.

Knowing we'll be running soon, I stretch forward to lengthen my hamstrings, glad to be wearing shorts and a sports vest. "How have they found us? We haven't even started yet."

Ashkai opens his eyes. "Our enemies grow stronger and more powerful with every day that passes."

I straighten and begin rotating my upper body, thinking, *Not as strong or powerful as you,* but saying, "What about the apartment?"

Emanating peace and calm as always, Ashkai looks at me and uses telepathy to say, *Do not underestimate the challenge we are facing.*

I smile and shake my head. Then I also use thought-speak—which all humans are capable of; it just takes a great deal of effort and training to develop—to say, *Sorry, Master.*

Speaking aloud, Ashkai says, "Are you ever going to stop calling me that?" The edges of a smile are there along with a raised eyebrow, his easy sense of humor never far away. Before I can answer, he moves on: "The apartment is too dangerous; we can never return to it. We must lose them in the city."

I'm about to ask why we weren't warned—Ashkai has a spy on the inside (a member of the Chamber, no less), an ancient soul sympathetic to our cause—but I can sense now is not the time. As I'm thinking about that, an image of a pale-skinned man standing in a snowstorm fills my mind, his colorless eyes trying to tell me something, but it's no more than a flash frame. I think there was a woman standing next to him, but I can't be sure . . .

18

We break into a jog, passing a large, muddy pond. As we're leaving the park on the corner of Fifty-Ninth Street and Fifth Avenue, Ashkai says, "Ten o'clock," and my eyes go there, finding a man and woman on foot, weaving through traffic toward us. Somewhere on their bodies will be a tattoo of either a phoenix, a fish, or a lotus flower. Phoenixes represent the lowest order of agents—rookies, so to speak—who do not pose a huge threat unless their numbers are overwhelming. Fish are more experienced and formidable, but again, one on one, I would always bet on myself. Lotus flowers are a different challenge altogether. They have achieved enlightenment and, as such, are not bound by the laws of nature, something that makes them extremely dangerous.

While thought-speak is a skill I'm getting better at, I can only exchange with those I have a connection with. Tuning into a conversation between strangers in the middle of a huge, bustling city while running for my life is well beyond what I'm capable of. The same doesn't apply to Ashkai, which is not surprising when considering his soul has been in existence since long ago and that he once spent fifty-two consecutive cycles in deep, isolated meditation. In fact, my master is so old that he has reincarnated on every one of the seven inhabitable planets. So far, Earth has been my only home.

"I can't hear them," Ashkai says. "I can feel their energy, but I can't break through."

We're jogging still, heading south on Fifth Avenue past the Grand Plaza, avoiding the flow of Saturday morning pedestrians *(how little they know!)* by hugging the edge of the sidewalk closest to the road, sun beating down on our backs, needing to get in among the taller buildings ahead, where it will be easier to vanish.

"What's the problem?"

"I don't know," he replies. "But it's as if something is keeping me out."

After a few blocks, Meta on my mind, we see four Flooders waiting to intercept us. To avoid them, we break down Fifty-Sixth Street, heading west, shaded by the looming architecture of the city, a selection of national flags fluttering in the breeze above our heads. The hot smells of rotting food and exhaust fumes agitate our lungs. Thirty seconds on, we see more agents, so we head down a narrow, garbage-infested alley, only to be cut off at the other end as well, forcing us to stop in our tracks.

There are so many, I think. *Too many to fight*, but before my doubts have time to become fears, I hear Ashkai's thought-voice reminding me that every problem has a solution and that to find it, we must stay calm, present, and connected.

More than anything, he continues, *we must embrace what's happening as if we chose it ourselves.*

A tall, wiry, Middle-Eastern–looking man wearing a badly stained apron appears from a door to our left. He's standing next to a row of large trash bins and is about to light a cigarette when he notices what's going on, first looking left at the Flooders approaching from the west, then at those coming from the east, and finally at the two of us.

"Step aside," I say. "Now." He does, just in time, allowing us to sprint through the door into a busy, hot, working kitchen that smells of spices and burned onions, with pop music blaring out of a radio. A large woman holding a knife shouts obscenities as we crash into her restaurant and race past the diners. I catch a glimpse of my lean, honed body in the mirrored wall, the outer shell of twenty-one-year-old Suzi Aarons from Los Angeles, the rich Jewish girl who vanished into thin air three years ago. She was overweight and shy back then, but a lot has changed.

Out on the street, we come face-to-face with two more agents. They try their best to stop us, but their best isn't good enough, and we leave them nursing broken limbs as we race on, taking detours when we have to—*my god, they're everywhere*—but mainly heading south. Then, after what must be ten minutes of hard running, Ashkai guides me into the sea of people, offices, and shops that make up Rockefeller Center.

"This way," he says, the two of us slowing to a brisk walk, trying to blend in, our breathing almost back to normal as we approach the GE Building, the art deco skyscraper that wouldn't look out of place in a Batman movie.

We enter the air-conditioned lobby, which is grand and spacious with marble floors, thick pillars, and a high, painted ceiling complemented by ornate, richly colored walls. I presume we're going to exit on the other side, maybe slip into another building, when Ashkai approaches a security guard and whispers in his ear. At first, the man flinches, but then he visibly relaxes, smiles even, and that's when I know my master is more concerned for our safety than he is letting on.

As the guard opens one of the mechanical gates, giving us access to the elevators, I ask Ashkai, in an urgent whisper, why he used his powers to manipulate and control a Sleeper (our term for souls who do not remember past lives), especially as it's something he routinely forbids.

Does he really think they're going to catch us?

Before he can answer, I hear my name whispered, the voice quiet and otherworldly, hitting me from all directions. Instinct forces me to stop and turn, and before I know it, I'm looking at the only person in the world I truly hate: Meta. I know for certain it's her, even though this is our first and only encounter. My sworn enemy, who in this life can't be more than eleven years old, stares into me, her eyes ablaze with an indigo fire. I'm mesmerized by her energy and power, and find myself edging nearer, as if the floor beneath is carrying me forward.

She says, "Hello, Samsara," and I feel deeply loved and safe. Part of me knows this is a trap, but I'm unable to resist.

"Hello," I reply, gliding, floating, and that's when Ashkai appears and shoves me into an elevator, bringing me back to the here and now. I watch him press the button for the fiftieth floor and then feel his hand reach for mine, the two of us crammed in the corner now, his grip warm and gentle. He looks into my eyes, projecting love, compassion, and strength.

I'm about to tell him what happened, how she so easily had me in her grasp, when he says, "Not everything is as it seems."

When we eventually get off the elevator, we find ourselves in NBC's offices, which are busy despite it being the weekend. Instead of turning right with everyone else, Ashkai hangs left, and as I'm trying to keep pace, a walled fire alarm shatters, seemingly unaided. A loud, persistent noise kicks in, accompanied by an automated female voice saying, "Fire. Please leave the building

ED LEISURE+CULTURE

immediately," over and over. I can't help but smile at my master's ingenuity. After all, there must be thousands of Sleepers in this skyscraper, all of whom are about to accompany us outside.

But will that be enough to hide us from her?

We're among the first to enter what looks like a seldom-used stairwell, but we are only two flights down when we spot three Flooders coming the other way, tranquilizer guns at the ready. The agent in front has a lotus flower tattoo on his neck. We turn back, but it's slowgoing, as civilians are gushing in, some of them pointing out how we're heading in the wrong direction and we should forget our personal belongings, better safe than sorry. Ignoring them, we reenter the fiftieth floor, only to be met by more Flooders spilling out of the elevator.

"With me," Ashkai says, and moments later, we're back in the crowded stairwell, going up again. After two flights, Ashkai starts shouting that a bomb is about to explode. The resulting panic further inconveniences our pursuers as we duck into a service corridor that takes us through to an adjoining section of the building. The next door we encounter requires a swift, hard kick from Ashkai. A few seconds later, we find ourselves outside, on a section of roof about the size of three basketball courts, most of the space occupied by satellite dishes and air-conditioning units. It quickly becomes clear there's nowhere to go, just more skyscrapers to the north and west—we're on a section that juts out slightly—and only the distant streets via the south and east.

I turn to my master, only to be confronted by his back, my stomach sinking as the penny drops. "You intend for us to jump, don't you?"

Instead of answering, Ashkai raises his palms, using them to help channel his will, which, at this moment, is to rip up satellite dishes, air-conditioning units, and anything else available, creating a makeshift barricade in front of the door, an obstacle that will buy us a few minutes at most.

With metal tearing from concrete, Ashkai glances over his shoulder and says, "First we must prepare for death."

"Prepare for suicide, you mean."

"Suicide is letting them take us alive." Goddamn it. I like this life. I like being an adult. I like knowing who I am.

"We can fight."

"Their numbers are too many, and they are armed."

"What happened to there always being a solution to every problem?"

"Sometimes the solution is also the last resort."

"I refuse to believe that."

Ashkai turns his gaze to the door again, palms aloft, remaining silent and focused until the job is done. Then he walks over to me.

"Samsara, the only thing that matters is how you choose to die. Everything else is a distraction. You must not cross over feeling angry or afraid. Feel your breath, clear your mind, repeat the mantras, and know we will be together again soon . . ."

He's interrupted by the sound of our enemies attempting to force the door open. Almost immediately, they give up, but soon afterward, sections of the makeshift barricade begin floating away. Ashkai reaches behind with his right hand, palm facing the door now, sending counter energy to hold everything in place.

"We don't have much time. Travel bravely and with an open heart and know that I will see you very soon."

He kisses me gently, then looks into my eyes and uses thought-speak to say, *Be thankful, journey well, and blessed be your next life.*

I nod, giving in to the inevitable, and watch as my master turns to focus his full attention on keeping the door closed, all so I can prepare and make ready. As soon as I jump, Ashkai will follow, the duration of the fall providing all the time he needs to find peace.

I reflect on the fact that neither of us is carrying our cyanide pill. We have them for emergencies such as this but have gotten out of the habit over the years. It's been a long time since we've had to use them.

I walk away and lift myself onto the lip of the building, staring east across the New York skyline, Roosevelt Island in the distance, then glance below at the distant streets busy with yellow cabs and people. I close my eyes and breathe deeply, summoning the death mantra, repeating the ancient words over and over.

Soon, I hear Ashkai's voice in my head. "You are ready."

I respond with, "As it ends, so it begins," a traditional farewell among my people, a phrase that embodies the cyclical, balanced nature of all things, a solemn promise to see that soul again.

Bending my knees, about to leap, I'm hit by a strong gust of wind. Then comes the sound of propellers and I'm overcome by dread. I open my eyes and turn just as a helicopter appears on my left; it had been previously shielded by the southern face of the skyscraper. There's a single sniper leaning through its open door. He's wearing a baseball cap and sunglasses, and has a strangely pale complexion. My master has currently got his back to me. His side is facing them. I open my mouth to scream a warning, but it's too late . . .

Even though he has drug-filled darts sticking out of his left side and two in his jugular, Ashkai is still able to push the helicopter away with a thrust of his hand. The pilot struggles to regain control as my master spins to face me. After a beat, he falls to his knees. The barricade dismantles in an instant, allowing Flooders to pour through the door like a swarm of ants. I'm about to run to Ashkai's side and fight with everything I have when he looks up and raises a palm in my direction.

"Don't do it," I shout as a pulse of energy hits the center of my chest like a huge, powerful wave, sending me flying off the building's edge.

My arms start flailing, hands grabbing thin air, as fear, anger, and bitterness engulf me. I use my mind to project it all at Ashkai, wanting him to know how scared and alone I feel. I'm terrified of how badly I'm going to die and that I'll be lost in the spirit realm for eons. What he did was wrong.

We are a team; we should have been side by side. What sort of ending is this?

I hear his thought-voice, still calm, still peaceful, saying, *Samsara, as it ends, so it begins. By freeing you, I have planted the seed for my own liberation. You will die. You will be reborn. And when you have your Flooding, I have no doubt you will find me.*

And just like that, the dark, angry fog dissipates, and I become instantly aware—*such clarity!*—of how selfish I am being. After all, Ashkai is the one who has been captured, the one facing the unspeakable terror of the Long Sleep. For the first time in our

24

history, *he's* relying on me, *he's* scared, *he's* exposed, and all I have been thinking about is myself.

My heart fills with love and compassion, determination and hope. For the second time today, I use telepathy to apologize to my master, adding, *I will find you.*

I don't expect a reply, but I get one—briefly—as Ashkai tries to tell me something about the spirit realm, how I must go there after my Flooding. But I'm forced to tune him out; death is demanding my full attention. I twist my body so that I'm facing the streets of New York. In doing so, I spot something utterly bewildering. There's a bed on the sidewalk directly below me, and there's a girl asleep on it.

Thinking how familiar she looks, I shout, "Wake up! Get out the way!" Before I've even finished the sentence, it dawns on me what's happening . . . that I'm Rosa Clark now, I'm asleep on Eyeliner's bed, and I've been reliving the final moments of my last passing. I'm trying to remember if I died well, and if not, how long I was trapped in the world between worlds and how many days, months, or years elapsed before I found a new body, the same one I'm about to smash into. But more important than that, I want to know if I have made any progress tracking Ashkai down.

And if not, what the hell am I doing sleeping?

FOUR

I'm already upright in Eyeliner's bed when my eyes snap open, T-shirt soaked through with sweat, my breathing heavy and labored, mind swirling and confused. Still seeing Ashkai on his knees, I leap to my feet and hurry to the desk tucked between the bay windows. I fire up the iMac. Diffused sunlight seeps through the cheap, white blinds, giving the room a hazy, golden hue.

I clench my jaw with frustration as the computer takes an age to boot, remembering Meta's eyes, her awesome, terrifying power. The screen becomes a black Harley Davidson straddled by a blonde wearing red heels and a white bikini. The big smile on her face provides a stark contrast to how I'm feeling. I go online and search for *suzi aarons new york suicide*, press enter, and then check my watch: 10:42 a.m., which means I had just over three hours sleep.

I click the top link. It takes me to a *Huffington Post* article from 2012, the journalist exploring why, in the United States, more men than women choose to end their lives jumping off skyscrapers, particularly in the Big Apple. The lady speculates about the data and then points out there are exceptions, like twenty-one-year-old Suzi Aarons from Los Angeles, who'd been missing for three years before she leaped to her death from the GE Building. The date was September 3, 1998.

I lean back and start doing calculations, beginning with Rosa Clark's birth: September 25, 1999. My consciousness would have entered her fetus forty-nine days after conception, which is when the brain's pineal gland forms, the portal through which spirits are able to access the physical plane. No doubt I beat out countless other souls vying for the unborn avatar. It may seem like there are plenty of babies born on Earth, but there are even more souls awaiting birth.

I only lost four and a half months; I did pretty well, considering. A person's state of consciousness at the moment of death, positive or negative, is amplified a thousandfold by the spirit realm, so to arrive there carrying anger, fear, and bitterness (as so many do) is to sentence him- or herself to an ordeal of indescribable horror, one that can take many Earth years to conquer and overcome.

The Chamber of Infinites has been hunting Ashkai for thousands of years because he refuses to adhere to their stupid, archaic, stifling laws. They are so out of touch that they won't do anything without consulting their oracles: seven individuals who, it is claimed, can predict the future. But they are often wrong, and the reason is simple: nothing is fixed or certain, especially fate.

Ashkai believes the world is ready for the truth, needs it, and that individual souls have the right to make their own choices and be given the opportunity to develop, learn, and grow.

What's so wrong with that?

Plenty, according to the Chamber of Infinites. They claim it's dangerous and counter to the laws of the universe to accelerate the evolution of souls. How can that be when the vast majority of our initiates have benefited immeasurably, thanking us for opening their eyes, and going on to contribute positively and lovingly to the human experience?

The truth is this: the Chamber of Infinites—made up of forty-nine elders and chaired by Meta, their de facto leader—is just another bureaucracy invested in the status quo, concerned solely with its own survival. They are the guardians of all the power and knowledge amassed by Flooders over the ages, and they don't want to give any of it up. They're content to leave the less fortunate in a state of ignorance, suffering, and spiritual inertia, arguing that's just the way it is.

While working myself up, a truly horrifying reality begins to take shape: *What if it's already too late?*

What if instead of sentencing Ashkai to the Long Sleep (from which he can be awakened), Meta condemned him to the *Decimatio*? I quickly remind myself that the Chamber of Infinites—unlike The Shadow—is an official organization bound by ancient laws and customs. The *Decimatio* is black magic and only employed by those who serve "The Demiurge," my people's term for the heavy accumulation of negative energy built up over hundreds of thousands of years, energy that has become conscious, energy that seeks to corrupt, destroy, and terrorize. The Chamber are misguided and deluded, but they aren't *that* bad; at least I hope they're not.

Needing a plan, I look around for inspiration. My gaze eventually settles on the "I Love London" mug beside the keyboard. It's half filled with cold, gray coffee. I could do with a hit of caffeine right now and am about to give Eyeliner a shout when the dark liquid inside the cup triggers something in my mind. Ashkai tried to tell me about the spirit realm as I was falling, that I needed to go there.

But why?

I only know of two surefire ways to access that plane of reality. The first is to die, so I can rule that out. The second, which is what my master must have been referring to, is to drink the sacred medicine, a concoction that temporarily alters the internal settings of the mind, allowing it to pick up frequencies and vibrations outside normal human sensory perception.

The spirit realm is a wondrous, deeply intricate domain made up of complex, entangled layers of sound, light, and energy. It is also inhabited by intelligent entities. Some are good and helpful, others bad and malevolent, the rest somewhere in between.

Journeying to the other side is risky. The Chamber has skilled shamans who patrol it, searching for the portals that open when physical beings alter their consciousness and cross over. Ashkai knew how to conceal us in that world, but I do not. In each cycle of life, my Flooding reaches me through such a gateway, breaching of its own accord, which is why I have to run so soon after receiving it.

I first drank the plant brew (which takes many forms) in ancient Egypt four thousand years ago. Guided by Ashkai, a powerful, wise, and compassionate shaman, I was able to access the startling truth about the nature of existence and who I really was.

And while it's a grueling ordeal full of painful, often harrowing experiences, I've drunk the medicine many times since, but only when initiating others and never without my master. Still, if he wants me to go there, that's what I'll do. One way or another, I'll procure the necessary ingredients, even if it means jumping on a plane to the Amazon, although there must be an easier way.

Before I can fully apply myself to that problem, I need two things: money and information, and I think I know where I can get my hands on both. Feeling renewed hope, I throw on the rest of my clothes and grab my bag. I'm about to walk out the door and leave the house quietly when something occurs to me, something that will save valuable time.

Moments later, I sneak out the bedroom and down the stairs. I can hear people talking, and I can smell marijuana. The sound is coming from the back of the house. I lean over the sloping banister to have a peek.

Eyeliner is sitting at the kitchen table with a couple guys his age, a hipster-looking one with a blond quiff saying, "Here's one for ya: say the bird kills herself, or has another fit and dies, would you have a quick look at her tits before calling the old bill?"

All of them are laughing now, even Eyeliner, but at least he adds, "What's wrong with you, dude?"

"I don't mean bang her, just a quick peek's all I'm sayin'. What's the harm in that?"

Eyeliner is telling the guy he needs professional help as I creep down the rest of the stairs and out the front door. After closing it gently and turning to face the street, I pause to breathe the crisp, fresh October air, feeling enlivened by it. I can hear a single bird tweeting. The trees and hedges are the earthy colors of autumn.

I stop on the pavement to scan the street, my eyes quickly finding a black Vespa on the far side of the road to my right. I swing my leg over it and put Eyeliner's helmet on, the one I grabbed from the desk—keys as well—just after scribbling a note promising to return everything later.

After starting the engine, I see an image of that blonde in heels straddling the Harley Davidson, remembering how happy she looked. Ignorance is bliss, I reflect, as I straighten the bike and set off.

***

Five minutes later, in order to avoid paying a visitor fee at the wrong end of the grounds, I pull up outside the unused Chester Road entrance to Highgate Cemetery: forty acres of Grade I listed land, which means it's left well alone by succeeding governments and local authorities. As a result, the 53,000 grave sites, entombing the bodies of the 170,000 people who have been buried here since 1839, are in a state of ghostly but charming disrepair, nearly all covered in a skin of ivy and moss and writhing with insects and other small, scurrying wildlife.

After parking Eyeliner's moped and placing the helmet inside the compartment under the seat, I approach the locked gate, rucksack over my shoulders. There's nobody around, and in seconds, I've climbed over it. I head northeast through the maze of leaf-covered pathways, each one flanked by long rows of stone crypts, some plain and simple, others splendid and ornate, boasting life-size statues of men and women; animals such as lions, dogs, and birds; and even musical instruments, including harps and pianos. That's not even mentioning the array of blank-faced angels, plump cherubs, and weathered crosses. Many of the structures are cracked and leaning at angles.

Glancing up now at the canopied trees, which are glowing amber as the light filters down, I breathe air damp and redolent with earth and decaying vegetation, all of it contributing to the spine-tingling eeriness of the place.

There are other living people here, mainly couples pointing out intriguing things and taking pictures, elderly loners as well, ambling along, hands behind their backs, pausing to read inscriptions here and there. But by the time I reach the resting place of celebrated nineteenth-century feminist and freethinker Emily Rose—that of her body at least—I'm totally alone.

As I look down at the inappropriately plain, nondescript granite tombstone, I can't help but recall what a wonderful, smart, and charismatic woman Emily was, and still is, no doubt: such a brave, battling soul who was committed to equality, freedom, and individual sovereignty, a person who refused to accept the ignorance of her age.

When Ashkai and I encountered her in 1829, she was already

independent, fearsomely intelligent, and angry about the various injustices of the world, all traits that suggest the soul in question is old, robust, and inherently good, three crucially important qualities for the work we do. After spending time getting to know this intriguing woman, assessing her suitability for initiation, we were as certain as we could be that she was ready for the truth.

While standing over Emily's gravestone, memories swirling in my mind, I'm compelled to close my eyes. I find myself back in that darkened Amsterdam basement, almost two hundred years past, watching Emily take the sacred brew from Ashkai and drink (having just witnessed him and me doing the same), then place the cup down, still wincing at the unpleasant taste as she lies back, bundles of dried sage burning in all corners of the room.

I listen as Ashkai, the humblest of shamans, wearing yet another body, living in yet another age, guides her through the spirit realm's alien and often nightmarish terrain, warding off negative entities by blowing plumes of tobacco smoke from a pipe and singing the ancient, healing songs known as *icaros*, gently opening her heart, mind, and energy channels, working and working until eventually it begins . . .

Emily writhes in both physical and psychological agony as the combined power of her past lives, her Flooding, first appears as particles of light, bright as the sun, emerging from a stormy portal in the center of the room, only visible to us as a result of our deeply altered states of consciousness. Those particles merge to form two thick beams, which then plunge without mercy into our initiate's chest and forehead, forcing her body to convulse. And so begins the information overload, the experience of all experiences, one that will visit her during every cycle from here on in, changing everything forever.

As the images fade, I open my eyes and take some breaths, wondering where Emily is now.

While we provide aftercare for new initiates, encouraging them to seek us out during subsequent lives for continued guidance and support, it's not uncommon for them to disappear for numerous cycles as they come to terms with their new reality and place in the world. Often, they do amazing things with those lives, free of the terror of nonexistence. Some of the greatest artists, scientists, and world leaders have been our initiates, working their way toward full acceptance.

I remove my backpack and place it on the floor in front of me. Then I lean forward to open the zip before rummaging inside for the trowel I stole from the shed before leaving Exeter. As soon as I pull it out, I hear something and have to shove it back in. I straighten and look to my right, I see an old man approaching, white hair poking from underneath his green hunting cap. He stops to ask if I'm here visiting a deceased relative, his voice posh and commanding, his terrier sniffing at my bag and feet.

"No," I reply, wanting to keep this as short as possible, hoping he didn't see the trowel. "Just looking around. I was getting my camera out to take a picture."

He raises an eyebrow and then glances at Emily's gravestone and chuckles, pointing his walking stick at it. "Oh dear, seems this one was a feminist. I'm guessing we're not wanted in the photo!" He continues on his way, calling his dog to heel, adding, "We're not all bad, you know."

The moment he and his dog disappear, and while contemplating what that raised eyebrow meant—*did he see it wasn't a camera?*—I walk behind Emily's tombstone. Once there, I place my bag on the floor and get the trowel out. I start clearing away layers of vegetation and earth at the base of the granite headstone, moving as quickly as I can, pausing occasionally to make sure nobody is around.

With the ground prepared, I start digging, and after a few minutes, having gone down a foot or so, I hit on something solid and flat. I focus on widening the hole and eventually reveal the edges of a nineteenth-century walnut jewelry box, roughly the size of two hardback books, one on top of the other. It's wrapped tightly in numerous layers of decaying and frayed cloths. The strings that had been holding everything in place have long since perished.

I have a flashback of the person I was when I buried this, the daughter of a violent and abusive alcoholic who raped me again and again, month after month, year after year . . .

As horrific as that life was, there's no point in dwelling on it now, which is why I refocus my wandering mind and pull the case out of the ground. I turn and rest my back against the tombstone. I'm about to peel the layers of material away so I can open this thing and see what's inside, when a man shouts, "Hey, what are you doing back there?"

I place the box inside my bag along with the trowel, and I stand, swinging the straps over my shoulders so both arms are free, watching as a middle-aged man and a younger woman, both wearing yellow sport shirts and black trousers, the woman's mousy hair in a ponytail, come to a hurried stop. They're just feet from me now but still on the main path. They are out of breath and obviously deeply offended. The lady says, "Have you been digging? You can't do that. Whatever you've taken, you must put back immediately."

"This is a misunderstanding," I say. The old man with the dog must have reported me as suspicious. "I haven't taken anything. This is my great, great grandma's plot. I wanted to bury a family heirloom here out of respect."

That throws Ponytail. "You should have asked permission. You can't just come into a graveyard and start digging; anyone knows that."

I tune out what she's saying and plant my eyes on her colleague, who is speaking into a two-way radio, asking for security to head for the east cemetery, aisle twenty, row fourteen. They have an intruder.

I figure that's my cue, and I dart right, bounding over graves now, ducking in and out of trees and undergrowth as I take the shortest possible route out of here. I hear the woman say "Stop, come back!" as her colleague tells security I'm running southwest. Before I know it, I'm out from under the trees and cutting across a section of open lawn. I see other members of staff in black and yellow appear from a building over to my left, one making a half-hearted attempt to intercept me as I approach the gate I climbed over about half an hour ago. I hurtle over it with ease, then open the seat of the bike to put the helmet on before pulling away, a man shouting at me from the other side of the gate as I lean back to conceal Eyeliner's number plate with my left hand, not wanting to get him in trouble.

As I turn the first corner, my mind has already moved to more pressing matters, contemplating where I can go that's quiet and private in order to open the box I closed well over a century ago. I hope there will be information in it to jolt a memory or inspire an idea because right now, I haven't got much to go on.

FIVE

I slip my bag off and place it on the empty bench. Then I sit and look out across the women's-only section of Highgate Pond, a gentle breeze rippling its wide, metallic surface, Eyeliner's Vespa parked five minutes away on the quiet, countrylike road behind me. My gaze finds a lady wearing a white cap and black goggles as she dives into the icy water on the far side of the lake, and I think how the place hasn't changed much in two hundred years. I'm glad about that. I appreciate being in the open, surrounded only by trees, grass, and blue sky.

The reason I came to Hampstead Heath, other than it being nearby, is it's out of the way, and privacy, along with some room to breathe and think, is exactly what I need right now.

Regardless of my tranquil surroundings, I'm both scared and excited as I reach into my bag and pull out the old jewelry box. Bits of earth crumble on my lap as I peel away the layers of cloth enveloping it, eventually revealing the weathered, damp, and partially rotting walnut exterior. I'm reminded of the person I was the last time I saw this, how sad and desolate I felt, petrified and desperate. I wonder if that's why my memory is so patchy as to what's inside.

Praying it's something useful and that this won't have been a waste of time, I slowly lift the lid. I'm greeted by a second package of sorts, its hidden contents wrapped tightly in some kind of dark, waterproof material, the texture and smell of it making me dizzy. I'm about to unravel the thing when everything goes black and woozy. I'm a helpless bystander as my consciousness is sucked from Rosa Clark's body by some irresistible force of the universe, then catapulted across time and space, the trees and grass and water gone as I become the person I was at the end of the nineteenth century: Elsie Farish.

I'm back in our central London home. It's two in the morning, and I'm reaching inside the cupboard under the stairs, working by candlelight, as we haven't had electricity installed yet. Using scissors to cut a large section from her father's Mackintosh raincoat, Elsie is still petrified, even though we had our Flooding recently, even though Samsara won't let anything bad happen again; we're about to leave this hellhole forever. But that's no surprise when considering the unspeakable and evil things he has done to his daughter over the years, done to *me*: Mr. Farish, depraved sadist and sociopath, heavy drinker and soon to be failed businessman.

Wait until everyone finds out what a pathetic loser you are.

I grab the bag full of valuables I've stolen from Elsie's parents (they're still living as if nothing is wrong), including a walnut jewelry box crammed with rings and necklaces. I leave the satchel in the hallway and head upstairs to the master bedroom one last time, my candle lighting the way. Mother is in bed alone, as usual, her energy drained by sadness, her husband on one of his epic drinking sessions. I realize it's been almost a week since I saw him.

If I lay eyes on that disgusting creature again, I'll kill him. That's why I must leave before he returns. Mother's parents are dead, and her brothers have long since emigrated to America, which means when I'm gone, that man will be the only person she has in the world.

Losing her child will be tragedy enough, even though it's a feeling she knows well . . .

I caress a lock of her beautiful red hair and say, "*Shh*, go to sleep," as she stirs. I should hate this woman for turning a blind eye, for letting Elsie suffer, but I haven't got it in me. Besides, she never had it much better, the remnants of an old bruise on her face even now. But it was losing two daughters, my sisters—the first during childbirth and then three-year-old Bella to a fever—that really broke her.

Doesn't she realize they had a lucky escape? No, because she thinks this life is all there is. I'm sad for a moment that I can't tell her that her daughters are most likely alive again, hopefully in a better home.

I've died as a child. In many ways, it's easier than as an adult, at least if the death is from illness.

I get to the bottom of the stairs and am about to extinguish the candle and leave when I hear someone approaching the front door. I hold my breath as Mr. Farish—*who else could it be?*—fumbles with and then drops his keys.

Elsie's tall, skinny body becomes rigid and afraid, which is why Samsara takes over, blowing the candle out and placing it on the floor. I look on from the shadows as the man of the house stumbles in, holding a paraffin lantern that's running low on fuel and therefore not emitting much light. The guy is six feet tall and barrel-chested, wearing a tombstone shirt, black suit, frock coat, and bowler hat, beady eyes magnified by the metal-rimmed spectacles that seldom leave his face.

I hate you so much.

I start thinking about the countless souls this psychopath must have tortured across the ages, and then I decide: the universe has put me here as its karmic enforcer, giving me license as executioner to hand out a slow, painful, and merciless death. After all, the more scared and desperate he is at the moment of his crossing, the more he will suffer and the longer it will take his consciousness to find and secure another human body.

The needs of Mrs. Farish cease to matter as her husband, lamp out in front of him, stumbles forward. He's just a few paces from crashing into me when he realizes something isn't right and then stops, peering into the darkness through his misshapen eyes (one is smaller than the other), saying, "Lizzie, that you?"

He can't see me yet, but when he does, he's in for a surprise: I don't have long, curly red hair anymore (I cut it short when Mother went to bed) and am wearing clothes too big for me, clothes I pulled out of the attic last night and adjusted as best as I could, clothes Father used to wear when he was younger and thinner, but was just as cruel; these include a dusty, old, flat cap.

Remaining in the shadows, breathing his familiar stench of alcohol, tobacco, and sweat, I say, "No, Father, Mother's asleep." Then I step into the dull light, my face expressionless and calm, head tilted and to the side. "So if you want to fuck me, now is a perfect time."

It takes a moment for the words to sink in, my strange

appearance as well, but when they do, his face contorts into an ugly snarl. "What is this?" he asks, thinking he's talking to a frightened, weak little girl, someone he's been able to abuse and dominate for eighteen years with nothing but feeble pleas opposing him—pleas that soon stopped—when in fact, he's staring into the eyes of his worst nightmare, unaware I'm the last person he's ever going to see.

In this life, at least . . .

I move closer. Every cell in my body, every person I've ever been, every person I'm *yet* to be, tells him that this is the end of the road; we see through his brash, confident businessman act, and we know who he *really* is: a sorry, pathetic creature who feeds on the suffering, fear, and pain of others, one who needs those things to survive. He's a true servant of The Demiurge.

Thinking, *I've met your kind many times before*, I say, "You disgust me," interested to see how he'll react to that.

I almost laugh as the look on his face goes from one of perplexed anger to disbelieving shock, his cheeks flushing red as he attempts to strike me with his left hand, the other hand still holding the lamp. I bring my forearm up to block before landing a counterblow, slapping him hard, making his spectacles fall to the ground, and I think, *That's on behalf of you, Mother.* I spit in his face, thinking, *That's for you, Elsie.* Then I say, "You like it rough, don't you, Daddy?"

He launches for me, clumsy, drunk, and heavy, roaring like a moron. I lean back and pivot, using his momentum to my advantage. He trips and reaches his hands out to brace himself against the lower stairs.

The lamp smashes, and flames erupt; there's more oil in there than I thought.

Mother...

As if to punctuate the moment, there's a crack of thunder. A storm's brewing. It's going to be a big one.

Mr. Farish stands, but rather than deal with the fire, which I don't think he's even noticed, he turns and surges for me again. Same as before, I drop a shoulder at the last moment. Sixteen stone of man hammer into the front door as I whip my coat off and turn to smother the flames. Within seconds, he launches another attack. Whatever happens, I can't let him pin me down. Elsie's body isn't equipped for that kind of close combat yet. Relying on my instincts, I use my hands to push myself off a stair while simultaneously extending my left leg hard and fast, hearing the bridge of his nose snap as he stumbles back, the fire still burning behind me. I can feel its heat . . .

The anger in Mr. Farish's eyes has been replaced by fear and confusion. Blood is gushing out of his nose and between his cupped fingers. He's also making a strange, guttural sound, giving me time to think. I need to end this quickly so I can stop the house from burning down. The fumes are already making it harder to breathe.

I'm standing on the bottom step, so I hop over the banister to avoid the encroaching fire. The man I am going to kill advances again, more carefully this time.

He wipes his bloody face with a sleeve. "Little bitch, wait till I get hold of you."

I take in my surroundings: flaming stairs to the left, wall to the right, man who wants to murder me ahead. I momentarily turn toward the kitchen, only to discover I left the cupboard door open after I finished cutting the raincoat, and now the door is blocking my way. I don't like being hemmed in, so I keep as much space between us as possible, considering my options while watching the pedophile edge forward, his hands out in front to grab me as he says, "You've been possessed; that's the devil inside you."

If he lunges or does something else rash, I'll be able to use his size and strength to my advantage once again, breaking his neck this time.

"The only thing inside me is your baby," I say. It's a lie, one designed to antagonize him so that he comes for me. The truth is he couldn't get me pregnant if he raped me a thousand times. The reason is simple: I am barren. It's a curse I carry across the ages. Ashkai believes it to be the result of an emotional trauma suffered in one of the lives I lived before he awakened me. If he's right, it's something I have yet to remember.

"You're lying," Mr. Farish says, taking another step, wiping his

39

face once more. "And even if you are with child, you won't be for much longer."

I get a rush of blood then—anger, fury, and bitterness emboldening me—causing me to feel protective toward a baby who does not exist, and I think, *Breaking his neck would be too kind, too quick, too merciful*, as an idea forms. I know instantly it's one I should ignore.

I hear *You can do this; you can do this; you can do this* repeated in my mind. Before I know it, and even though there's nothing from my past that suggests I'll be able to pull this off, I've extended my right arm and spread my fingers wide, hearing that same inner voice start to shout, ordering me to do it and do it now!

Who else but Elsie? Wanting to give that poor girl something to smile about, for her to feel strong for a change, I close my eyes—a big risk—and visualize the inside of Mr. Farish's chest and lungs. I imagine an ethereal version of my hand, a limb of light and power, bridging the gap between us, then passing through shirt and skin, muscle and cartilage, rib and sternum, eventually feeling the contours of his dark heart, clasping it like a ball, squeezing.

At the same time, I attempt to connect with the molecules, atoms, chromosomes, and cells that comprise his human body, appealing to the intelligence of his DNA, showing it the evil nature of the man, asking for help to constrict lungs and windpipe as I apply more pressure to his heart.

I hear a strange noise and I open my eyes. Father is struggling to breathe, holding a hand to his chest, his face pale and drawn, afraid and desperate, hearing Elsie say, *"Yes, yes, yes!"* as she assumes total control. Elsie remembers how he used to sneak into her room when she was a little girl and climb on top of her, saying it was their little secret, that Mummy wouldn't understand, and that he only did this because he loved her so much.

The more ancient part of my soul gets out of the child's way, watching from afar as she squeezes tighter, then tighter still, forcing Mr. Farish to his knees, his mouth gasping for air and eyes begging for mercy. He keels over and falls to the ground. I hear a sizzling sound and realize, when the smell hits, that the flame-heated floorboards are cooking the right side of his face.

40

I'm in a sort of dream state, reveling in his pain and suffering until I'm startled by a high-pitched scream coming from the top of the stairs. It scrambles my brain, and all of a sudden, I'm not sure what's happening or where I am. I feel hot and disoriented. Hearing a loud banging from somewhere, I slowly regain my senses, remembering the fire—*dear god, it's out of control*—remembering Mrs. Farish.

She'll have to jump.

I'm about to tell her to go to my bedroom at the back of the house when I hear that thudding again. It's people outside trying to get in, asking if we're okay.

Our neighbors must have heard the fight and Mother screaming.

Next thing I know, they've broken the door down, and Mr. Kirkenham from across the road is telling me to go outside. It's pouring rain, and he's soaking wet. I feel dizzy and have a burning sensation at the back of my throat; I cough as I say "Mother . . ." He promises to save her and turns his attention to that task. I notice another man grabbing the heels of Mr. Farish's body, dragging it to safety, the thing totally unresponsive now, a slab of charred meat.

I hear Mr. Kirkenham tell Mother to stop screaming and listen, that everything will be okay. There's no attention on me, so I grab my bag and slip out the back door into the storm.

Part of me knows what I did was wrong as I cut across the garden, coughing and wiping smoke from my eyes. I regret leaving that poor woman a childless, bankrupt widow. I'll get some money to her somehow. I wish I had an ounce of Ashkai's patience and understanding. How I envy his ability to always meet hate with love and darkness with light.

Another part of me thinks, *You did her a favor; you did Elsie a favor; you did the world a favor.*

That part feels good.

***

When my eyes eventually open, I'm utterly drained and aching all over. I spot the woman with the white cap gliding across the lake's shimmering surface. I imagine what it would be like to take my clothes off and dive in; to immerse myself completely; to feel the cold and see the sun's rays splinter, dance, dazzle in the water; to breathe that radiance deep into my lungs and forget everything.

For eighteen years at least . . .

I hear somebody approaching from behind, ripples of charged energy crashing into me—*not a good sign*—and turn, ready to fight when . . .

. . . is that Eyeliner?

All doubt is erased when he shouts, "Where the hell's my bike?" I'm trying to work out how he found me while I pack everything and stand, my back to the lake.

He comes to a halt on the other side of the bench, looking flustered and annoyed, saying, "I want my keys, I want my helmet, and I want to know where my bike is, as well as anything else you've nicked."

He must have a tracking device on the moped, I think. *Although why does he need me to tell him where it is?*

As I'm mulling the puzzle over, Eyeliner juts a hand out, obviously wanting it filled with keys. He's got a serious, no-nonsense look on his face. He's wearing jeans and a black leather jacket (iPad mini sticking out of a pocket) and is currently telling me what a bad person I am, how all he's done is try to help. He reminds me that he put a blanket over me when I was cold, fed me, and gave me a place to sleep. He trusted me, only to be stabbed in the back. He finishes his self-righteous rant with, "I bet that whole seizure thing was just an act, all part of the scam."

That pisses me off. "What are you talking about?"

"You coming over all mysterious and vulnerable, so I'd let you in my house. How you pretended you were knackered so I'd leave alone while you helped yourself to my stuff."

"I didn't steal anything . . ."

"Don't even bother."

"I left a note . . ." I begin, but he interrupts.

"Since last night you've passed out on a bus, randomly shaved your head, stolen my bike, and vanished into thin air, so why would I believe a stupid message you left? You were probably just buying time so I wouldn't call the police."

"I was going to bring it back."

"If that's true, why didn't you just ask if you could borrow it? That's what normal, law-abiding people do."

"You would have said no."

"Of course I would have said no! I've only just met you. What about insurance, you thought about that? You have a license? You even care?"

I don't answer, and he mutters something about having enough shit on his plate. Then he looks left, right, and over his shoulder. "Where is it anyway? Don't tell me you sold it?"

I ignore his questions. "How'd you find me?"

He shakes his head and sighs. "Thank god I did."

"How did you find me?"

Again, no answer, and it's obvious from his body language he's hiding something. I'm about to ask a third time when he reaches for my bag on the bench.

"The hell are you doing?" I ask, yanking it close, feeling a shooting pain in my head and worrying about that while Eyeliner says, "Chill out, just need to grab something."

"What?"

He points to a side pocket. After a pause, I open the zip and stick my hand in, surprised to find an iPhone in there, especially as I don't own one.

"You planted this, didn't you? And used that iPad to find me?"

"None of this would have happened if you hadn't stolen my bike and disappeared."

Normally something like this would make me angry, but I'm sort of okay about it, I guess because I can tell Eyeliner didn't mean any harm. And in a strange way, which I don't understand yet, I'm happy to see him.

"Let me get this right," I say, unable to resist cutting him down a peg or two. "You have the audacity to accuse me of stealing when you're nothing but a creepy, lowlife stalker?"

His face flushes red. "I wasn't stalking you. As if . . ."

I hold the phone up. "What do you call this then?"

"You're unpredictable and weird," he says, part of him clearly ashamed, the rest frustrated and defensive. "I was worried you might disappear and wanted to be able to find you if you did."

"What I said. Stalking."

He leans over, grabs the phone, and shoves it in a pocket. "Just gimme my keys and tell me where my bike is."

I reach into my pocket and hand them over. "Go back to the road. Turn left; it's about a hundred yards along. Can't miss it; helmet's in the seat."

He nods, wishes me a good life, and walks away.

It might be because he's shown me kindness in the past, because I'm worried about having another seizure, or because I'm an idiot, I'm not sure. All I know is I don't want him to go yet.

"How come you lied to me?" I say.

He stops and turns. "Huh?"

"About your name? It's not George, is it?"

That surprises him. "You nick my passport as well?"

"No, you're just a terrible liar."

He smiles, and I can sense things softening between us.

"But a pretty good stalker, it seems."

I reply, "The best," and am about to say *Don't worry about it. None of my business*, but he gets in first, saying, "I didn't want you to judge me." There's a hint of shame in his eyes.

"Because of your name? How bad can it be?"

He looks at the floor, then off into the distance before coming back to me. "I thought you might recognize it, especially after you thought we knew each other when we met at the bus station."

"You famous?" I ask, at the same time remembering the pills he tried to hide from me, wondering if that's connected.

"More like infamous."

"Kill someone?"

"Nah, not yet."

"You wanna tell me?"

"What my real name is or what I did?"

"Both. Either. None. Up to you."

He looks at his watch. "It's a long story, and I'm cold."

"What's the time?"

He glances at his wrist again. "Quarter to one."

"Wanna get a bite to eat?" I ask.

"You hungry?"

I smile and say, "Lunch time, isn't it?" Then I say, "You mind if we go back to yours, though? I'm getting a headache and don't want to take any chances."

Eyeliner looks concerned, so I reassure him, explaining I'm fine, just better to be inside if things take a turn for the worse, which they won't.

When that conversation runs its course, I ask what he thinks of my suggestion.

He winces, takes a deep breath, and looks out across the lake, making a show of thinking it over. He gets his phone out and says, "Let me just call ahead, tell my housemates to lock up the silver."

SIX

Eyeliner, who's carrying my bag on his back, says when we reach the scooter, "You okay getting the bus? The NW3 goes by mine, and there's a stop up that way, it's how I got here. Or I could order an Uber for you?"

"I've got a better idea," I say, sticking a hand out, wanting a break from all the serious, heavy stuff. "Hand over the keys."

"Why?" He narrows his eyes, the edges of a disbelieving smile forming.

"Why'd you think?"

"So you can nick it again?"

"Very funny. So I can give you a lift home."

"But I don't need a lift home. Besides, we only have one helmet, and even if we had another, you'd be *my* passenger." He pats the seat of the Vespa. "You know this belongs to me, right?"

"I do, yes, but it's not far, and I'm a great driver. Come on, live a little."

"Live a little? That's a good one. Anyway, you said you're not feeling good. What if you start having a fit? What do we do then, die a little?"

"That's precisely why I want to drive; it'll give my brain something to focus on. That always helps, so just hand over the keys and stop worrying. We'll be fine; put your arms around me. I promise you'll be safe."

I can tell he likes the sound of that. Putting his arms around me, I mean.

"Have you even got a license?"

"No. But I'm a natural."

"That's reassuring," he says, pulling the keys out. "Just don't kill us, all right, and stay off main roads; I know a good route."

I take the keys, open the seat, and offer the helmet.

"You wear it," he says.

"No thanks," I say, getting on and starting the engine. "It smells bad."

He smiles. "That's because I like to shit in it." The two of us chuckle as he fixes the strap under his chin and gets behind me, putting his arms around my waist, and says, "Hey, slow down" after I set off faster than I should.

We're heading east toward Archway, sticking to back streets, less than two miles from our destination. Eyeliner gives directions and reminds me to concentrate, saying that if a police car sees us we're screwed. My stalker is freaking out because he can hear a siren in the distance.

He's saying other stuff back there, blabbing on as usual, but it's difficult to hear everything, especially on the longer stretches of road where I'm able to open the throttle as far as it will go, appreciating how refreshing the cool air feels against my face.

There's a T-junction ahead, and Eyeliner tells me to go right when we reach it; we're almost there. I'm about to say, "I hope you're a good cook" when his body tenses and he starts saying "shit" and "fuck" over and over, losing it because a police car has appeared from the intersection we're approaching.

I'm caught off guard by how quickly my flight response kicks in, the surge of adrenaline forcing me to turn and head back the way we came. I tell Eyeliner to cover the number plate with one hand and hold tight with the other.

"No way, don't be crazy. What the hell are you doing?" It's a very good question.

But it's too late for regrets because we're already running, sirens blaring to our rear, lights flashing. It dawns on me how much of an impulsive idiot I am; after all, what could the police have done? We hadn't crashed; nobody had been hurt. I could have just smiled and told them we were sorry, that my boyfriend was giving me a quick lesson on a quiet road. They might even have let us off with a warning.

So why did you run?

Because I've been doing it for so long, because it's all I know . . .

Something strange starts happening to my peripheral vision, the very fabric of reality flickering, distorting, and bending around me. Electrons, photons, and subatomic particles rearrange themselves into different moments from my long past. Memories and scenes morph in and out of each other, becoming clearer, more convincing, sucking me in . . .

I see Demaris of Sparta, dress torn, muddy, and wet from the rain, being chased down by three Persian warriors, their army raping and pillaging after victory on the battlefield; then Red Cloud of the Kickapoo tribe fleeing on horseback across the open plains, her trackers distant specks on the horizon; Yamato of Hokkaido, northern Japan, hiding in a mountain cave, snow falling outside, shivering, hungry, and afraid; Necalli, the young Tlascalan virgin, just hours from being marched to the summit of Tenochtitlan's Great Pyramid to have her heart cut out—an offering to the gods—somehow slipping through the bars of her fattening pen before dawn, swimming across Lake Texcoco, vanishing into the jungle, defying all odds.

Why can't they leave me alone? I think, remembering what happened the last time I ran, how Ashkai was taken from me after I saw him collapse on that rooftop, how I wanted to help but was not able to, and how I was forced to run even when I was ready to stand and fight.

I hear an urgent voice cutting through the white noise, getting louder, saying, "Sam, fuck sake, stop, just stop, it's not worth it," the words pulling me back into twenty-first century London, seeing the tarmac and houses, the police car still on our tail.

There's a red mini approaching, so I take the next right to avoid it while Eyeliner tells me to pull over, that I have no choice now. There's a delivery truck ahead blocking the entire road; guys are pulling furniture out. I glance in my wing mirror as those blue lights come flying around the corner, hemming us in. Deciding on a change of tactic, I slam the brakes and lean into the resulting skid, executing a perfect 180-degree turn before fully engaging the throttle again, seeing an Asian lady behind the wheel of the police car, a bald, white guy next to her, my eyes telling them to make a decision: *move or kill two teenagers.*

At the last moment, the female officer yanks the wheel to one side and smashes into a parked Jaguar, leaving enough of a gap for our scooter to jink through. I know that by the time she gets over the shock of the impact, we'll be long gone.

I wait for Eyeliner to tell me what a crazy bitch I am, how he wishes we'd never met, but he doesn't say a word.

***

Five minutes later, I pull up outside Eyeliner's house, turning into a free space when he says, "Get off, I'll do it," the first words he's spoken since we lost the police car.

"Okay," I reply, leaving the engine running and standing beside him. In an attempt to lighten the mood, I say, "Bet you wish I'd taken the bus, huh?"

He slides forward but doesn't respond. I tell him I'm sorry, but all I get is more silence.

"Come on, I know you're dying to say something?"

He looks at me, his face expressionless and cold in the helmet. "You're right," he says, eyes forward when he adds, "Goodbye, Sam," and pulls away, leaving me standing there like an idiot. I realize he's still got my bag on his back. I'm running now, shouting after him, but it's too late.

The jewelry box!

Watching my belongings vanish around a corner, I tell myself not to overreact, that he was so pissed off he obviously wasn't aware he had it. I'm reasoning he just needs to blow off steam, which is fair enough. He'll be back in ten minutes tops. And if he's still sulking then, fine, I'll take my bag and get out of here for good. I'm not sure what the hell I'm playing at anyway, wasting time like this, and for what?

I glance at my watch and take a seat on the low wall outside Eyeliner's house, my back pressing into an overgrown bush in his front garden. I look at the brown and yellow leaves lining the pavement, piles of them bunched around the wheels of cars.

What if he's gone back to the police officers to see if they're okay? What if he brings them here? What if he looks inside my bag? What if he throws everything in the river to spite me?

I'm starting to feel the cold and don't want to risk another headache, so I stand up, go through the squeaky metal gate, and knock on the door, deciding that if he's going to make me hang around, I might as well do it in the warmth of his bedroom.

The hipster answers. He's wearing skinny jeans and a tight-fitting maroon shirt fastened to the top, looking ridiculous because he's not as slim as he thinks. Remembering what he said to Eyeliner about ogling my breasts, I jostle past, saying, "Hiya," with a big smile on my face, acting as if I have every right to be here. I'm about to head upstairs when he says, "Oi, what's goin' on? You can't just come in my house. Who are ya?" He sounds like he's from one of the home counties, Essex or Kent maybe.

I stop and turn, about to explain that I'm George's friend when I remember that's not his name. I improvise. "You know who I am."

He glances at my shaved head. "The bird Tammuz met on the bus?"

"Told you," I say, hiding my surprise, which isn't easy considering Tammuz is the Sumerian deity of spring and harvest, an ancient symbol of death and rebirth.

"You nicked his bike. He's out now trying to find you."

"He succeeded," I reply.

He laughs. "Which means you failed."

"You're very rude, you know that?"

"I'm rude?" he says, pointing at his chest, getting agitated while I think more about Eyeliner's real name, shocked by it, but with no idea why he's "infamous."

The hipster continues: "You nick my mate's motorbike then barge in 'ere like you pay rent and I'm rude? That's classic, that; this has got to be a wind-up."

"The stealing thing was a misunderstanding. We worked it out; why else would I be here?"

There's a pause, and I can tell he's not sure how to handle this.

"Hold up," he says, poking his head out the door. "I can't see his bike."

"That's because he's on it. Einstein."

"Why ain't you with him?"

"I needed to use the bathroom. He's just popped to the shops to grab stuff for lunch. He'll be back any minute."

"I'm calling him," he says, pulling his phone out.

"Good," I say. If Tammuz answers, I'll hijack the conversation and tell him to bring my bag back.

"Mate, it's Jamie. That bird who nicked your bike is 'ere, just barged in, reckons you said it was okay, but I wanted to check 'cos it don't make sense. Call me back, yeah."

Jamie hangs up and tells me I need to wait outside, and if Tammuz phones and says it's okay, he'll let me know. I tell him that he doesn't have to worry, Tammuz and I are cool, and I add, "Anyway, it's cold outside; where're your manners?" He's not convinced and doesn't care, explaining I have to leave because "birds," however fit, aren't allowed in unsupervised, so I tell him that's fine, but only if he makes me. Then, for some reason I'm not sure of, I lift my top with one hand and pull my bra down with the other.

"That's to save you the trouble in case I have a fit and die."

The look on his face is priceless, somewhere between shocked and aroused, which is an improvement on smug at least. I turn and head upstairs to Tammuz's bedroom, slamming the door behind me.

***

I'm sitting on the floor next to the bed, meditating. I've taken my jacket and boots off.

I am absolute existence. I am a field of all opportunities. I am the universe.

I'm disturbed by the front door opening and closing downstairs. Moments later, I hear people talking. I recognize Jamie's voice, then Tammuz's . . .

Why didn't I hear him pull up?

I've still got my eyes closed, but the light within is fading fast. I know I'll be forced to let the feeling go soon. I'm bracing myself because somebody is bounding up the stairs.

Tammuz blusters in, and a tense, negative energy crashes into me, along with his words. "Get out," he says, which is when I open my eyes, seeing my only friend standing in the middle of the room with my backpack hanging off a shoulder. Relieved about that, I watch the look on his face go from angry to bemused.

"You meditating?" he asks, like it's the most ridiculous thing he's ever seen.

I smile, determined for this not to turn into an argument, beaming love and compassion at him. "Yes, wanna join?"

"You're so weird . . ."

I ignore that and say, "It suits you."

"What does?"

"Your name, Tammuz. I like it."

He shakes his head, letting me know that's totally irrelevant. "What are you doing here? You trying to take my life over or something?"

"I was waiting."

"For what?"

"The bag you stole from me." I smile so he knows I'm only kidding.

"I didn't steal it," he replies. "I forgot I even had it. Anyway, why didn't you wait outside? What makes you think you can come in here without me? I only met you a few hours ago."

"I was cold," I say. "And I didn't know how long you'd be."

"That's such crap."

"It's the truth."

"If you were so cold, why'd you strip in front of my mate Jamie? He said you flashed him."

"I had my reasons."

"What reasons? Do you fancy him?"

I laugh. "As if . . . He's a cretin."

"You're properly mental, you know that?"

"Seems to be the general consensus in this house."

"You on the run?"

"From who?"

"The police. Is that why you shaved your head and nearly killed us both?"

"I made a mistake. I shouldn't have reacted like that; I'm sorry."

"You didn't answer my question."

"No, I'm not."

He passes a hand through his hair and glances out the window. "Sorry isn't gonna get my bike back."

"What do you mean?"

"I just dumped it on a housing estate."

"Why?"

"The police might have my number plate. Now if they turn up, I can play dumb, say it was nicked."

"Didn't you cover it like I said?"

"I had other things to do, like trying not to die."

"If the police don't show by tonight you can get it back, or tell me where it is and I'll grab it for you."

"That's a big if, especially if they see you here. My face was mostly covered by the helmet, but you they got a proper look at. That's why you have to go. They could turn up any second."

I uncross my legs and pull my boots on. "You're right."

I stand and grab my jacket from the bed, pulling it on as I step closer to Tammuz, letting him know I want my bag. He holds it in place while I maneuver around to slip my arms through the straps. When I turn to face him again, I've ended up in his personal space somehow (*or is he in mine?*). It's awkward and charged, and for a moment I think about rising on my tiptoes and kissing him, but it's a stupid idea, so I ignore it.

I take a step back. "Before I go, you mind telling me something?"

"Depends what it is."

"What are you 'infamous' for?"

He shrugs. "Does it matter?"

"I guess not."

"My surname is Hartman. Google me."

"Thought you were supposed to be *my* stalker?" It was meant as a joke, but his capacity for humor still hasn't returned.

"Thanks for everything," I say. "You're a good person, and I'm glad I met you. Sorry for messing your day up . . . see you around, maybe?"

I'm walking toward the door when he says something

unexpected: "If not in this life, maybe the next."

I stop and look at him. "Why would you say that?"

He shrugs again. "What?"

"About seeing me in another life?"

"Dunno, just an expression, why?"

I study Tammuz's eyes to see if he's hiding anything, but it doesn't look like he is.

"No reason," I say, writing it off as a coincidence, even though I know there's no such thing. "I'm just interested in that stuff."

"What stuff?"

"Reincarnation, past lives."

He laughs. "No wonder you're not scared of dying."

I stare at him, I don't know why, and things go quiet as we look at each other for longer than we should. I'm pulled in by those blue, intelligent eyes, sensing a deep vulnerability in them.

"Take care, Tammuz," I say.

He nods, and I head downstairs, surprised at how fast my heart is beating, even more surprised that I'm thinking about him when I should be focused on what's inside that jewelry box—and, of course, my master.

It's the side effects of your Flooding. In a few days, everything will be okay.

I'm opening the front door, about to step outside, when I hear Jamie's annoying and unmistakable voice.

"Hey, B cup," he says. "Check this out."

I turn, and he's standing in the hallway, hands on hips, a stupid, smug look on his face, massively pleased about something.

I'm about to ask what he wants, but then I glance down and see it.

"Now we're even," he says.

I lunge forward as if I'm going to attack, and he flinches. The house idiot looks pathetic, standing with his dick hanging out. I turn and walk away.

SEVEN

I leave Tammuz's house and head southeast down Holloway Road. The perfect blue sky hanging above, deep and peaceful as a lake, feels like it belongs to a different time and place, one that boasts green fields, rolling hills, and sunsets to take one's breath away. But instead, it presides over this corner of north London that has scratchy pubs, dilapidated pawnshops, and unpleasant city smells (exhaust fumes and rotting food the most prominent). The locals, who look poor and tired, are black, white, yellow, and brown, a rainbow of sorts, only one that has nothing to offer its observer other than a dirty look.

They are all meat robots, I think. *Alive but not living, conscious but not awake.*

I walk into a McDonald's and cut across the large, brightly lit canteen, weaving between huddles of school kids, shop assistants, and workmen in fluorescent jackets, all of them scoffing burgers and fries and slurping milkshakes. The sickly, sweet smell of the food is making my stomach groan, which is when I remember I've only had toast today. I slip into the disabled toilet in the far corner and tell myself to be patient; I'll grab something healthy and nourishing soon as I'm done.

The walls are a dull, dirty yellow, and the floor is old, worn-down linoleum. It also smells bad, so all in all, the vibe isn't great, although at least I'm not hungry anymore. I rest my bag on the cistern. Then I lower the toilet lid and wipe it thoroughly, using dampened paper towels, and only sit when I'm satisfied it's clean and dry. I grab the backpack and place it on the floor between my feet, catching myself in the full-length mirror on the back of the door. I look tired, pale, and weak. I make a mental note to start getting my strength up, which means lots of good food and regular, strenuous exercise.

I reach inside the bag, pull the jewelry box out, and open it. I remove the enclosed package, heavy with jangling metal, and rest it on my lap, placing the wooden container on the floor. After unraveling the thick, rubberized fabric, I'm finally confronted with what I buried all those years ago.

The first thing I see is the sparkle of gold, silver, and amethyst rings as well as a beautiful necklace made of freshwater pearls and cameo shells, all of it cold and slightly damp. There's also an emerald pendant, a gold and enamel locket, a pair of diamond drop earrings, and a collection of Victorian coins: gold sovereigns, half crowns, guineas, shillings, and farthings.

That's what I'm looking for, I think, delving my fingers into the pile of precious metals and stones, unearthing and pulling out a second, much smaller parcel, just two inches by two inches.

I take real care to untie the string and then remove the pieces of paper inside, gently unfolding each one until I have four leaves, each the size of a postcard and very thin and delicate. While the ink from the dip pen I used all those years ago has run, smudged, and faded in places, most of it is okay and legible, which is a huge relief.

Physical objects such as these often act as portals, giving me direct and immediate access to key moments from the past. That's why, when I look in the mirror opposite me, I'm not surprised to see a clear image of Elsie Farish hunched over her father's desk in the early hours of the morning, working by candlelight, just twenty-four hours before she committed murder and ran away. Pretty red ringlets brush against pale cheeks as she carefully records, in that neat, flowing handwriting, everything she could remember that felt important.

I look away from the mirror and turn my attention to the notes themselves.

The first page is dedicated to treasures I have buried in the United Kingdom, the ones Elsie could remember, anyway. There's one beside an ancient, two-thousand-year-old yew tree in Berkshire and another two hundred paces south of Stonehenge's central megalith (the related memories coming back to me now), although I can't imagine I'd be allowed to start digging there. I remember when Stonehenge was deserted, considered a weird, spooky pagan monument, back before tourists reclaimed the past.

I move on to another section entitled *Allies*. Here I had written about Ashkai and the fact that we were together in our previous life cycle, when I was a serf named Inga from Ryazan, western Russia. The year of her Flooding was 1824. Ashkai had been born a Spanish noble and was very wealthy.

Thankfully, my master was successful in his attempt to reach out and appear in my dreams, letting Inga know how to find him. Even though no oceans stood between us, getting to him was far from easy. As a serf, I had no rights and no money, so I had to steal, lie, and even fight when necessary. It is a journey I will never forget. I wouldn't have made it without the fighting skills and strategies and knowledge of human weakness I remembered from past lives. Even so, I learned so much about who I am and what I am capable of.

I stop reading for a moment and close my eyes, already smiling. That's because the words on the page have enabled me to relive the embrace we shared in the doorway of his Madrid home, the kiss, the merging of our energies, the absolute bliss. I long for that feeling again, knowing there's only one way to attain it.

When I eventually open my eyes, feeling a mixture of sadness, hope, and frustration, I scan forward until I reach the heading *Enemies*, under which I have listed the Chamber of Infinites, Meta, and The Shadow, gasping because I'd forgotten what happened to Elsie the night after her Flooding:

An intruder appeared in my dream. He assumed my master's form, but it was not he, of that I am certain. Who was the imposter and what did he want?

I don't have the answer to that puzzle, and there's more to learn, so I move on, having to wait until the final paragraph for my biggest, most valuable clue:

Met Rebus (when I was Inga). Ashkai's spy inside the Chamber of Infinites. He was peculiar and kept staring at me. I think he was trying to scare me, but why? And who was the woman standing beside him?

Contemplating those questions is tantamount to stepping into a time machine because just like that, I'm the wiry, auburn-haired Russian girl with those wide, blue eyes, sitting in the window of the *Vis En Brood Café* in central Amsterdam, 1832. It's snowing, and the canal to my left is frozen and dotted with ice-skaters. The sky is ashen and featureless, and the docked boats covered in coats of ice will not be going anywhere for a while. It's a picturesque winter scene. Ashkai and Rebus are at the center of it, standing beside a small, wooden bridge. Rebus, it turns out, has albinism. His hair, beard, and skin are as white as the snow at his feet.

They're about twenty paces from the café, but whatever they're discussing can't be for my ears; otherwise, why be out there? Especially as we just spent half an hour having a cagey breakfast together. We ate grilled herring with rye bread washed down with chicory tea. I was sitting quietly while they exchanged pleasantries and small talk in Dutch. But that was just camouflage because their real conversation was telepathic. I tried to listen in but couldn't break through, maybe because I wasn't welcome.

After finishing breakfast, Rebus stood and said he had an appointment. My master offered to walk him out, and here I am, excluded and alone, itching to know what they're discussing. Something in my gut is telling me I won't like it . . .

Rebus, like my master, is very ancient and advanced; that much is obvious from the rich, layered energy he emanates, not to mention the position he holds in the Chamber, something Ashkai only told me about on the way here. I don't know how long Rebus has been in the Chamber or exactly why he conspires against it, but the fact he does is admirable, reminding me not to write him off completely, to give him the benefit of the doubt.

Eventually, the conversation, which looks heated, ends with Rebus storming off. He crosses the bridge and disappears into a narrow alleyway between buildings.

Moments later, Ashkai reenters the café and sits opposite me, brushing snow from his thick, wool coat, otherwise showing no signs of feeling the cold. My master serene, calm, and accepting, as always. Handsome as well, with youthful, olive skin, a goatee, and wavy, brown hair, save for that strip of gray in the center of his forehead.

Speaking ancient Egyptian, I say, "What's his problem?"

Ashkai tries to pour tea from the pot on the table, but it's empty, so he gestures to the waitress for a refill. Then he looks at me and says, in the same language, "Speak freely, Samsara."

"He vexed me."

"Why?"

"The man is obnoxious."

Ashkai smiles. "He's complicated."

"Was he talking about me out there?"

"Yes."

I sigh because my master has an annoying habit of only answering the question I asked, when it's obvious I want him to elaborate. "What did he say?"

"It's difficult to explain."

"Please try."

"He wanted to know if we could trust you."

That makes me angry. "How did you answer?"

"I explained I've known you for many thousands of years. That I awakened you, that I trust you utterly, and love you deeply."

His words soften me. "What's he so suspicious about?"

"He feels threatened."

"By Meta?"

"It's more complicated than that."

"Why did he storm off?"

"We have very different points of view."

"On what?"

"Everything."

"Will he still help us?"

"In what way?"

"He's your spy, isn't he?"

"What gives you that idea?"

"You've told me before you have a friend within the Chamber."

Ashkai smiles as a father would to his daughter. "As long as we continue to place the happiness of others before our own and strive to improve the human experience, the universe will protect and guide us. And that's the only friend we need."

The short, chubby waitress arrives with a fresh pot of tea and fills our cups.

After she leaves, I say, "That means we're on our own," feeling strangely calm about that. Then something occurs to me I'm less at ease with. "What if this is a trap? What if Rebus has given our position to the Chamber?"

Ashkai drinks some tea. "Then we take our cyanide," he says.

"That's comforting," I reply, lacing the statement with sarcasm.

After a beat of silence, Ashkai excuses himself to use the outside lavatory to the rear of the café, cutting through the kitchen to reach it.

I glance out the window, holding my tea in both hands and blowing on the water to cool it. I smile when I spot a young couple skating along the canal, arm in arm. I follow them with my eyes until they disappear underneath the bridge I'd been looking at before, and I almost drop my cup when I see Rebus standing there glaring at me, snow swirling around him in eddies. Beside him is a woman with a striking, otherworldly appearance, sharp cheekbones, and eyes so dark they look empty. A voice in my head startles me, jerking my attention back to Rebus, who has the look of a powerful Nordic god. His voice echoes in my skull, deep and resonant as he says, *I see you. I know what you are. Even if he doesn't.* I jerk my head toward the kitchen, hoping to see my master, but he is not there. When my gaze returns to the bridge, it is empty.

I'm expecting Meta's agents to appear from all directions. I reach for my poison, but everything carries on as normal. Moments later, Ashkai returns and sits, looking at me before asking, "What's troubling you, Samsara?" He reaches across to hold my hand. "You seem afraid."

I empty my mind of thoughts and make up a lie.

The first I've ever told him.

EIGHT

I buy a grilled chicken wrap from a Turkish restaurant and sit at a table to eat. There's a big TV on the wall, and the news is on. A pretty blonde lady with large breasts is interviewing a representative from COSMOS, the huge multinational technology company. As well as specializing in Internet-related services (they're starting to give Google and Facebook a run for their money), they do a lot of other really cool stuff. Right now, for example, the COSMOS rep, a geeky, Asian guy wearing glasses, is explaining how fragments from a large comet are going to smash into Mars this coming Friday, just after midnight, so technically early Saturday morning. COSMOS, who has partnered with NASA, will be live streaming the event across the world, free of charge.

"Weren't the dinosaurs wiped out by a comet?" the pretty blonde news lady says, grimacing comically.

"That's right," the technology geek replies, smiling, even flashing an awkward glance at her cleavage. "But Mars is over fifty million kilometers away, so we have nothing to worry about."

After eating and catching up on current affairs, I walk into one of the many pawnshops on Holloway Road. The place is packed with electronics, mainly: TVs, stereos, PlayStations, and Xboxes. My internal monologue is telling me to focus on the task at hand: getting a good price for the contents of my walnut jewelry box. The problem is, I'm still in shock about the things I remembered. I have no idea what it all means or how to process the information.

What happened in Amsterdam? What did Rebus mean when he said he knew what I really was? And who was that woman?

I shake my head to clear it, and then I approach the counter. The skeletal, tough-looking old lady sitting on the other side of the thick pane of glass, deep wrinkles lining her sun-damaged face, puffs on a cigarette and raises an eyebrow when she sees my heap of jewelry and old coins. "If it's nicked, I'm not interested,"

61

she says in a raspy voice.

I want to ask who she's kidding, that half the stuff she buys is stolen, but instead play the game, saying my grandmother died and left this to me, and I want to use the money to travel and broaden my horizons.

The Cockney-sounding lady says, *"Mmm,"* then spends ten minutes analyzing each piece one by one, inspecting the metal and stones with a loupe. She comes over, seeming bored and uninterested, like there's nothing special here. It's all part of an act to lower people's expectations before ripping them off. I tell her I'm planning on shopping around for the best price, adding, "So let's not waste each other's time."

She looks up and stubs out her cigarette. "I'll giva ya two grand all in." She says it like she'd be doing me a favor. "And I've got all the time in the world, luv."

I say, "There's gold, silver, diamonds, emeralds, pearls . . . And it's all vintage and in perfect condition. It's worth ten times that, and you know it."

"What planet you on?"

"Thankfully not Mars," I mutter.

"What did you say?"

"Forget it," I reply. "Give it back; I'll try your competitor over the road."

"You'll 'ave no luck there, tighter than a duck's arse, that lot," she says, looking at one of the rings again. She moves on to the pearl necklace, rubbing a finger over the perfectly matched, ten-millimeter pearls. Elsie's grandmother wore that on her wedding day. "Two thousand, two hundred n' fifty."

"Least I'll take is £5K," I shoot back. "Either that or I remove the pearl necklace."

Grandma lights another cigarette and stares at me, her eyes shrewd, perhaps showing a hint of respect. Not too many eighteen-year-olds can negotiate like I do. She offers an extra £250 for everything, but I refuse. Then she offers a hundred more, and I laugh and tell her I don't have time for this. Finally, she says, "Most I'll go is three grand, including the necklace, but that really is your lot, not a penny more. Take it or leave it."

"Fine," I say after considering the offer, certain as I can be that that's the highest she'll go, unwilling to waste time going from place to place haggling over a few hundred quid. "I'll take it, although I don't know how you sleep at night."

She smiles at last, revealing smoke-stained teeth. "Like a baby, luv." Then she rests her cigarette on an ashtray and grabs the pearl necklace, which has an elegantly carved shell cameo centerpiece.

"How do I look?" she asks, draping it around her neck, and for a moment I'm Elsie again, six years old, watching Mother getting ready for a night out. Mrs. Farish turns from her dressing table to ask the same question of her daughter: *How do I look, pumpkin?*

"Like a princess," I say (as I said then), and the old lady bursts out laughing.

"Nice try, sweetheart, but we've already done the deal." Still chuckling, she counts out a thick wad of fifty-pound notes and stuffs them in a brown envelope. She hands it over via the security drawer, and I slip £300 in a pocket for easy access. The rest goes in my bag.

I'm about to leave when she says, "Goin' somewhere nice?"

I don't know what she means at first, but then I remember I told her I was using the money to travel, which might not be so far from the truth.

"To another dimension," I reply, and she says, speaking to my back now because I'm heading for the door, "Sounds cold."

I step onto Holloway Road and look at my watch: 3:27 p.m. I scan right, then left, and spot an Internet café a few doors down, where I go and grab a computer in the far corner of the room. There are fifteen or so PCs, divided by thin, cheap partitions. Half of the cubicles are occupied by rowdy teenage boys in school uniforms, chunky headphones covering their ears, cans of coke beside the keyboards they're hammering. I hear gunshots, explosions, and curses, the atmosphere and smell reminding me of Rosa's little brother Joe, who spent hours, even days when he could get away with it, playing brutally violent war games.

I feel a deep sadness at the tendency for souls (more now than ever) to waste precious lives and opportunities, unaware they'll keep reincarnating, keep suffering, until they learn the lessons required for spiritual development and growth, allowing them to edge ever closer to the ultimate goal, which is to merge with the Absolute Light from whence they came, infusing the oneness of all things with wisdom and love, strength, and tenderness.

At least, that's how it used to be . . .

The problem is human suffering. Although meant as a catalyst for positive change, it has unexpectedly become conscious in its own right. And like all living things, this malevolent energy—this darkness—seeks to ensure its own survival. That means poisoning hearts and minds and attacking anything it perceives as a threat. The forces of love and light are at the top of that list, forces that Ashkai and I have worked tirelessly to protect. But there is only so much we can do, especially when we've had to expend precious energy and time evading those who hunt us.

"Our enemies keep us focused," I remind myself, although they are my master's words, not mine.

"They are a gift," he would often assert. "A constant reminder of what we are fighting for."

"And what is that?" I asked, many lives ago, the two of us paddling a canoe down the Amazon, the sky, trees, and scattered caiman eyes tinged pink by the setting sun. The rainforest was abuzz with its myriad expressions of life and spirit, a fitting home for Mother Ayahuasca, the ancient visionary brew we were seeking.

"We fight for the truth and for the light and for souls to know what we know. For what is knowledge if it cannot be shared and enriched by others?"

"Why does our own kind impede us?"

"Because they sleep even though they are awake."

"How?"

"By succumbing, as many do, to the alluring and grasping, self-serving nature of ego."

"Is it too late for them?"

"Nobody is a lost cause, Samsara; never forget that. Darkness cannot survive in the presence of light."

"As you wish, master," I say, but that's where our dialogue ends because the chubby boy two booths away has started swearing loudly, angry because his computer has crashed. He flips his keyboard and argues with the owner of the shop, demanding his money back. The owner tells him to shut the hell up and stop moaning.

There's a pair of headphones on the desk, so I put them on to block out the noise, thinking about Meta now, the Chamber of Infinites, and, of course, Rebus. I hear those words in my head again: *I see you now. I know what you really are. Even if he doesn't.*

What did Ashkai's so-called friend mean by that? And why didn't I come clean to my master?

The truth is, I don't know why I kept Ashkai in the dark. It was instinct, a feeling in my gut to keep quiet, but to what end, I'm not sure. I just hope that decision isn't the reason he was eventually captured.

Could it all be my fault? I wonder, but the implications are too overwhelming to bear, so I force myself on. *What did Rebus mean about who I REALLY was?* Then I remember what my master told me, that his old friend felt threatened. Maybe Rebus thought he was being watched by Meta and other members of the Chamber, and his cover had been blown?

Then again, if Rebus was so paranoid, why risk meeting Ashkai face-to-face? There were other ways for them to communicate. Had Meta already gotten to Rebus? Was our spy a double agent working against us?

It's possible. But then, why weren't we ambushed? We were exposed and vulnerable.

This is useless and a waste of time, so I yank my headphones off and throw them down, frustrated because questions just lead to more questions, the mystery deepening at every turn.

"Not you as well," the manager shouts from across the room. "What happened, crashed?"

I look over my shoulder and say, "Nothing, I'm fine," and he loses interest, but not before pointing out I'll be charged if anything's damaged.

I nod, letting him know I won't be any trouble, and turn to my screen, resolving to stop asking questions and start finding answers. I type *ayahuasca* into Google now, looking for current information regarding the powerful and sacred medicine of the

Amazon. If I can get my hands on some, I'll be able to access the spirit realm, which is where Ashkai told me to go.

I open the Wikipedia entry for ayahuasca, and it outlines what I already know: that the brew is made by the genius combination of two specific Amazonian plants, which are then pounded and boiled with water, producing a gloopy, dark, foul-tasting tea.

The first ingredient is a shrub called chacruna. It contains the most powerful psychoactive known to man: dimethyltryptamine (DMT), venerated by Flooders as the spirit molecule.

The human body, however, possesses a stomach enzyme that breaks down and metabolizes DMT on contact. The solution to this problem turned out to be the eponymous ayahuasca vine itself. The job of this plant is to temporarily deactivate the gastric enzyme causing the block, allowing the spirit molecule to be absorbed into the blood and fast-tracked to the brain's pineal gland, or "third eye," where the work is done.

When asked how their ancestors knew to combine these two unassuming shrubs from the tens of thousands on offer, shamans always give the same answer: the plants told them.

Time to find out what else they know.

I search for places in the United Kingdom that facilitate ayahuasca ceremonies.

I systematically work my way through the links offered up, going from chat forums to newspaper articles and blogs to psychotherapy sites and even the odd celebrity account of his or her "life-changing" experience.

So the good news is, the medicine has grown in popularity in the West, particularly over the past twenty years. The bad news: information on how to get hold of it in the United Kingdom is sketchy at best, with people pointing out it's a word-of-mouth thing. It's not surprising when considering DMT is a Class A drug (Schedule I in America), meaning serious prison time for those caught in possession.

In some ways, it's smart. Governments want their people docile, unquestioning, and obedient. People are easier to control that way and less prone to trouble, each person knowing their place in the hive. They're stuck in the endless cycle of working, consuming, and being afraid, believing they might win the lottery one day, or maybe get promoted at work, and that happiness is something to strive for but never actually achieve.

At the same time, the ruling classes aren't stupid. They know people require the means to escape and let go every now and again, to break from the life they're not living. So people should drink alcohol and pass out, smoke cigarettes, and if they're really depressed, visit their doctors, who will prescribe expensive pills (made by large, profit-driven pharmaceutical companies) that will make them feel better about their shitty lives without having to change a thing. It's fine to alter consciousness; it's even okay to get addicted to substances, but only ones we—your benevolent leaders—endorse because we care about you and know what's best.

All that other stuff that challenges the mind and forces people to ask questions about the nature of reality and the purpose of life, well, they're called "bad drugs," and people need to stay away from them.

Thinking about this stuff makes me angry, so I clear my mind and open Rosa's Gmail account. The first things I see are messages from her mum, dad, and brother. Though it's difficult and unnerving (in none of my previous lives did relatives left behind have this means of getting in touch), I force myself to keep focused on what *really* matters. I love them, of course, but there is a bigger picture here. My loyalties lie with Ashkai, and I can't let myself become distracted or emotional.

After taking a deep breath, I start firing off e-mails to websites, journalists, and self-styled "psychonauts" who have written about the medicine, asking if they're aware of ceremonies taking place in London. But who knows if any of them will even reply? I could easily be the police, after all.

I sigh, stretch, and glance at my watch. I've been here over an hour, and staring at this screen has given me a headache. It could get very bad very quickly, so I log off and walk toward the manager, who's sitting behind a desk and playing with his phone. The wall behind him is covered with posters.

I'm about to cough so I can pay and get out of here when one of the images grabs my attention. It's for a videogame called *God of War* and features a powerful-looking skinhead warrior with a facial scar holding a sword of fire and magic. It's an arresting scene, full of drama and adventure, so my gaze lingers for a moment, particularly on the word "God," which reminds me of Tammuz and the fact his parents named him after a deity, one associated with death and rebirth, no less. I'm wondering what the universe is trying to tell me about him. I feel the clues stacking up.

The birthmark on his neck, the feeling we'd met before, his living less than a mile from Highgate Cemetery, a comment about seeing me in another life, the sexual chemistry . . .

Then I remember what he told me when I asked what his big secret was: *My surname is Hartman. Google me.*

I sit back at the computer and do exactly that. At first, nothing jumps out, so I add "young criminal" into the mix, figuring that whatever he did to become "infamous" likely involved breaking the law in some way. It's a hunch that pays off.

I open the first link. It takes me to a newspaper article from last summer. There's a picture of Tammuz, head down, being harassed by paparazzi, a lawyer-looking guy in a sharp suit ushering him through the crowd.

I scan the headline and read the story.

Like a ripple on a lake, a smile spreads across my face.

NINE

By the time I get to Tammuz's, the sky is a soft, reddish glow. It's less than half an hour till dark, and it's getting colder, too. Remembering I don't have anywhere to stay and I'll need to find a hotel later, I ring the bell and watch my breath steam the air, hoping the house idiot doesn't answer.

But of course, he does, rolling his eyes and saying, "You keep showing up uninvited, we'll have to get a restraining order."

I look down at his groin. "I prefer talking to that; it's more interesting."

He grabs it and says, "You better believe it." Then he says, "You wanna meet him again, just let me know. Crazy or not, I still would."

I'm about to tell him thanks, I'll bear that in mind when Tammuz shouts from the top of the stairs, asking who's at the door.

The idiot looks over a shoulder. "Who d'ya think?"

Tammuz says, "Oh man, tell her to go away."

"Tell her yourself, dude," Jamie replies. Then he winks at me and struts off, disappearing into a room on the right.

Tammuz appears with damp, messy hair, looking like he's just had a shower, smelling clean and fresh. He's wearing slim jeans and a crinkly white T-shirt but no shoes or socks. It's the first time his arms haven't been covered since we met, and it turns out he's big into tattoos.

The first thing he says is to come inside; he's still worried about the police. He closes the door, adding, "What do you want?" The two of us stand in his gloomy hallway that smells of dust, boys, and cooking.

"To speak to you. It's important."

"Go on, then."

"Can we go upstairs?"

"What if the police show?"

"If they had your number plate, they would have been here ages ago, so don't worry about it."

"Easy for you to say."

"Easy 'cos it's true. Actually, let's go get your bike; we can talk on the way."

"I dunno . . ."

"You leave it much longer, it really will get stolen or trashed and for absolutely no reason."

"What's the time?"

Without looking at my watch, I tell him it's gone five; the thing with the police was hours ago.

He thinks for a moment, then says, "Okay, let me get changed. Wait here."

When he's midway up the stairs, I ask if he's got a spare helmet.

He stops and turns. "Yeah, why?"

"Couple of reasons: First, I learn from my mistakes. Second, I don't want to be left alone on a rough estate. I'm just a girl, after all."

He says, "Shame you don't drive like one."

***

Five minutes pass.

Tammuz appears wearing a jacket and carrying two helmets. He offers to put my bag in his room, saying it's a bit of a walk, but I tell him, "Don't worry; I need the exercise."

When we're outside, I explain how sorry I am about everything, but he cuts me off.

"Why'd you come back, Sam?" he asks, saying it gently, though.

I glance at the sky with its splashes of red, orange, and turquoise, using the time to think, knowing I need to tread carefully with this.

"Beautiful, isn't it?" I say.

"What?"

"The colors."

He looks up. "I guess . . . but that's not why you came back."

"You always in such a rush?"

"Says the girl who nearly killed us today. Wish you'd stopped to appreciate the sky then."

"I said I was sorry."

"What do you want, Sam?" His tone was firmer this time.

So much for easing him in. "I need a favor."

"What kind of favor?"

"An introduction."

"To who?"

"People you've been involved with in the past."

"What do you know about my past?"

"I looked you up online like you said, saw what you got in trouble for, and I think you can help me get something I need."

He laughs. "If it's a criminal record, I'm your man, but from what I've seen, you don't need help with that."

I keep quiet, and he taps the helmets together a couple times, then says, "What did you read? Most of it's bollocks."

We turn left, and in the distance I see a disheveled gray tower block, one of many architectural scars on the horizon, guessing that's our destination.

I say, "That you were a drug dealer and got busted with enough Class As to see you sent down for a decade, including a garbage bag full of magic mushrooms. But you only did six months, so everyone freaked, saying you got off lightly because of your rich, powerful father and his connections, which is why the story made the papers. That about right?"

He clanks the helmets together again. "It was a grocery bag, not a trash bag, and it was a first offense. I was young, too, only seventeen, and if my old man did anything, I never knew about it. He despises me anyway."

"Doesn't mean he wouldn't look out for you."

"If he did pull strings, it was because he was embarrassed having a son in prison, especially one with tattoos and shitty grades."

"What about your mum?"

"She's all right, but they're divorced. She lives in Devon with her special friend now. That's who I was visiting at the weekend."

"She's the reason we met, then?"

"I'll try not to hold it against her," he says, barging me gently with a shoulder to let me know he doesn't mean it, not at this moment, at least. I nudge him back.

We walk in silence for a while, passing an empty bus stop when Tammuz says, "Go on then, what's the favor? And don't tell me you need me to score for you."

My eyes give the game away.

"Forget it," he says. "Don't even bother; they'd throw away the key this time."

"Hear me out," I ask. "All I need is an introduction to someone; that's it. You won't have to break the law."

"Why'd you need me? You're a pretty girl. Go to a club and ask around. Take ten minutes if that."

"What I need is very specific."

"Oh god, what weird shit are you into?"

"Heard of ayahuasca?"

He nods. "Never done it, but it's similar to magic mushrooms and LSD, right, just more hardcore and spiritual?"

"Kind of."

"There was something on Facebook the other day about how it helps cure crackheads and alcoholics. The guy being interviewed said it was like twenty years' therapy in one night."

"It's a powerful medicine," I say, feeling hopeful. "Any idea where I can get some?"

"Sounds like serious stuff."

"It is, but I've worked with ayahuasca before. I know what I'm doing."

"So speak to the people you got it from before."

"I can't."

"Why?"

"Long story," I say, followed by, "I really need your help, Tammuz," as I reach out to touch his arm.

"You sick or something?"

"Why would you say that?"

"You said it was a medicine . . . you act like you have a death wish . . ."

"No, I'm fine, it's a different kind of problem . . ."

Tammuz says, "If it was weed or coke or pills even . . . but this stuff . . ."

He shrugs, and I start probing, asking where he used to get magic mushrooms and how that contact might be able to help. He keeps deflecting, saying he isn't in touch with people like that anymore. He's trying to get his life on track.

I can sense he's getting frustrated, so I stop pushing and change the subject as he leads me onto the grounds of the estate, its tower block looming directly over us now, an obelisk in the darkness.

We walk down a gentle slope, veering round to the right. Very soon, a car park comes into view, tucked in beside a long row of garages.

Tammuz stops dead, keeping us in the shadows. "Damn, we're too late."

"Why?" I say, following his gaze, spotting a black guy wearing a bright orange jacket and leaning on a moped, chatting with a girl. The bike's front wheel points our way, a nearby lamppost illuminating the scene.

I smile. "Don't worry; it'll be okay."

"I recognize the guy in orange; he's bad news. Let's go."

"Who is he?"

"Tried to mug me a couple weeks back," Tammuz says, sounding jittery.

"Pulled a knife as I was coming out the tube; thought I was gonna die. Turns out he targets people like me all the time. Same thing happened to a mate of mine."

"What do you mean people like you?"

"Middle-class white boys."

"What did you do?"

"What do you think? I ran very fast in the opposite direction."

I feel myself getting angry, hating the idea of Tammuz being scared like that. "He chased you?"

"Who cares? Let's just go before he sees us."

"Gimme the keys," I say. "Wait by the road; I'll be up in a sec."

"Not a chance," he says, grabbing my arm. "Come on, we're going."

I shrug him off. "I've got this under control."

"Forget it," he says. "There's no way either of us are getting stabbed over a hairdryer on wheels."

"Nobody's getting stabbed," I say, heading toward the car park.

Tammuz calls after me and says, "Come back you idiot; this is stupid!" but I keep going, and I hear "Fuck sake" followed by his footsteps. I feel him just behind me now.

When I'm close enough to Orange and his girlfriend, I say, "Thanks for looking after it for us," my body language friendly and relaxed as I come to a halt beside the front wheel of the bike. I notice the guy has cane rolls and is about the same age as Rosa.

The girl, who's white, screws her face up and sucks air through her back teeth. She's all forehead, plucked eyebrows, and big jewelry. "Da fuck you say, bitch?"

I use my eyes to let her know I'm not afraid; I'm the person in control here. "We're here to pick our bike up."

"What bike?" Orange says, still leaning on the seat, smoking a cigarette. The girl echoes, "Yeah, what bike, skank?"

He tells her, "Hush, I've got this," and she sucks teeth again.

Behind me, Tammuz says, "Let's go, Sam."

Orange stands, and he's bigger than anticipated. He looks over my shoulder and says, "Was I talking to you, bruv? You hear me arx you a question?"

Tammuz doesn't respond, and the bully puffs his chest out and snarls. "Nuttin' to say all of a sudden, bruv? Cat got your tongue, yeah? Mind your business then before I bitch slap you, can't you see the men are talking?"

Forehead girl bursts out laughing and points at me. "Nah, allow it! He just called you a man, innit, proper dissed you coz a' your skanky hair. You got cancer or what? And what's that nasty mark on your face, bird shit?"

The guy tells her to shut her mouth, and then looks at me and smokes, scanning me with his eyes like I'm hanging meat. "What bike?" he repeats, licking his lips and smiling.

"That one," I say with a nod. The girl is making a phone call now.

He glances at it. "If dis is your ride, babe, what's it doin' in my yard?"

"We were seeing a friend."

"They live 'ere?"

"Yeah."

"What's their name?"

"None of your business."

He lets out a big, confident laugh. "Everything here is my bidness," he says, stepping closer. "Sure we can work summit out, doh, know what I'm sayin', fine ting like you." He puts his hand on my shoulder, and I'm about to break it when Tammuz steps forward and tells him to leave me alone. Tammuz's voice is trembling.

The mugger explodes into a rage, flicking his cigarette away and pushing past me, getting in Tammuz's face. He says if he chats shit again he's getting shanked. Forehead is laughing and on the phone, telling someone to "get round here coz some chiefs are being disrespectful and Robbie's on a madness." Robbie says, "Wait a minute, you look familiar, bruv, where do I know you from?"

Tammuz is so scared he can't speak, and Robbie erupts again, grabbing fistfuls of his coat. "I arxed you a question, bruv, where do I know you from?"

"Nowhere," Tammuz says. "I mean, I don't know . . ."

I take my backpack off and put it beside the front wheel of the bike. I walk up to Robbie. He's got his back to me, shouting in Tammuz's face. I tap his shoulder, and when he turns, I slam the angle of my right hand into his throat, then my left hard into his solar plexus. Finally, I kick the heel of my right boot into his left knee so he's incapacitated, pushing him onto the tarmac now. He's whimpering and gasping for air.

I understand Robbie's life has been hard, and he's just trying to survive like everyone else, but that doesn't make it okay to bully and terrorize people he perceives as weak. He had a choice to make a moment ago, just like he did the day he decided to try and mug my friend. Both times he chose badly, and I hope this experience might help him see that.

I look at Tammuz, who's stunned and pale, telling him to put his helmet on and hand me the keys, which he just about manages.

I grab my bag and put it on his back, taking the second helmet for myself now, all the while keeping an eye on Forehead, who's shouting into her phone, saying, "Man, dem need to get here quick."

To me, she says, "You're dead, you and your pussy-hole boyfriend."

That's when I hear something and look left as a group of teenagers fly around the corner by the far end of the garages, running toward us. I count four guys and two girls.

Helmet straps hanging loose by my cheeks, I jump on the bike and Tammuz gets behind, saying "go go go." I pull away just in time, but two of the chasing pack are fast and won't give up. They reach out to grab us, forcing me to swerve left and right. I struggle to pick up speed on this hill. Just when I think we're okay and the exit is in sight, one of them manages to get ahold of Tammuz, yanking him to the ground, along with my bag.

I manage to steady the moped and pull over. I stride toward Tammuz, who's on the ground. Someone wearing a baseball cap is holding him down and punching him.

The other runner, who's looks Indian and has big, bulbous eyes, opens his arms wide and asks where I'm going, so I kick him hard in the chest and drive the heel of my right palm into his left temple, brushing him aside as I continue forward.

Tammuz is protecting his face, so doesn't see me ram my foot into the top of his attacker's skull, clearing him out of the way. As I'm helping Tammuz up, another boy appears and throws a punch. I turn my head so that he connects with the helmet I'm wearing. The guy says, "you fucking bitch" as I remove the helmet and slam it into his nose, causing blood to gush everywhere. The next person comes for me with a knife, so I break his wrist, hearing bones crunch and separate as I kick high into another person's throat, parrying blows now as I strike out at elbows, lower spines, shins, and groins, making sure none of them get near Tammuz, utilizing the helmet as both a deadly weapon and protective armor.

Very soon, they're backing off, assessing the damage and telling me from a distance that I'm a dead bitch. Robbie's back on the scene in his orange jacket, saying how he and his boys are gonna run a train on me.

I say, "Good luck with that," and then grab Tammuz's arm and lead him toward the bike, picking his helmet up on the way, as it came loose when they pulled him to the ground. My bag is still on his back.

After starting the bike, against a background of curses and threats, I ask if he's okay. He says, "Yeah, but I'd really like to go now."

TEN

When we get to Tammuz's house, I park his bike and, looking over a shoulder, say, "If you're planning on disappearing, I'd like my bag, if that's okay?"

I'm glancing at the sky now, clouds scudding across a three-quarter moon, starting to feel cold, the adrenaline rush from the fight fading.

"You're all right," he says, and when we're standing on the pavement, I lean forward to kiss him on the cheek. The only problem is we're both wearing open-faced helmets (which I somehow forgot), meaning I head-butt him instead.

"Sorry," I say. "Was trying to give you a kiss."

He smiles, but I don't want him to get the wrong idea. "On the cheek."

He says, "Of course." Then, "What for?"

"As a thank you."

He looks confused.

"For standing up for me."

He smiles. "I didn't do anything other than get the crap beaten out of me."

"That's not true. You stepped in and told that guy to leave me alone, and you stood by me, even though you didn't want to be there."

He shakes his head and smiles, then leans forward and nudges his helmet against mine. "That's my thank you then," he says.

"But you were attacked," I reply. "That wasn't supposed to happen."

Tammuz pulls his helmet off and says, "I'm not gonna lie; that's the most scared I've been my whole life, but it was worth it. Where'd you learn to fight like that?"

"They had no right to get in our way, and he shouldn't have tried to mug you."

"Who the hell are you?" he asks playfully, with a smile.

I remove my helmet and change the subject, wanting to know if he's okay, especially after being pulled from the bike, but he assures me all is fine. He says that the bag broke his fall, and he took most of the punches on his forearms. He raises his arms as he adds, "Got my tattoos to hide the bruises."

"That's something," I say, and then add, "I should go," while reaching for my bag, which is scuffed and out of shape.

"Where you staying?" he asks, helping it onto my back.

"Hotel."

"Which one? I'll give you a ride."

"Was hoping you could recommend somewhere."

"I can," he says. "Stay here. Hotels in London are crazy expensive, even the crappy ones. Save your money."

I say, "That's a kind offer, but . . ." and he interrupts, "You can have my bed. I'll sleep on the sofa."

I pull a face, letting him know it's a bad idea, and he says, "It'll be a chance to spend some quality time with Jamie. I've seen the chemistry between you two; why fight it?"

I tell him he's funny and then explain I've got stuff to do, but he insists. He says he'll make a few calls. He might know somebody who can help with the Amazon medicine thing, and the only reason he didn't mention it before is because he hasn't spoken to the guy for a while. "He's not the friendliest bloke you'll ever meet but knows his stuff when it comes to substances that get you high."

I say, "That's amazing," and "Yeah, I'd love to stay, but only if you call your contact tonight." Tammuz says, "Okay, cool," and we go inside. I can't resist blowing the house idiot a kiss when he pops his head out of the lounge to see what's happening.

Tammuz suggests I wait in his bedroom while he makes the call from downstairs. I can tell he's nervous about reaching out to this person.

I sit on the bed, and five minutes later, he appears and tells me that his contact said to come round tomorrow at one. I ask where he lives, and Tammuz says Highbury, which isn't far.

"He have ayahuasca or know where we can get it?"

"We'll find out tomorrow. He doesn't talk business on the phone."

"Thank you, Tammuz," I say, standing, giving him a hug, kissing him on the cheek properly this time, wanting to go further, to feel his lips against mine and to run my fingers through his dark, messy hair, but I hold back. It's a bad idea and will only complicate things.

We go downstairs, and Tammuz prepares some cheese on toast in the kitchen. The sink is piled with dishes, and an ashtray overflows with cigarette and spliff butts. Tammuz points at a cleaning roster on the wall and says, "This is what happens when it's Jamie's turn."

"I'm tired," I say after eating. "No problem," Tammuz answers, "I'll change the sheets." I tell him not to bother.

Alone in his bedroom, after doing some push-ups, sit-ups, and yoga poses, I take a shower and go to bed, wearing black knickers and a tight yellow T-shirt, trying to ignore the part of me that doesn't want to be alone, hoping that Tammuz will slip into bed while I'm sleeping, that I'll wake and he'll be there . . .

Go for it, Tammuz, be brave, I think, and despite the warmth between my legs demanding attention and a streetlamp seeping through the paper-thin blinds, tiredness soon takes hold and I feel myself drifting, knowing my mind will continue to work on things while Rosa's body replenishes. I'm thinking about how I'm Ashkai's only hope, as I leave normal consciousness and enter the world of dreams.

As if on cue, a majestic, astral jaguar emerges from the void. Ashkai's spirit animal pads toward me, leaving paw prints of fizzing, animated light, the beast glowing with vibrancy and color, getting closer. I watch as the predator's head morphs into the face of the Theban prince I fell in love with four thousand years ago.

This is a dream, I think. *And I am in control.* I relish that as I focus on the tingling wetness between my legs while visualizing the beautiful, nubile sex slave I once was, trained since childhood in the art of physical pleasure. And what a joy it was to satisfy the mighty prince Ashkai, especially as the favor was always returned.

The ethereal, ancient me, oiled and ready, reaches out to caress the half man, half beast, while Rosa licks fingertips, the same hand brushing past erect nipples on its way down, almost there, so close, when somebody lifts the duvet and climbs into bed. I feel the warmth of their breath on the back of Rosa's neck.

Tammuz, I think, dreaming lucidly, aware of the fact I am straddling two dimensions at once. *Not now!*

This boy is just a silly crush, whereas Ashkai is my light, my love, my soul mate, and I am angry with Tammuz for imposing like this, especially as I will have to wake and tell him to leave, knowing the jaguar will likely be long gone by the time I fall asleep again.

I feel Tammuz's hand slip under my T-shirt and cup a breast. I open my eyes now, turning to tell him no, but instead of seeing the kind person who covered me with a blanket on that bus, I find myself looking at the house idiot, Jamie's smug face just inches from mine, his right cheek flat against the pillow. I am instantly furious and appalled, but when I try to push him away, I discover, to my horror, that I'm paralyzed.

I try to scream but only manage a pathetic whimper. Delighting in my predicament, Jamie laughs, revealing a mouth of rotting, black teeth. His pupils burn red, skin melting, the idiot transforming into a hideous, green witch.

The demon lunges and straddles my midriff, pinning my arms (not that I can move them). Its hideous, wart-covered face advances toward mine, cheek by cheek now, whispering something, saying she wants what I have . . .

Could I still be asleep? I think, the question garnering hope.

"Your light is special," the wench says, sounding impressed before turning nasty again. "I must feed." She's shouting now. "Give me what's mine."

The creature, frenzied and angry, leans back to glare at me, but by now I have a pretty good idea what I'm dealing with.

"You are a succubus," I say, regaining composure, seeing by the look in her eye that I am right. "You wasted your human lives, didn't you? And now your light is too dim, too weak, too damaged for the demands of a physical body. But you long still for pleasures of the flesh. Which is why you prowl the dreams of others, stealing their life force, biding your time for a return to the Earth plane."

The wench leans close and screams, "Give me your light!" but I know this entity is powerless without fear. And I am not afraid.

"Be gone," I say, sensing my jaguar nearby, ready to pounce. But I don't need help dealing with this scum energy.

I say, "Leave me, succubus, for I will give you no light," but instead of disappearing, the wench starts to whimper and groan.

"I have erred," she says, eyes changing from the color of lava to a deep, midnight blue. "Have mercy." But this is not my work. I watch her green skin crack and splinter, each fissure releasing a shard of energized, sentient light, a voice calling to me . . .

"Samsara," it says, as if travelling across a vast distance. "I am coming. I see you."

By now the succubus is gone, but I am not alone, for she has been replaced by a being of immense beauty and power, one with soft, wide lips, short, dark hair, and piercing indigo eyes, an aura of the same color cocooning her naked, goddesslike form. Just like the wench, she is straddling me, but my arms are free, and I am no longer paralyzed.

How did you find me? I ask using thought-speak, and Meta says, out loud, "With love." Her voice resonates in such a way as to make me feel better than I've ever felt, so safe, peaceful, and warm.

She says, "Do not fight, little one," but I hear the jaguar snarl, and it helps bring me back. I'm calling my master's name now, invoking the power of his spirit animal, asking for its light to merge with mine.

I become aware of a change in my physical energy, an almost painful tingling, and I look over to my right. There is a huge, dappled feline paw where my hand should be. My head is also transforming. There's an indescribable feeling of my brain rearranging as I become part cat, part woman. I roar with a mixture of desperation and rage. Simultaneously, I unfurl my claws and swipe for Meta's head. But in the moment before contact, everything changes—no more Meta, no more indigo light, no more jaguar—and I'm back in the land of the living, scouring the side of Tammuz's face with my nails.

"Ahhh, fuck!" he says, recoiling. "Sam, it's me. You were having a bad dream."

I'm upright now, sweating and out of breath, the room ablaze with morning sunshine.

"It's okay," Tammuz says, holding a hand to his cheek and edging toward me. "Everything's okay now, you're safe."

But I'm not. And neither is he.

ELEVEN

"I am so, so sorry, Tammuz," I say, sitting at the kitchen table, palms cupping the mug of chamomile tea he just made. There's a window on my right with a view of two bicycles and a neglected back garden. Even though it's a fairly clear day, down here, in among the tightly packed houses made of dark brick, everything feels industrial and bleak. To make matters worse, I'm still badly shaken from the events of last night. I'm also dealing with a thumping headache. I have to breathe and relax if I want to avoid another seizure.

Inside, I tell myself that just because Meta found a way into my dreams, it doesn't mean she knows where I am. I reason that if she did, I'd have been captured by now instead of sitting here drinking herbal tea.

"What the hell happened?" Tammuz asks.

My gaze is drawn to the scratches on his left cheek. After getting out of bed, I snapped a leaf from the aloe vera plant in the bathroom and used its gel to soothe his wounds. Even so, I feel guilty and low. It's glaringly obvious I have to get out of his life before something really bad happens.

"I had a nightmare," I reply, promising myself after today—ayahuasca or not—he'll never see me again. I feel sad about that. I wish I wasn't wearing his jumper that's way too big for me, and I wonder what it is about his smell that makes me feel so safe and at home.

He says, "You sounded like a wild animal. It was nuts, howling and roaring . . . woke the whole house up. Jamie was fuming. I thought you were either having a fit or being murdered, which is why I came in."

I point at his face. "And that's how I thanked you."

"Was it because of the fight last night?"

I rub my temples to ease the pain. "No . . . maybe . . . I don't

84

know . . ."

"Were you being tortured or something, in your dream I mean?"

"I'm not sure; it's patchy . . ." I look away to let him know I'd rather not go into details.

He adds more sugar to his coffee. "You weren't the only one had a weird night."

"Nightmare?"

"Not exactly. Seriously messed-up dream, though."

"About?"

"You," he says, holding my gaze.

I raise an eyebrow."

He says, "It was nothing kinky, don't worry."

"I'm not."

Tammuz takes another gulp of coffee. "Good." He's trying to be cool, even though he's blushing.

"Details, please?" I ask, happy to be changing the subject.

"Other people's dreams are boring, aren't they?"

"Not when they're interesting."

"Okay, but I want to hear yours as well, whatever you can remember. I deserve that at least, don't I?"

"You first," I say, rubbing my temples again, thinking I'll just make something up when he's done.

"Deal," he says, and we clink mugs.

"I warn you, it's properly out there," he says, sitting back, running a hand through his hair. "I woke in the middle of the night, at least that's what I thought . . . and standing at the bottom of the couch was this woman or angel or goddess or something. She was beautiful, though, really, really beautiful, and there was this light everywhere . . . and it all felt, I dunno, really . . . sort of . . . real, I guess, realer than this even, does that make sense?"

I nod, trying to hide my concern. "Yes, it does."

He sits forward and reaches for my hand. "Everything all right? You've gone pale?"

"I'm fine; keep talking," I say, pulling away, feeling a shooting pain in my left temple, hoping this story isn't going where I think it is.

"Tell me if it gets boring."

I force a smile.

How could Meta possibly know about Tammuz?

He says, "So the angel or goddess or whatever she was glides over, floating like a cloud, and strokes my head, and I get this amazing feeling all over, as if I'm coming up on ten pills at the same time, only better . . . really loving and peaceful, sort of healing as well, hard to explain. Next thing I know, she starts speaking to me in my head, if that makes sense, saying she needed my help."

He pauses, and I say, "With what?" feeling like the left side of my brain is about to implode.

"Sure you're okay?"

"Yes," I snap. "Tell me."

He gives me a funny look, part concerned, part annoyed, before saying, "Finding you. How weird is that?"

"You're sure she meant me?"

"Totally . . . even said your name. Only it was different, foreign sounding, Sam something . . . I can't remember exactly, but it was definitely you, 100 percent."

"What did you tell her?" blinking now, things going blurry . . .

"I told her you were with me, but she wanted details. Before I could carry on, this pantherlike creature appeared out of nowhere, only it looked like it was made of smoke or vapor or something. It attacked her. I was so scared I woke up and couldn't get back to sleep afterward."

Trying desperately to suppress the buildup of pain and pressure inside my skull, I say, "Describe what she looked like."

"Why, what's going on?"

"Just do it," I say. "Now."

He says, "You're acting crazy again," followed by, "short, dark hair, high cheekbones, full lips . . . She had this light around her as well, like an aura I guess, and these incredible eyes . . ."

"What color were they?" I ask. "Her eyes, I mean," praying he says green or brown, anything but . . .

"Indigo."

My last thought, following an epic explosion of pain in my head, is: *I'm going to pass out,* which is exactly what I do.

***

What's on my face? I wonder, feeling heavy and lethargic.

I open my eyes, but light pours through like boiling water, and I retreat into darkness again.

I'm lying flat. I try sitting up and fail. Something is holding me down.

Am I dreaming? Has Meta found me? Is this the Long Sleep?

"What's going on?" I say, but it's difficult to talk with this thing on my face.

I'm sensing people around, lots of noise and bumps and motion, and hear Tammuz say, "She's moving."

This is followed by a girl saying, "Hello, Sam, you're all right, sweetheart; everything's okay. My name is Stephanie, and I'm a student paramedic. You're in an ambulance on the way to hospital."

I had another seizure, I think, remembering Tammuz's dream, feeling frightened and exposed now, like an injured mouse being pawed and prodded by a cat.

What game is Meta playing?

I half open my eyes, adjusting to the light, and see Stephanie looming over me, her youthful features coming into focus. Even though there's a strap across my chest and another at thigh level, I'm able to bend my right arm at the elbow, my hand exploring my face now. The student paramedic tells me to leave the oxygen mask on; it's helping me breathe. She explains that I've suffered a seizure, but I'm much better now, and she adds, "Your boyfriend's here, so you've nothing to worry about."

"We're just friends," Tammuz says.

I lift my head. He's in a foldout chair down by the rear of the vehicle. I give him a tired wave. Stephanie, who's wearing green and looks to be early twenties, is closest, and I can sense somebody else in the corner behind, most likely the senior paramedic in charge.

I take the oxygen mask off and say, "I can breathe fine . . . need to loosen these straps; they're too tight."

"I'll sort that," Stephanie says, getting to it, explaining the straps were so I wouldn't hurt myself on the journey, especially as I was having a seizure. Then the girl is asking questions, wanting to know my medical history and if something like this has happened before, what medication I'm on, and if it's okay to take a blood sugar reading.

Thinking on my feet, I say, "Yeah, fine, do what you have to." I tell her I've had epilepsy since childhood but that I stopped taking my prescription recently as I was suffering side effects. I tell her I can't remember what the pills were called, but yes, I will see my GP, definitely, don't worry, I'm fine, honestly, feeling much better now.

I have to go through the same routine at the hospital with the doctor (who runs more tests). She lectures me about what a bad idea it was to stop my medication, instructing that if the side effects are a problem, I should consult my GP about other options.

I say thanks, apologize for the trouble, and ask if I can go now. After more questions and another lecture, she eventually says okay, and on the way out I grab Tammuz, who's sitting by a vending machine, looking ridiculous in his faded jogging pants, T-shirt, and brown leather shoes, which he must have thrown on at the last minute. I realize I don't look much better drowning in his jumper and wearing the paper slippers the hospital provided, my legs bare and exposed.

"Let's go," I say, following the Way Out signs along the wide blue corridor, the air infused with antiseptic and death. I feel a lot better knowing the seizure helped clear out some of the negative energy I was carrying.

Tammuz falls in beside me. "What'd the doctor say?"

"That the two of us look like idiots."

He doesn't understand that I'm joking. "Really?"

I glance at his shoes. "You especially. He said it was depressing for the other patients."

He follows my gaze, his brain eventually catching up. "Next time I'll call my stylist instead of an ambulance."

We skirt around an overweight man pushing a trolley full of medical equipment. "You shouldn't have called anyone; I was fine."

"You were fine?" Tammuz says, losing patience and raising his voice. The two of us press against the wall now, letting a large family past. A very old woman is at the center. "I'll remember that next time you're foaming at the mouth and shaking like crazy, eyes popping out of your fucking head."

The old woman, who looks frail and unwell, cuts Tammuz a disapproving look, so he lowers his voice. He asks me what's *really* going on, saying he knew someone at school with epilepsy, but his fits were nothing like mine. He adds, "I thought you were dying."

There's a line of taxis outside, and before long, we're on our way back to Archway. I tell Tammuz not to worry because that's the last seizure of mine he'll ever see.

"You going back to Exeter?"

The black cab smells of cheap leather and stale perfume.

"Your place first, then Highbury to see your friend, then yes, I'm going home."

Tammuz throws his head back and laughs. "There's no way I'm helping you"—he glances over his shoulder at the driver, whispering now—"score drugs . . . not in your condition. What if you die or something? You can forget it."

I can see he's deadly serious, which means I have to change his mind. I look out the window, making myself sad, waiting for tears to form before saying, "If I tell you something, you have to promise not to go on about it and ask loads of questions, understood?"

The energy in the taxi softens. "Yeah, of course, tell me what's going on."

I make as if I can't get the words out, then say, "I'm sick. I mean, really sick. I've been treating myself with ayahuasca for a while now; it's the only thing that works. But the person I was getting it from disappeared two months ago, and since then, my seizures have been getting worse. That's why I'm here, and that's why I need your help. If I don't start treating myself soon, the damage to my brain could be irreversible. That's why I need you to introduce me to your friend. After that, I promise you'll never have to see me again."

Tammuz looks shocked. "I'm so sorry, Sam . . . what's . . . um, what's . . ."

"What's wrong with me?" I say. "It's a neurological thing, really rare, more chance winning the lottery, lucky me, huh?"

He looks down at his feet. "What about your doctor? There must be something they can give you."

The question annoys me, though it shouldn't. I'm just so tense right now.

"You think I'd be going to all this trouble if there was a pill I could take? You think I'm stupid? You know what? Forget it, not your problem, I'll just grab my stuff and go."

Immediately, he comes to sit beside me. "I'm sorry, okay? No wonder you've been acting crazy." He smiles. "Of course I'll help, whatever you need."

I wipe away tears and tell him he doesn't have to; I've gotten him in enough trouble and I'll work it out. He puts a hand on my shoulder and says, "*We'll* work it out," which is when I know everything's back on track. To make certain, I lean in and kiss him on the lips, just a peck. I see in his eyes how much he wants me and know I shouldn't give that power up easily.

Tammuz is a good person, and I feel bad manipulating him, but Ashkai's life is on the line.

And Meta's not the only one who can play dirty.

TWELVE

Tammuz says, "This guy we're going to see, he's unpredictable. Let me do the talking." Then, after a pause, "Even if he starts losing his shit. That's just what he's like. Don't do anything stupid, is what I'm saying. I know how to handle him."

"What's he got to lose his shit about?" I ask.

"He's high-strung. And he drinks vodka like it's water."

"What's he got to be stressed about?"

"Everything."

I roll my eyes and sigh. "Just spit it out."

He says, "You never let anything go, do you? I sort of owe him money, only I don't, depends how you look at it."

"How can you sort of owe him money?"

"When I got busted, the drugs they found were Viktor's. That's his name."

"How much was the stuff worth?"

"A grand, £1,500, maybe, but I kept my mouth shut and went to prison, so we're quits far as I'm concerned."

"How'd you get involved with someone like that?"

"By going out with his daughter."

"When?"

"School. I was fifteen."

"Was it serious?"

He starts fidgeting. "At the time . . . feels so long ago now."

It's a quarter past one in the afternoon, and we're on a bus to Highbury, on the top deck with nobody in earshot. The sky is thick with clouds, and my bag is between my legs, as I plan on disappearing very soon. I want to put distance between Tammuz and me so he's out of harm's way, although Viktor might have other ideas . . .

"What was her name?"

Tammuz, sitting on the seat in front of me but angled round in

91

my direction, says, "Dina," with a hint of sadness in his voice.

Is that jealousy I feel?

Whatever it is, I ignore it. "When'd you see her last?"

"Three, four years, something like that."

"Why'd you break up?"

"We didn't. Viktor sent her back to Russia to live with his sister. He thought I was a bad influence, which is hilarious coming from him."

"What happened?" I ask, remembering (once again) how I journeyed across that vast land in 1824. My name was Inga then, a scrawny serf, and I was searching for Ashkai. Over the course of a year, traveling thousands of miles, I survived subzero temperatures, starvation, illness, and attacks from other travelers who wanted what little I had. But I fought and endured, and my search was successful. I take heart from that, as Tammuz says, "We were caught smoking a spliff at school; that's all, big deal. Crazy bastard sent her home the same week. I haven't seen her since. I was devastated, so I confronted him about it, wanted to show I was serious about his daughter, thought he might respect me. Biggest mistake I ever made."

"Why?"

"He threatened me, said I was lucky to be alive, but I stood my ground, told him to go for it, that all I cared about was Dina. Then, he asked how he could trust someone who gave his daughter drugs, and I said I'd do anything to prove myself. He said, 'Okay, well, come work for me then, that way I'll see what kind of man you really are.'"

"Doing what?"

"Running errands, delivering packages, stuff like that. He's got loads of businesses, restaurants and dry cleaners mainly, and I was going between them a lot. I quickly realized he was dodgy, but I was losing it. My e-mails to Dina were going unanswered, and her phone was dead. Dumb, I know, but things were bad at home, and I wasn't thinking straight."

"With your dad?"

"I prefer to call him Judas, but yeah; he went ballistic after the spliff thing and stopped my allowance, said he wasn't going to fund my habit. I told him to keep his stupid money, promised myself I'd never ask him for anything ever again."

"And Viktor was paying you?"

Tammuz nods. "Very well."

"What was in the packages?"

"Not a clue, didn't look, especially after what he said he'd do to me if I did.

But it was never about that. He was just feeling me out."

"For what?"

"Turns out, his main business was drugs, and he wanted me to sell weed at school. He'd been playing me from the start."

"But why? It sounds so small-time."

Tammuz laughs. "You didn't go to my school. Everyone was loaded and posh and destined for big-time, well-paid jobs. Viktor was thinking long term, but I didn't care. I was popular; I had money; and when you're sixteen, seventeen, that's all that matters."

"The article I read . . . it wasn't just weed they caught you with, was it?"

"That's because people started asking for harder stuff after a while, coke, ecstasy, mushrooms, so I spoke to Viktor, and he made sure I had everything I needed. By then, I thought I was untouchable."

"What about Dina?"

"He let me speak to her on the phone a few times, but after a while, it started hurting less. There were other girls as well . . . they probably only liked me for the drugs, but I didn't care. I still thought about Dina, but I got so caught up in everything, a year flew by"—he clicks his fingers—"just like that."

"Then, something happened that scared the crap out of me, so I spoke to Viktor, told him I wouldn't be able to work for him anymore, even introduced him to someone who could take my place.

"Viktor said it didn't work like that, but I insisted. He told me to sell what I had and that he'd think about it, but two days later, the police raided my parents' house, found my stash, and sent me to prison for a year. I was out after six months with good behavior, but by then, Mum and Dad had broken up. Judas tried to blame me for destroying the family, even though I knew for a fact he'd been screwing my Mum's best friend for years."

"Sounds like a real dick," I say, wondering if Viktor was the one who handed Tammuz over to the police. The timing, the fact that Tammuz was no longer useful, messing around with the guy's daughter . . .

Tammuz says, "Complete and utter, but that's life, huh? Can't choose your family. I moped around, feeling sorry for myself for ages, but Mum helped snap me out of it, said I had to prove the bastard wrong, show him I wasn't a loser. She even dragged me down to college last year so I'd enroll."

"Why didn't you move to Devon with her, start over?"

"This is our stop," he says, standing. "Because it's the most boring place on Earth." Looking over a shoulder, he adds, "Sorry, no offense . . ."

We're on the lower deck when the bus stops. As we're getting off, I say, "Still not talking to your dad?"

"No, and I never will," he says, turning left. Specks of rain tickle my face. "Mum got half his cash, and he got a new family; everyone's a winner. Good riddance, you ask me."

Even though he's putting on a brave face, it's obvious this is upsetting, so I change the subject. "Seen Viktor since you got out?"

He shakes his head. "Been staying as far away from him as possible and everyone else I used to know."

"So why we heading there now?"

"Because he can get hold of anything."

"Even for someone who corrupted his little girl and vanished, owing him money?"

"I'm hoping he doesn't see it like that."

"You and me both."

***

"This is it," Tammuz says, leading us into the front garden of a three-story Georgian house on the corner of a pretty crescent. A little park is opposite, and Range Rovers and BMWs line the pavement.

We climb the steps, and Tammuz rings the bell. The rain's starting to come down a little harder now.

I loosen the straps of my bag. "Viktor didn't mind you bringing someone?"

"He doesn't know."

"How come?"

"Didn't have a chance to tell him."

"Won't it look weird turning up with a stranger?"

"Probably," says Tammuz, and I can tell he's nervous. In fact, it's obvious he doesn't want to be here at all, and definitely not on his own.

The door opens, revealing a short, stout man wearing a roll-neck jumper and a navy baseball cap. He's in his midforties with stubble; his nose bends left slightly. One look at his lumpy, scarred hands, and it's obvious the boxing he's into doesn't involve gloves.

"Pree-vyet, Sergei!" is Tammuz's attempt at "hello" in Russian. His pronunciation is terrible. He sticks a hand out. "How's it going?"

But Sergei, a man with the destructive, poisonous energy of a killer, is looking at me.

"Who this?" he asks, in a thick Russian accent.

Tammuz pulls his hand back. "Sam. She's cool; don't worry."

"I look worry?"

Tammuz forces a laugh. "No, of course not, it's just an expression, means you can trust her . . . where's Viktor? I'll explain."

"Tell your woman wait in park."

Your woman, I think, biting my tongue.

"But it's raining," Tammuz says.

Sergei points at me. "She have hood on jumper."

"Can I use your bathroom?" I ask, improvising, flashing teeth. "I'm gonna pee my pants."

"Go behind bush," Sergei says. Tammuz tries to reassure him, but the brute is having none of it, telling me, "Go now, wait in park," and he says to Tammuz, "You, inside, Viktor waiting," which is when I take matters into my own hands. I speak Russian to Sergei, telling him this isn't the welcome I was expecting from a

95

brother.

He scans me head to toe. "You speak Russian?" saying it in his mother tongue. Tammuz poses the same question in English.

Still addressing Sergei, I say, "My father is from Ryazan." That was Inga's place of birth. The best lies never veer too far from the truth.

He grunts. "I am from Kolomna; you know it?"

"Yes," I reply. "I have relatives there."

He glances at Tammuz. "Boyfriend?"

"No, but we have known each other many years."

Pointing at the scratch marks, Sergei says, "You do that to his face?"

"Yes, it's a long story."

Sensing he's being talked about, Tammuz says, "What's going on? What did he say about me?" So, I reach out to touch his arm reassuringly.

Sticking to Russian, Sergei asks, "Why has he brought you here?"

"To introduce me to Viktor. Do you work with him?"

"He is my brother. What do you want?"

"I have something for him. It's very important."

"What?"

The rain is heavy now, so I glance skyward. "Can we talk inside?"

"Answer now," he says. "Or leave."

Improvising again, I slip my bag off and rest it on the floor, opening the side pocket now, reaching inside to grab a handful of fifty-pound notes. Straightening, I say, "When Tammuz went to prison, he owed Viktor money. I'm here to settle that debt."

Sergei orders me to put the money away, but I continue waving it in his face until he has no choice but to usher us inside. He says, "Wait here," when we get to the lounge, and he disappears into an adjoining room via a sliding door, which he closes after him. I see a glimpse of a kitchen through there, and classical music seeps through, along with the smell of garlic and onions.

Tammuz is a ball of nervous energy. "Fuck, Sam, you speak Russian and didn't mention it?"

"Lower your voice," I say, stuffing cash into the front pocket of my jeans, taking in our surroundings: high ceiling, crystal chandelier, dark wooden floors, glass coffee table, open fireplace, flat-screen TV, an aerial photograph of central London on the wall, and Union Jack cushions on the sofa. There are Russian influences as well—some traditional red dolls and a watercolor of the Kremlin—but they are few and far between.

"I'm good with languages," I say, glancing at the family photographs placed throughout the room, most featuring a very pretty girl with a beauty spot on her left cheek.

Hello, Dina.

The large, powerful-looking guy with the receding hairline and wide nose has got to be Viktor. There's something familiar about that face . . .

"Why didn't you tell me you could speak Russian?" Tammuz says. "Pretty crucial information, don't you think?"

"Didn't ask."

"Why the hell would I?" he says. "And where'd you get all that money? You steal it?"

"I've told you, I'm not a thief."

"Why were you giving it to Sergei?"

"I was offering to pay your debt to Viktor."

Color drains from Tammuz's face. "He ask for it? Tell me exactly what he said."

"No. I offered."

"You fucking *what*? Why? I didn't say you could do that."

"To get us in."

Tammuz carries on swearing but stops when Sergei reappears. The Russian looks at me, saying, "Viktor will see you alone."

Tammuz is getting more and more agitated. "Speak English. What's going on?"

I ignore him.

"What about Tammuz?" I ask.

Sergei replies, "He stays with me."

I nod, and Tammuz demands to be looped in. I tell him Viktor wants to see me alone, and he says, "That doesn't make sense," before raising his voice. "Hey, Viktor, what's going on—"

Sergei cuts him off with a shove. "Shut up mouth," he says,

speaking English, the accompanying glare promising worse if Tammuz doesn't fall into line.

"I won't be long," I say, grabbing my bag. "You need me, I'm just through there, okay?"

"This isn't happening," Tammuz says. "You stay; I'll go," but he only gets as far as the sliding door.

Sergei closes it behind me, saying, "That was last chance." His tone is aggressive. I'm ready to burst in there if I have to, although it sounds like Tammuz has gotten the message.

I focus my attention on Viktor, who is sitting at the far end of a white marble island with gas stove built in. Steel pans are overhead, and knife handles stick out of a large wooden block. Beethoven's *Moonlight Sonata* emanates from an expensive-looking speaker, the haunting piano melody reminding me of Ashkai, who is a huge fan of classical music.

Viktor is facing my direction but hunched over a bowl of steaming red soup. A chunk of bread, metal-rimmed spectacles, and what looks like an alcoholic drink are also on the counter. Glass doors frame Viktor. There's a good-size garden out there, a weeping willow in the corner, its branches and leaves heavy with rain.

Speaking Russian, I say, "Sorry for disturbing your meal," while walking toward him, bag hanging by my side, picking up a whiff of vodka, noticing a black and white photograph from the late nineteenth century of Tower Bridge on the wall, the thing partially built, an event I witnessed firsthand.

When Viktor—older than Sergei, strong shoulders, weathered face—eventually glances up, I'm struck by a powerful sense of déjà vu, dizzied by it, and I'm trying to process what that means as I come to a halt adjacent to him and put my backpack down. "Can I sit?"

Viktor grunts and waves a hand, which is when I notice something about the right side of his face. The skin below his ear and around his jawline is mottled and discolored. It's obviously a birthmark, which means it's connected to a previous life cycle, most likely one of his deaths. Racking my brain for connections, I perch on a stool and say, "Look at me, Viktor," speaking Russian, needing to put the pieces together. Instinct tells me it's important.

After removing the spoon from his mouth, Viktor, who is as ugly as he is arrogant, uses a napkin to wipe his pink and fleshy lips. Speaking English, he says, "What so special about your face I should look at it?" He has less of an accent than his brother, but has a deeper, more commanding tone. I can feel the toxicity of his aura. The air is thick with it.

He's wearing a white shirt speckled with red soup, its top three buttons undone and with a thick carpet of hair poking through. He has rings on his fingers and a tattooed neck that reads *"nikomu ne doveryayut"* (trust no one).

"It's not my face I'm interested in, it's yours."

He takes a drink and flashes his wedding band. "You are too late." He reaches for his glasses and puts them on, taking a good look at me now. "My wife is away in Russia, so maybe I make exception this time."

The bespectacled leer offers a very good clue as to who this man is *(I would know that look anywhere)*, but it's something else about his now magnified eyes, something I missed before, that confirms his identity.

"I am offended," I say, surprised by how calm I'm feeling.

"Because you are pretty? You want be ugly? World lonely place for ugly woman."

"I am offended because you don't remember me."

"I know you?"

"Very well."

He narrows his eyes, one of which is larger than the other *(just like him!)*, in half recognition. "Ah, one of Zlata's whores, yes? You have long hair before? You should grow back; short hair for man."

"No. I am your daughter. At least, I used to be."

His joyless smile unveils crooked, coffee-stained teeth. "Come sit on lap then; be good girl for Papa."

"Does Dina sit on your lap?"

His expression changes. "You know my daughter?"

"I know you fuck her." I say it to test the water, no longer thinking about ayahuasca, Meta, or Ashkai; instead, I wonder how this demon energy was able to return to the Earth plane so quickly.

I'm hoping, for Dina's sake, history has not repeated itself.

Why have our paths crossed like this? There must be purpose in it. Am I to inflict pain and suffering on you, as you did to Elsie for so many years, or is this an opportunity to choose love over hate?

I know in my heart and in my bones it's the latter; that's what Ashkai would advise. I just don't think I'm ready, not yet . . .

He looks at me as if I'm nothing. "Pretty face but dirty mouth like whore."

"At first I thought it was strange for a Russian to have Union Jack cushions and pictures of London on his wall, but your affinity for this city makes total sense now. Do you remember your life here, Mr. Farish? I hope you don't mind me calling you that?"

He points at his temple, index finger twirling. "Crazy like rabid dog."

"And that birthmark on your face, does it still burn?" I'm remembering the smell of Mr. Farish's charred flesh, his corpse being dragged away from the blazing fire. *Too bad that he doesn't remember it.*

Did you make it to the window, Mother? Were you brave enough to jump?

"It seems I did not do enough to banish you from this world," I say. "That tells me you are an old soul, which means you should know better."

Viktor chuckles. "This joke, yes?" and then in Russian, "I do not have time for games. You told Sergei you had come to pay the boy's debt, but there is more to your visit. What do you want? And choose your words carefully, for I am not a patient man."

I want to hurt you, my inner voice whispers, Mozart playing on the speaker instead of Beethoven now, but I know that is not an option. To punish Viktor for Mr. Farish's crimes would be deeply wrong and something the universe would hold me accountable for. The truth is, I don't know this man; I may think I do, but I don't.

"I have come to ask you a question," I say, also speaking Russian, the voice in my head saying, *He is still a monster; look at how he manipulated and exploited Tammuz.*

Viktor tips the rest of his drink down his throat, the veins in his face suffused with red. He's an alcoholic, just like Mr. Farish.

"Ask."

Now is my chance to get things back on track, to start enquiring about where I can get my hands on ayahuasca and explain that I'll pay well over the odds if necessary, but instead I say, "Why did you hand Tammuz over to the police?". . . as if it even matters . . .

"He is your boyfriend?"

"No."

"What is your relationship?"

"We are friends."

"He told you I went to the police?"

"No."

"For what reason do you accuse me?

"Because you are an arrogant man who cares only for himself."

Stop looking for a reason to hurt him, Samsara.

"Because he quit working for you and was no longer useful."

Focus on what you came here for.

"And because he loved your daughter and you didn't want to share her."

Viktor unfolds his arms and removes his glasses, placing them on the marble work surface. Seeing him do it triggers feelings of shame and vulnerability. Mr. Farish always took his spectacles off before hitting his wife or abusing his daughter. Stuff like that is very hard to forget, let alone forgive.

"You are very brave," Viktor says, his face somewhere between angry and impressed. "I deal with ruthless men, cruel men, murderers, and thieves. Even these dogs, who fear nothing, fear me. But you, who I could crush like a bug"—he slams a fist down—"face me with the courage of a lion. Is that what you are, little whore, a lion?"

I remain silent.

"Why aren't you afraid?" he asks.

"Because I am stronger than you."

The corners of his mouth turn up, but it's more of a snarl than a smile. "What makes you so sure?"

"Fear empowers you. Without it, you are nothing. I learned this long ago."

"Power and fear are the same; they are brothers."

"Evil men are feared. True power comes from love."

"You speak like a woman," he says, opening a drawer to his right, "a very stupid one." With practiced ease—though I could have stopped him if I wasn't distracted and, let's face it, curious—Viktor points a gun at me, silencer attached. "I am known for my temper," he says. "Many times I have made bad decisions because I am angry. That is why I have started listening to classical music, so I can be calmer, more reasonable. How do you think I'm doing?"

I use the footrest of my stool to stand and lean forward, letting the nozzle of the silencer press into my forehead. I feel no fear at all.

His eyes widen with astonishment. "You claim you are my daughter," he says, "but you would make a much better son." Snapping his arm back, he attempts to strike me with the butt of his gun. The big Russian is slow, so I have time to duck, lying flat against the cool marble as he swipes thin air. That's when I do something I know I will regret.

Viktor roars and leaps out of his seat, dropping his gun in the process, dealing with the bowl of hot soup I stupidly pushed onto his lap, the one that's just hit the floor and smashed into pieces. When he looks up, I'm standing beside my stool, survival instincts taking over.

Viktor, who has madness in his eyes, bends for his weapon. In that time, I grab two things: a large steel pan from above the stove, which I use to intercept the two bullets aimed at my head, and a knife from the wooden block. Throwing fast and precisely, I bury the knife's blade in my attacker's throat.

Viktor drops his gun and reaches for the knife, his eyes burning with fear and rage, chest hair and shirt turning the color of his trousers. He splutters the word *"shlyukha"* (whore) before looking over my shoulder, hissing, *"ubit yeye"* (kill her).

I turn and see Sergei in the doorway, eyes fixed on his older brother, a man he clearly idolizes. His face reflects shock and loss, but the emotion is quickly replaced by cold calculation.

"Tammuz," I shout, Viktor falling with a thud. "Run!"

Instead of coming for me, Sergei closes the sliding door and disappears into the lounge.

Viktor is lying on his back, and I have to dig under his heavy, still-twitching body to retrieve the weapon he tried to kill me with.

You were defending yourself, Samsara. You had no choice.

I straighten as the doors to the lounge slide open. Tammuz is being pushed through the gap, nose bleeding, eyes streaming, Sergei holding a gun to his head with its silencer attached. These guys are dedicated to the art of killing discreetly. Using Tammuz as a human shield, Sergei fires at my head. I hit the floor and curl into a ball, the bullets shattering one of the glass doors behind me as cold air and heavy rain gush in from the garden.

"Please don't hurt me," Tammuz says, voice trembling. "I don't want to die."

I sit upright against the base of the island, Viktor's corpse by my feet. I check that there's a bullet in the chamber and say, "Stay calm, Tammuz. This will be over soon."

He says, "I haven't done anything. Just let me go, please. I haven't done anything."

As if that ever matters.

The second glass door is still intact, and I can see their reflection in it, Sergei still shoving Tammuz forward. The island is on their right, so I crawl back to where my bag is on the opposite side, keeping low, knowing there are only two possible outcomes here.

Tammuz and I die or . . .

I make a run for it and dive into the lounge, more bullets missing their target as I roll and stand in the same movement. I tuck the gun into the back of my jeans and race for the front door, slamming it behind me so that Sergei hears, pulling my hood up in case of witnesses and running down the concrete stairs, hardly noticing the driving rain. Turning left and left again, I grab a trash can and use it to leap over the wall into Viktor's garden. Entering the kitchen via the missing door, I pull the gun from my jeans as I head for the lounge, skirting the broken glass.

I hear Sergei before I see him. Tammuz is yelping and begging for mercy.

I peer into the lounge and see Sergei, his back to me. He pulls his baseball cap off and throws it on the floor, putting the gun on the glass coffee table.

Tammuz is a tight ball on the sofa, trying to protect himself from the fists hammering down like meteorites. Sergei pauses at intervals to ask questions, his voice measured and efficient. "Who is she? Where she go?" Tammuz is saying he only met me yesterday and that I'm from Devon, swearing to god that's all he knows.

"Tell me where she is or I cut balls."

"No need," I say, speaking English. "I'm right here," pressing the gun into his bald spot. Then in Russian, I say, "You so much as flinch, I'll kill you." Then back to English with, "Tammuz, listen carefully . . ."

Sensing he's no longer in immediate danger, Tammuz uncurls and stands, shuffling in the direction of the front door, scared and disoriented. "What happened in there?" He points toward the kitchen. "Is Viktor dead?"

"We can talk later."

"I'm not interested in your lies," he says, pulling his phone out. "I'm calling the police."

"Viktor tried to kill me, Tammuz. It was him or me. I had no choice."

"I don't want to hear it. Everything you touch turns to shit."

Before he's able to dial the third nine, there's a gun pointing at his head.

"Put that down. Now." Then in Russian, "Do not give me a reason to kill you, Sergei."

Tammuz looks up. "You're out of control."

He's right. I'm a loose cannon, dangerous, unpredictable, and as much as I tried to show Viktor how fearless I was, the truth is I'm petrified of absolutely everything. I'm out of my depth and drowning, and I don't know what to do.

Desperate for Tammuz to stop judging me and because I am determined to find a way out of this mess, I present a hunch as truth. "You went to jail because of Viktor," I say. "He tipped the police off; did you know that?"

"What?"

"You were no use to him anymore, so he threw you under the bus."

"Is that why you killed him?"

"He tried to shoot me. This is his gun. I was defending myself. None of this was supposed to happen."

Sergei sees an opportunity and takes it, using his right arm to knock the weapon from my hand, lunging for me. I trip over the edge of the glass coffee table and collide with the hard wooden floor. The impact knocks the wind out of my lungs, and Sergei takes my neck between his huge, rough hands and squeezes. Rosa's body, which weighs 110 pounds, is useless in close combat, especially against a man who's double her size and trained to kill.

I try to smash the heel of my hand into his temple and then into his solar plexus, trying to bring my knees up next, but I'm weak and getting weaker, thinking it would take a steamroller to get Sergei off me. Viktor's brother is gripped by fury; he's hungry for revenge.

Tammuz throws himself into the fight, giving me hope, but Sergei backward head-butts him in the face, and he disappears from view.

Angling my head as much as I'm able to, I look around for something I can use, and there it is: Viktor's gun, just out of reach to my right.

Thousands of years ago, soon after my initiation, when Egypt was still the center of the world, Ashkai revealed many truths to me, including how separation is nothing more than an illusion of mind. He taught me that all things, material and nonmaterial, are comprised of the exact same energy, all of it drawn from a single, unified source. There is intelligence in every proton, every electron, every atom; consciousness is fundamental and present in all things.

I visualize the gun gliding toward me, pulled in by beams of light emanating from my outstretched fingers, but it's difficult to focus on the task. I can feel my eyes popping out of my head, and I can see swirling geometrical patterns: mandalas forming and pyramids sprouting, and colorful, organic tentacles reaching out to envelop me, all of it intelligent and conscious. I am having these visions because I am dying, because my body is releasing huge amounts of biologically endogenous DMT (ironically, the exact thing I came here searching for), opening a portal for my soul to pass through, meaning at least eighteen additional years of darkness and suffering for my master . . . I'm finding myself inside a hallway now, seeing a door and a number—4320—although it's little more than a flash frame.

I look at my outstretched hand, then the gun, then my hand again, praying, begging, but all, it seems, for nothing.

I have failed, I think, facing Sergei, looking into his determined, murderous eyes. *Please forgive me, Master.*

I'm in the process of letting go, of giving in to the drift, when something happens: movement in the corner of my eye!

Crouching next to me is . . . an animal of some sort . . . a panther I think . . . and unless I'm mistaken, it appears to be made of black smoke. Not only that, it's using its right paw to nudge the gun toward me.

A voice in my head says, *Your work is not done, Samsara.*

It doesn't quite sound like Ashkai, more of an impression of him, but I don't have time to think about that because I'm losing consciousness. In fact, I'm not sure this is really happening, still not convinced when something solid and cold slides into my palm.

Don't give up, the voice adds. *You are closer than you realize.*

I bring my hand to Sergei's head and pull the trigger.

Darkness crashes over me like a wave.

***

Nothingness until . . .

A voice.

Tammuz's voice. Urgent and afraid.

He's telling me over and over to wake up, but I have no idea what he's talking about. Then he says, "Sam, listen to me. Even though you're the craziest person I've ever met . . . even though you stole my bike . . . even though it's cheesy and doesn't make any sense . . . I think I've fallen in love with you. In fact, I know I have. So do what you always do and fight. Do you hear me? Fight."

A warm, comforting breeze hits then, with Tammuz's scent on it. I think, *He loves you, Samsara.* The thought and the scent combine to make me feel peaceful and at ease until a switch is flicked and I bolt upright.

"Are you okay?" I ask, looking around the room, breathless and confused.

"Yes," he replies, a relieved look on his face. "I am now."

I notice how wet my lips are and that I can taste Tammuz on them, realizing he gave me mouth-to-mouth—*that breeze!*—feeling so happy to be alive, so grateful that I rise onto my knees and start kissing him, pulling his top off at the same time, gripped by an uncontrollable passion and hunger, wanting him so badly it hurts. Tammuz tries to stop me, pointing at Sergei's corpse next to us, blood and brains everywhere, but I'm determined and forceful and get what I want.

THIRTEEN

After hanging his coat on the back of the door, Tammuz sits on the edge of his bed and puts his head in his hands. He's got a black eye and cut lip to go with the scratches I inflicted this morning, and his hair is wet from the rain.

"This can't be happening," he says. "They'll give us life for what we did."

I put my bag down and sit next to him. I reach out to touch his shoulder, but he flinches. I edge away, a foot or so between us now, and I'm sensing how deeply shocked and panicked he is.

"I killed them, not you, so if anyone's going to prison, it's me and only me."

Tammuz looks up and stares out of the bay windows to our left. There's nothing but heavy clouds and evening gloom, rain drumming against glass.

He says, "I aided and abetted. In the eyes of the law, that's just as bad." He runs his fingers through his damp hair before adding, "They took my fingerprints last time I was arrested; I'm in the system . . ."

"We wiped the place down. There's no trace of us being there."

"All it takes is one."

"We were thorough. I made sure of that. And don't forget, Viktor and Sergei were drug-dealing Russian gangsters. The police will think some rival operation took them out. They'll never connect us to what happened."

"What if someone saw us?"

"Saw what?"

"Us arriving or leaving?"

"That doesn't prove anything. And when we left, I had my hood up, and you were wearing Sergei's baseball cap. Our faces were hidden."

"What about DNA evidence?"

"Tammuz . . . they have to suspect us first. They won't."

"Even if they don't catch us, we killed two people, Sam. I don't know if I can live with that."

Can I trust you not to crack?

"*You* didn't kill anyone. I did. And it was self-defense both times. If I'd hesitated, we wouldn't be sitting here right now because we'd be dead. You need to stop feeling guilty and remember that."

Tammuz looks at me, his face battered and bruised, eyeliner smudged and fading. The fond thought goes through my mind that he doesn't need help looking beautiful as he says, "What happened with Viktor? How did it go so wrong?"

Before coming to Archway and because I insisted, we went via South London to discard of the evidence that connected us to the double homicide: two guns, a steel pan, a knife, flannels we cleaned up with, and a baseball cap, all concealed inside a trash bag. Neither of us spoke as I headed down back alleys to drop things down drains or into the Thames, knowing Tammuz would be asking questions as soon as we got back here. I was preparing answers in my head, telling myself this is more of a theory than a lie.

"Viktor told me he tipped the police off about your stash," I say.

"Why would he do that? He had nothing to gain."

"He thinks you lied to him."

"About what?"

"Loving his daughter."

"He knows how much I cared about her."

"He found out you were seeing other girls."

"Bollocks. There's no way he could have known that."

"He had Sergei spy on you."

"Why?"

"Because you were involved with his daughter, because you worked for him, because he was a control freak."

Tammuz's face is a picture of frustration, anger, and disbelief. He says, "Nothing happened until almost a year after Dina left. I hadn't spoken to her for so long. I wanted to, but Viktor always had an excuse for why she wasn't available. I didn't know if I'd ever see her again . . ."

After a short pause, he says, "Even if all this is true, why would he tell you? It doesn't make sense."

"He was drunk and shooting his mouth off."

Tammuz doesn't seem to have trouble believing that. "What else did he say?"

"The same week he found out you were cheating . . ."

"I wasn't cheating! I thought I was never going to see her again."

"Same week he found out about that you told him you didn't want to work for him anymore. Timing couldn't have been worse."

"So he called the police?"

I nod.

"What if I'd got scared and handed him over?"

"Was that an option?"

"No, he'd have killed me, but he didn't know I'd assume that or make that choice."

"Maybe he did. You're not that hard to read. And it would have been your word against his anyway."

Tammuz stands and paces the room, muttering and swearing, trying to process everything. After thirty seconds or so, he stops. "Please don't tell me you killed him for that?"

"I told him he was a bully and that what he did was wrong . . ."

Tammuz interrupts. "So how did he end up with a knife in his throat?"

I look down at the floor, genuinely embarrassed about this part. "I pushed a bowl of hot soup onto his lap."

Tammuz drops his head and sighs. "You did what? That's ridiculous. Why?"

"I was angry . . . I lashed out without thinking."

He says, "Why doesn't that surprise me?" followed by, "He hit you?"

"He pulled a gun and tried to shoot me. After killing me, he would have put a bullet in your head. I did what I had to do to keep us alive."

Tammuz looks out of the window again but finds nothing to console him. "This is so messed up . . ."

I glance down at the well-worn carpet, noticing faint stains that look like countries on a map, imagining how many people must have lived in this house over the years. All those lives. All those memories. And some of those are out there now as new people, with no memory at all . . . it always saddens me to think of people being so oblivious. "I'm sorry, Tammuz. I wish I could go back in time and undo it, but I can't." With my eyes on him, I say, "I'm not a bad person; you have to believe that. I had no choice. I shouldn't have provoked him, I admit it, but I had no idea he'd try and shoot me. Everything spiraled out of control in a matter of seconds."

Looking at me intently, he says, "Why do you always have to fight? Why can't you just walk away sometimes? What are you so fucking angry about?"

Without thinking, I say, "It's not anger that makes me do these things; it's fear."

Admitting to feeling afraid, to being vulnerable, brings on a torrent of emotions: sadness, anger, confusion, frustration, despair, shame . . . and I'm panicking now because the last thing I want is to cry.

"Who are you, Sam, who are you really?"

Shoving all of those feelings into a little box, I stand and say, "You need to take your clothes off and shower."

Tammuz pulls a face. "Does death turn you on?"

"We need to get rid of everything we were wearing so there's nothing to connect us to the scene."

"Then what? We just carry on like nothing happened?"

"Then I get out of here, forever this time."

He says, "You run away a lot, don't you?" but it's more of a statement than a question.

His words hit a nerve, probably because they're spot on. I open my mouth to speak, but nothing comes out. Looking into his eyes, I find it almost impossible to keep a lid on that box.

Seeing I'm not going to respond, Tammuz says, "What about us?"

I get flashes of the sex we had, reliving the animalistic roughness of it, the underlying tenderness, the perfect fit, the uncanny communication, him touching me just where and when I wanted to be touched and likewise . . . recalling how much I wanted—*no, needed!*—him inside of me. I think about all that for one glorious second, then push it aside.

"There is no us," I say, flat and cold. "It was a mistake."

Tammuz glares at me as if I'm the biggest, most evil bitch on the planet.

"Fuck you, Sam," he says, leaving the room, which is just as well because when I start crying, it's difficult to stop.

**

Still alone in Tammuz's bedroom and feeling a little better after letting it all out, I sit at the desk in front of the bay window and use the computer, opening Rosa's Gmail account as I think, *What's my next move, Master?* Give me a sign.

There are numerous messages from Rosa's mum, dad, brother, and other worried people. I make a mental note to create a filter so I won't feel this tug in the future, but for now but I ignore them, instead drawn to the subject heading *Sacred Ceremonies* from lotusmeditations@gmail.com.

My heart quickens.

When I fired off those e-mails yesterday enquiring about ayahuasca ceremonies, I wasn't holding out much hope of receiving any replies, especially as the brew is illegal in the United Kingdom.

I open the message:

> *Dear Rosa,*
>
> *A friend forwarded your enquiry as she thought I might be able to help. I hope that's okay.*
>
> *Unfortunately, the medicine is banned in the United Kingdom. Though I am aware of some low-profile ceremonies conducted there, there are none I would be able to recommend at this point.*
>
> *If you follow the link below, you will find information about the Inner Light Retreat. They are based in Spain, where ayahuasca can be drunk legally. As you will see, their next gathering is in six weeks, and the ceremony will be conducted in English. Maybe that could work?*

www.innerlightretreat.com

I have better contacts in Los Angeles, where I live, so if you are ever passing through, let me know.

I hope that is helpful and that you find what you are looking for.

Love and light.
Kaya Benu
www.lotusmeditations.com

At first I was deflated—*I can't wait six weeks!*—but then I clocked the name of her business: Lotus Meditations.

For Flooders, the lotus flower represents enlightenment, and I already know there's no such thing as coincidence. Furthermore, the last time I had eyes on my master, just before he pushed me from the GE Building in New York, I was inhabiting the body of a girl called Suzi Aarons, a Jew who had been born and raised in California.

It has to be a sign.

I check out Kaya's website. It turns out she runs a meditation studio based out of Venice Beach. It prompts me to start searching for flights to the West Coast of America.

With hope rising in my chest, I am reminded of what that voice said, whomever it belonged to, as I reached for the gun I needed to kill Sergei:

Don't give up. You are closer than you realize.

FOURTEEN

I hear the bedroom door opening, so I close the Internet browser and turn in my seat.

As soon as I've showered and disposed of the clothes we were wearing at Viktor's earlier today, I'll head straight for Heathrow. First thing in the morning, when the British Airways desk opens, I'll purchase a ticket to Los Angeles in cash. Once in America, I'll locate the girl who e-mailed me, source some ayahuasca, cross over to the spirit realm, and . . .

And what, Samsara?

I'm hoping I'll know when I get there, that when I leap into the abyss, a net will appear.

Tammuz, towel around waist, clothes under arm, says, "Bathroom's free; there's a clean towel in there." The look on his face shows me he's calmed down a little.

"Thanks," I say, standing. As I head for the door, scanning the array of tattoos on his left arm, I'm startled to see an image of the Great Sphinx of Giza covering his shoulder. Rays of sunlight emanate from its head. Three pyramids stand in the background.

I stop and say, "What made you get that?" I lean in for a closer look, spotting a small ankh in the center of the sphinx's forehead, the Egyptian symbol for eternal life.

Tammuz maneuvers his body so he can see what I'm referring to. "This one?" he says, pointing at it.

I nod, and he says, "I'm a Leo; that's what gave me the lion idea. My tattoo guy added the other stuff."

"You been to Egypt?"

"No, you?"

"Yes," I say, "many times." I'm still analyzing the curious image, at a loss as to what the universe is trying to tell me about this man, if anything.

"Cool."

I look into Tammuz's makeup-free eyes, and he holds my gaze, feeling the instant buzz of electricity. I step back to break the spell, saying, "The sphinx is older than they think, you know."

He takes a moment to respond, as if he heard me on a delay. "How old do they think it is?"

"Around 4,500 years."

He looks impressed. "How much they off by?"

"Eight millennia, give or take."

"Eight thousand years?"

"Yup."

"Bullshit."

"I know for a fact it's true."

"How? Were you there when it was built?"

"No, but I know someone who was."

Tammuz laughs. "Course you do. Bet you've met aliens as well?"

"Depends what you mean by aliens."

"Were you dropped on your head as a kid?"

I smile and say, "It's possible." Then, "Put the clothes and the shoes you were wearing in a trash bag. I'll take it all with me when I leave."

After showering and wrapping a white towel above my breasts, I head back to the bedroom. Tammuz, who's wearing jeans, a green hoodie, and black glasses, is sitting on the edge of his bed looking at his iPad, utterly engrossed, the energy in here much more tense then it was fifteen minutes ago. It takes him a moment to even realize I'm there, but when he does, he slams the screen facedown and looks up.

"You okay?" I ask.

After staring at me for what feels like an eternity, he says, "No."

"Why?"

"You seriously have to ask that?"

"What were you looking at?"

"What do you think I was looking at?"

"I don't know; that's why I'm asking."

After a pause, he says, "I was checking to see if there was anything online about what happened."

"And?"

"There's something on BBC news about a possible gang-related shooting in North London. It didn't go into any details, though."

"See, it will never come back to us."

"You don't know that."

Silence.

On the floor beside him is a black trash bag. Clothes are sticking out of the top of it. I go to grab my backpack so I can take it to the bathroom and get changed. Tammuz stands and says he'll leave me to it. He asks if I'm hungry and want a sandwich or a cup of tea, and then he tells me he's on edge, but he's sorry for being rude.

"That's okay," I say, and even though I'm starving, I tell him no thanks, that I've got to go soon, and add, "Has that got everything in it?" I gesture toward the trash bag. "Shoes as well?"

"Yeah," he says. "But I'm coming with you."

"Where?"

"To get rid of it."

"I can handle it."

"The stuff in there could send me to prison for the rest of my life. I'd like to make doubly sure it gets disposed of properly, if that's okay?" His tone is frigid but also scared. I don't want him to be scared. I also feel irrationally offended, as if he should realize I've cleaned up crime scenes in a dozen lives. Granted, most were before the age of modern forensics. I suddenly remember Rosa's dad watching crime shows and understand why I'd found myself riveted to the pesky little details, though at the time I thought it was gross and morbid.

"Don't you trust me?" is the lame result of these colliding thoughts.

"I barely know you."

"Fair enough," I say. "I'll be downstairs in ten minutes; then we go."

Tammuz is about to leave the room when I say, "They suit you."

He turns, his face letting me know he has no idea what I'm talking about.

"The glasses, they make you look . . . distinguished." I don't mean it. Ever since Mr. Farish, I've not been a fan of men in spectacles, but I wanted to say something nice, and that's all I could think of.

He gives me a half smile, the saddest smile I've ever seen, and leaves the room.

I grab my bag and pull out a fresh pair of skinny jeans, my red TOMS sneakers, and a gray sweatshirt with "GEEK" written on it in big black letters, something Rosa thought was cute. After emptying my pockets, I stuff all of today's clothes into the trash bag. Then I'm out of the door and down the stairs, shouting for Tammuz, so he knows I'm ready to go.

"That was quick," he says, coming from the kitchen, no longer wearing glasses, with a half-eaten sandwich in hand.

Trying to lighten the mood, I say, "Unlike you, I don't have makeup to put on."

He grabs a black leather jacket that's hanging on the banister, smiling as he says, "I have no idea what you're talking about."

***

When we hit Archway underground station, I say, "Give it to me," meaning the bag full of clothes Tammuz has been carrying. The two of us are huddled under his tiny umbrella, arms interlinked. The rain has died down a little, but the air is wet and cold. My TOMS are soaked through, but I'll be able to buy new clothes at the airport, not that I'll need much in sunny California.

Tammuz hands it over. "What's the plan?"

"Wait here," I say, adjusting the straps on my backpack before jogging toward the tall, looming office building next to the station. I'm approaching a homeless couple with a brown Staffordshire bull terrier. Its ribs are showing. The three of them are sitting on the floor underneath an architectural overhang, their faces beaten and tired. They have cans of strong lager on the go.

Speaking to the woman with hollow cheeks, I stoop and say, "Here are some dry clothes for you both. They should fit." I pull a fifty-pound note from my jeans. "Your dog looks hungry."

The woman beams a toothless smile and starts to get up, but I tell her there's no need. I hear them talk excitedly to each other in

Polish as I turn and walk away, the man shouting, "Thank you, we appreciate, thank you."

"You trying to frame homeless people?" Tammuz asks as I step under his umbrella, the two of us face to face.

"You're so cynical," I say. "Philanthropy is a hobby of mine."

"I thought we were going to burn them."

"The homeless people?"

"Very funny. The clothes."

"Not the right weather for it," I say. "We did the next best thing, though."

"What now? We go our separate ways?"

I nod.

"What's your plan? You have anywhere to stay?"

"I'm a big girl, Tammuz."

"So that's it, we never see each other again?"

"Depends."

"On what?"

"Whether or not we're meant to."

Tammuz pinches the bridge of his nose in frustration. "You have a phone number?"

"No."

"An e-mail address?"

"No."

"You blowing me off?"

Unable to resist the obvious joke, I say, "As romantic as that sounds, I have other plans."

Tammuz lets out a disbelieving laugh. "I'm not going to dignify that with a response." His eyes sparkle with an idea. "Your turn to wait," he says, handing me the umbrella, diving into a nearby corner shop. Two minutes later, he reappears holding a lottery ticket.

"My number's on the back," he says. "And if you win Saturday, you better call me."

I tuck it into my jeans without looking. "I will."

During the silence that follows, the mood changes.

He says, "Did you mean what you said before, about us being a mistake?"

I decide to be honest. It's the least he deserves. "Yes and no."

"What does that mean?" he says. Then he adds, "I'm worried I'll never see you again."

"Considering everything's that happened, wouldn't that be a good thing?" I give him a smile that's meant to be both kind and mysterious, but I have no idea how it comes off.

He shakes his head. "Absolutely not."

"I heard what you said earlier."

"When?"

"When you thought I was dead. You said you loved me. I think it helped bring me back."

"It's true. I know how cheesy that sounds and that it doesn't make any . . ."

I stand on my toes and kiss him. "As it ends, so it begins."

He opens his eyes. "What's that supposed to mean?"

"It means we'll see each other again."

"When?"

I shrug. Then I turn away from him, enter Archway Station, and buy a ticket to Heathrow. After passing through the ticket barrier, just before stepping onto the escalator and disappearing underground, I feel compelled to glance back and see if Tammuz is still there, to look into his eyes one final time.

But I don't.

FIFTEEN

My eyes snap open, and my body flinches.

The light is bright and suffocating, and for a split second, everything is fuzzy and nothing makes sense. There's a strong, cloying smell coming from somewhere; it's heavy, musky, overwhelming.

When things come into focus, I'm confronted by a young black girl looking down at me; she has a cream-colored beanie hat, thin eyebrows, and red lips, her hand pulling away from my shoulder.

"Relax, babes," she says, smiling. "This is da last stop, figured you'd want wakin' before da train took you back to where you started." The pungent odor belongs to her: a heady mixture of flowery perfume, stale clothes, and tobacco.

I look out of the window, see Terminal 5 signs, grab my bag, and stand, swinging my arms through the straps while saying, "Thanks, I appreciate it."

"Lucky day, innit?" she says, getting off at the same time. She's seventeen or eighteen with that West Indies–infused London swagger, reminding me of the girl with the big forehead from last night, Robbie's sidekick, only not a psycho bitch.

Beanie glances at my bag. "Where you headed?"

"Los Angeles," I reply, walking along the platform toward the escalator. Everything in this station is made from glass or chrome, giving a clean, clinical, futuristic feel to the place.

"I'm, well, jel," she says, keeping stride. "I'd kill to go there."

The escalator is carrying us to street level, and I can already feel the cold, wet air blowing in from outside. "There must be an easier way," I reply, following up with, "What about you?"

She sucks air through her back teeth. "I ain't goin' nowhere, babes; this is da closest I'm gettin' to LA for now, one day doe, even if I have to hijack a plane, innit."

I force a smile. I'd rather be left alone, but she just did me a favor, so I'm trying not to be rude.

We step off the escalator and follow the exit signs. "Know of any cheap hotels around here? My flight's not till tomorrow."

At first, Beanie seems thrown by the question, but then her face brightens, and she points across my body, saying, "Check out dat guy's smug face."

I stop and turn to my left. There's a large advertisement for the Premier Inn.

It's a picture of a middle-aged black man tucked into a purple and white bed, cuddling a teddy bear. He looks like he's having the best, most contented sleep of his life. Something I'm in desperate need of.

"Perfect," I say, turning to Beanie. "Where is it?"

She shrugs. "Dunno, babes, I ain't from round here, just visitin' a friend, innit, must be close doe . . ."

"Don't worry," I say, pointing at the London Underground employee standing on the other side of the ticket barrier up ahead, both of us walking again. "I'll ask her. Thanks for waking me up. I owe you one."

Beanie's phone rings and she stops to answer. "That's okay, babes, just bring me back a present, yeah?"

Looking over my shoulder, I wave and say, "You got it."

The staff member gives me directions to the hotel and a rundown of nearby places to grab a bite. There's Subway opposite the station, so I opt for that, devouring a six-inch Veggie Delight in seconds.

It's late by the time I arrive at the Premier Inn, and there's only one person manning the desk: a chirpy, slightly, strange man in his midforties sporting a combover and thick-rimmed glasses. After introducing himself as Walter, he asks for my passport. I could show him Rosa's; it's something I packed before leaving Exeter, but I want to stay off the grid as much as possible, so I concoct a story about how my mum is picking me up first thing and she has all my stuff, adding that he can scan my ID in the morning. I flirt as well, laughing at his geeky jokes ("I hope your passport photo isn't as bad as mine!"), making him feel good.

Mission accomplished.

My small, neat room on the fourth floor smells of polish, dust, and stale cigarette smoke. White sheets are on the bed and there's a purple throw. The room has a wooden desk and chair and a flatscreen TV.

I strip down to knickers and a T-shirt, have a quick wash, and slip into bed. Even without a teddy bear to cuddle, I'm asleep before my head hits the pillow.

No dreams, just darkness until two indigo eyes appear above me. Then four. Then eight. Then sixteen. The number grows exponentially until there are literally millions of them, slotted side by side like puzzle pieces, blinking as one, watching me.

Words accompany the image, something along the lines of "There you are," although I don't hear an actual voice.

I notice that I am naked. I try to move, only to discover my legs are heavy and unresponsive. The sky of eyes changes shape now, its outer edges swooping down as a vibrant red begins to shimmer across its surface. Then orange, yellow, and purple, and then every hue and quality of light imaginable, all of it dancing and pulsating in a way that feels organic and alive.

"What do you want?" I shout as this thing, whatever it is, becomes a sphere around me. Tentacles emerge from it and move in my direction.

"Wake up, Samsara." I definitely heard a voice that time, and I know who it belongs to.

Meta.

The tendrils edge closer, each one capped with a single eye.

"What do you want?" I ask again, still unable to move. I look down to see what's wrong with my feet, but they have disappeared, or rather, the sphere has absorbed them, shins as well. A horrible thought occurs to me, that I'm being eaten alive and slowly digested.

"You are in danger," the voice says.

"Let me go," I shout, panicking, afraid of what will happen if I am fully consumed by this thing.

The iridescent sphere of light and color blinks and says, "Wake up, Samsara. NOW."

At the same moment, a tentacle touches the center of my

forehead. The eye attached to it delves into my mind, and I see an image of Rosa back in her hotel room tied to a chair. Something is covering her mouth. Then, to my utter surprise, I *become* the chair, which is cheap and badly made . . .

Seconds later, I'm viewing the world through Rosa's eyes again, although her perspective has changed. Down at floor level now, I see two embroidered letters straight ahead: "BU," white thread on black fabric. I feel compelled to reach out and touch them, as if that will save me somehow. Before I'm able to, a charge of electricity pulses through my body, and just like that, I am no longer in the world of dreams. Nonordinary reality is replaced in an instant by the ceiling of my hotel room.

I sit upright.

Aside from my labored breathing, everything is silent. I am dripping with sweat. I look at the clock on the television directly in front of me: 1:45 a.m. Below it, tucked underneath the desk, is a small wooden chair. It's the one I was bound to in my dream. I remember how fragile and creaky it was.

I shake my head and laugh, seeing the funny side of how messed up I am, surrendering to it.

It has stopped raining, and the sky has cleared. I know because a shaft of moonlight is shooting through a crack in the curtain. I take some deep breaths, get out of bed, and go to the bathroom, the carpet dry and prickly under my feet. The extractor fan kicks in when I turn on the light. It's loud and invasive. I splash water on my face and look in the mirror, inspecting the red marks on my neck (the result of being throttled yesterday), remembering how lucky I am to be alive, to still be in with a chance of rescuing my master.

I think about taking a shower but decide against it. What I need is more sleep, and the British Airways desk doesn't open for a few hours. I should probably give some thought to the dream I just had, but then again, what's the rush? I'll have plenty of time to unpack it while crossing the Atlantic. Besides, the symbolism is pretty obvious: I feel trapped and powerless, hence being tied to the chair, and watched by Meta, which explains the sphere of eyes. I have no idea what those embroidered letters were about, but then again, maybe they weren't about anything.

I dry my face, switch off the bathroom light, and walk into the adjoining room. I notice how silent everything is without the extractor fan. I stop in my tracks before reaching the bed, sensing human energy close by, energy that does not belong to me, energy that was not present two minutes ago. But before I can do anything about it, before I can turn and fight, something hard and heavy hits the back of my head. I see the moonlit floor approaching and feel a breeze against my face.

Nothingness envelops me.

***

I become aware of music. It's tinny sounding, as if being played on a mobile phone.

The track has a high-tempo reggae beat and fast, aggressive Patwa lyrics that are impossible to decipher.

I can smell weed.

My head is lowered, my chin against my chest, and my eyes are closed. I resist the urge to open them.

Someone nearby says, "She's dead, cus. You licked her hard, you know."

A man. Londoner. Young. On my left.

Another person speaks: "How can she be dead if she's breavin', bruv? Look at her chest."

Male. Similar age. Also left of me but farther away.

"What you doin', man? That's rank!" says the first speaker, sounding amused and grossed out at the same time.

Who are these people? I keep my eyes closed, wondering if this could be a continuation of the dream I was having, if getting up and going to the bathroom was just something I imagined.

But I know that's not the case. I was awake, and these people broke into my room.

How did they do that so quietly?

My mind flashes back to the altercation over Tammuz's moped, mainly because of the pattern and tone of their speech. Could this be Robbie's work? If so, where is he, and how did he find me?

The two voices came from my left, and I can feel somebody else's presence in front of me. Could that be him? I think that accounts for everyone, but I can't be certain of my judgment, especially after taking a blow to the head.

The guy who thought I was dead suggests something else. "What're we waitin' for, man? People coulda' seen us or heard somfin'. I'm already on probation. I say we take the cash and bounce."

My money, I think, still trying to work out who my abductors are, what they want, and how I can hurt them.

First things first: what are the facts?

I'm sitting on a chair with my wrists secured in front of me, palms together. Something has been stuffed into my mouth, and there's duct tape across my lips. No point screaming then. More binds across my stomach and chest attach me to the chair. My ankles are strapped. To make matters worse, I'm wearing only the knickers and T-shirt I went to bed in.

I remember my dream and the strange episode with the chair, the very one I'm bound to now. My internal compass is telling me I'm facing the door. That means bed on the left, desk right, window behind. I think about the image I was shown when that tentacle delved into my forehead: me sitting as I am now, tied up as I am now, Meta—or someone posing as Meta—telling me to wake up, that I was in danger.

The person in front of me speaks for the first time. Confirming my initial suspicion, he says, "Listen up, bruv; no one cares what you say. Plus, I told you 'nuff times we ain't goin' nowhere till I get my wheels. You get me? Then we're teaching this bitch a lesson while her pussy-hole boyfriend watches. Be none of dis face-to-face white boy shit either, nah man, allow it, I'm flipping her over like the dog she is. Woof woof."

Laughter.

He's talking about Tammuz. I raise my head, opening my eyes, discovering I am farther back in the room than anticipated.

The desk, which Robbie is perched on, is over to the right. Because of where he's sitting, I can't see the digital clock on the television—*how long was I unconscious?*—but I can see my money and a thick roll of silver duct tape.

Beyond the desk is a short, narrow hallway that leads to the door. I assess my options while looking into Robbie's eyes, telling him without words that whatever happens to Tammuz will be returned to him tenfold. The anger in my chest makes me feel I could explode, sending forth deadly shards of bone and teeth to maim, kill, and disembowel. If Ashkai were here, he would tell me that anger clouds the mind and impairs judgment and that true strength comes from stillness and love. But he isn't here. I am alone. And I must do things my way.

Robbie, spliff in one hand, tire wrench in the other, looks me up and down, his expression somewhere between a leer and an angry snarl.

"Wagwan my liqqle ninja, sleep good?" Cane rolls, orange bomber jacket, thick, gold chain on his left wrist, chunky watch. I absorb everything I can, searching for weaknesses.

I look left. Sitting on the bed are two others I recognize: closest, perched on a corner, is the mixed-race guy (wearing a New York Yankees baseball cap) who dragged Tammuz off the moped. He's gnawing at his fingernails and has the air of someone who doesn't want to be here. I'm guessing he's the one who suggested they quit while they're ahead.

Farther away, his back against the headrest, feet up, is the wiry Indian with bulbous eyes who tried but failed to take me down on the estate. The music is coming from his phone. He sees me looking at him and brings his hand up to his face, inhaling deeply through his nose. It's a strange and confusing gesture until I see he's holding a pair of my knickers.

The contents of my bag have been spilled onto the floor, and the mini bar has been raided: miniature vodkas and whiskies, bottles of beer, packets of peanuts, and chocolate wrappers; the place is a mess. There's a large, half- drunk bottle of Jack Daniels next to Robbie. He must have brought that with him. I look over a shoulder to see if there's anyone behind, but there isn't.

I fix my eyes on Robbie and try to get inside his head, try to influence his thoughts and decisions, but it's easier said than done.

Under the right circumstances, it's something I believe I could do. But these are anything but: I'm tied up, and the marijuana smoke is making me light-headed. I'm also afraid and angry, and the music is driving me crazy.

Robbie stands and leans forward, giving me a brief line of sight on the television: 2:28 a.m. I was unconscious for over half an hour.

He takes a hit on the joint and blows three smoke rings in my face. "You wanna speak, innit?"

I nod, eyes stinging.

"I take this off"—he points at the duct tape over my mouth—"you ain't gonna scream or make a peep, are you?"

I shake my head, still trying to penetrate his, silently saying, *Let me go, Robbie, let me go,* over and over, at the same time listening to the psychopath say, "Cos if you do"—he gets a firmer grip on the wrench—"I'll crack your skull like a melon."

He makes as if to strike, and I flinch. Robbie laughs and looks at his friends, saying, "See what I'm tellin' you? Just needs breaking in like da rest of em."

They laugh, and Robbie says, "You're gonna be a good girl, yeah, do what I tell you?"

I nod.

Robbie passes the joint to the Indian and offers one last warning. "Don't mess with me, Rosa, this ain't no game, you know."

My passport.

Robbie says, "And we know where you live."

I nod again, and he peels off the tape, doing it roughly and without care.

I use my tongue to empty my mouth, and a white ankle sock (that belongs to me) lands on my skinny, bare thighs. It's stupid, but having it there makes me feel less naked and exposed.

Keeping my face flat and emotionless, I say, "What do you want?"

Robbie slides the tip of his wrench along my inner thighs and knickers and pushes my sock to the ground. Glancing between my legs, he says, "Everything you got." After a few more seconds of ogling, the message in his eyes crystal clear, he backs off and settles on the corner of the desk. "You think you can come to my yard and pull that Bruce Lee shit and get away with it?" He sucks teeth. "Nah, man, it's eye for an eye round my sides. You fucked me, now I fuck you; dems the rules."

I glance at the stack of fifty-pound notes on the desk. "Take the money and leave. While you still can."

The guy who's wearing the baseball cap says, "She's right, man, this is gettin' on top . . ." But he stops speaking when Robbie stands and looms over him, wrench at the ready. Robbie says, "One more word about bailin', bruv, I dare you, just one more word, come on, what you got for me?"

Silence.

"Come on, big man, let's hear you bitch and moan some more."

Cowering, Baseball Cap says, "Okay, bruv, allow it, allow it, it's cool, man, it's cool, chill, bruv."

The Indian gets to his feet. "Allow it, Robbie, allow it, man, you know what he's like." Then to Baseball Cap: "My days, Choppy! Why you always gotta be such a pussy?"

"I know, I know," he replies. "I'm sorry, man, sorry . . ."

Robbie stares for a beat longer, Choppy coming over all servile and submissive, letting his master know he won't talk out of turn again. Seemingly satisfied, Robbie softens, the two of them bumping fists now, saying, "Respect."

Robbie returns to his spot on the desk and faces me, picking up where we left off, never letting go of that wrench. "Dis ain't about money, boo," he says. "You disrespected me in my own yard, and man dem cannot allow such liberties to go unpunished, you get me?"

"Where is Tammuz?" I ask.

"Your boyfriend?"

"He's not my boyfriend."

"Is it?" he says, nodding. "Why's he comin' to save you then?"

"What do you mean?"

"He's on his way, innit."

"Why?"

"Cos we texted him a picture of you tied up. He called beggin' us not to hurt you, crying like a bitch; one of my boys went to grab

128

him."

"How did you find us?"

"I had my people scouting for you," he says, looking pleased. "It was my number one priority, you get me?" He holds a finger up. "Number one."

I remain silent, trying to work out what's going on, my head swimming with questions and scenarios, when a piece of the puzzle falls into place.

"The girl on the train," I say, remembering her cream beanie hat and friendly smile. "She was following me?"

Robbie glances at his friends. "She can fight, she's buff, and she's smart, too. Wifey material, innit?" Then back to me: "Everyone who saw your face was out scouring; we had eyes on the high street, at the station, outside Tescos. . . " He throws another look at his friends. "These chiefs kept tellin' me it was a waste of time, but I don't give up easy."

"How did you get Tammuz's number?"

"Found a lottery ticket in your jeans. Guess what, it was a winner."

Addressing the Indian, Robbie says, "Give Dane a buzz, yeah? Tell him stop messin' around, we ain't got all night, man, and I'm getting horny, yunartamean?"

"What if Tammuz brings the police?" I ask, ignoring the disgusting wink Robbie just gave me. The music stops at the same moment; the Indian is making a phone call. "You thought about that?"

Choppy seems even more nervous, probably because I mentioned the police, but he doesn't say anything; he looks at the floor and bites his nails.

Robbie loses his temper again. "This question time or sommit?" he says. "Shut yer mouth, girl, before I slap you up."

"Leave Tammuz out of it," I say. "He hasn't done anything. I'm the one you want, and I'm already here."

Robbie stands, even angrier now, spreading his body wide, making a show of how crazy he is. "I look like I takes orders from bitches? I'll do whatever I want to whoever I want when I want, you get me?"

Looking up at him, I say, "You and your friends are going to rape me while Tammuz watches, is that your plan? Because I'm telling you now, that isn't going to happen."

Robbie leans into me, his breath humming with marijuana smoke, dry-roasted peanuts, and Jack Daniels. I notice for the first time how wasted he is. He says, "Baby girl, by the time we're done taking turns on you, you ain't gonna be able to walk for a month."

"You'll have to kill me first."

"And bang a corpse? My days! I ain't into that weird shit."

"You're disgusting," I say, spitting in his face. He backhands me, so I spit again, saliva hitting his orange jacket. He's furious now and raises his right arm to strike me with the wrench. Part of me wills him to swing with everything he's got because fuck him; the other part realizes I have to stay alive, for Tammuz if not myself.

"Please do that again, I beg of you," he says. "Spit at me again; see what happens."

I take a moment to compose myself.

Trying a different approach, I say, "Please, Robbie, don't do this."

"Is it? The ninja can beg! What happened to all da tough talk?"

The Indian gets up off the bed. "Bruv, bruv, Dane's outside."

"What's he sayin'?"

"He's got him."

"Moped, too?"

"Yeah, man, all good."

Moments later, there's a knock, and Robbie tells Choppy to answer the door. Robbie returns to his position on the edge of the desk, wrench on lap. He swivels right so he can welcome our new arrivals. Even though I have to crane my head a little, I have a good view of what's happening. I see Tammuz's face first. He's being shoved forward by a large black kid (who must be Dane) with short, spiky dreadlocks. Tammuz says, "You okay, Sam, they hurt you?" His face is pale and fear-stricken.

Robbie puts on a silly voice and mimics him. "You okay, Sam, they hurt you?" Then, as Dane, helmet in hand, pushes Tammuz onto the bed, Robbie adds, "Sam. The fuck is Sam?"

"Huh?" Tammuz says, his whole body trembling. Choppy walks to the other side of the room now, standing behind me somewhere.

Robbie says, "Don't they speak English where you're from? I said, who's Sam?"

Tammuz glances in my direction. "She is," which is when Robbie bursts out laughing.

"How many names you got, boo?"

I ignore him.

"Lying about who you are, bag fulla cash, airport hotel . . . You're running from somfin', innit? And it must be pretty deep if you need to get out the country. What you do?"

"I killed someone," I say.

"Who?"

"A man who underestimated me."

"You got something against men?"

"Only ones who try to rape me."

Robbie grins. "Is it, babes?" He stands and walks toward me, stopping when his groin is just inches from my face.

"This ain't personal, you know, it's bidness. You disrespected me, and I can't have that, yunartamean?"

"Take the money and leave," I say.

"Don't worry, I will," he replies. "But first I'm gonna take my dick out, and you're gonna suck it. The harder you work, the sooner it's done. Try anything stupid and his head"—he points the wrench at Tammuz—"gets taken off, then yours." Robbie steps back. "Do what I tell you, play nice, and both of you walk away from this. We got a deal?"

"Before you put anything in my mouth, you better say goodbye to it."

I clap my teeth together hard and fast.

"Ouch," Robbie says, followed by, "I hear you, Rosa or Sam or whatever your name is, foreplay ain't your thing."

He's talking to his boys now, telling them to cover my mouth with duct tape, that he wants me facedown on the bed. Things are starting to get very real.

Tammuz tries pleading with them, saying he can get money, lots of it, and that his dad is rich, but Dane slaps him and tells him to shut up. Meanwhile, the Indian is walking toward me, grabbing the duct tape, saying, "I get twos, yeah?"

131

Despite having memories spanning thousands of years, and despite having suffered in every way imaginable, I feel afraid, powerless, and very, very stupid.

This is your fault, Samsara, I think, fully aware that our individual realities are only ever a reflection of our deepest thoughts and feelings.

"Whatever you focus on grows," Ashkai always said, and he was right.

Tammuz stands and says, talking to Robbie, "I remember how we know each other."

Dane squares up to him. "What you chattin' about, you idiot?"

Still talking to Robbie, Tammuz says, "The other night, you asked if we'd met before. Well, we have."

Robbie puts a hand on Dane's shoulder so that he backs off. "Where?"

"Outside Archway Station a few weeks back," Tammuz says, his voice trembling. "You tried to mug me."

"What d'ya mean tried?"

"I ran. You chased me, but I was too fast."

Robbie's eyes light up. "Oh shit, I remember this chief," he says, becoming animated, enjoying himself. "You can move, innit, bruv!" Talking to the room now: "Soon as I pulled my shank, he was out of there, gone, I'm tellin' you, a white Usain Bolt." Looking back at Tammuz, he says, "What can you do a hundred meters in?"

"Huh?"

"What's your hundred meter time?"

"I don't know."

"What about in school, they must have clocked you, innit?"

Tammuz looks confused, fear fogging his mind. I'm thinking if I can get him to calm down and focus, then maybe I'll be able to get a message through. Robbie says, "You stupid or sumfin'? I said what was your time in school?"

"Twelve, maybe thirteen seconds . . ."

"Nah, man, allow it, you're quicker than that, or can you only run when a nigger's chasing you? Bet if we took you outside now, you'd break the world record, innit?"

"Why don't we go and find out?" Tammuz says, heading for the

132

door.

Dane pushes him back. "Where'd you think you're going?"

"Tammuz," I say, speaking loudly. "Look at me. I need you to look at me and nobody else. Focus on what I'm about to say and look at me."

Our eyes meet, and I open my heart to him, repeating in my mind, *We are connected; we are one,* while saying, for the benefit of the room, "We need to do what they tell us, Tammuz, it's our only chance."

"Listen to your girl," Robbie says. "She's speaking sense at long last."

I carry on talking, telling Tammuz to stay calm, that it will all be over soon, but my real message, the one I'm sending telepathically, is of a very different nature.

Speaking aloud, I say, "Do you understand, Tammuz?"

Something has happened, but I'm not sure what. I listen for his thoughts, but all I'm able to pick up is fear.

"You heard the lady," Robbie says. "You understand or what?"

Tammuz looks confused, and I wish I had more time, but Robbie and his friends are losing interest in our little scene. Praying something got through to Tammuz, that he'll have the courage to act even if it didn't, I let out a huge, terror-filled scream, shouting, "Help, Room 407, help!" Robbie explodes into action. He's half a second from taking my head off with that wrench when Tammuz rugby tackles him from behind.

Yes!

I tense every muscle in my body as they smash into me hard and fast. The fragile chair collapses under our combined weight as we hit the floor.

Tammuz is trying to put Robbie in a headlock but loses his grip in the fall, and they struggle. Robbie, who must have dropped his wrench, uses his superior size and strength to elbow and eventually roll Tammuz over, the two of them wrestling on the floor beside me now, the base of the bed hemming them in. The Indian and Dane are trying their best to get involved, but with limited space and a constantly moving target, they're finding it difficult to land any meaningful blows.

I bite at the tape around my wrists and yank my arms apart. I'm about to reach forward to free my ankles, worried how long that will take, when I see something that makes everything slow down. Robbie's backside is right next to my face, and the pockets of his jeans have embroidered letters on them: FU on the left, BU on the right. My hand is already inside the latter, knowing there will be something in there I can use.

Robbie is too busy with Tammuz to notice what I've done, same with Dane and the Indian, but Choppy is a different matter. He's standing directly above, looking down at me, wrench in his right hand. His eyes are full of indecision *(or is that compassion?)*, and he fails to act as I open the lock knife I just pickpocketed and use it to release my ankles and midriff before stabbing Robbie in his upper right thigh, the blade hitting bone before I pull it out again.

Robbie screams, but by the time anyone knows what's happening, I'm up on my feet and have the blade against his throat, pulling him to his knees while telling Choppy to drop the wrench and get in front of me where I can see him. I order the others to back away from Tammuz, who's curled up on the floor in a tight ball.

Choppy complies, edging past me and stepping over Tammuz to join his friends.

"Don't try anything stupid," I say. "It will end badly for you."

"My days, you stabbed me," Robbie says, holding a hand over the wound. "Just relax, yeah, babes, lemme go so I can get this looked at, yeah? You'll never see my face again. I wasn't gonna do anything, swear down, we just wanted to scare you . . ."

I press the blade into his throat to shut him up, breaking the skin so he and the others know how serious I am. "Tell your guys to back off. Now."

"Back off, man," Robbie says. "Back the fuck off."

The three of them retreat, and I tell Tammuz everything's okay and that he can get up. Tammuz is not looking too bad considering, messed-up hair and red blotches on his face, but no serious damage from what I can tell.

"You good?"

He nods, checking himself over for injuries.

"I'm going to give you instructions," I say, talking to our four friends. "Follow them, and you live. Hesitate even once, any of you, and I open his throat. Is that clear?"

"Yes," Robbie says. "Do what she says, man."

I tell Choppy to pack my bag without forgetting my money or passport; Robbie is bitching how he's bleeding to death and needs a doctor. I instruct Tammuz to bind all of their wrists and tape their mouths, promising Robbie I'll tourniquet his wound if they all play nice.

"Do it," he says, and I honor my word.

We shove all of them into the bath, the group sitting side by side with their legs over the edge. I have a quick wash in the sink before getting changed in the bedroom as Tammuz secures their ankles with duct tape and asks where the keys to his moped are, hearing a muffled response followed by the jinglejangle of metal.

I enter the bathroom and pull the tape from Choppy's lips.

"How did you get into my room?"

He coughs. "The man who works here, he gave us a key."

"Where is he?"

"In his office. The girls are watching him."

I can hear a police siren in the distance. Someone from a neighboring room must have made the call.

"Why do you hang out with these people?" I ask.

"What do you mean?" Choppy says. "They're my mates, innit."

"You're not like them."

"Course I am," he says. "What do you know about me?" but I can tell it's more for their benefit than mine.

I grab the knife and cut his binds. "Go."

He looks confused. "I ain't going nowhere without them."

I push him into the bedroom and toward the door, out of earshot. "Go now," I say. "And don't you dare warn the girls, just leave."

"Why you doing this?"

I shove him into the communal hallway, the police siren getting louder. "Because you did the right thing."

Dropping the tough guy act, Choppy says, "I didn't know he wanted to rape you. I ain't into that shit."

I nod.

He turns and starts running.

I close the door, grab my bag, and tell Tammuz we're leaving. I hear loud, muffled sounds coming from our three captives. Unable to resist, I pop my head in and smile at Robbie, the big, bad gangster making the most noise of all, showing me the whites of his eyes and gesturing wildly at his bloody leg to let me know I can't leave him like this.

But I can and I do, saying, "Looks like you're the one who won't be able to walk for a month, bruv."

SIXTEEN

Seconds after we pull away on Tammuz's Vespa—I'm wearing the spare helmet that was in the seat compartment—two police cars skid to a halt outside the hotel's entrance, officers streaming out of both vehicles. It's inevitable that Robbie and his crew will be serving prison time for this, especially with the manager's testimony, as he was obviously forced to comply under duress.

"Can you take me to the airport?" I shout, fresh, cold air rushing by, the road and pavements black and glistening. Tammuz can't hear me. I repeat the question, but it's no good. He turns down a residential street and parks.

After kicking out the stand and getting off, he says, while removing his helmet, "Jesus, Sam, if that's even your name, do you know what that animal was about to do?"

I nod, and he asks how they found us.

I take my helmet off but remain seated, pausing to watch the planes overhead, one of them readying to land. I feel revitalized and strong in spite of everything, and I hope it means I'm through the worst of the side effects associated with my Flooding. Either way, a switch has definitely been flicked somewhere deep inside of me.

"They saw us outside Archway Station."

"You're joking," Tammuz says after letting the comment sink in. "What're the chances?"

"Pretty high actually. Robbie had people all over the area looking for us."

"He tell you that?"

"Yes."

"How did they overpower you? Why didn't you just kick their arses like last time?"

"They broke into my room and hit me over the head," I say. "Caught me by surprise." I rub the spot with the tips of my fingers, and Tammuz moves around to take a look, telling me there's a bump but no blood. He touches it gently, saying I should get it looked at; I might have a concussion. I disagree, of course, and he knows better than to push me.

He changes the subject. "Did they touch you . . . before I got there?"

"Touch me how?"

"You know exactly what I mean."

"Luckily for them, no."

He softens and says, "Thank god," and then he says, "They were going to rape you," staring into my eyes, talking as if I don't know that already.

"But they didn't," I say, curious to know if Tammuz heard my voice in his head, unsure of how to broach that subject, not wanting to open Pandora's box. "Thanks to you."

"It was so close," he says. "We got lucky."

"There's no such thing as luck. We were presented with a problem, and we worked together to solve it."

"We were presented with a problem," he repeats, looking at me as if I'm insane. "What the hell kind of thing to say is that? It wasn't a crossword; they were going to rape you. How can you be so calm?"

"I try not to dwell on the past or what might have been."

"How very Zen," he says. "Unfortunately, I'm the opposite. I can't help dwelling on the past, like when you told me your name was Sam, or how we had sex after you killed someone. For some reason, I'm finding that stuff difficult to shrug off. What do you suggest, some deep breathing? Burning incense, chanting maybe? That should sort it out, right?"

Ignoring the sarcasm, I say, "My name *is* Sam."

"Just stop it, will you? I'm sick of it. Tell me who you are and what's going on. After everything we've been through, it's the least I deserve, don't you think?"

"Yes," I say. "But that is the truth."

"Who the hell is Rosa then?"

"She's also me."

"How can you be two people?"

138

"They are only names, labels, they mean nothing."

He sighs. "Let's forget Sam for a moment. Tell me about Rosa."

"What do you want to know?"

"Who is she?"

"I told you, she's me."

Through gritted teeth, Tammuz says, "Fine. How old are you, Rosa?"

"Eighteen."

"Where do you live?"

"Exeter. Until recently."

"Are your parents there?"

"Yes."

"They know where you are?"

"No, and it has to stay that way. I'm making these decisions for a very good reason, so don't try and be a hero. I mean that."

"Don't worry. I'm done trying to save you."

"Good," I say, surprised by how much that hurt.

Tammuz pauses, bracing himself for whatever he wants to say next. "Are you ill?"

"No."

"Unbelievable," he says, becoming animated. "What about the fits?"

"They're genuine, but it's not epilepsy."

"What is it then?"

"Something else."

"Something else. Are you serious? I can't believe you let me think you were dying; that is so dark."

"Why? We're all dying, even you."

"Now you're just being a dick."

"You want the truth, here it is: I thought you could help me get something I needed, so I manipulated you. For what it's worth, I'm sorry. You're a good person. That's why I tried to get out of your life."

"What if you're not meant to get out of my life?" he says, forcing me to realize something very interesting: every time I've tried to put distance between us, events have conspired to thrust us back together again.

Why?

"If you're not ill," Tammuz says, "why do you need that ayahuasca stuff?"

"It's a long story; you wouldn't understand."

"Try me."

"No."

"Fine," he says. "I give up. Where next?"

"What do you mean?"

He glances at a plane overhead. "Where you going?"

"Hong Kong."

He nods.

"That's a lie," I say. "But you know that, don't you?"

"Yes," he replies. "I'm learning. Need a lift to the airport?"

"If it's not too much trouble."

"Which terminal?"

"Three," I say. It's another lie, but the less he knows about where I'm going, the better. My life is only going to get more dangerous and complicated, and I don't want to be responsible for another person's safety, especially his.

Five minutes later, Tammuz drops me off and wishes me a safe flight. I want to hug him, but he's being standoffish, so I keep my distance and say thanks and goodbye and disappear into the terminal. I feel alone and afraid but also fired up and determined, ready for whatever this crazy life decides to throw at me next.

SEVENTEEN

After getting the shuttle to Terminal 5, I wait for the British Airways desk to open, and then I buy a return ticket to Los Angeles, which costs £850. My backpack qualifies as hand luggage, and I have a couple hours to kill, so I eat and look around the shops, buying a few T-shirts, a pair of sunglasses, extra underwear, shorts, and makeup. Before boarding, I get $1,500 at the currency exchange, leaving me with around £900 sterling.

Because of the eight-hour time difference, we land the same morning of departure (Wednesday) at 11:25 a.m. I had three hours of dreamless, heavy sleep on the plane but don't feel properly rested, which isn't surprising, considering the events of the night before.

I'm remembering my life here as Suzi Aarons, how I was overweight and depressed before my Flooding in the mid-1990s and convinced I only had friends because of who my father was—a rich and powerful movie producer—and the advantages that afforded me, such as VIP access to all the best parties and a white Mercedes convertible. I soothed my secret pain and self-loathing with food and then forced myself to vomit because of how disgusting and worthless I was, living that cycle over and over until I was awakened and set free. I had realized yet again, as with every life, that the personality I had developed to cope with the uncertainty of the world, and the ego associated with it, had concealed from me my true nature and purpose.

I jump in a taxi outside LAX. Predictably, the sky is blue and the sun is shining. I tell the driver I'm looking for budget accommodation in the Venice Beach area. He takes me to a freestanding two-story building called Ocean Park Getaway. The exterior is pastel blue and sand yellow, and the beach is just a few blocks west. Even better, a single room is only sixty-two dollars per night.

I pay cash for a few days in advance. They insist on taking a copy of my passport for their records, which isn't ideal. I head to my surprisingly large but sparse en-suite room on the ground floor. There's no air-conditioning, so I open a window, turn on the ceiling fan, and lie down, looking at the rotating blades from my position, hypnotized by the movement and sound. Everything softens as I begin to fall asleep. I fight it at first but then give in to the sheer power and pull of the other world, knowing I have arrived when a man says, "Sleep, little owl, sleep," the words echoing between unseen walls as if spoken inside a huge, cavernous, subterranean chamber.

It is very dark, and I raise my right hand to within an inch of my face but see nothing.

"Master?"

While I do not recognize the voice (although it is reminiscent of the one I heard when Sergei was trying to kill me), he is the only person who calls me that.

The air is cool and damp against my skin, and the floor has the rough texture of stone. I realize that for the second dream in a row, I am naked, confused, and utterly vulnerable. I can hear a girl screaming in the distance. I feel intimately connected to her, but I can't put my finger on why.

"Yes," the voice says. "I am here."

"Where? I can't see you," I say, feeling panicked. "I need light."

"There is no light here. Only darkness."

Could this be the imposter? I think, recalling the strange dream Elsie had the night after her Flooding, the one she wrote about in her notes before burying them in Highgate Cemetery.

"You have done your part, little owl, but you must be very careful," the man says. "For there are many who want to destroy what we have. We can't let that happen."

I'm not sure what he means. I want to ask questions but decide against it; experience has taught me that Ashkai (if this is really him) won't give a straight answer. Indeed, the more I probe and rationalize, the more complicated and confusing everything will get. And the lesson is always the same: *stop trying to solve problems at the level of mind and go deeper.*

I try to do exactly that by following my breath, visualizing a flowing, liquid light connecting throat, chest, and stomach.

"Stop doing that," the voice says, which is when I know it is not my master speaking. I do my best to shut the imposter out as I travel deeper within myself. It's a very calming exercise, and before long, all thoughts, worries, and concerns fade away. And the good news doesn't end there because the suffocating darkness of moments ago has been replaced by an expansive and perfect clear blue sky.

Even better, I am flying across it: soaring like an eagle, spinning like a ballerina, somersaulting like a carefree child, that is, until I become aware of the mighty Amazon rainforest below, its thick, brown waterway slaloming through green, verdant jungle, an immense and powerful serpent. There's a canoe down there, a mere speck from my vantage point. I dart down and zoom in, knowing exactly who I'll find: Ashkai and Ainia, a girl I once was, both of them nut brown, lean, and in the prime of life. I estimate this to be about forty cycles ago, roughly two thousand years.

After buzzing around like a curious hummingbird (I am formless and invisible), getting a good look at both of their faces, I settle upstream a few feet above the water. I'm looking over Ainia's exposed shoulder at Ashkai, who's sitting at the back of the boat, rowing toward me. The canoe is centrally positioned in the river, a good place to be when passing potentially hostile tribes, of which there are many.

There are caimans in the water and insects and birds in the sky. Everything is warm, damp, and earthy. Ashkai has a six-inch bone from the right leg of a spider monkey piercing his nose and a bow and arrow at his feet. He says, "Human beings are born with limitless potential and infinite wisdom."

"Why are most of them so stupid then?" Ainia asks, her sharp, angular cheekbones decorated with dye from the genipapo tree.

"Is a babe stupid for reaching out to touch a flame?" Ashkai responds. At one point, he glances up in my direction, just for a beat, and a smile teases the outer edges of his mouth.

"No," Ainia says. "But that is different."

"Why?"

"Because they know no better."

"Can't the same be said of man? At the level of consciousness, are they not also babes?"

"But if people are inherently good, as you have always maintained, why do they behave so despicably?"

"They are afraid, and fear smothers light," he says, looking at my position above the water again. "That fear can become so entrenched, so powerful, that it begins to take on a life of its own, a conscious parasite that feeds on its host."

"For what purpose?"

"For the purpose of transforming that soul into dark, hateful energy."

"So fear itself is something to be afraid of?"

"Only if you want to empower it further. It might not feel like it, little owl, but love is the predominant force of the universe. It's what holds everything together, and it is who we all are at the deepest, most fundamental level."

"Why does learning such a simple lesson take so long?" Ainia says. "And involve so much misery and heartache?"

"Pain and suffering, if channeled correctly, can be great teachers."

"Of what?"

"Of surrender, of acceptance, and ultimately of the truth."

"And what is the truth?"

Ashkai looks over Ainia's shoulder a third time, holding my gaze, even though I am lighter than air and completely invisible. He says, "Let go of your fear, Rosa, and you will see."

As if mirroring my state of shock, everything darkens: the sky, the jungle, the water. The river reptiles, some of them very large and agitated, start surrounding the canoe, thrashing their long, thick tails and snapping their teeth. Others are coming toward me. To avoid them, I shoot upward until I'm hovering about twenty feet above the water.

How can I let go? I think, thrusting the question into my master's mind.

His reply, as it can often be, is cryptic. "You must remember in order to forget."

Remember what? I ask, noticing that Ainia is no longer on the boat, no longer anywhere . . .

Ashkai stops rowing, grabs his weapon and stands. "You must leave," he says, stringing an arrow and taking aim, eyes looking straight through me.

What are you doing? I ask, but instead of responding, he lets fly, the caimans nudging the boat, trying to unbalance him.

Because I have left my physical body behind, the projectile passes through me harmlessly. Seconds later, I hear the arrow thud into something solid. I turn to discover a black hawk with white-tipped wings screeching and tumbling through a still darkening sky. The instant the bird splashes into the water, it is torn apart by snapping jaws and teeth. But the threat is not over. Thousands upon thousands of the same birds are pouring through a swirling black hole rimmed with gold, a portal from another dimension or place. Their wings are tucked in unison, a battering ram of feathers and claws just seconds from reaching us.

Turning back to Ashkai, worrying for his safety, I use telepathy to say, *Why is this happening?*

"The fear inside of you is fighting to protect itself."

From what?

"From your light and from my love."

What should I do?

"You must return to the physical realm, and you must do so now."

Following his orders, I visualize Rosa on the bed. I attempt to reenter her body, but nothing happens. Even though I can feel her heart beating wildly, I can't punch through. I watch helplessly as Ashkai kicks a reptile away. He unsheathes a second arrow and holds it close to his mouth, whispering what sounds like an ancient spell. But it's too late because the birds have arrived, their claws and beaks somehow sinking into me, even though I am without form or substance.

I am deeply afraid and also blind because it is completely dark now, as dark as the subterranean chamber I found myself in at the start of this journey.

A beam of sunlight shaped like an arrow cuts through the void and pounds into me. I burst into flames, and the birds release their grip. I am plunging toward the river now. There is a large caiman with its jaws open, waiting to devour me.

Time slows, and I have a moment of clarity, realizing that everything in this dream has been about fear, my fear.

If it belongs to me, surely I have power over it?

I am not afraid, I say, embodying the statement, believing it. *I AM NOT AFRAID.*

As I surrender, let go and trust myself, no longer trying to control what happens; the light of the sky returns, and the predators vanish. I crash into the cold, bracing river and immediately feel clean, safe, and renewed.

I am in Rosa's body, swimming naked beneath the surface, the water like silk against my skin. I am surrounded by hundreds of dolphins with long, thin noses, each animal saturated with color and light. The magnificent coral reefs and the many odd creatures that live among them have the same mesmerizing quality.

Part of me wants to stay here—*such beauty, such peace!*—but it's not an option.

It's time to wake up.

It's time to face my fear.

It's time to fight.

EIGHTEEN

By the time I shower and change, throwing on flats, denim shorts, and a yellow, long-sleeve T-shirt, using concealer on my face to hide the violence of the past few days, it's just after half past three in the afternoon. I'm thinking about Ashkai and Ainia, the Amazon and caimans, the portal and hawks. I'm aware something special happened during that dream. There's a feeling in my bones and my blood that I can do anything I put my mind to.

Moving objects without touching them, bar nudging a small pebble a centimeter or two, and that only after prolonged periods of deep meditation, is not a skill I have mastered. Undeterred by that fact, I am standing in the middle of my hotel room, staring at the circular handle on the door, asking the myriad pieces that make up the whole, elements forged by the heat and power of exploding stars, the genesis of all matter, to do my bidding. I become aware of a girl's voice in the hallway but manage to block it out as I laser in on the task at hand.

You are me, I think. *And I am you.* I feel the curve of metal in my empty right palm. I'm gripping tightly and rotating slowly. I'm elated, but not surprised, when there's movement. I watch the handle turn—*Yes!*—and the door swing open, but then I crash back to Earth when a skinny, blonde girl appears, phone in one hand, doorknob in the other, wheeled suitcase behind.

"I'm so sorry," she says, startled and apologetic, early twenties, pretty face. "I thought this was my room." Closing the door now, she says sorry over and over before explaining the situation to the person on the other end of the phone. I take a deep breath and consider making a second attempt, but the moment has passed, and I have work to do.

They have free Internet at the hotel, so I jump on one of the computers in reception, using Google Maps to work out how far it is to Kaya's meditation studio. It turns out it's just a fifteen-minute walk. I step into the California sunshine, Ray-Bans on, and enter a vibrant world of street performers, political graffiti, muscle men, and medical marijuana outlets. I get all the high I need from the Pacific Ocean, her vastness and power just a stone's throw away.

Kaya's studio is located in the basement of a four-story building that's also home to Love Yoga and an enterprise called Float Works. On the way in, I spotted a sky-blue Mini Cooper covered in "Lotus Meditations" branding, thinking it's the kind of thing a manager or owner would drive, meaning Kaya's probably on site.

The first thing I notice as I step out of the elevator is the large arrangement of plants and flowers directly below a circular skylight, wafts of lavender and jasmine tickling my nostrils. Beyond that, standing behind a long white counter, and below a wall quote that says "Bring your mind home," is a man in his late thirties, athletic and toned with dark hair and brown eyes.

"Hey, how you doin'?" he says, smiling, raising a hand, slightly effeminate, "Joey" on his nametag. "Welcome to Lotus Meditations."

"Thanks," I reply, taking in the neutral, sleek, modern décor, flowers providing splashes of color, and scented, flickering candles lining the bookshelves.

"Is Kaya around?" I ask, noticing the display of magazines on the front desk. All of them are the same issue of *Cosmo*, a beautiful blonde with washboard abs gracing the front cover. Emblazoned around her are provocative statements, such us *How To Climax Together* and *Meditate Your Way To Better Sex*.

"She's teaching right now," Joey says, nodding toward the closed door on my left, then glancing at the clock behind him—3:52 p.m.—adding, "Take a load off; she'll be out soon."

"Thank you," I say, sitting on the bench adjacent to his counter and underneath the bookshelves.

"I love your accent," Joey says. "Where you from, Australia?"
"England."

His eyes sparkle with excitement. "Amazing. London?"
"Yes."

"I was just there in May, loved it, so much fun. You on vacation?"
"Kind of. Arrived today actually."

148

"Fantastic. Welcome to Los Angeles. You a friend of Kaya's?"

"Not really. We've been e-mailing, though."

"She's the best, make sure you catch her breathwork class if you have time; it's incredibly powerful. You meditate?"

"When I can," I say, standing. "There a bathroom I can use?"

"Over there," he says pointing to his left. By the time I return, there are people leaving the studio, putting shoes on and grabbing bags, all of them saying thank you to a lady standing by the exit. I assume this is Kaya. She's mixed race and has ringlets of dark brown hair. She's in her early forties and slender with good posture and smooth, glowing skin.

Not wanting to disturb her, I return to my seat and wait. On his way to the empty studio, most likely to get it ready for the next session, Joey winks and says that she won't be long. I'm looking at the right side of Kaya's face from where I am, instinct telling me she's someone I'll like and get on with. I hope she feels the same, especially as I'm going to need her help.

As soon as the last person leaves, I stand and clear my throat. "Hi, Kaya," I say, walking toward her, hand extended. "I'm Rosa, you e-mailed me yesterday about . . ." I stop midsentence, watching the color seep from her face as the energy in the room goes from calm and tranquil to anxious and spiky.

Kaya steps back, saying, "How did you find me?"

"I don't know what you mean," I say, after a bewildered pause, realizing she knows me or at least thinks she does. "Have we met?"

"You need to leave," Kaya says, pointing toward the elevator. "Now."

"Why, who do you think I am?"

Joey reappears. "Everything okay?"

"This girl needs to leave," Kaya says, her employee standing between us now. "I don't want her here."

"Let's go," Joey says, stern and professional. An older couple appears out of nowhere, startled looks on their faces, asking Kaya if they should come back later.

"No, it's fine," she says, talking to them but looking at me. "Just head through. I'll be in shortly."

"Time to leave," Joey says, putting a hand on my shoulder,

ushering me toward the elevator. I don't appreciate being touched by people I don't know. I lash out and shove him, although I'm aware it's an overreaction. Kaya marches over to the counter now, reaching for the landline.

"That's it," she says, dialing. "I'm calling the cops."

"Why?" I say, pressing the issue. "What have I ever done to you?"

"I have an intruder on my property," Kaya says into the phone. "And they're violent, so please send someone quickly." She starts giving the address and answering other questions, all the while looking straight at me, her eyes brimming with . . . not anger, not hate, but fear.

"I don't know who you think I am," I say, "but you're wrong about me. I'm a good person."

Kaya holds the phone against her chest. "Then go," she says, which is exactly what I do.

For now.

***

Forty-five minutes later, the branded Mini pulls out of the car park and onto the main street. I get a glimpse of Kaya as she turns right, heading away from the coastline, moving quickly.

From the backseat of my parked taxi, I dart an arm forward and utter the famous line, "Follow that car." I'm speaking to Janet, the African American driver to whom I agreed to pay a hundred bucks an hour for as long as I needed her.

While pulling out, she says, "Who we following?" There are pictures of cute kids on the dashboard and a miniature Jamaican flag hanging from the rearview mirror. Everything smells of air freshener and cocoa butter.

"It's my boyfriend," I say, wanting to motivate her. "I think he's cheating, and I need to know one way or the other."

"Say no more," Janet replies, picking up speed, getting to within three vehicles of our target. "Girl, where there's smoke, there's usually fire. Especially when a man's involved."

At the second set of lights, Kaya indicates off the busy road onto quieter residential streets, eventually turning into a driveway in front of a lime-green craftsman house with a eucalyptus tree out front.

I keep my head down as we cruise by. Janet says, "That's who he messin' with? Looks twice your age."

"Doesn't make it hurt any less," I say, glancing left. Kaya is hurrying toward her front door, looking over a shoulder before opening it.

What's she so scared of?

Janet parks a few houses down, and I give her a hundred-dollar bill.

Thirty seconds later, I'm on Kaya's front porch. Maybe she forgot to lock the door? No such luck. I peek inside, but there are net curtains over the windows, meaning I can only make out shapes and outlines. Seeing what look like a piano, a sofa, and a mirror on the wall, I snap my head back because somebody entered the room.

Moving quickly and quietly, I make my way to the back of the house. Once there, I discover a cute deck with a rocking chair and a huge array of potted plants: pansies, violas, basil, oregano, perennials, shrubs and . . .

I do a double take.

Is that what I think it is?

I lean forward and laugh quietly to myself. After all, I'm looking at an ayahuasca vine! Just as I remember, it's thick, knotted, and fibrous like a strong piece of rope, with large green leaves growing on the outshoots. I do a quick scan of everything else up here but fail to locate the second ingredient required for the shamanic brew: *Psychotria viridis*, aka chacruna.

Why have one without the other?

I become aware of a police siren in the distance as my gaze returns to the ayahuasca vine and the ceramic pot holding it. I notice circular marks and scuffs on the white decking, the kind of superficial damage you'd expect if, say, there was a spare key under there for the cleaner. I'm about to stoop and investigate when the back door swings open.

"Give me an excuse, and I'll pull this trigger," Kaya says, her legs apart, double-handed grip on the semiautomatic pistol aimed at my head.

"I'm not looking for trouble," I say, palms raised. "I just want to talk."

"How did you find me?" Kaya asks, wearing black leggings and a loose- fitting gray cardigan. "It wasn't supposed to happen like this."

"It was the other way around," I say, ignoring her second comment.

"What are you talking about?"

"You wrote to me yesterday. I was looking for a place to drink ayahuasca in the United Kingdom."

She thinks for a moment. "Rosa?"

I nod.

Pause.

"What's it been, two, maybe three weeks?"

"Since what?" I ask, the police siren getting louder . . .

"Your Flooding."

My heart quickens with fear, excitement, and hope.

"You're like me," I say.

"I am nothing like you." Her voice is laced with disdain.

"What is it you think I've done? Tell me so I can explain myself or apologize if I've wronged you."

"It's not what you've done, Samsara; it's what you're going to do."

"How do you know my name? And what are you talking about? I have dedicated my lives to helping others."

"The only thing you're dedicated to is Ashkai, and he is not who you think he is."

Instinct takes over, and I step forward. "What do you know of my master? Where is he?"

"Any closer," Kaya says, raising her voice, "and I'll put you to sleep for another eighteen years."

"And when I awaken, I will find you and return the favor."

There's a knock at the front door.

"This is LAPD," a male officer says. "We're responding to a 911

152

call regarding an intruder."

"Leave now," Kaya says, talking to me, keeping her voice low. "Or get arrested for harassment and trespassing. You won't be much use to your master then."

"I'm not the person you think I am."

"Yes, you are. You just don't know it yet."

"Have you always been such a bitch?" I ask, and Kaya starts counting down. "Five, four . . ."

Another knock. "Can you open the door please; do you need assistance?"

"Two, one . . ."

"It didn't have to be like this," I say, turning, slipping into the narrow alley behind the house, promising myself the next time I see that woman, she won't have any choice but to tell me everything I need to know.

NINETEEN

Many hours later, in the dead of night, I get out of the taxi a quarter mile from Kaya's house and start walking. I'm wearing jeans, a T-shirt, and a zipped-up hoodie and feel exhausted. My mind has not stopped working since this afternoon, posing question after question after question . . .

How did Kaya know my name? What does she think I am going to do? What is the nature of her relationship with Ashkai? What did she mean about him not being who I think he is?

It's approaching 2 a.m., and that chilly ocean breeze is making me wish I'd thrown on a jacket. The residential streets of Venice are eerily quiet, that is, until a helicopter passes overhead, drawing my gaze, forcing me to notice the crescent moon and dusting of stars, each one slashing trails of light across the dark expanse of the boundless universe. Yet another question enters my head: *how many stars are out there?* It's one I have pondered many times before, which might explain why it has stirred a long-forgotten memory . . .

I suddenly feel dizzy and am forced to sit on the sidewalk. I close my eyes, knowing that I'm about to have another one of my flashbacks. The signs, by now, are unmistakable.

When I open my eyes, things have changed. For example, instead of sitting, I am on my feet. Instead of being alone, I have Ashkai by my side. He says, "There are more stars out there than grains of sand on Earth."

We are in ancient Egypt, and I am the luckiest slave to have ever lived.

"Including the great desert?" I ask, the two of us enjoying a midnight stroll through the royal gardens of his Theban palace. I'm still coming to terms, both physically and mentally, with the reality-shattering ordeal that was my Awakening. That's not to say I'm not feeling good—on the contrary, I have never been better—but Ashkai has stressed it will take time to fully process the experience.

"Including every desert and every beach, even on lands yet to be discovered," my master says, wearing a linen wraparound from the waist down, his long, dark hair, gray streak included, tickling those broad, powerful, battle-scarred shoulders.

"How is that possible?" I say, aware of Ashkai's bodyguards, who are always close by, knowing how much they resent and despise me for rising up from my position as a slave, not that I'm the only person he has taken under his wing. Ashkai recently adopted a street urchin. The little girl, who is deaf, blind, and dumb, managed to evade the Royal Guards during a recent parade. She reached out and held his hand. Since then, she has been like a daughter to him. In fact, just half an hour ago, the two of us tucked "Angel Face" (his nickname for the child) into bed, showering her with hugs and kisses.

"Anything is possible, Samsara. That is what I hope to teach you."

"I suppose I can fly, then?" I say, knowing how much Ashkai enjoys being teased.

"Did you not fly during your spirit journey?"

"That was different."

"Why?"

"Because I didn't really become an owl and soar the skies and heavens."

Ashkai's expression is one of playful confusion. "Why did you speak of such things if they did not occur?"

"Because they did occur," I say, smiling. "But even in the midst of it, when I was up among the stars, a small part of me was always aware of my body lying on the floor."

Ashkai thinks for a moment. "Let me ask you this: why do you choose to believe that element of your experience over everything else?"

"It's not that I don't believe . . . I mean, nothing will ever be the same again. I'm just pointing out that I didn't *actually* fly."

After walking past a pond, its surface scattered with brightly colored water lilies, my master says, "Have you ever awoken from a nightmare only to sigh with relief when you realized it wasn't real?"

"Many times."

"The same thing happens when we die. What was real becomes a dream and what was a dream becomes real."

I stop walking and turn to face the man to whom I owe everything, the warm air infused with citrus from the nearby lemon trees, insects and frogs making their noises. "Then I must have died," I say, contemplating my life now compared to just six months ago when I was nothing more than a commodity to be used and discarded. "Because what you describe has already taken place."

"You will not always be this happy, Samsara. The gift of remembering has many downsides."

"For this moment alone, it is a price worth paying."

Looking at me as a wise father would his young, naïve daughter, Ashkai says, "I hope you still feel that way in four thousand years."

At that moment, it's as if a huge hand from above snatches me up and hurls me across the ages, returning me to the modern era. I'm back in Rosa's body now, sitting upright on the curb, shocked and afraid because of what I just remembered.

Four thousand years has passed since that night, I think, telling myself it must be a coincidence before remembering I don't believe in them. I'm feeling angry, confused, and hungry for answers as I stand and run the rest of the way to Kaya's house, relieved to see her car in the driveway and that no lights are on.

After catching my breath, I sneak around back and climb onto the deck, moving slowly because the wooden panels are squeaking under my feet. I pull out my flashlight (purchased this afternoon) and use it to locate the ayahuasca plant. Next, I get on my hands and knees and tilt the ceramic pot forward, lowering my face to the ground, peering underneath. At first, it appears I was wrong to think gaining access would be so easy, but then the narrow beam of light catches something shiny. I move a fallen leaf out of the way, and there it is: the key for the door, which I open as quietly as possible.

I edge into Kaya's kitchen and grab a knife from the rack on the counter. From my position in the middle of the room, I take another step, and the floor creaks. I look down and discover I'm standing on a trap door. There must be a basement down there. Moments later, I'm edging past a small dining table and into the lounge. I can smell the same tones of lavender and jasmine that greeted me when I arrived at Kaya's meditation studio yesterday. I was unaware then that I would be breaking into her home less than twelve hours later.

Ever since my dream involving the Amazon, hawks, and Ashkai's arrow of fire, my senses have felt sharper, almost preternatural, and right now, they are telling me another human is nearby. I pause and focus on that frequency, the air rich with life, and for a moment, I'm able to pick up what must be Kaya's heartbeat. It's slow and steady, giving me confidence she's asleep.

My flashlight finds a small antique piano in the far corner of the living room, and then a sofa with a red throw covering it. Soon after, I'm looking at the first of two heavily worn, mismatched leather chairs before exploring the shamanic and psychedelic art on the walls.

I look around for signs of other people, framed photographs of kids or a husband, but there's nothing to suggest anybody lives here other than Kaya.

From where I'm standing, I can see the eucalyptus tree in the front garden. On my right is an archway that leads to a small hallway and three additional rooms. The door for what I'm guessing must be the master bedroom is closed, but the other two, toward the back of the house, are open, revealing a study and a bathroom, both of which are empty, meaning there's only one place Kaya can be.

Because my eyes have adjusted pretty well, and because I need one hand to hold the knife and the other to open the door, I pocket the flashlight while simultaneously telling myself to be careful, as she'll likely have that gun close by and be willing to use it. I move quickly, bursting in and leaping onto the bed only to discover that what I thought was Kaya's sleeping body is, in fact, a pillow stuffed under the duvet.

"Hello, Samsara," a man says.

I daren't turn or make a move in case he has a gun.

"Who are you?" I ask.

In place of an answer, two projectiles slam into my back.

Everything starts to melt and dissolve. I spill onto the bed like liquid.

***

I have descended into a deep and all-encompassing dream.

Somebody I do not know and cannot see tells me to open my eyes, repeating it over and over.

"Let me sleep," I want to reply as I'm floating through heavy, impenetrable fog. "I am tired." But I can't get the words out. There is also something about the energy and tone of this strange male entity that is making me feel uncomfortable.

Voice raised, he says, "Open your eyes, now."

"I am too weak."

"You are stronger than you could ever imagine," the man says, but I ignore him, giving in to the drift when I hear, "Since when did you stop obeying your master?"

The comment gives me a jolt. I am still fast asleep, but my awareness has sharpened.

"I am not fooled," I say, peering through the gloom. "You are an imposter."

"No, I am a beacon of truth."

"Then show yourself."

"I am waiting."

"For what?"

"For you to be ready."

"Why do you pretend to be Ashkai?" I ask.

In place of an answer, the voice says, "He has been lying to you."

A deep anxiety washes over me. "About what?"

"Everything."

"If what you speak is the truth," I say, "then I am alone in the universe."

"How can that be when I am always by your side?"

As if motivated by his words, the surrounding fog reshapes

itself into an outstretched hand, index finger aglow with a dark, ominous fire.

Do not touch it, I tell myself, but before the thought is complete, I already have, the resulting explosion of energy and power healing and invigorating me on both the spiritual and physical planes.

I quickly realize something before opening my eyes: I'm no longer asleep. I'm back in the material world, experiencing the here and now. Not only that, I am in grave danger, the like of which I have never encountered before. I don't know how I know that, I just do.

When I open my eyes, a scene of absolute horror begins to unfold like a black flower from hell.

A large man wearing a feathered headdress is straddling my midriff. Eyes closed and wearing a purple gown made of silk, he is uttering spells of black magic, speaking Nahuatl, the ancient language of the Aztecs, all while holding a large obsidian blade in a double-handed grip, the gruesome instrument of death pointing ominously downward.

I am naked and lying on the floor in a darkened, smoke-filled room. There are plastic sheets underneath me. My arms are stretched out crucifixion style, but thankfully, they are not tied down. There are flickering candles encircling us. I have to assume that this person, whoever he is, shot me with a tranquilizer gun before moving me here. The exposed piping in the ceiling and air conditioning unit to my right suggests we're in a basement somewhere, most likely Kaya's.

He wants my heart, I think, instantly afraid but also furious and hateful, remembering the girl I was at the turn of the sixteenth century, Necalli, the fifteen-year-old Tlascalan bride whose wedding day (and life thereafter) was destroyed when a hundred or so Aztec soldiers, eagle and jaguar warriors among them, ambushed her village and slaughtered all of the unsuspecting men in what felt like seconds. Fathers, uncles, brothers, and friends were cut down like corn.

They spared all of the virgins that day, including me, but only so we could be transported to Tenochtitlan—modern-day Mexico City—the Aztec capital, where an even worse fate awaited us, one that involved being marched to the top of the great pyramid, where so-called priests would tear out our still-beating hearts, all to satisfy the ravenous and bloodthirsty appetites of the malevolent forces they worshipped.

Through a combination of luck, guile, and determination, I was able to escape that hideous fate. Can I do it again?

"Yes," whispers the voice from the fog. "But you must embrace the darker side of yourself."

The man speaking Nahuatl—eyes closed, voice trembling—says, "I summon the weak, the damned, and the depraved, demons and monsters, devils and ghouls . . ."

The *Decimatio*, I think, watching as a small portal materializes in and around that terrible weapon of human sacrifice.

He doesn't want to kill me, I realize. *He wants to annihilate my soul.*

Individual wisps of black smoke begin making their way through the portal. There are just a few at first, but then they start gushing through like raw sewage. Some of the spirits are drawn to the feathers, candles, and pipes in the ceiling, while others come straight for me, hovering above my chest and head. I can sense how ravenous and desperate they are, like a pack of starving wolves, and how quickly they'll consume my soul.

Switching to English, the man with the knife says, "For Mother Earth!"

In order to take aim, he opens his eyes for the first time. On seeing I'm awake, he panics and brings the knife down hard and fast. Before impact, before certain and enduring death, before all hope of rescuing Ashkai evaporates forever, I black out. When awareness returns, I find that I am holding the man's wrists, stopping the jagged point less than a centimeter from my solar plexus.

The look on his face is one of astonishment, shock, and fear until he pulls himself together and leans forward on the knife. He is heavy and determined, and even though my will to survive has given me superhuman strength, it's clear I won't be able to hold out for long.

"Fight!" the voice tells me. "Do not give up."

He is too strong, I think, feeling pressure on my ribcage, skin breaking, blood seeping through . . .

"Be angry; be hateful. That's where your power lies."

How?

"By using the fire I gave you."

I'm able to picture it burning deep down inside of me. I let the flames spread into every part of my body, and as they do, I feel myself getting angrier, stronger, and more determined.

"You can do anything you put your mind to," the voice says, and out of nowhere, I am reminded of how much Elsie, the girl I was in the late nineteenth century, hated and despised her rapist of a father and how she was able to channel those dark and destructive energies into powerful, reality-altering thoughts.

But Mr. Farish was weak, I think. *This man is formidable. How can I overpower him?*

The voice says, "By believing in yourself," and that's when something clicks.

Of course, I think, as if it's the most obvious thing in the world. *My potential is limitless.*

"You are special," the voice says. "You are strong." Each word is infused with such power and energy. It's like nothing I've ever known, and it feels incredible.

Something inside me, something dark and hidden, guides me then, giving me an idea. Wasting no time, I visualize a protective force field cocooning Rosa's delicate body. When that is done, I let go of the man's wrists with complete and utter confidence. Despite his best efforts, the knife doesn't move until I want it to. I take over the workings of his mind, forcing him to turn the weapon around. I feel resistance and fear, his soul fighting back, but I brush it aside as I would an annoying fly, forcing him to stab through cartilage and bone, muscle and heart, inflicting a wound from which there is no coming back.

As warm blood gushes onto my stomach, the man falls to the side, his head slamming into the ground, the feathers in his headdress catching fire on the candles.

His last words are "I had no choice."

The man dies then, and the light of his soul is set upon by the desperate and hungry spirits who had been waiting to feed. The voice from the fog whispers, "I am proud of you."

TWENTY

I am awake but badly shaken and confused.

I can feel the aftereffects of the sedative I was given. Maybe that's why I keep phasing in and out of awareness. One minute I'm lying naked on the floor, sobbing and covered in blood, and then I'm standing underneath a shower watching red swirls at my feet. The next thing I know, I'm wearing my clothes, although I have no idea where I found them or any memory of getting dressed. I only register I am in Kaya's house when I see the psychedelic and shamanic art on the walls.

Where is she?

I lie on the sofa with the red throw and stare at the ceiling. It's still dark outside, but the living room light is on. For some reason, Tammuz is the last person I think about before falling asleep, which explains how I've ended up in his bed, dreaming now. After pressing my nose into his pillow, I look up and discover that my friend, wearing jeans and a black jumper, is standing over me. He is leaning forward trying to give me something, so I pull the duvet back and sit up on my calves.

"I want you to have this," he says.

I realize to my horror Tammuz is holding a human heart. The veins and arteries have been severed, but the organ is still beating. Blood is dripping onto my bare thighs. He also has a gaping hole in his chest and what looks like a deep knife wound in his neck.

I stand and say, "What are you doing?" while trying to help. Tammuz doesn't let me. "Who did this to you?"

"It's okay. I don't need it anymore."

After a struggle, I manage to shove his heart into the cavity only for it to fall through his back onto the floor. I get on my hands and knees and retrieve it, but by the time I straighten, everything has changed.

I'm standing on top of a building peering down at the streets of

New York. It's daytime.

A voice to my rear says, "You made me a promise, Samsara."

I turn and see Ashkai as he looked the last time I saw him, handsome and young, with skin like chocolate.

I am dreaming, I remind myself, but it's a hard concept to hold on to.

"The question is, will you keep it?" Ashkai continues, standing about fifteen paces away.

"Why did you lie to me?" I ask, getting sucked in, losing perspective.

"After everything we have been through, you abandon me at the first sign of doubt?"

The comment cuts deep, and I feel instantly stupid, guilty, and ashamed. After all, what am I basing my suspicion on other than a few bad dreams and the testimony of a stranger?

"Nothing makes sense anymore," I say. "I don't know who I can trust, and that includes myself."

Ashkai lowers his gaze, worry and concern etched on his face. "Who gave you that fire?"

I look down at my outstretched hands, and hovering above each palm is a single black flame.

A voice to my right says, "You know the answer to that question, brother."

I turn, and Rebus is standing a few paces away, skin whiter than a wedding gown. He says, "My soldier failed, but he will not have died in vain; I promise you that, old friend. I will never give up."

My master looks at him and then back at me. "Who gave you that fire?" he repeats.

"I don't know," I say, wondering where Tammuz's heart has gone. "But it saved my life."

"Only so it can use you."

"Liar," the fire in my left hand whispers. "Enemy," adds its counterpart.

"I can control it."

"Then you would be the first."

I lean forward and try to blow the flames out, but nothing happens.

"It's a part of you," Ashkai says, and I start to feel panicked, clapping my hands and rubbing them against my clothes. But all that does is make each fire spread, first along my arms and torso, then down my legs, and finally up over my face and head.

"How can I stop it?" I ask.

"By filling your heart with love and light," my master says, but I can think of nothing more impossible. To make matters worse, I'm at the center of a raging inferno, and my skin is starting to crackle and blister.

"Help is coming," Ashkai says.

He raises a hand and sends forth a pulse of energy, hurling me from this building for the second time.

***

Before hitting the ground, I awaken with a start, returning to the here and now.

I sit upright on Kaya's sofa and pull my legs into my chest.

I'm facing the window and can see the eucalyptus tree out front. Morning light is streaming in, and birds are tweeting.

I check my hands and arms and prod my face, looking for marks and blisters, but it seems I'm okay.

I glance at my watch: 6:27 a.m. I'm struggling to come to terms with everything that has happened: the man who tried to butcher my flesh and obliterate my soul, the strange entity who gave me the energy and belief to fight back, Ashkai's warning about the dark fire, his promise to find me.

Could the encounter with my master have been in any way real? Or was it just a paranoid fantasy? Furthermore, why did Rebus appear on that roof, and what did he mean when he said his soldier had failed? Did Rebus order my assassination? I can't help but remember the rude, obnoxious, pale-skinned man I met on that bitter winter's day in Amsterdam almost two centuries ago, how he and Ashkai spoke privately outside the *Vis En Brood Café*. And then there was *that* message, using telepathy to tell me he knew who I *really* was, the suggestion being I was dangerous in some way.

There's another possibility, one that involves the death cult known as The Shadow. While I have never encountered any of its members—Ashkai made sure to keep us as far away from them as possible—I know that their sole purpose is to snuff out all expressions of love and light.

Was the man in the basement one of them?

Confused, frustrated, and getting nowhere, I clear my mind and gaze through the window again, this time looking at Kaya's Mini in the driveway.

Where is she? How does she fit into all this? Could she be the same woman who was standing next to Rebus in Amsterdam?

In an ideal world, the two of us would sit and have a civilized conversation, but Kaya decided against such a peaceful and pragmatic approach, choosing fear and suspicion instead. It's a decision that is going to come back to haunt her.

Searching the house is the obvious next step. I start in the lounge and dining area before heading into the bedroom and then the study, emptying drawers, cupboards, and shelves, pulling books, DVDs, and artwork to the floor. I get excited when I find a laptop, only to discover that it's password protected. I try *Kaya*, *Lotus Meditations*, *Rebus*, and *Ashkai* without success.

I think to when Kaya pointed a gun at my head. Her reaction clearly stemmed from fear. She would have assumed I was going to return. In fact, I pretty much told her that would happen.

So what does she do? Reach out for help, of course, and in this case *(if my wild speculations are correct)*, that meant contacting Rebus. He then ordered one of his "soldiers" to take me out. Permanently.

Even though we've spent less than three minutes in each other's company, Kaya didn't strike me as the type who's into ripping people's hearts out of their chest; hence that was why she didn't want to be here. But that doesn't explain Rebus's absence. If he hates me as much as I think he does, why not do the job himself?

Maybe he lives in another country, I think. *Or he doesn't like getting his hands dirty.* I start to wonder if it was his idea for Kaya to leave her car in the driveway, so I'd assume she was home.

I'm reminded of what the man in the basement said as he passed, that he had no choice. Are they all just following orders, Rebus included? Is Meta's propaganda machine *(who else could it be?)* poisoning their hearts and minds? The possibility is a frightening one because if they were willing to give my soul to the *Decimatio*, then wouldn't they have done the same to Ashkai?

No, I tell myself. *He is still alive; I can feel it.*

Whatever their motive, as far as Rebus is concerned (if he is indeed to blame), I'm no longer a problem. Then again, Rebus will be perturbed when his assassin doesn't check in. The question is, does he have a contingency plan?

I've been ransacking Kaya's place for about twenty minutes, rifling through paperwork, photographs, and notebooks, pocketing things of value as I go: rings, necklaces, and small amounts of cash. I venture into the kitchen, a room I have thus far avoided, and feel instantly nauseous. The trapdoor to the basement is in here. Looking at it forces me to remember how I clambered through, naked and covered in blood, like a goblin escaping the depths of hell.

There's a stepladder in the pantry, so I grab it and head back to the master bedroom, standing in front of the fitted wardrobe now, wanting to see what's on those upper two shelves. In among the sheets, travel bags, beach towels, and bedding, I find a shoebox, those preternatural instincts telling me I've landed on something important.

I climb down and sit on the edge of the bed so that I'm facing the stepladder and Kaya's hanging clothes. The window, which looks out front, is to the left of me, and the door leading to the hallway is directly behind.

I open the shoebox. Inside is Kaya's gun, the same one she pointed at me yesterday. It turns out it's fully loaded. Scraps of paper, old concert tickets, and photographs are underneath it. I flick through the images and . . . bingo: one is of a man with alabaster skin, early to midforties, walking out of a building.

It has to be Rebus.

There is a long row of yellow cabs in the edge of frame, which suggests New York. There's also a familiar corporate logo in the lower ground window behind him. I adjust my eyes and focus on it. There's just one word—COSMOS—written in white against a dark, starry background. I know the organization well; everyone does. In fact, they were on the news just recently, talking about a large comet that's on a crash course with Mars.

The photograph is in good condition—no smudges, no frayed edges—which suggests this is the human body Rebus's consciousness currently occupies. He's tall and strong and, with that shaved head, looks like the kind of guy you wouldn't want to piss off. Although, for me, that ship has sailed.

I pocket the image and continue my search, but nothing else catches my eye unless I'm missing something . . .

I should be buoyed by the discovery of the photograph—it proves my suspicion that Rebus and Kaya are connected—but instead, I feel numb and deflated, wanting to lie down, fall asleep, and never awaken. I think, *How did that happen?* because I don't remember placing the barrel of the gun against my right temple or the moment I started contemplating how easy it would be to start over. I feel a deep-down desire to hurt and punish myself.

Why not just do it?

There's a noise to my left. I look toward the window and blink rapidly. Staring at me, his face full of pain, worry and disbelief, is somebody I know.

"The hell are you doing?" the person shouts, banging the glass a second time. "Put that down."

I must be dreaming, I think, looking at Tammuz, whose face has softened as the hand holding the gun falls of its own accord.

"That's it," he says. "I'm finding you a psychiatrist."

TWENTY-ONE

I place the gun on the bed and head into the hallway. I open Kaya's front door. I'm expecting to see nothing. I must be hallucinating after all, but there he is. Tammuz, his face dusted with stubble. He's wearing the same black jumper as in my dream. I'm relieved the similarities end there.

"You've been in America less then a day," he says, stepping inside, carrying a brown leather bag, "and already you have a gun. What do they do, hand them out at the airport?"

After closing the door, I reach out and prod the center of his chest.

"I see you haven't lost any of your charm," he says, glancing at my hand. "What was that all about just now? Tell me it wasn't loaded."

I step forward and place my right cheek against his sweater. Tammuz puts his bag down and embraces me, and we just stand there for a while. I wish this moment of peace and calm could last forever. But of course, it doesn't. Tammuz says, after kissing the top of my head, "Did you do this?" He drifts away from me toward the lounge, which is a mess. "Where's Kaya? She know you're here?"

That's when the novelty wears off and suspicion sets in.

Talking to the back of his head, I say, "How did you find me this time?"

He ignores me and keeps walking toward the dining area, which, in turn, becomes the kitchen. I don't have the energy to explain the scene in there, let alone the basement, so I raise my voice and say, "That's far enough."

Tammuz turns to face me, the red sofa on his left. "Why, what's through there?"

I take a few paces. "How did you find me, Tammuz, and how do you know Kaya?"

"I don't know her," he says, dodging my first question.

"How do you know her name?"

He starts mumbling something about a dream he had, but I cut him off, saying that unless he wants a gun pointed at *his* head, he better answer my damn question. And yes, it is loaded.

"That's not funny."

"It's not meant to be. Now spit it out."

He says, "Just relax, okay?" Then: "I read Kaya's e-mail."

"What e-mail?"

"The one she sent you about ayahuasca."

"You hacked into my account?"

"Don't be ridiculous. I went to check my e-mail, but you were still logged in."

"So you thought you'd snoop around? How dare you invade my privacy like that?"

He laughs. "Says the girl who hasn't stopped lying since the moment we met. By the way, how's that life-threatening illness of yours?"

"So you've never met Kaya or spoken to her?"

He shakes his head. "Not once."

"How did you get her address?"

"Does it matter?"

"Yes. Very much."

"Why?" Tammuz asks, running a hand through his mess of dark hair. "After everything, don't you trust me?"

I stare into his eyes, waiting.

He gets the message.

"I landed yesterday afternoon and went straight to Lotus Meditations . . ."

Something occurs to me, and I interrupt. "How did you get into the country with a criminal record?"

"I just took my chances. Nobody asked any questions. I guess I'm pretty small-time in the grand scheme of things."

"If they catch you, you'll be banned from America for life."

"It's a chance I'm willing to take."

"You're such an idiot," I say.

"Thanks a lot." Then he adds, "After landing, I went straight to Lotus Meditations. The address was on Kaya's e-mail. I asked the guy working there if she was around, but he wasn't very helpful. I couldn't understand what his problem was until he started talking about the crazy English girl from earlier, asking if I was anything to do with her.

"I told him I was your brother and that I was worried because you hadn't taken your medication. He calmed down after that but had no idea where you were. I figured you might come back, so I went to the Starbucks across the road and started doing some research on my phone. That's when I came across this article Kaya had written for *Cosmopolitan* magazine. It was about sex and meditation.

"I left it a couple of hours and then phoned her studio. I was expecting that guy to pick up, but it was somebody else. I asked if Kaya was there, but she wasn't, so I explained I was from *Cosmo* and that we needed her home address; otherwise we wouldn't be able to process her invoice."

"And they just gave it to you?"

"I'm here, aren't I?" Tammuz says. "I got here at six thirty last night, but nobody was home. I hung around for a while, but as soon as the sun went down, it got pretty cold and I was knackered, so I called it a night. I was up early and couldn't get back to sleep, so I came here, hoping to catch Kaya before she went to work.

"I was on the other side of the road killing time when I saw movement in the house. It was still really early, so I decided to take a look through the window before ringing the bell, and there you were. Holding a gun to your head. Another brilliant piece of decision-making to add to your collection."

"I didn't pull the trigger, did I?"

"What about next time?"

I think for a moment, weighing up his story, searching for signs he might be lying or keeping something from me, but his blue eyes, mesmerizing and sharp, look honest and trustworthy, as usual. I'm thinking again about how hard it is to shake this guy and whether or not that's significant.

"You're pretty resourceful, huh?" I say.

"I was worried about you."

I have more questions, but they'll have to wait.

171

"You need to leave."

He scans the lounge, taking in the mess. "What are you looking for?"

"Just go, Tammuz; we'll speak later."

"When?"

"Wait for me at the Ocean Park Getaway. That's where I'm staying."

"Where is it?"

"Not far. Google it."

"How long will you be?"

"Less than an hour."

"You promise?"

Losing patience, I grab his hand and usher him outside, picking his bag up on the way, telling him to go to the hotel and wait for me. He tries to respond, but I close the door in his face. Looking through the spyhole, I see him stand there for a beat before turning and walking down the patio steps.

I have one place left to look, and I want to get it over with as quickly as possible. I take a few moments to brace myself before making my way into the kitchen. Once there, I get on my hands and knees and peer into the basement. The first thing I see is that circle of candles, all of which are still burning, apart from the two or three that were extinguished when the man toppled over.

Because of the candlelight, I can just about make out the corpse's bare feet in the shadows next to a sizable pool of blood. His purple gown has ridden up slightly, and I can see he's wearing jeans underneath. He'll probably be carrying a phone and a wallet, and those are two things I'd very much like to get my hands on.

I climb down the metal ladder and locate the light switch. The obsidian blade is sticking out of the man's chest. The plastic sheets I had been lying on are crumpled and smeared with blood. The headdress, made of alternating black and white feathers, is only partly burned. I don't remember doing it, but I must have put the fire out soon after killing him.

The spirits who devoured his soul are no longer present. The portal has also disappeared, although there is a lingering negative energy that is giving me goose bumps. Other than that, everything is pretty normal: rolls of toilet paper, canned goods, and other provisions in the far left corner; a washing machine and dryer on my right, along with a sink. A box of Christmas decorations, three pieces of luggage, camping equipment, and a good-size wine rack to add to the clutter.

After extinguishing the candles, I approach the dead body and stand over it, steering clear of the blood. I wasn't able to register what he looked like before, but now I can. He's black, under forty, and has prominent cheekbones. He has curly (rather than afro) hair and lips that are narrow but rounded. If I had to guess, I'd say he was from East Africa: Somalia or Ethiopia, somewhere like that.

I get down on my haunches and pull up his purple gown. His front pockets are empty. I'm in the process of trying to roll him forward into the blood when a phone starts vibrating somewhere on my left. I stand and turn, homing in on the sound, quickly determining the source: a navy-blue Jansport backpack that's tucked underneath the wooden counter running along the far wall. It didn't catch my eye before—*why would it among everything else?*—but it certainly has now.

I grab the bag and rest it on the work surface. I can see by the light shining through that the phone is inside the small front compartment. I open the zip and pull it out.

The number is withheld.

I swipe the screen and put the phone to my ear.

Speaking in an urgent whisper, a woman says, "Bacchus?"

I remain silent.

"Bacchus, are you there?"

"He can't get to the phone right now," I say. "Want me to pass on a message?"

"Samsara?"

"Who is this?"

"You're alive?" She says it as if she's relieved.

"Who are you and how do you know my name?"

No longer whispering, the mysterious woman says, "Get out of there, Samsara, now!"

173

TWENTY-TWO

"Who is this?" I ask, but the phone goes dead.

Could it have been Kaya? Did she have second thoughts about her involvement in my demise? The woman's voice was lowered and rushed, so it's hard to be certain one way or the other. But who else could it have been?

Erring on the side of caution, I pocket Bacchus's phone and throw his bag onto my back. I'm climbing out of the basement, poking my head into the kitchen when I hear a noise and stop.

There's somebody opening the front door. As long as the person isn't sporting a lotus flower tattoo, I'll be able to take them out, no problem. But then I hear two men whispering, walking toward the back of the house, and I'm not so confident.

What if Rebus is one of them?

I'm still shaken from the phone call and make a very bad decision: I go back the way I came, closing the trapdoor behind me, but I realize at that moment that there's no way they won't check down here, especially as there are handprints and smears all over the kitchen floor. Preparing for battle, I extract the obsidian blade from Bacchus's chest and wipe it on his jeans so as not to leave a trail of blood. After switching off the light and removing the bag from my back, I slip underneath the wooden counter along the far wall next to the washing machine, dragging two pieces of luggage in front of me.

Instead of looking around the house, the strangers gravitate directly above. I can only hear male voices; their words are muffled and undecipherable. I move the bags slightly, giving myself a narrow gap to peer through, although right now, the room is pitch black. When the trapdoor opens, a shaft of light hits the floor several feet from the dead body, which thankfully is still hidden in the shadows.

"Bacchus?" a man says, speaking with a thick German accent.

"There's blood on the floor and on these stairs," says a second man, whose accent identifies him as American, his voice gruff and authoritative.

"What do you think happened?" asks a third. He is significantly younger than the others, in this life at least.

Germany answers, "Something other than the plan."

"Let's go check it out," America says, and they start coming down when there's a noise from somewhere, maybe a loose book falling from one of the shelves I ransacked in the living room. America changes his mind.

"We should clear the rest of the house first," he says while closing the trapdoor, plunging the basement into darkness.

Please don't lock it, I think, but of course they do, the metal bolt sliding into place. I get out from where I am and switch on the light.

I pull out Bacchus's iPhone. There are eleven missed calls from a person named "Jord." The icon on the screen reads *slide to call*, so I do. After three rings, a man answers: "Where the hell are you? We're at the house now."

It's the same guy who just made the decision to clear the rest of the house before coming down here.

I hang up and try to access the contacts page, but this time, it asks for a security code. Frustrated, I switch the thing off and shove it into a pocket.

I think about my four thousand years of training, about what Ashkai would do if he were in my position. I try to imagine what his advice would be, even whispering to him, "I need you, master, tell me what to do," but I get nothing in return.

I look at the dead body.

Something occurs to me. It's an idea that quickly evolves into a plan. It's far from perfect, but anything is better than just hiding and hoping for the best.

Doing what I have to do isn't easy and it takes effort, but by the time the trapdoor opens again, seconds after I unscrewed the light bulb, everything is in place.

"Let's take a look," Jord says, and I stop breathing, keeping totally still.

Following a short pause, the young one asks, "What's that?"

The three of them peer down from the safety of the kitchen. I'm guessing they have a flashlight. "You were just on it, back that way."

While they were upstairs sweeping the house, I rolled Bacchus's corpse underneath the counter, concealing it behind Christmas decorations, luggage, and camping equipment. I am lying where he was, facedown, positioned so that his blood appears to be flowing from my body, obsidian blade tucked under the upper part of my chest.

"This doesn't make sense," Jord mutters, and the young one asks, "Is it her?"

Jord says, "I don't know." Then he says, "Salazar, you come with me. Cato, stay here and keep watch. If anything happens, you know what to do; don't hesitate. Do you understand? We can't take any chances."

"You can count on me, sir."

The other two begin their descent, leaving Cato in the kitchen. That means if my plan works, which is unlikely, all he'll have to do is lock me in and call for backup. Is that what the guy in charge meant by *don't hesitate*?

One problem at a time, I think. Jord says, "Where's the light?"

I consider launching an attack while they're still finding their bearings, but I hesitate, and the moment passes.

"I have it," Salazar says, flicking the switch over and over. "It's not working."

"That's because there's no bulb," Jord says.

"Explains the candles."

"What on earth happened here?" Jord says, obviously referring to me, the blood, and the general carnage of the room.

The German, who is edging closer, says, "It's got to be her, right?"

"Maybe, maybe not," Jord replies, "but just in case, put a bullet in her head."

"Why?" Salazar asks. "Nobody could survive losing that much blood."

Jord takes a step forward. "Do I have to do everything around here?"

"Please sir," Salazar says, his tone both professional and pleading. "I have it."

I don't hesitate. I swing both legs up and around and to the left, sweeping Germany's feet from under him as I grab the sacrificial blade and rotate onto my back. Salazar is falling toward me now, his body turned in the direction of the ceiling, his flashlight spinning in the air.

When he slams into me, muscular and heavy, the knife, which I am holding in place above my chest, pierces his left shoulder blade, grinding through skin, bone, and heart.

Jord, who also has a flashlight, is firing shots but has so far only managed to hit his partner. I tuck my head and bring my arms around. I grab Salazar's right hand, the one that's still holding the weapon he was about to kill me with. The German is more dead than alive, and it's not difficult to take control. I press his index finger repeatedly. The bright flash of each bullet illuminates Jord's bearded face, which is being transformed into a mess of blood and mangled flesh.

Before the American has even hit the ground, I maneuver Salazar's hand, now completely lifeless, so that the gun is aimed high over my left shoulder. I get a glimpse of Cato—baby face, ginger hair, silver necklace—and pop off two more rounds. Both miss, and he slams the trapdoor shut. I pull the trigger again and again, aiming for the lock, but the magazine is empty.

I push Salazar to the side and stand. I pick up a flashlight. Jord is facedown on the floor, his weapon close by. I hope there are at least two bullets left: one to destroy that lock and the other to kill Cato. I'm reaching for Jord's gun when the trapdoor, which is behind me, opens. I have to assume Cato is armed. Driven by adrenaline, I dive right in the direction of the counter along the far wall. As I hit the floor and turn, a handmade Molotov cocktail slams into the center of the room, the resulting explosion consuming Jord and Salazar and also the gun I was half a second from retrieving.

Cato throws in another before locking the trapdoor. I manage to roll out of the way, and it smashes into the Christmas decorations, luggage, and camping equipment. A huge fireball engulfs the whole area, including the work surface above, but the flames are a secondary concern. If I inhale too much of that dark, acrid smoke, I'll be dead in under a minute.

The basement is now flooded with heat and light, and everything smells of burning flesh.

I'm able to find a small, dirty towel in the far corner of the room, which I wrap around my nose and mouth. It will buy me some time but not much. I grab an empty linen basket and make a beeline for the sink. By the time I have filled it, both fires have increased significantly in size and power. I throw the water onto the one consuming the far wall, as it poses the biggest threat, but the water barely makes a dent.

I open the washing machine; it's empty. I move on to the dryer, which, to my relief, is filled with white cotton sheets and towels. I grab a handful and run them under the sink. By now the whole room is thick with poisonous fumes, and my eyes, which are stinging, are becoming useless.

Armed with wet laundry, I hurry to the raging bonfire in the center of the room. Once there, I wrap two sheets and a towel around my right hand and arm and throw the rest onto the flames in the general area I last saw Jord's gun. I reach into the blaze now, feeling around, but then have to pull out because of the unbearable heat and sickening fumes.

I've started coughing and have thirty seconds or so before I pass out, which means if I don't get my hands on that gun, it's all over. I'm about to reach in again and suffer third-degree burns if that's what it takes when . . .

"Sam, are you in there? Sam!"

Coughing and spluttering and on the verge of passing out, I turn and look up. Through the dark, scorching smoke I see what appears to be a sphere of soft yellow light. Realizing the trapdoor is open, I make a dash for the metal stairs and start climbing. But there's a problem: my arms and legs have turned to jelly, and I'm losing clarity. When the inevitable happens, and I slip and fall, someone grabs me from above, yanking my beaten, bruised, and burned body into the kitchen.

"Are you okay?" my savior repeats over and over as my cough mutates into a delirious laugh. The irony of my situation, at this moment at least, is the funniest thing in the world. Fire saved me from the *Decimatio*—saved me from the man who tried to remove my heart—only to try and kill me hours later.

It's so funny, it hurts.

TWENTY-THREE

Fresh from my long and soothing ice-cold shower, I walk into the bedroom wrapped in a towel and grab my bag.

"Where you going?" Tammuz asks, sitting on the edge of the bed.

I gesture toward the bathroom. "To get changed."

"Do it here if you like. I'll close my eyes."

Is he making a move?

The timing isn't great, but the same was true after I put a bullet in Sergei's head. I remember how animalistic and aggressive I was, how I needed it to happen.

I put my bag down and smile. "How do I know you won't peek?"

"Would it matter? I mean it's nothing I haven't seen before."

"Sure about that?" I say, letting the towel drop, my body a patchwork of cuts, bruises, and burns. None are particularly serious, and everything should heal okay with the correct care, but for now, I look like I've been put through a wood chipper.

Tammuz stands and approaches, putting his hands on my naked shoulders. "We gotta get you to a hospital."

"I can't afford it," I say, reaching for the towel, covering myself.

"What do you mean?"

"There's no such thing as free healthcare here, and I don't have insurance."

"I'll put it on my credit card."

"Trust me; it's not as bad as it looks. There's a pharmacy on the corner; I'll be able to get everything I need from there. Actually, do you mind going for me?"

He steps back, eyes narrowing. "What, so you can vanish again? Until you tell me what the hell you're involved in and why people are trying to murder you, I'm not leaving your side."

"Even if it gets you killed?"

"Yes . . ." He hesitates. "Even if it gets me killed. That's how much I need to know. That's how much I care."

After pulling me out of the basement from hell just over an hour ago, Tammuz gave me water, washed my face, and wrapped me in the red throw that had previously been covering Kaya's sofa. With emergency vehicles wailing in the distance and the smoke and fire worsening, Tammuz led me out via the back door, but I wouldn't go anywhere until he agreed to take the ayahuasca vine with us.

"Is that what all this is about?" he'd asked. "A stupid plant?"

As soon as we got back to my hotel room, Tammuz fired more questions: "What happened back there? Who was that man and what did he want? Who are you really?"

Instead of answering, I hit back with a few of my own. "Where did you come from? What happened to the ginger-haired guy who tried to kill me? How did you know I was in the basement?"

As always, Tammuz broke first, explaining he was halfway to my hotel when he thought better of it and turned back, worrying I'd never show up. He was two hundred yards from Kaya's house and had just heard what sounded like gunshots when a man with ginger hair came running out and sped off in a car. Tammuz got into the kitchen through the back door and knew instantly there was a fire coming from below. Because the room was filling with smoke, he missed the trapdoor to begin with. Then he took a step forward and heard a creak under his foot . . .

After getting changed in the bathroom, I tell Tammuz I'm heading out to grab a bite and that he's welcome to join.

He starts freaking out, saying I owe him an explanation and that he wants it right now, adding, "And if you lie to me again, I'm done, for good this time. No more stopping you getting raped or pulling you out of fires. You'll be on your own, no matter what stupid dreams I have."

"What dreams?" I ask, thinking that's the second time he's mentioned that today. "Has the woman with indigo eyes returned?"

"No," he says. "And anyway, I'm not answering any more of your questions until you answer some of mine."

"Fair enough," I say. "Let me eat, and I'll explain everything."

"The truth this time?"

"Nothing but."

***

We find a cute little café and sit outside, facing each other. To my right and Tammuz's left is an undulating skate park full of cool kids wearing baggy jeans, colorful T-shirts, and baseball caps. Beyond them is a row of palm trees lining a wide, spacious beach, which in turn gives way to the deep and glistening Pacific Ocean.

Wafts of coffee and fried food are carried over the salty breeze. Our waitress pours water for us, and I order salmon and scrambled eggs. Tammuz opts for a cup of tea with yogurt and granola. Before our food arrives, I excuse myself and go to the bathroom. As I'm walking through the restaurant back to our table, I get a line of sight on Tammuz as he puts something into his mouth, washing it down with water. It reminds me of the morning we met when I was in his bedroom, having just shaved my head. Tammuz was clearing a space on his messy, cluttered desk when he stumbled upon a container of pills. It was obvious from the way he behaved that he didn't want me to see what they were. I consider asking him about it, but then I remember it's none of my business.

I sit, and our food quickly arrives. I'm ravenous and consume every last morsel in record time.

Tammuz says, "I've kept my side of the bargain. Now it's your turn."

I look at his pretty features and messy black hair. There's a tingle of happiness in my chest. "What do you want to know?"

"The truth."

"About what specifically?"

"Stop playing games."

"I'm not; I just don't know where to start."

"The beginning is as good a place as any."

"That would be a VERY long story."

"I'm not here for a story. I want the truth."

"What if the truth is inconceivable and impossible to believe?"

"Let me be the judge of that."

Ideally, when this conversation is over, Tammuz, who I want more than anything to be safe, will get as far away from me as possible. For that to happen, he needs to think I'm lying, but I'm not sure I've got it in me, not after he flew halfway across the world to save my life. I realize something: I might be able to kill two birds with one stone by being totally and utterly honest. He'll think I'm a crazy, pathological liar and run a mile, but at least I'll have a clear conscience and know I did right by him. For once. It makes me sad to imagine him running, but that's just selfish.

I sit upright and rest my palms on the table. There is a scattering of people eating brunch and drinking healthy-looking smoothies, but I don't care what they hear or think. I'm staring into my friend's eyes, trying to connect with him on a deeper, more meaningful level.

"My full name, my real name, is Samsara . . ."

Tammuz's face lights up. "That's it," he says, slamming his hand on the table. "That was what the lady with the eyes told me . . ."

I interject. "So you have seen her again?"

"No. I'm talking about the first time, the night before you tried to claw my eyes out. She called you Samsara. It's been bugging the hell out of me."

"She cannot be trusted," I say.

"Excuse me?"

"If she appears again, do not listen to what she says, and get away if you can."

"Are you suggesting she's a real person?"

"Her name is Meta. She is very dangerous."

"But it was just a dream," he says with doubt in his tone, remembering how moved and shaken he was at the time. "You know the difference, right, between dreams and reality?"

"The line is much more blurred than you imagine."

He sighs. "Sure it is."

"If she wasn't real, how was she able to give you information about me, information that was correct?"

He thinks for a moment. "You must have told me your full name, or I overheard you or something, maybe when you were sleeping . . ."

"Anything is possible," I say, remembering my goal is to tell the truth, not convince him of it.

"What's next, a story about how you were abducted by aliens? You promised the truth."

I say, "Just shut up and listen." I pause. I've never said this to a Sleeper. Then I say, "The truth is, I'm four thousand years old and counting.'"

He rolls his eyes and goes to speak, but I beat him to it, saying that if he interrupts again, this conversation is over.

"Fine," he says. "If nothing else, it will be entertaining."

"You're not even twenty," I say, "and look at the baggage you carry around: the hate you have for your father, losing Dina, selling drugs, falling out with Viktor, going to prison . , , And that's just what you've told me. Imagine four thousand years of that stuff. Imagine the number of enemies you'd have built up? Well, mine happen to be very dangerous and extremely resourceful.

"In my previous life cycle, before I was reborn as Rosa, they found us. By us, I mean my master and me. I escaped, but he was captured. I am fighting for the liberation of his soul. *That's* what all this is about."

Something, I'm not sure what, seems to have struck a chord with Tammuz, his expression much less derisory now. He says, "On the bus from Exeter, while you were still asleep, you called me master. Did you think I was him?"

I nod. "I was confused and disoriented."

Tammuz lets that sink in and takes a deep breath before saying, "I'm going to suspend disbelief for a while and see where this goes. Who are *they* and why are they chasing you?"

"Souls who remember past lives are known as Flooders. There are many of us, a worldwide community, in fact, with its own government and laws. Meta is essentially the prime minister or president of that government, and like all politicians, she is corrupt and motivated by her own vested interests."

"Which are?"

"To stagnate human consciousness and stop people realizing their true potential."

"Why, what does she gain?"

"Power. In a truly enlightened world, there would be no place for Meta and her followers because all knowledge would be shared and everybody would be equal."

"And that's what you and your master want?"

"It's what we fight for."

"How?"

"By initiating and enlightening as many souls as possible."

"What does that involve?"

"Helping people remember. It's that simple."

"Remember what?"

"Their past lives: who they really are, where they came from, the nature of reality, but most of all, their true purpose."

"And what's that?"

"To contribute positive energy to the universe, to love and be loved, to grow and improve and learn."

"Have I had past lives?"

"Yes."

"Could you help me remember them?"

I don't like where this is going, so I decide to downplay my expertise in this area. "No, only a shaman such as my master can safely guide new initiates. It is an extremely hazardous undertaking."

"Surely you've learned a thing or two in four thousand years?"

"Wisest is she who knows she knows nothing," I say. "And four thousand years is a mere blink of an eye."

"What do you need ayahuasca for?"

"It's a gateway to the spirit world. I am hoping to find answers there."

"What kind of answers?"

"About where my master is and how I can find him."

"What if he's already dead?"

"Death, as you perceive it, is an illusion."

"So we all live forever?"

I ignore his question. "You said before that if I lied again, you were done with me."

"And I meant it."

"So a four-thousand-year-old, reincarnating girl who uses

plants to access parallel dimensions is believable now?"

"Two days ago I would have laughed in your face."

"What's changed?"

"The night I dropped you at Heathrow . . . I had another dream."

I sit forward, heart doubling in speed. "Was it her?"

"No, it was somebody else."

"Who?"

"A man."

"What did he say?"

"That I had to find you and protect you."

"What did he look like?"

"Tall and powerful . . . like a warrior or . . . a pharaoh or something."

I can tell Tammuz is holding back. "There's more, isn't there?"

"Yes," he says, fidgeting.

"Okay. What are you waiting for?"

"It's ridiculous, but he told me he was your master. He said you carried something very powerful and that the future of the universe depended on keeping you safe."

"Did he tell you his name?"

"Yes."

"What was it?"

"Ashkai."

TWENTY-FOUR

"I read online it tastes like battery acid," Tammuz says, referring to the ayahuasca vine he's stooping over, the one he lugged all the way from Kaya's house at my insistence.

"You get used to it," I mutter, although I'm not really listening, sitting upright on the bed in my hotel room, pillows wedged between my back and the headboard. I'm studying the iPhone I took from Bacchus, the man who tried to kill me. Earlier this morning, when I was undressing to shower, I discovered it in the right pocket of my denim shorts. My first reaction was panic—after all, Tammuz tracked me down in London after hiding his phone in my bag—and I almost flushed it down the toilet. Fortunately, I came to my senses just in time, realizing it was switched off anyway.

Besides, the man who owned it is dead. How likely is it that Rebus is on a computer somewhere attempting to locate the whereabouts of his "soldier's" phone? Surely he'd assume it went up in flames along with Kaya's house. Even so, after everything that's happened, I don't want to take any chances, especially with Tammuz here. I'm going to turn it on soon and see if anybody calls or sends a text (the security lock prohibits anything else); I just need time to regain my strength and composure before inviting danger and chaos back into my life. I also need breathing space to work some things out, such as why Ashkai—or Ashkai's imposter—is communicating with Tammuz.

While contemplating my ever-growing list of problems and mysteries, I have been distantly aware of Tammuz trying to get my attention.

"Samsara!"

I look up and see him standing at the foot of the bed. "Sorry, I was miles away."

He says, "I thought you'd gone to the spirit world without me." Then he adds, "Isn't there another plant you need to make this stuff?" gesturing over his right shoulder toward the vine of souls, which is in the far left corner of the room.

"You've done your research," I say. "And yes, there is."

"Is it really a medicine?"

"Yes, and so much more."

"What kind of things can it cure?"

"It depends on a lot of factors, such as the set and setting and the shaman leading the ceremony."

"Let's assume the set and setting are golden and that you've got the best shaman in the world. What sort of things could be achieved then?"

"That's a difficult question to answer. Can you be more specific?"

Tammuz thinks for a moment, and it's pretty obvious he's of two minds about something. "It doesn't matter," he says. "That other plant you need, where can we get it?"

"The Amazon."

"Didn't Kaya have one, or did we lose it in the fire?"

"I don't think so. I looked everywhere."

"What about her meditation studio?"

"What about it?"

"When you come out of the lift, there's that indoor garden thing, you know? Maybe she keeps one there."

A bulb lights up in my mind as I cast myself back to yesterday afternoon: arriving at the building in Venice, taking the elevator to the basement. When the doors opened, the first thing I saw was a large arrangement of plants and shrubs directly underneath a skylight.

I spring to my feet, pocketing the iPhone. "There's only one way to find out. Wait here while I go check."

Tammuz does not look impressed. "Hey, it was my idea."

"Don't be so childish. I'm trying to protect you; it could be dangerous."

"All the more reason for me to come. In fact, it's a direct order from your master."

"What?" I ask, confused and exasperated.

"He said I had to protect *you*, remember?"

I realize Tammuz will follow me, whatever happens.

188

"Fine," I say, "but you do exactly what I tell you, understood? Your life could depend on it."

"If what you say is true, death is nothing to be afraid of."

It's a comment borne of ignorance, which is why I say, "You have no idea what you're talking about."

***

Before leaving the hotel, I purchased a straw hat and large black sunglasses, both of which I'm wearing now.

I say, "You go in first and distract whoever's on reception. I'll be right behind. If the plant is there, I'll need time to grab some of its leaves. Whatever happens, ten minutes from now, we meet at the Starbucks across the road."

"What if Kaya's here?"

Her name alone fills my stomach and chest with bitterness and bile. "I doubt we'll get that lucky."

"Who is she and how does she fit into all this?"

"That's a very good question."

We've been in this car park, standing behind a white van for ten minutes. It's a hot, sunny day, and I'm sweating a little. Tammuz is sipping on a refreshing-looking drink crammed with ice and slices of lime.

A group of people recently left the building and others have been trickling in. Tammuz Googled the studio's schedule and discovered that a meditation class—called *The Healing Power of Crystals*—started at 3 p.m. That was four minutes ago, meaning it should be pretty quiet down there.

I watch Tammuz, who's wearing a black T-shirt and faded gray jeans with white Nikes, cut across the car park and enter the premises. I count to thirty before following him inside. The air-conditioning is a welcome respite from the heat, especially as I'm not dressed appropriately, wearing jeans and long sleeves to conceal my cuts, burns, and bruises. I want to slip into the basement incognito, so instead of taking the elevator, I search for the stairs, eventually finding them at the far end of the corridor.

The hat and sunglasses are a precaution in case Joey happens to be working again. I doubt he'll take it kindly if he sees me vandalizing Kaya's garden.

I exit the stairwell onto the lower ground floor and pause to take in my surroundings. I can hear Tammuz's voice in the distance. He's apologizing for something. Straight ahead, roughly twenty paces, is the impressive collection of plants and shrubs. To the right of all that greenery and color (enhanced and beautified by the sun's rays pouring through the skylight) is the archway entrance to Lotus Meditations, with its new age books, wall quotes, and scented candles. From behind the long white desk (where guests are met and greeted), looking straight through the foliage, you have a direct line of sight on the elevator, the one that's just pinged. I figure somebody's running late for class.

I spin to face the wall and pretend to read a notice board. I shoot an inquisitive glance to my right just as a ginger-haired man wearing a blue bomber jacket appears.

Cato! I think, at the same time hearing a voice from behind whisper, "Enemy."

I look over one shoulder, but nobody is there. It's incredibly strange and disconcerting, but my priority at this moment is to capture and interrogate the coward who tried to kill me, the same one who just flashed a brief look in my direction before disappearing from view. There was definitely fear and worry in his pale blue eyes, but from what I could tell, he didn't recognize me.

The intelligent thing would be to stop and assess how best to handle this situation—after all, what if Meta is nearby?—but it's hard to keep a level head when you bump into a man who tried to lock you in a basement and turn you into a bonfire. And anyway, isn't the element of surprise a plan in itself?

I follow Cato into Lotus Meditations, coming to a halt just after entering. On my right are two toilets, one unisex, the other disabled. Directly ahead is the long white desk that has a display of crystals on it. The door to the studio is to the left of me. Three floating bookshelves lined with new age literature and scented candles are in between the desk and door. Standing in front of those with his back to me is Cato.

He's talking to Tammuz, but Tammuz isn't really listening. That's because he's preoccupied with a huge puddle on the floor that's peppered with bits of ice and lime. While pretending to be concerned about the mess he "accidentally" made—one that Cato has trodden though—my friend's body is angled in the direction of the toilets. He hasn't noticed me yet; neither of them has. I hear a noise and turn so that I'm facing the same way as Tammuz. As I do, Joey appears from the unisex lavatory carrying a stack of paper towels.

"Class has already begun," he says, looking at me quizzically. It's as if he recognizes me but can't quite connect the dots. "Next one's at four if you'd like to sign up?"

"Thanks," I say, slipping seamlessly into the accent I had in my previous life when Los Angeles was home, also turning away so that he can't see my face. I edge toward the long white desk now, looking at the display of crystals, some blue, some yellow, some jagged, some smooth, the price tags informing me the small ones are twelve dollars, the large, eighteen. The *Cosmopolitan* magazines are still there, so I begin flicking through one of them.

"Take your time," Joey says, looking over a shoulder. "You need anything, I'll be here cleaning up this guy's mess." He laughs then, telling Tammuz he's only joking. Tammuz goes along with it, even though I can tell he's confused and uncomfortable, looking at me, then Cato, then me, then Cato again, putting two and two together.

Turning his attention to Joey, projecting a nervous, edgy vibe, Cato asks, "Where's Kaya?"

"She's gone away for a few days," Joey responds while bending to place paper towels on the floor. "Can I help?"

"Where? I need to speak with her urgently." Cato's tone is rude and abrasive, and Joey visibly bristles.

"Allow me," Tammuz says, taking the paper towels. Joey says, "Like I said, she's gone away for a few days. What's this about?"

"There's been a fire at her home."

Joey gasps. "Are you serious?"

"You must have a phone number for her. Give it to me."

"Was anybody hurt?"

"You, unless you give me her fucking number."

"There's no need to be so aggressive," says Joey.

"I'm sorry," Cato says, reaching into his jacket, pulling out a gun. "How about we start again?"

Tammuz tries to interject, but Cato tells him to shut up, which he promptly does.

"Hey, Mister," I say, bringing my arm back.

Cato is looking right at me when a smooth, eighteen-dollar crystal smashes into the center of his forehead. His neck snaps back and his legs buckle as he drops the gun and falls sideways into what's left of Tammuz's drink.

"Oh my god," Joey says. "Oh my god."

I grab the gun and revert to Rosa's English accent, asking Tammuz, "You okay?"

Joey, drained of color, is struggling to process what just happened.

"Oh my god," he says again, shuffling toward the telephone at the far end of the white desk.

My gaze follows him. "What are you doing?"

He looks at me, startled. "Calling the cops."

"Don't do that."

He picks up the phone. "Are you crazy? He pointed a gun at my head!"

I remove my hat and sunglasses and place them on the bench underneath the bookshelves. "Now I'm pointing a gun at your head."

Joey's mouth hangs open, recognition in his eyes.

"The last thing I want is to hurt you," I say, "but try something stupid, and that's exactly what I'll do, understand?"

He nods.

"Now put the phone down and come here."

He advances slowly and carefully, as if in the presence of a rabid dog.

"Sit there," I say, gesturing toward the bench.

After doing so, he says, "There's cash in the register; just take it and go."

I crane my head to look at the clock on the wall: 3:12 p.m.

"When do they finish?" I ask, nodding toward the studio on my left.

"Three fifty, but there's another class straight after."

"People get here early?"

"Sometimes, yes."

Cato starts moving. He's disoriented and groggy.

I look around and notice a door at the far end of the long white desk. It's on the side that Joey stands on when greeting customers. "Where does that lead?"

Joey follows my gaze. "To an office."

"Anyone in there?"

"No."

"Where's Kaya?"

"She e-mailed yesterday saying she had to leave town for a family emergency. What the hell's going on? Is she in trouble?"

I say, "Both of you help him up and take him to the office."

Although it's a struggle, Joey and Tammuz eventually get Cato on his feet.

"Sit him down," I say when we're inside the tiny, windowless office that consists of a chair, a desk, and a printer/fax machine. "Face him my way."

When Cato—who has his wits about him again—is in place, I ask Tammuz, without using names, to pat our hostage down, telling him to do it slowly and methodically and to also look out for tattoos.

"Why?"

"Just do it."

"That's everything," Tammuz says two minutes later, pointing at Cato's belongings on the floor: tan leather wallet, Audi car keys, Samsung Galaxy, six-inch hunting knife. We found the tattoo as well. It was on the underside of his left wrist: a small phoenix with flaming wings. That makes him a junior agent.

"What about his necklace?" I ask, wanting to be sure there isn't something attached he could improvise as a weapon.

Tammuz pulls the silver chain from underneath his T-shirt. There's a small piece of what looks like jade attached to it, a stone synonymous with the spirit world.

193

"Want me to take it off?" Tammuz asks.

"No, leave it," I say, kicking everything, including the knife, behind me and against the wall. I offer the gun to Tammuz and say, "Take Joey out there and keep an eye on him."

Tammuz replies, "There's no way I'm touching that. Seriously, you can forget it."

I know how stubborn he can be, so instead of pressing the issue, I turn my attention to Joey. "Give me your wallet."

He looks confused and afraid. "What for?"

I point the gun at his face, and less than three seconds later, I have what I asked for. I pull his driver's license out, reading, "Joseph Donovan, Three-Eight-Six Burnside Avenue." I slip it into a pocket, handing everything else back. "I know who you are," I say, staring at him intently. "I know where you live. I recommend you do as you're told."

"Please don't hurt me," Joey says, "I have a son."

That throws me. "Aren't you gay?"

"My son is adopted. We're all he has."

"Be smart then," I say before telling Tammuz, "Close the door behind you and make sure he doesn't run."

"Are you going to hurt him?" Tammuz asks.

"Yes," a voice whispers. "Hurt him, kill him; make him pay."

I look left and right and behind, but nobody is there.

"Jesus, not now," Tammuz mutters.

I fix my eyes on him.

"I wasn't talking to you," he says.

"Who were you talking to, then?"

"Nobody. It doesn't matter."

"Did you hear a voice?"

The expression on his face is one of incredulity. "Yeah, yours."

I want to press him further, but now isn't the time.

"Go," I say. "Now."

He ushers Joey out of the room, and I lock the door. After shoving the gun into the back of my jeans, I stoop and grab Cato's knife, feeling the sharpness of its edges as I approach my prisoner, and I say, "You're wondering how I survived that fire, aren't you?"

"The how is immaterial," he says. The man is afraid but not yet

194

overwhelmed.

Cato's tattoo offers a strong indication he is less capable than me both physically and mentally, but that's not to say he isn't dangerous.

"Who are you and why are you trying to kill me?"

He smiles, but there is no joy in it. "It's true, then."

"What is?"

"That you don't know what you are."

"Enlighten me."

"I can't do that."

"Why?"

"Because an enemy who is ignorant is easier to defeat."

"Are you sure about that? Your friends are dead, and you are at my mercy."

"That's because you have a powerful ally. He talks to you even now, doesn't he?"

Did he hear the voice? I wonder, at the same time saying, "Ashkai?"

Cato spits on the ground. "He is nothing but a traitor and a liar."

I lean forward and press the tip of the blade against his throat. "Do you know where Ashkai is?"

He shakes his head.

I move the blade down a few inches. "One way or another, you're going to tell me what you know."

"Do it," the voice in my head demands. "Make him suffer."

"My brothers are waiting for me on the other side," Cato says, straightening his back. "It would be an honor to be reborn alongside them."

If I hesitate or waver, even for a second, he'll think I'm weak. That's why I tell him to take his jacket off. When he does, I shove as much of it as I can into his mouth. While convincing myself this is nothing to do with the voice and everything to do with finding my master, I hammer the blade into Cato's right thigh just above the knee, going all the way to the hilt, holding my free hand over his face to muffle the noise.

"Kill him," the voice says, and murderous intentions wash over me. I realize with disgust that I am enjoying this man's suffering.

When the worst of the screaming is over, I remove the jacket and say, "That's as good as this is going to get unless you tell me where Ashkai is."

Eyes bulging, brow dripping with sweat, Cato says, "He's here! He's here!"

I turn the knife. "Where?"

He screams again. This time, there's nothing to absorb the noise. "America."

"Be more specific."

"New York."

I try to get more details, twisting the blade again, but he swears that's all he knows. My instinct is he's lying. I decide to start with the fingers on his left hand, willing to do whatever it takes, when somebody tries, unsuccessfully, to open the door.

"He ran," Tammuz shouts, banging against it. "People are here; we have to go."

"Kill him," the voice says, and I slap the side of my face three times.

"It's already too late," Cato whispers, but his diction is unclear. One look at him, and it's obvious why: the small green stone attached to his necklace has found its way into his mouth.

"He's inside you even now," Cato adds before biting down on the cleverly disguised amulet, releasing the deadly poison inside.

Within seconds, Cato's body starts to shake violently, his mouth foaming, eyes bulging.

Aware there is nothing I can do to save him, I gather his belongings and unlock the door. When I step out, there is a large group of startled and afraid people staring at me, some of them on the phone. They must have evacuated the studio on account of Cato's screaming.

I scan their faces, searching for Tammuz, but he's nowhere to be seen. I get out from behind the white desk, break into a jog, and head for the stairs at the far end of the corridor. To get there, I have to pass the indoor garden. As I do, the sun's rays refract through the skylight in such a way as to be miraculously concentrated on one plant in particular, making it shine, glow, and pulsate with life.

Chacruna!

I reach over and grab as many leaves as I can before exiting the building. I place them on the passenger seat of Cato's Audi. I'm trying not to draw attention to myself as I edge out of the car park and merge with the steady flow of traffic. I listen for the sadistic, cruel voice, but all I can hear is the engine purring.

And that's just fine by me.

TWENTY-FIVE

There's a voice in my head again, but this time, it belongs to Cato.

"You don't know who you are."

What did he mean by that and all of the other strange, cryptic things he said? Telling me I had a powerful ally who "talks to you even now," that it's too late because "he's already inside you."

Could Cato hear what I was hearing, or did he know something I'm not privy to? Or was he just a crazy, brainwashed, low-level agent caught in the intricate web of propaganda and lies spun by the black widow herself, Meta? To a certain extent, probably yes, but that doesn't mean there wasn't truth in what he was saying, especially when I consider everything that has happened these past few days, much of it perplexing and unexplainable.

Then there's Tammuz. What was that "Jesus, not now" all about? Could it have been a response to the voice? And if so, was it the first time he'd heard it? Tammuz's tone suggested a certain familiarity, as if he'd reached the end of his tether with someone he knew well.

It's possible that someone was me. Since entering his life, it's been problem after disaster after nightmare. But I don't believe that's the case. His comment was targeted at somebody or *something* else. The question is, who or what?

I've parked Cato's Audi in an alleyway close to my hotel but am still in the driver's seat with the engine running, air-conditioning on full blast. Part of my mind is racing, trying to work out what the hell is going on, while the other is being lulled and hypnotized by the sound generated by the air vents, imagining how cold it would need to get before the blood in my veins thickens and eventually freezes. Would that be enough to cool the dark, whispering flames that appeared in my hands during a recent dream? Remembering how one minute I was trying to put Tammuz's heart back into his chest and the next . . . I was on the summit of the GE Building in New York, my master wanting to know where I got the fire from and saying it was a part of me now and that the only way to extinguish it was to "fill your heart with love."

But the entire mystery has a much earlier genesis. After all, there's the imposter who has been invading my dreams, a male energy who masquerades as Ashkai, the same one who warned me when I was moments from being murdered. In fact, if it hadn't been for his gift of heat and fire, I wouldn't have awoken. My story would have ended.

Was it the fire bullying me to hurt Cato? Was it the imposter? Are they one and the same?

Then there's the biggest question of all, one I have avoided through a process of denial and delusion. Why did Ashkai take such a keen interest in me in the first place, a lowly sex slave who was nothing more than a commodity to be used and abused by powerful and cruel men? Why pluck her from obscurity and embark on a rich and textured relationship spanning the ages? And why did he say, as we strolled though his royal gardens after my initial Awakening, that he hoped I was still happy about the decision in four thousand years?

Well, that time is now, and unfortunately, happiness is not the emotion that best describes my state of being. Even so, I need to stay focused on the only thing that matters: finding my master. Ashkai has been keeping me in the dark about something important. That much has become obvious, but I have to believe he had my best interests at heart. The alternative, and also worst-case scenario, is that I have been used and manipulated for thousands of years, a pawn in a game I didn't even know I was playing.

Considering that possibility, however far-fetched, brings on feelings of sadness and vulnerability, which are better than the all-consuming bitterness and anger that follow as I punch the steering wheel over and over and scream at the top of my lungs.

Soon after come tears, along with the realization that I'm acting like a child.

I sigh and start massaging my forehead but stop immediately because my fingers and palms feel like the surface of the sun. I hold my hands out to inspect them, but other than looking a bit red and blotchy, which is to be expected after repeatedly thumping the steering wheel, there's nothing out of the ordinary, unless the flames are still there but unseen, flickering and hungering for the one thing that makes them stronger: negative, destructive emotions.

I place my hands over the air vents to cool them, and I close my eyes, only opening them again after a sustained period of slow and mindful breathing.

It has done the trick. I feel better. But what do I do now? Where do I go?

Cato told me, albeit under extreme duress, that Ashkai was in New York. As somebody who worked for Rebus and ultimately Meta, Cato would have been aware of the events that unfolded on the roof of the GE Building back in 1998. Is that why the Big Apple popped into his head? Or was there some truth in what he was saying?

In the absence of other leads, I make a decision to set off for New York as soon as possible. I just need to make a detour along the way. I'm thinking about that as I look at the bundle of chacruna leaves on the passenger seat. Instead of butterflies, it's as if I have a swarm of bats trying to escape the confines of my stomach.

I now have the tools needed to leave my body and cross over to the spirit realm. To find answers to my questions, I may need to venture deeper into that world than ever before.

Am I ready? I think. *Am I strong enough?*

There's only one way to find out.

***

I turn down the corridor toward my hotel room and see Tammuz slumped on the floor with his head in his hands. He hears me coming and gets up. The look on his face is an unnerving mix of emotions; fear, relief, and anger are the most prominent.

I nod and open the door. As soon as it's closed, he says, "I've got one question for you, then I'm out of here."

The air is sticky and warm, so I turn on the overhead fan. Then

I throw Cato's sports bag onto the bed. It was in the trunk of his car. After emptying his clothes out, I refilled the bag with my DMT-enriched leaves. After all, it would have raised eyebrows if I'd walked around with them on display. The last thing I want is for people to notice me. A loaded gun and a Samsung Galaxy are also in the bag. The latter, like the iPhone I have, has a security lock. Cato's wallet, I discarded, but not before taking three things from it: $240 in cash, a New York State driver's license, and a sleek black card with HOUSE OF PHOENIX spelled out in raised gold letters. Beneath that, but smaller and in lowercase, are the words "east village." The image of a bird with wings of fire is on the reverse.

It has the look and feel of a private members' card for a club or association of some sort, one, it seems, that's frequented by junior agents. I need to do some research online. Maybe Tammuz will let me use his phone? If not, I'll jump on one of the hotel's computers in the lobby.

I sit on the edge of the bed and say, "I'm listening" as a refreshing breeze blows down from above.

Tammuz takes a few steps and looks down at me from the center of the room. "Is he dead?"

"Does it matter?"

"Of course it matters."

"Why?"

"Because there's no way you can say it was self-defense. If you killed him, it's murder. Now is he dead or not?"

"Yes. But I didn't kill him."

"Then who did?" But before I can answer, he says, "I heard the screaming. Everyone did. What were you doing to him?"

"Extracting information."

"You sound like a psycho."

The comment irritates me, though there's shame in there, too, and I feel my whole body tighten. "Psychos lock people in basements and set them on fire."

"So it was revenge, is that it?"

"I thought you just had one question?"

"You haven't answered it yet."

"He killed himself. Does that make you feel better?"

"What? How?"

"Remember that green stone on his necklace?"

"Yes."

"Turns out it was full of poison."

After giving me an incredulous look, as if he's never met anybody more full of shit, he says, "You read that in a spy novel?"

I get to my feet. "You know what? I'm sick of you interrogating me and judging me."

"Well, I'm sick of people dying."

I walk over to the door and open it. "This thing between us, whatever it is, is over. I don't want your help, and I sure as hell don't want you following me around like a lost puppy."

Tammuz rolls his eyes, but it's obvious his pride has been hurt.

"Haven't you got the message yet?" I say, wanting to do more damage. "Just fuck off back to England and leave me alone."

"No."

"Get out."

He shakes his head.

"I suggest you leave before I make you."

Tammuz stands. "You're pathetic. You know that?"

I get a rush of blood and start marching toward him. My plan is to shove him into the corridor, but then I see fear in his eyes, and it shames me.

What's happening? I feel as if I'm waking from a terrible nightmare. *I'm turning into a monster.*

I come to a halt and drop my head. "I'm sorry. I would never hurt you."

The pressure in the room dissipates. Tammuz steps forward and puts his arms around me. The gesture of kindness strips away the last of my defenses, and I start to cry.

Tammuz doesn't say anything. He just holds me, and for a brief, blissful moment, it's as if we are one.

TWENTY-SIX

After pouring a very large dose of the thick black liquid into a paper cup, I say, "If in exactly three hours I'm not back and you can't wake me, what's going to happen?"

Tammuz glances at his bottle of water. "You get a cold shower and a slap on the face."

"Until then, what do you do?"

"Keep an eye on your vital signs, watch Mars get pummeled, and stop us getting eaten by coyotes, the usual stuff."

"And what don't you do?"

"Drink any of that, although I still can't see why not." He's pointing at the repurposed Coca-Cola bottle I've just poured from.

"Do we have to go over this again?" I say, placing the bottle inside my backpack for safekeeping. "I need you clear-headed in case anything goes wrong. Also if . . ."

"Okay, okay, I get it."

"Thank you," I reply, even though he's just telling me what I want to hear. That's fine as long as he sticks to the plan.

It's 8:30 p.m. on Friday, October 11. We left my hotel three hours ago and took an Uber to Runyon Canyon's northern entrance on Mulholland Drive, up in the Hollywood Hills. The huge, undulating park covers the eastern section of the Santa Monica mountains, and the panoramic views of Los Angeles are glimmering and spectacular, especially on a clear, balmy night like this.

Yesterday, after the unfortunate incident with Cato and the argument that ensued, Tammuz and I lay on the bed for what I thought would be a short nap. Instead, we slept, dreamlessly in my case, for twelve hours. Rather than waking energized and refreshed, I felt weak, heavy, and incredibly guilty for wasting so much time.

I spent the early morning focused on just two things: beating myself up and gathering the paraphernalia needed for brewing ayahuasca: a portable gas stove, a wooden mallet, a sharp knife, distilled water, and a large steel pot.

I also turned on the cell phone taken from Bacchus, the man who tried to kill me in Kaya's basement. Almost immediately, an icon appeared, indicating a voicemail had been left overnight. In order to access it, I needed the security code. I tried 1, 2, 3, 4, and other obvious combinations but didn't have any luck. Cato's Samsung ran out of juice while we were sleeping, and when I sent Tammuz out to buy a charger, he came back with the wrong one. He was going to rectify his mistake, but I told him not to worry about it for now.

Preparing the medicine, which involved cutting, pounding, and boiling the two Amazonian plants, took all day. The plan was to drink in my room with Tammuz holding the space, but it turns out that Fridays are pretty raucous at the Ocean Park Getaway. Most of the clientele are in their early twenties, so I guess it's to be expected. I ran through various alternatives before settling on what felt like the best two: check into another hotel or find somewhere outside that was quiet and safe. Being immersed in nature helps set the right tone for spiritual journeys. All I needed was a suitable location.

That's when I remembered Runyon Canyon. Suzy Aarons, the person I was before Rosa, used to walk her Pomeranian up here regularly. A quick Internet search revealed the park was still open for public use and that it closed every day at sunset. We arrived a little before that and hid in the bushes until the dog walkers, runners, and wardens had cleared out. We had around two hundred acres to play with, so staying out of sight wasn't too difficult.

The moon and stars coupled with the twinkling lights of the city have enabled us to see pretty well. We had to use our headlamps when climbing to reach this secluded, high ridge, but other than that, they have remained switched off. I chose this spot within the canyon because of how hard it is to reach and because it affords 360-degree views, meaning nobody will be able to sneak up on us. To the west we can just about make out the lights of the Pacific coastline, south are the skyscrapers of downtown, north is a sheer drop into a valley, and east is Griffith Park with its famous observatory, which will be buzzing with activity this evening.

That's because just after midnight, around which time I should be returning to normal consciousness, twenty fragments of a disintegrated comet are going to collide—astronomers predict spectacularly—with Mars.

I put the cup to my lips and pause, getting a whiff of that familiar stench of decaying earth, along with hints of ammonia and sick.

Speaking excitedly, Tammuz asks, "So, does it really taste like battery acid?"

Reclining on my blanket, bag doubling up as a pillow, I say while wincing, "Imagine a snake covered in razor blades slithering down your throat."

"That good, huh? How long before it kicks in?"

"*Shhhh,*" I say, looking up at the endless expanse of darkness peppered with stars and planets and a glowing moon. "I need to focus."

"Okay, sorry."

Setting an intention is important, so I close my eyes and visualize Ashkai, not as the great Egyptian prince of old, but as the African American who ended my life in order to save it. I think about all of the great things he has done and how much I love him, but it's difficult to stay on track. That's because the memory of what happened in New York—and everything since—has unsettled me, releasing a torrent of questions I don't have answers to, questions that are making me angry, suspicious, and afraid.

Who is my master really, and what has he been hiding? Who is the imposter, and where does the voice come from? What about those dark, whispering flames and, of course, Meta? What does she want, and how close is she to finding me?

"You all right, Sam?" a voice asks. I open my eyes. Leaning over me, his hand resting gently on my thumping chest, is Tammuz, only he looks different. His stomach is aglow with a pulsating internal light that's making his entire body shine and bloom at two-second intervals. The effect is mesmerizing until I notice something dark and sinister hovering above his left shoulder. It's an intelligent entity; that much is obvious. It has long, veinlike tentacles that have attached themselves to various parts of Tammuz's body. I've seen things like this before, spiritual vampires who siphon energy from their hosts. That's why Tammuz's light is pulsating when it should be continuous. His life force, his soul, is being sucked dry.

While the situation is bad, it's not unusual. Negative entities attach themselves to human beings all the time. Even so, this is bigger and more powerful than any such parasite I have encountered in the past. Left unchecked, it will cause Tammuz serious psychic and emotional damage. It's something we're going to have to deal with, just not right now.

"I think you were having a nightmare," Tammuz says. "Everything okay?"

"Yes, don't worry," I whisper. "Let me be."

There's a buzzing sound coming from inside my head. I close my eyes. I know from experience it's only going to get louder and more overwhelming. In fact, it won't stop until the medicine has finished retuning the chemical infrastructure of my brain, the means by which human consciousness can perceive and interact with planes of existence otherwise inaccessible.

Tammuz says something else, but it's hard to hear him over the noise. And anyway, he's a million miles away now.

Everything is vibrating and shaking. It's as if an avalanche is approaching.

I hear a woman's voice inside my head.

"Are you ready?" the stranger asks, her tone flat and emotionless. "Here it comes."

Almost instantly, a deluge of fragmented colors and shapes smash into me, carrying me forward. The impact is so violent and powerful that it manages to break me into pieces, each one flying off in a different direction.

The sensation of forward momentum is quickly replaced by a swirling feeling, as if I am inside a huge washing machine. All around are millions upon millions of different colors, shapes, and geometric patterns. There are also pyramids, hieroglyphs, and large stone heads with reptilian eyes. While moving, I glimpse a piece of myself in the maelstrom and try to lock onto it, but it quickly gets lost in the chaos.

Who is the me seeing me? I ask. *Who is the I asking?*

That's when my grip on things start to loosen, and panic sets in. My journey has barely even begun, and I already feel like I have gone totally crazy.

"You drank too much," Samsara says.

"What's happening to me?" Rosa screams.

"Make this stop!" Suzy demands.

I hear Elsie next, then Inga, followed by every other person I've been, all of them berating me—whoever "me" is—for being so naive and stupid.

"What have you done to us?" they shout in unison. "Make it stop."

The woman speaks again. "Fear or love?" she says, cutting through the noise and confusion. "It's your choice."

The spinning stops, and I become aware of two portals. The one farthest away is shining with light and tranquility. The other is its opposite: a dark whirlpool of nothingness. It's sucking all of the colors, shapes, pyramids, and hieroglyphs into its vortex. Somehow, I am immune to its pull.

Even though I can't fully conceive of what it is, I know I must choose love, and that love is represented by light. I start moving toward it, but as I do, a piece of my being, a fragment I was separated from when the avalanche hit, whizzes past and disappears into the nothingness.

My instinct is to follow after it—*what if I need that; what if it's important?*—but Ashkai always told me that love is the preeminent force of the universe, that it's the only truth there is. Because of that, I continue toward the light.

I hear another voice then. It's the rasping entity who spoke to me before Cato killed himself.

He says, "Before you save your master, you must save yourself."

"But I have to choose love," I say.

"Self-abandonment is hate, not love."

I'm just inches from the white portal now. It's so beautiful and inviting, but maybe he's right; maybe saving myself is what this journey is all about. And isn't facing fear different from choosing fear?

"Of course it is," says the voice, and I turn, allowing the darkness to take me.

***

I am running down a long, narrow, dimly lit corridor. I am afraid, but I don't know why. *Am I being chased?*

I look over a shoulder, but nobody is in pursuit. There are numbered doors on either side of me. I reach a T-junction at the end of the hallway and stop. I look left down one seemingly endless corridor and right down another. The floors and ceilings are cold, gray concrete, and the walls are bare and white. I can see perfectly, but there are no lights or windows, which means I should be shrouded in darkness.

Directly in front is a frosted glass door. The number 5183027 is engraved into it. The handle is round and metal. I look left, right, and behind. From what I can tell, all of the doors, bar the numbers, are identical. As I take it all in, a feeling of déjà vu washes over me. The sensation is subtle at first but quickly grows stronger. It's clear I have been here before. I just don't know when or under what circumstances.

I check myself over, feeling my face and head for clues. It seems I am in the body of Suzy Aarons, the person I was the last time I saw Ashkai, just before he threw me from that building in New York. I'm even wearing the clothes she died in: black shorts, white sneakers, gray sports vest.

I become aware of an unpleasant but familiar taste in my mouth, and things start coming back to me, things like Rosa, Tammuz, and drinking ayahuasca.

I look at the numbered doors more closely. They trigger something in my mind.

I remember being here!

While that is good news, it also represents a problem. Having drunk the medicine, I should have risen and crossed over to the spirit realm. But instead, I somehow descended into the corridors of my own subconsciousness. My first and only other visit here took place thousands of years ago when my training was at its most grueling and intense.

Back then, after wandering the labyrinthine halls for what seemed like an eternity, I built up the courage to open one of the many doors. It wasn't a random choice, however; I was drawn toward it like a bee to a flower. The number displayed was 4320, digits I have seen during visions and dreams these past few days. Before I could open the door, Ashkai appeared and raised a hand.

"It's better not to disturb anything down here," he said, projecting his own consciousness into the deepest and most private recesses of my mind.

"Why?"

"Behind each door is a moment from your past, everything you've ever done, thought, or felt, and it's crucial they remain separate from each other."

"For what reason?"

"It has to do with your Flooding and making sure the information you receive is truthful and real. At this level, if memories are disturbed, they can become distorted and misleading, negatively impacting the lives you have yet to live."

I didn't fully understand what he meant, but it didn't really matter. My master said it was a bad idea, so it was a bad idea. But that was a long time ago, and things have changed. The problem is, I don't know where door 4320 is located, nor do I feel drawn in any particular direction. Keen to explore nonetheless, I reach for the handle in front of me. At that moment, I hear the woman in my head again, her tone ethereal and soothing.

There you are.

I turn to the hallway on my left and see a shining orb, about the size of a tennis ball, hovering roughly twenty feet away.

Wrong door, the light says as I move toward the strange but clearly benevolent entity.

The floating apparition remains still, and I'm able to get very close. The light, which has a liquid quality, is brilliant and should be hurting my eyes, but it isn't. The being is emitting a low humming sound, and I can sense it's as interested in me as I am in it.

I am you, says the sphere, communicating telepathically. *And you are me.*

Of course, I think, remembering the part of myself I followed into the unknown. *That's why I came here.*

I reach out a hand.

Patience, the orb says, retreating. *I must take you somewhere.*

Speaking aloud, I say, "To door 4320?"

Yes.

"What's there?"

Pain and suffering.

"Will it be worth it?"

That depends.

"On what?"

The choices you make.

"Take me," I say, and with the words uttered, the light being shoots down the corridor like a bullet, moving away from me into the far distance.

"Wait," I shout, breaking into a run. "Slow down."

When the light being comes into view again, it has stopped at another intersection.

Follow, it says, darting right, and the game of cat and mouse goes on and on, down hallway after hallway, past door after door and crossing after crossing.

I notice that the ground is sloping downward and that the air is getting brisk. Not only that, the look and feel of everything is changing. Although I can't pinpoint when it happened, the doors are now made of wood instead of glass and some even have padlocks on them. The floor, once bare concrete, is covered with animal skins that have become rigid in the cold. The walls, previously clean and white, are dark and alive with images of stars, planets, and constellations.

It's becoming apparent that door 4320 is hidden deep within my subconscious, meaning it will be harder to navigate out. And there's something else to consider, something disconcerting: I haven't seen my guide for what feels like a very long time.

What if I have been tricked? What if I'm stuck here forever?

It's a frightening prospect, but I don't have to dwell on it for long. The orb has come into view again, hovering in the distance.

Only this time, it's not waiting for me at an intersection. This time, it's outside a door.

We have arrived.

I come to stop and lean forward on my knees. It's very cold, and my breath, labored and heavy, is steaming the air. I turn my head and look at the door. It has been boarded up with panels of dark wood, each one covered with a thin crusting of ice.

"This is different," I say. "Who did this?"

You.

"When?"

You already know the truth, my guide says. *All you have to do is remember.*

Before I can reply, she passes through the barricade and disappears.

"Wait," I say, thumping the cold, hard wood. "How am I supposed to get in?"

My question goes unanswered.

I try pulling the panels off, using my right leg as leverage, but they are heavy and securely nailed. I attempt three shoulder barges followed by numerous kicks, but it soon becomes clear all I'm doing is wearing myself out.

If only I had an ax, I think, flinching because of a thudding, clanking sound behind me. I turn, and there on the floor, beside my feet, is exactly what I thought of. I grab the ax and palm it from one hand to the other. In doing so, I notice an explosion of goose bumps on my arms. It's freezing down here, and I'm not dressed for the occasion. By way of a solution, I imagine Suzy Aarons in jeans and a long black coat with sturdy boots, smiling because that's exactly what she's wearing now.

Halfway through hacking the barricade to pieces—the door beyond (including the number 4320) in clear view—it dawns on me that I could have just imagined it away. After all, this is my mind, and everything I am seeing is a projection of sorts, a way of making sense of the mystery that is my own subconsciousness. In essence, I am the architect of everything I am seeing and experiencing. That means I have a great deal of power here, but only if I am able to remember where I am and what's going on, two things that are easily forgotten under such challenging and emotionally turbulent circumstances.

It's more satisfying to use the ax. I swing it again and again, not stopping until the obstruction has been reduced to a pile of chips. The oak door it was protecting has an ornate, golden handle. After putting the ax down, I turn the handle and push, revealing complete and impenetrable darkness. I close my eyes and visualize light, but when I open them again, nothing has changed.

I take a step forward, then another. On the third, I slip and plummet about thirty feet. I hit the hard ground with a thud. At first, I think I must have broken my legs, but other than some cuts and bruises, I seem to be okay. And there's light down here! I clamber to my feet and look around, discovering I am in a huge, natural cave with cathedral-like proportions.

I angle my head toward the hole I came through and the door beyond, but I can't locate any sort of gap in the stone above.

I scan the cave, unsure of what my next move should be. The orb spirit is nowhere to be seen, but up ahead, next to the opening of a narrow tunnel that bends off to the left, are two burning torches that have been stuck into divots in the ground. The walls and protuberances have been painted with images of bison, aurochs, deer, and other more unusual depictions of humans transforming into animals.

The air is damp and cold, and there's trickling water nearby. I walk toward the two flames to see what's down that tunnel. I'm still approaching the entrance when a woman starts screaming. She sounds far away at first, but her guttural shrieks—*is she being tortured?*—quickly get louder and more immediate. The person is obviously in excruciating pain, and I can't help but feel panicked and overwhelmed, especially as her suffering is bouncing off the walls, crashing into me from every direction.

I've barely had a moment to process what's happening when two lean, powerful men appear from behind my left shoulder, moving with speed and purpose. They have the demeanor of seasoned warriors and are carrying torches of their own. Wearing only loincloths—*are those knives strapped to their waists?*—the men vanish into the tunnel.

"Where are we?" I shout, following after them. "Where are you going?" They don't react in any way.

Can they see me? I wonder. *Is this even real?*

The tunnel, also alive with art, is fairly wide but only a fraction taller than me. The people I'm following, whose torches are casting menacing, shape-shifting shadows, have to stoop as they run.

"Wait!" I shout, noticing that the man on the right has lighter skin than his slightly shorter companion. In fact, it's as if he has been covered with chalk.

I stumble on a raised ledge and fall to the ground, but I'm back on my feet in no time. The distance has grown, but I can still see the men up ahead. At one point, their flames vanish around a corner, and everything goes black. Seconds later, when I regain line of sight, I force myself to find an extra gear, slowly closing the gap now.

We must be nearing the girl because her screaming is getting louder.

The tunnel begins to widen and open before finally spilling the two warriors, closely followed by me, into a horseshoe-shaped space with no other exits. In addition to the flames being carried by the men who led me here, there is a freestanding torch to my left.

The room is significantly smaller than the one we came from, maybe a tenth of the size, and the ceiling is covered with thousands of painted handprints, all of them surrounding a large red circle.

There is a thin blanket of smoke in the air, pungent with strange herbs and spices.

There are roughly fifteen people, men and women, seated in a circle on the floor toward the back wall, directly opposite the entrance to the tunnel. They all seem to be naked and are holding hands. They are chanting quietly. In the middle of the group, on a raised platform, is a girl with her legs spread, screaming at the top of her lungs. Her entire body (including her face) has been smeared with some sort of dark paste. A young man is stroking her hair.

Standing behind both (facing me) is an older woman with a striking appearance, swaying from side to side. She's wearing the head and skin of a cave lion, and her entire body, like the girl's, has been painted black. Her eyes are closed. In each hand is a small wooden container emitting smoke.

There's something about this place I don't like. In fact, it's as if I'm in the presence of pure evil. I have an instinct to turn and run, but I resist it.

My gaze returns to the girl on the floor, and I become aware of a dark mass of energy hovering above her left shoulder. The man tending to her is leaning directly into it. All in all, it's a strange and somewhat terrifying scene, but there's at least one bit of good news: the girl is not being tortured; she's having a baby. I can see its head.

I feel relieved but also jealous; the experience of being pregnant and giving birth is one that has eluded me. Whenever I think about the fact I have never been somebody's mother, it makes me sad, but there is no time for wallowing in self-pity, especially as everything has descended into madness and chaos. The men I followed here weren't coming to offer help. Instead, their plan was to spread violence and carnage, using their torches and knives to bludgeon, slice, and murder.

Some of the group are caught by surprise and massacred in seconds. Others among them, six men in particular, react quickly. They put up a brave and valiant fight but are no match for the cold-hearted assassins they face. Determined to protect the mother and her baby, I leap into the melee to engage one of the intruders. When I do, something happens that knocks the wind out of me: the man I was about to attack has a gray streak in his otherwise dark, shoulder-length hair.

My master is looking straight at me. He has a broad nose and a thick beard. He raises his knife and thrusts it toward my chest. I'm too shocked to move, and I brace myself for the end, welcoming it, but instead of cleaving my rib cage, the blade passes through harmlessly and hammers into the man standing behind.

Ashkai steps through me to continue his rampage, and I find myself, disoriented and confused, within five feet of his lighter-skinned accomplice. I watch as the highly skilled and ruthless killer parries an attack from the lion woman, countering with a fatal blow of his own. The warrior spins in my direction, his milky chest streaked with blood, and I look directly into his pale, soulless eyes.

He isn't just light-skinned, I realize. *He's albino.*

Rebus, gripped by a ferocious bloodlust, is making his way toward the girl who is in the final throes of labor, her child's head almost through. I want more than anything to help, but I am less of a thing than the smoke surrounding me, a helpless bystander as the man with dead eyes, his back to me now, leans down and tries to snatch the innocent babe from between its mother's legs.

When I first entered this room, there was a young man, possibly the infant's father, stroking the girl's hair. He never left her side. Now, he's just hurled himself at Rebus. He might as well have run into a wall. Rebus, almost nonchalantly, stabs the tall, slender boy three times in quick succession—*tat tat tat*—before shoving him onto the ground. Rebus turns to look at the girl again, but before he can grab her baby, another man barges into him.

I don't know how it happened, but I'm now standing directly above the boy with the knife wounds: two in his chest, one in his neck. Rebus and the pregnant girl are behind me.

For some unknown reason, this young man, who has brown hair and blue eyes, is of great interest to me. I want to help him, but in my current state, that isn't possible, not that there'd be any point anyway.

"I am sorry," I say.

He's on his hands and knees looking through me toward the girl, his gentle, intelligent eyes full of regret and despair. The life seeps out of him then, and his body slumps to the ground. My eyes are fixed on the horrible wound in his neck and the blood gushing out of it in short bursts, which slow as his heart stops beating.

I'm about to lower onto my haunches to take a closer look when Ashkai shouts something in a language I don't understand. I glance up. Ashkai has an arm extended and a pained expression on his face. I turn. Rebus is holding the newborn baby by its tiny, delicate ankles.

Ashkai says something else, and his partner replies, the man's tone overflowing with anger and indignation. After saying his piece, Rebus dashes the baby's head against the floor, ending the child's life before it even began. The mother, who's already on her feet, umbilical cord still attached, starts clawing at Rebus's face and eyes. Moving with the grace of a wave and speed of an arrow, Rebus spins the girl and slits her throat in the same devastating motion.

While watching her bleed out and fall to the ground, I lose the ability to breathe. I feel a strange tickling sensation in the front part of my neck and bring my hands up to investigate. I become aware of a warm river of blood gushing onto my bare legs and feet. A moment ago, I was in a long black coat and sturdy boots. I'm even more perplexed when I see those exact items on the body of the dead girl on the floor, the dead girl who now looks like Suzy Aarons.

She is now me, and I am now her.

I look at the tiny corpse on the floor, the umbilical cord still connecting us.

Maybe my son is still alive, I think, but when I try moving toward him, everything goes fuzzy, and my ears start ringing.

The next thing I know, I'm lying on my back, pulsing in and out of awareness, looking at the red circle on the ceiling and the handprints surrounding it.

The light being appears above my blood-soaked chest, materializing out of thin air, its voice in my head saying, *Fear or love? It's your choice.*

TWENTY-SEVEN

I become aware of the night sky. I'm seeing it through a complex and intricate weblike grid of overlapping red and blue lines.

Someone or something tells me to breathe, and the next thing I know, I'm gasping for air. It's as if I've just emerged from a long and life-threatening spell under water. With each inhalation comes a new batch of disturbing feelings and memories: Ashkai, Rebus, and the pulverized head of that poor, innocent baby.

Did any of that actually happen? I ask myself. Was the child really mine? And if so, why haven't I been able to remember until now? Did the deeply traumatic nature of the experience force me, on a subconscious level, to bury it? Are the emotional wounds I suffered the reason I have never been able to get pregnant again? Or did Ashkai mess with my mind in some way? After all, he was able to project himself into the most personal and private recesses of my subconscious mind in order to stop me from opening door 4320. Did he barricade it afterward so I wouldn't know the truth about what he is? A liar, a manipulator, a child killer!

My eyes well, and I want to scream, but I don't. I tell myself I shouldn't rush to conclusions. What if everything I saw was a deception of some sort? At the beginning of my journey, a female voice asked me to choose between fear and love. I selected the latter and started moving toward the portal of light. Before I was able to reach it, a fragment of myself disappeared into the ominous whirlpool of nothingness that was also present. I interpreted that darkness to be fear itself.

Another voice, one I recognized, spoke then, telling me I needed to save myself before rescuing my master.

It was the entity who tried to bully me into killing Cato. But he's not my only tormentor; there are also the imposter and the dark fire (unless they are one and the same), all of them conspiring to drive me totally and utterly mad. Bearing all of that in mind, it's at least possible that what unfolded in that cave—no matter how real it seemed—was nothing more than a paranoid, deranged fantasy.

I focus on the sky above and notice what looks like a shooting star. I worry that it's heading straight for me. And it's moving at speed. I brace myself for a collision, but nothing happens. I open one eye and then the other. Floating above my chest is the orb, its light flickering now.

Communicating telepathically, it says, *I have more to show you.*

Using only my mind, I reply, *More of what?*

The truth.

I don't know if I can trust you.

Can you trust yourself?

Speaking aloud, I say, "I don't know." Then I say, "I want to know where Ashkai is. I want to know if he's still alive."

I can show you, but first you must drink more medicine.

The Coca-Cola bottle filled with ayahuasca is in my backpack, which I'm currently using as a pillow. I sit up and pull it out from under me, realizing something at the same time: I'm alone.

"Tammuz," I say in a loud whisper. "Where are you?"

Nothing.

I check my watch: it's 11:42 p.m.

I stand and look around. Downtown Los Angeles a field of jewels. The air is a little cooler, and a strong breeze is rustling through the shrubs, plants, and trees. I can't see Tammuz, but on the floor where he had been sitting is the Coca-Cola bottle.

"Tammuz!"

The orb is still there, flickering like a faulty light bulb. The grid has all but disappeared.

Drink, the orb says.

I lean forward to grab the bottle, taking a large, unpleasant swig, thinking how Tammuz must have reached into my bag while I was watching the carnage in that cave, my friend keen to discover for himself what all the fuss was about. Knowing I would berate him when I awakened, he likely wandered off somewhere close. I am angry he went against my wishes, but I'm not surprised. I would have done the same thing in his position.

What if he's having a hard time? I remind myself he's a big boy and responsible for his own choices.

With the rancid taste of the medicine still thick in my throat, I lie down and close my eyes, waiting for whatever happens next.

***

We can resume our work, the light being says.

Time has passed; I don't know how much.

I open my eyes. The grid is back in high definition, and the sphere is as bright as the sun, although it doesn't hurt to look at it.

"What are we waiting for?" I ask.

Follow.

I start to sit up when I become aware of something unexpected: my guide is amused. She isn't laughing, but there's a playful energy surrounding her.

"What's so funny?"

You can't take that, the entity says, referring to my body. *Otherwise how will you be able to fly?*

It's a comment that reminds me of my Awakening, the night when Ashkai initiated my first Flooding. I wasn't bombarded with memories of earlier lives—he said it was because my soul was still very young—but I did get a glimpse of the bigger picture.

I left my body that night, transforming into a large, powerful owl with orange-yellow eyes, soaring the celestial heavens and even traveling through time, seeing advanced technological cites that my master said existed on other planets.

The light being instructs me to follow, and I focus in on my heart, going deep and then deeper still. Searching for the light of my soul essence, the spark each of us carries, our connection with source. Elated because I can see an owl emerging from the light, I watch the bird grow in size and magnificence. I become the owl and burst through Rosa's chest.

Switching to thought-speak, I say, *I am ready.*

Just as it did in that corridor when we first met, the sphere made of liquid light shoots off at a phenomenal speed, heading east toward Griffith Observatory. The white domed building, sitting on top of a large hill, is shimmering like a coin in the moonlight. Fortunately, the laws of the material world do not apply here. Any limits that do exist are self-imposed. Suffused with the belief that anything is possible, I tuck my wings and blast through the air like a rocket.

I am traveling on the razor's edge of reality, the narrow boundary between dimensions. The grid has disappeared, but right below me is a thin layer of what appears to be a transparent gel. The material world is beyond it. As I'm passing over the observatory, I see lots of people gathered on the lawn, their heads angled skyward, some peering through telescopes and binoculars.

While maintaining the same blistering pace so as not to lose track of my guide, I'm able to slow the speed at which I am seeing things. I spin so that I'm on my back, looking the same way as the crowd. But in place of stars, I see sparkling handprints, bright and innumerable. In the center of them is a big red ball, which I instantly recognize as Mars. It's a planet that many ancient cultures associated with war and destruction. That's appropriate because right now, fragments from a huge comet are bombarding it.

It's a living version of the painting I saw on the ceiling of that cave. *Is that why I'm experiencing this now, or are the events of this moment somehow connected to who I was in my unremembered past? If such a thing even exists . . .*

I turn to face the ground. I don't want to lose my guide. But instead of seeing the LA skyline at night, I find that I'm soaring above New York City. It's early morning, and the sun is rising over to my right, fingers of red and gold reaching out across Long Island and Queens. All those dull, gray buildings are radiant and alive.

The thin layer of gel has evaporated, and I can see everything in perfect detail.

Even though I can't locate my guide, I have a feeling we are almost there. I unfurl my wings now, slowing to a gentle glide. The streets below—I'm passing the Empire State Building—are busy with people and cars.

Letting instinct guide me, I swoop down between buildings,

sending a message telepathically to my spirit guide (even though I haven't seen her for a while), curious to know where I should be going next. In place of an answer, as my gaze sweeps over the mass of pedestrians in and around the Rockefeller Center, I hear a thud followed by a collective gasp. I bank in the direction of the noise. A crowd has gathered around something, so I fly above them to investigate.

They are looking at a dead, mangled body, arms and legs at impossible angles, the corpse facedown in an expanding pool of blood. The pavement beneath is cracked and dented. It won't be easy for the authorities to identify the victim, but I can: her name is Suzy Aarons.

Inside my head, I hear the word *follow*, and I look up. Directly above is my guide, and she's heading toward the top of the GE Building, slowly at first but picking up speed. I do exactly the same thing, the windows and concrete rushing by in a blur.

Before long, I have eyes on Ashkai. He is kneeling on the ground, tranquilizer darts sticking out of his torso and neck. Directly behind him is the door to the stairwell, its barricade long since dismantled. An army of hostile agents is pouring through it. The helicopter is up here in the sky with me. The pilot has just about managed to regain control after being hit by that pulse of energy sent by my master.

The pale-skinned man who shot him—the one wearing shades, a baseball cap, and a bulletproof vest—is still leaning out of the helicopter, holding onto one of the side rails. I didn't know who he was back then, but I do now: Rebus.

All roads, it seems, lead back to this man. But if he was once Ashkai's ally, feeding him valuable information about Meta and the Chamber of Infinites, what motivated him to switch sides?

It's another unanswered question to add to the ever-growing list. Although, at least one mystery is about to be solved: the one regarding what happened to Ashkai after he pushed me from this very building. It's true I have doubts about my master—how could I not after everything that has happened?—but it doesn't mean that I've stopped loving the man who has given me so much.

The most frustrating thing about being here is there's nothing I can do to change what has already happened; nothing I can do to stop the twenty or so agents who have formed a circle around my master, a man who's moments away from passing out; nothing I can do to impede Rebus, who has leaped from the helicopter onto the ground; and nothing I can do to halt the little girl who's just emerged from the stairwell, her shiny black hair tied in a ponytail. I remind myself that while Meta's body is that of a child, her soul is ancient and deadly.

But what is this? I watch, as the diminutive figure with indigo eyes marches toward the ring of agents. In her left hand is a gun, and she's firing at them. Meanwhile her tiny right palm has just released a huge cannonball of energy. It slams into the group and breaches their circle. Through the gap—*is this really happening?*—Meta aims her gun at Ashkai, who is still on his knees. Rebus dives in front of my master, two bullets slamming harmlessly into his armored chest.

Who is this child? I wonder, realizing I must have been mistaken about her identity.

The agents, all armed with tranquilizer guns, are returning fire. They've also formed a protective wall in front of Ashkai, who is now lying facedown on the floor.

The child is nimble, fast, and acrobatic, and is managing to evade the slew of projectiles aimed at her. Out of bullets, the kid dives behind an air-conditioning unit to reload. She comes out shooting.

I hear a voice inside my head, a woman saying, *You can't hide from me.*

I swoop and scan all of the faces on the roof, but nobody seems to be aware of my presence.

Up here, the voice says, and my owl eyes find the helicopter. It's hovering about thirty feet above the action. Leaning through the side door is a young woman. Like Rebus, she is wearing a baseball cap, shades, and a bulletproof vest. I didn't notice her before. *This is your fault,* she says.

Meta? I ask, but before the woman can answer, the little girl starts firing at the helicopter, forcing the pilot to maneuver out of harm's way.

222

I'm about to follow the mysterious woman when I remember that my master is in peril. Looking down now, I see Rebus and two others breaking away from the main group. Soon after, they are standing side by side, palms raised. Converging and focusing their efforts, the three men bombard the child with ball after ball of energy. One slams into a satellite dish and sends it flying, another shatters a window, and a third crashes into a wall, leaving a sizeable crater.

The child, who is incredibly skilled, dodges, weaves, and back flips but eventually falls victim to what is a relentless and overwhelming attack, crashing to a heap on the floor. The tranquilizer guns never stopped firing, but for the first time, their darts hit home, turning the poor girl into a human pincushion.

Everything stops.

Silence.

The girl, who is out of breath, stands and assesses the damage.

"Why have you betrayed us?" Rebus asks, his face full of pain and sadness.

The child replies, "You have lost your way, brother."

"Do you think I wanted to do this?" He points a finger at Ashkai, who has long since passed out. "Don't you know how much I love this man?"

Already unsteady on her feet, those indigo eyes losing luster and power, the girl says, "You have a strange way of showing it."

"I have no choice."

The child puts the gun to her head.

"We always have a choice."

Then she pulls the trigger.

TWENTY-EIGHT

I open my eyes.

I feel completely and utterly normal.

The sky is still dark over Runyon Canyon, but birds have started to sing. That means sunrise is imminent. That means the front gates will be opening. That means joggers, dog walkers, and other people who will find the fact I'm lying here, having plainly spent the night, strange and disconcerting, maybe even suspicious.

There is a deep chill in the air. It's so cold that my entire body is trembling.

I try to sit up. The head rush is overwhelming, and I lie back down. The medicine has worn off, but the journey of the previous few hours has taken its toll.

Who was the highly trained child, and why was she trying to kill my master? And what did she mean when she told Rebus he had lost his way?

In the lobby of the GE Building, just before Ashkai bundled me into that elevator and brought me back to my senses, I was convinced those powerful and entrancing indigo eyes could only belong to one person: Meta. Now I'm not so sure. Then again, Rebus did ask, "Why have you betrayed us?"

I try sitting again, more slowly this time. I'm hit by another head rush, but it's manageable.

I'm facing east toward Griffith Observatory, the horizon beyond tickled by the first feathers of light.

I look to my left, right, and behind. I'm on my own, which means Tammuz is still out there somewhere, unless he went back to the hotel without me.

I delve into my bag and pull out a bottle of water. Other than ayahuasca, I haven't had any fluids for almost ten hours, and I'm feeling dehydrated.

The more I drink, the thirstier I get. I drain the bottle.

All of that liquid in my stomach is making me nauseous, and the feeling is getting worse. I'm going to vomit, so I force myself to stand and hobble over to some bushes that are facing west toward more rolling peaks and hills, a few of which lie within the boundaries of Runyon Canyon. The Pacific Ocean is beyond those, although I can't make it out in the gloomy twilight.

The first thing that comes up is all that water. It's soon followed by an eruption of thick, gray sludge that smells truly awful, making me retch even more. While that's happening, I get a shooting pain in my bowels and start fumbling with my jeans, shoving them down to my ankles and squatting, putting my hand over my mouth so that it's not coming out of both ends at the same time.

I knew this might happen. Purges are common when working with the medicine, but they usually occur near the beginning of a journey rather than the end. Either way, it's not a big deal, it's just bodily fluids, and they're better out than in. In fact, I'm not the least bit embarrassed when I see Tammuz sitting on top of a nearby peak—arms wrapped around legs—facing my direction. Although to be fair, I think he's more interested in the sunrise, which is blooming into life behind me.

I packed plenty of toilet paper and wet wipes, so I'm able to clean myself up. I've got some fruit and a few granola bars in my bag. I'm not hungry, but I force half a banana down because I need the energy. Then I pack and start making my way over to Tammuz, who's still looking at the horizon. Not that I can blame him. The sunrise is spectacular, that bloodred disc poking its head between two hills, sending swirls of lilac and splashes of pink across the sky.

But then everything is more beautiful in the hours and days after an ayahuasca journey. It's one of the many perks. Maybe that's why I'm not upset with Tammuz, who has tears streaming down his face, for disappearing last night. It could also be the reason I feel a deep and meaningful connection with him as I sit and rest my head on his left shoulder, letting the magnificence of that view sink in.

Neither of us speaks. There are no words to improve this already perfect moment.

I must still be trembling because Tammuz takes off his jacket and covers me with it.

Some minutes pass, and I spot a jogger winding his way through one of the many trails below.

I sit upright, taking my head off Tammuz's shoulder. He's still crying but in a gentle, subdued way.

"Wanna talk about it?" I ask.

After a pause, he says, "I've never *really* seen a sunrise before, never really looked at it."

"Better late than never," I say, following up with, "What happened last night?"

He laughs and wipes tears from his face. "Everything happened last night."

"You had a powerful experience?"

Without taking his eyes off the horizon, he says, "You could say that." Then he says, "Right at the beginning, about half an hour after I drank, I was visited by this . . . this cloud of light. It was female and intelligent."

He pauses, but I let the silence endure, knowing he'll resume when he's ready.

"It was hovering above me, scanning my body, looking for something, but I didn't know what. Then four beams of light appeared out of nowhere and plunged into my body."

Tammuz shows me four spots spread across his chest and stomach. "They were heading for these trapped balls of repressed emotions, things that had been locked away deep inside of me for a very long time. The balls shattered and exploded, and the emotions inside came pouring out . . ."

"There was sadness and joy, anger and jealousy, love and hate. There was everything. It was so powerful, I thought I was going to die. There was a message as well, something like: "These are the things you haven't dealt with yet; here they are.""

"I had a memory of being a small boy, of how I felt invisible then, and heard the female energy say, 'You are loved, you are loved, you are loved,' while being caressed and held by her. I had no idea how much I needed to hear and feel that."

Tammuz stops there, and I tell him how amazing that sounds

and how not everyone has such a positive experience the first time they drink.

"That was just the start," he says, glancing at me. "After that, it was horrible."

"What do you mean?"

"Everything you told me was true. I know that now."

"About what?"

"Reincarnation."

"What did you see?"

He stares into the distance like a troubled war veteran, then says, "I found myself in this cave with paintings everywhere. It was thousands of years ago."

The sick feeling in my stomach returns with a vengeance.

"How do you know?" I ask.

"I just know. I was with my wife and some other people who were meant to protect us. We were hiding, but I didn't know why or who from. My wife was in labor, I could even see the baby's head, when these two maniacs appeared and started slaughtering everyone.

"The really fucked up thing is they weren't there for us. They wanted the baby. I did everything I could, but the men were too strong, and I was killed. As I was dying, I saw a ghost looking down at me."

Tammuz pauses before adding, "It was you."

"Interesting," I say, trying not to look freaked out, that banana disagreeing with my sensitive bowels. "I'm sorry you had to go through that. When people die during ayahuasca journeys, it's what they call an ego death. I know it doesn't feel like it now, but it's a good thing."

Brushing my explanation aside, Tammuz says, "You didn't look like you do now, but it was definitely you."

He saw Suzy, I think, casting my mind back to what happened in that cave,

remembering how that poor boy was stabbed three times, twice in the chest and once in the neck. I look at the same spot on Tammuz's body now, just to the left of his Adam's apple. In place of a gaping wound is a bright red birthmark, the one I noticed the night we met while waiting for the bus to London. I had an instinct then that the two of us were connected somehow; I just had no idea how deeply.

Tammuz's trip down memory lane coupled with his birthmark represents concrete proof my master has been lying to me. It's a crushing realization, but I don't let it show. The only half-positive thing I have left, the last glimmer of hope, is that Ashkai tried to stop Rebus from killing my baby. Did he have a last-minute change of heart, or had Rebus gone rogue? Is that why they fell out? Is that why Rebus shot Ashkai with a tranquilizer gun in New York?

"What do you think it all means?" I ask, hoping he hasn't put the other pieces of the puzzle together.

"You were there, weren't you?" Tammuz says. "You saw me?"

"No," I say, relieved because if he knew I was his wife and that the child was ours, there's no way he wouldn't mention it. "I was having my own journey."

"You're lying."

"Not everything that happens on ayahuasca is real, you know. Sometimes it's just crazy stuff your head makes up."

He starts defending his experience, telling me he *knows* it was real, so I stand and interrupt. "We better go."

Tammuz gets to his feet. He's not crying anymore.

"I don't want to fight with you," he says. Then he adds, "Did you get the answers you were looking for? Do you know where Ashkai is?"

"I think he's in New York. I don't know where exactly."

"That's not much to go on."

"I know," I say, turning so I can be sick. "But it's better than nothing."

TWENTY-NINE

Tammuz says, "Even though last night was hands-down the scariest and maddest experience of my life, I feel totally amazing today. Know what I mean?"

"Afraid not."

"What's wrong?"

"I'm frustrated."

"Because you don't know where Ashkai is?"

"There's that," I say, holding up Bacchus's cell phone. "But there's also this."

"Maybe the guy who owned it didn't have any friends."

"What's that got to do with anything?"

"Would explain why it hasn't rung all day. Let's be honest; he was a bit of a dick."

Tammuz is trying to be funny. I guess it's an attempt to cheer me up, but it's having the opposite effect.

"Somebody left a voicemail the night before last. I want to listen to it."

"Why?"

"Because I have a feeling it's important."

It's just gone 1 p.m. on Saturday, and we're at the Ocean Park Getaway. There's a crack in the curtain letting a shaft of sunlight through, revealing motes of dust in the air.

On our way back from Runyon Canyon, we stopped for some breakfast. My stomach was still sensitive, but I was able to keep food down and felt better as a result. Tammuz ate like a ravenous wolf, telling me how amazing everything tasted and how incredible he felt considering he hadn't slept for twenty-four hours. He spoke some more about his profound visions and experiences. I got the impression he was holding something back, something personal and important, but if he didn't want to elaborate, that was his prerogative.

On arriving at the hotel, we took turns showering before lying on the bed side by side. I was wearing tracksuit bottoms and a hoodie, and Tammuz was in boxers and a T-shirt.

Very quickly, tiredness caught up with Tammuz, and he fell asleep. I stared at the ceiling fan thinking things through, such as where I should go when I arrived in New York . . .

At breakfast, I used Tammuz's phone to Google the information on the black card I found in Cato's wallet—*phoenix house* and *east village*—but nothing of interest came up.

The only address I have in New York that feels in any way relevant is for COSMOS, the technology and Internet company that, as it happens, has its headquarters in the East Village. The photograph of Rebus I found in Kaya's house, before the place burned down, shows him leaving there. That doesn't mean it's going to be significant or that I'll find anything useful at the location, but it's as good a place to start as any.

After the twenty-four hours I'd had, it was only a matter of time before I finally drifted off, entering the familiar, and sometimes helpful, world of dreams.

I found myself back in that cave, but instead of being in the presence of pain, misery, and murder, I was surrounded by cell phones; in fact, I was standing knee-deep in them.

One was ringing. I searched franticly through the pile, phones sliding out of the way and toppling over one another, creating new piles, but eventually I found the one ringing and grabbed it. Just as I was about to answer, it went dead. A moment later a text appeared:

Important message. Enter four-digit code for access.

But I didn't know what the number was, and it's a problem I've carried over into the waking world.

I look at Tammuz, who's propped up on some pillows on my left. "Is there any way to hack into a person's phone and listen to their messages?"

"Yeah, journalists do it all the time to celebrities. You just need the owner's code, and you can do it remotely from a landline."

I roll my eyes. "Thanks, that's really helpful."

"I've got an idea," Tammuz says, looking mischievous. "Let's drink some more ayahuasca."

"How's that going to help?"

"The guy who owns that phone is dead, right?"

I nod.

"We can look for him in the spirit world and ask him to help us out with the code. Not as if he needs it now."

Something inside me snaps. "Do I look like I'm in the mood for your stupid jokes?"

Tammuz takes a deep breath. "Why've you got to be so serious all the time?"

I'm about to tear into him some more, needing an outlet for my anger and frustration, when I'm struck by what feels like an interesting idea.

I swipe the screen. I'm remembering what happened after I drunk the medicine. How I was lost in the corridors of my own subconscious. How I was led to *that* door with *that* number, the number I've seen again and again since my Flooding. The number 4320.

I input the four digits and . . . the screen comes to life. I throw my arms around Tammuz, kissing him on the lips.

"You're a genius," I say, which is funny because the look on his face is kind of dumb.

"What did I do?"

I jump to my feet and stride to the far corner of the room, my excitement quickly replaced by worry, concern, and fear.

What if it's nothing?

Standing in the shadows and turning away from the sunlight, I access Bacchus's voicemail, click on the new message and listen . . .

***

A woman says, "Samsara, if you get this, call me on 212-756-8934. And hurry; we don't have much time."

The area code for New York is 212.

I play the message over and over. I recognize the voice. It's the same person who called when I was in Kaya's basement, the person who told me to run.

Back then, I thought it might have been Kaya herself, but I realize now that's not the case. I don't know who this woman is or why she wants me to call her, but what have I got to lose?

Tammuz has come over to my side of the room. "How did you get the code?"

I don't respond, and he presses again. "Who is it? What did they say?"

"Please be quiet. I need to think. In fact, wait here; I'll be back in a minute."

"If you walk out of that door, I'm following you. I told you I'm not letting you out of my sight."

"You're not my fucking father," I snap. "Just wait here."

He looks wounded, but I don't care. I throw on some shoes and head to the front of the building, slipping down a quiet side street before dialing the number I've already memorized, shielding my eyes from the sun.

It rings once, twice, three times . . .

"Pick up," I whisper. "Please . . ."

"Hello?" a woman's voice says, a voice I recognize.

My already racing heart finds another gear. "Who is this?" I ask. Silence.

"Do I know you?"

"Yes and no," the woman says.

"What's that supposed to mean?"

"We have a mutual friend."

"Ashkai?"

"Indeed."

"He's a liar."

"Is that so?"

"Yes it is, which means you're full of shit as well."

"Don't you think you should hear what he has to say before losing faith? Maybe you don't understand the situation as well as you think."

"I've started to remember my past. I saw him do something terrible."

"Do you know why he did it?"

I think for a moment. "No."

"Then you still have much to learn."

"Do you know where he is?"

"I do."

"New York?" I ask.

"Yes."

"Where exactly?"

"I can't tell you over the phone."

"Why?"

"It's too risky."

"Who are you?"

"Meet me tomorrow at noon."

"Tell me who you are!"

"Be patient, Samsara. All will be revealed."

"Where?"

"Ashkai's favorite place in New York. Do you remember it?"

It comes to me instantly. "I do."

"Noon. Be there."

"How do I know I can trust you?"

"It's better you don't trust anyone. It's safer that way."

THIRTY

I tell Tammuz to go through airport security alone, explaining I'll meet him at the gate.

He wants to know why we can't go together, telling me he's worried I'll disappear, so I do my best to reassure him, while at the same time insisting we do it my way.

He eventually gives in, and I hang back, watching as he puts his bag on the security belt and enters the full-body scanner. Before disappearing around the corner, he glances back for one final look, his eyes asking, "What are you up to?"

We're at LAX, about to catch the red-eye to New York. But that's only if the next few minutes go to plan. If they don't, I could end up arrested and in jail. That's why I needed Tammuz to go ahead.

Everything will be okay.

I can do this.

I know I can.

I walk forward and place my hand luggage on the belt. Then I approach a middle-aged white man wearing a light blue uniform, explaining I have a phobia of technology, which means I can't enter the full-body scanner. I'm smiling and being cute, two things that have zero effect on Jayla, the large African American who has been assigned to pat me down.

She looks like she hates me already, so who knows how she'll react if what I'm about to attempt doesn't work.

I'm carrying a gun, the one I took from Cato. It's tucked into the back of my jeans, my baggy clothes concealing it.

This is a huge risk, but it's a calculated one. Besides, there's no way I'm going to New York unarmed. The girl on the phone said it herself; I can't trust anyone, and she's currently top of that list.

Before the episode in Kaya's basement, I wouldn't have had the confidence to attempt something so bold, but since then, since encountering that dark, foreboding fire, I have felt so much more capable, and dare I say it, powerful . . .

I remind myself of something important: using only the power of thought, I was able to force a man to stab himself in the heart.

If I can do that, I can do this.

"Extend your arms," Jayla says, and as I follow her instructions, I begin using my mind to probe hers. Using the power of my will, I am tuning into the frequency of her consciousness. Once I have found the right station (so to speak), I will make the necessary adjustments. The goal is to convince Jayla to believe in me and trust me so completely that whatever I say is accepted as bedrock truth, overriding her own thoughts and training. It's a form of deep hypnotism. It's also unethical, but these are desperate times.

I can feel something happening (it's the mental equivalent of a key overcoming a stubborn lock), so I lean forward and whisper that I'm an undercover FBI agent and that she will ignore the gun tucked into the back of my jeans. It's a matter of national security.

"I'm your friend, Jayla," I continue. "I'm on your side. You have nothing to worry about. Everything is going to be okay."

She looks dazed for a moment, even a little bit drunk, but then starts patting me down. I feel her hands on the gun, which is when doubt sets in.

What if I can't do this?

I'm expecting Jayla to raise the alarm, thinking I'll have to run and fight if she does, but instead she smiles, her eyes glazed and strange looking. Jayla ushers me forward, telling me to have a nice flight.

***

The following morning at 11:50 a.m., I'm on the ground floor of the American Museum of Natural History, which is located on the Upper West Side of Manhattan across the street from Central Park. Made up of twenty-seven interconnected buildings and housing forty-five permanent exhibition halls (I've done my research), as well as a planetarium and a library, it's rightly celebrated as one of the largest and most important institutions of history in the world, even if it does get lots of things glaringly wrong.

It's Sunday, and the place is buzzing with tour groups and families, excited children pointing things out to Mom and Dad, their teenage siblings looking as if they have better things to do.

Even though this could be a trap, I feel sharp, strong, and ready to defend myself. I just wish Tammuz wasn't here with me. I asked him to wait at the hotel, but aside from the fact he point-blank refused, it's obvious he has some sort of role to play in all this, which is why I decided to stop resisting the inevitable. I did make him agree to keep his distance in the museum and not to get involved if things became violent. He hasn't got a great track record of doing what I ask him; then again, if he did, we wouldn't be here now.

As I pass through the meteorite display and enter the Hall of Human Origins, by far Ashkai's favorite exhibition, I'm reminded of the last time he brought me here, not long before our enemies tracked us down. It is becoming clear he told me something important within these walls. I know because my brain is trying to piece together the details of what was said. So far it has failed, although I have a feeling it will come back to me soon. I just need to be patient.

The museum has been updated significantly over the past two decades. There are large screens displaying colorful, interactive images along with other technological advancements in lighting and sound. The basics are pretty much the same though, that is (in this room at least) the arrangement of skeletons and skulls and dramatic historical reconstructions of early humans doing things like making fire and hunting.

Right now I'm looking at two skeletons standing side by side behind a thick pane of glass, amber lights illuminating the scene. The collection of bones on the left, complete with that famous protruding brow, is Homo erectus. The figure on the right represents Homo sapiens.

"If you're going to name yourself, you might as well choose something flattering rather than true," a familiar voice says, only this one is male.

I turn to my right, and standing beside me is Ashkai. He's the person he was the last time we were together: tall, black, and handsome with that ever-present gray streak in his hair, along with those kind, brown eyes.

I look around the exhibition hall. Other people are still here going about their business, but it's as if they are occupying another plane of existence. In fact, everything outside my immediate field of view is opaque and blurry.

I realize what's happening. This is a flashback. I'm reliving a moment from my past, a moment that unfolded in this exact spot.

"Homo *stultus* would have been more appropriate," I say, repeating the exact words uttered by Suzy almost twenty years ago.

Ashkai laughs, but I can tell he's not himself.

"What's wrong?" I ask, speaking ancient Egyptian.

After a prolonged silence, Ashkai says, also switching to the language of the pharaohs, "I understand that Sleepers do not remember the lives they have lived, but even so, it's curious they believe in such fallacies."

"What fallacies?"

"About our past as a species."

Ashkai points at the skeleton on our right. "According to the current geological record, anatomically modern humans have lived on Earth for a hundred and fifty thousand years.

"The story goes that for about a hundred thousand years, we didn't make any meaningful progress. We were hunter-gatherers who were totally incapable of innovation. Then, out of nowhere, came the first signs of culture in the form of cave art. But civilization as we know it, according to those who call themselves experts, didn't begin until the rise of the Sumerians some five thousand years ago.

"It's a story of slow and assured progress culminating in the self-aggrandizing magnificence of the current age.

"As you know, the truth is much more complicated than that. Smart hominids, who carry the flame of consciousness, have been in existence since the long ago. And in place of a neat and clean ascent, their story on Earth has been marked by a series of dramatic ups and downs and new beginnings."

After a short pause, Ashkai continues, "It's impossible for Sleepers to conceive of this, but human souls once inhabited other planets across the universe."

"Don't they still?" I ask.

My master, who has sadness in his eyes, shakes his head.

"Why?"

"Because they have long since been obliterated . . . take Mars, for example, Earth's older brother. An advanced civilization flourished there before sowing the seeds of its own demise."

"What happened?"

"They gave in to the powers and temptations of darkness, letting fear and hate overwhelm them. As a result, they weren't ready when the great comet appeared from the sky, wiping the slate clean. This unfortunate episode took place close to a million years ago. If the people's hearts had been filled with love and their eyes had been open, they would have been able to work together to ensure some sort of future."

"Fear, hate, temptations," I say. "It sounds very much like the world we live in now."

"It does, only the stakes are even higher."

"Why?"

Ashkai looks into my eyes. "I have not told you this before, but Earth is the last habitable planet in the universe, as far as we know. If she is destroyed, the human story is over. Once and for all."

I let the gravity of his message sink in, wondering if that's the reason I've started to feel dizzy.

If Ashkai is correct, and he usually is, there is no room for error when it comes to our mission of awakening souls and bringing them into the light. I realize something else, something extremely unnerving. Ashkai, who is not usually prone to worrying about things that may or may not happen, is gravely concerned. And that means he knows something.

"What aren't you telling me?"

Ignoring my question, he says, "The world is riddled with so much bitterness and paranoia, and it's growing by the day. When the time is right, and we have both seen this happen many times before, a dark and powerful force—one must only look to Adolph Hitler as an example or Stalin or even Genghis Khan—will harness that hate and use it to cause damage on an unprecedented scale."

"You're talking about a world war," I say.

Everything goes black for about three seconds, and my hearing becomes muffled.

What's happening to me?

Ashkai says, "With the technology and weapons this civilization has at its disposal—and will have in the years to come—that means complete and utter destruction."

"What makes you think that is our biggest threat?" I ask. "Why aren't you worried about a comet hitting Earth? It ended life on Mars, why not here as well?"

"Because that is not this planet's destiny."

"How do you know?"

"It has been foreseen."

"By whom?"

My master turns to face me and places a hand on my shoulder. "There are things you do not know, things I have not been able to tell you."

"Such as?" I ask, but everything goes dark again.

When my vision returns, Ashkai is no longer there. Meanwhile, the skeletons and artifacts of the museum have started spinning around me as if caught in a huge whirlpool. I am feeling myself becoming unsteady when something strikes me across the face, bringing me back to the here and now.

"Pull yourself together," says the brown-skinned girl with indigo eyes. She looks about the same age as Rosa. "One of us has been followed."

She's dragging me out of the Hall of Human Origins, and for some reason, I'm not resisting. We're heading north into the Grand Gallery, a large, white room with a marble floor. A huge, sixty-foot canoe is hanging by wires from the ceiling, its bottom about two meters above the ground.

We're on the starboard side, running toward an exit. The only problem is there are three people striding toward us from across the room: two guys and one woman. My head is still fuzzy and I feel weak, but fortunately, guns don't require much effort. I'm on the verge of pulling mine out when the other girl raises her left hand in the direction of the boat. Almost immediately, two of its suspension cables snap, and its front half crashes to the ground, cutting our pursuers off, giving us time to slip out onto Seventy-Seventh Street.

The sky is dark with low hanging clouds, and rain is falling.

The girl bundles us into the back of a black BMW and tells the driver, who is smoking, to put his foot down. Just before we pull away, there's a bang on the window. I reach for my gun and point it at . . . Tammuz. I tell the girl to let him in, but she ignores me, the car skidding away at speed. I look out of the rear window. Through the droplets of rain, I can see Tammuz chasing after us, his face full of fear and desperation. The three people from the museum are behind him.

I shout a warning, but then we turn a corner, and he's gone.

THIRTY-ONE

I point my gun at the cool-looking Asian with a Mohawk just as he flicks his cigarette out the window.

The rain is coming down hard, and the windshield wipers are swishing left and right.

"Stop the car," I say.

He ignores me, so I lean forward and press the muzzle into the side of his head. "I'm not leaving my friend behind."

Mohawk glances at me through the corner of his eye, but then returns his attention to the busy, wet road, weaving through traffic at high speed.

"Don't listen to her," says my kidnapper. "Keep going."

Mohawk speeds up, so I point the gun at his boss instead.

"Tell him to stop, or I'll pull this trigger."

This is the first time I've been able to properly look at her since she grabbed me in the museum, everything after that whizzing by in a blur of adrenaline and confusion. The girl, who is no more than twenty years old, in this life at least, has a very striking appearance. She's Latino, beautiful in an interesting and androgynous way, with short, tousled hair and full, pillowy lips.

As I'm looking into her indigo eyes, something strange happens. At first, it's just a bit of dizziness, similar to what I experienced in the museum before she appeared, but then I realize I've forgotten where I am or even what my name is. But it doesn't matter because I feel so incredibly good and safe, a voice in my head saying, *Don't be afraid. We're on your side; just go to sleep . . .*

What a great idea, I think, drifting away like a summer cloud, hoping this feeling lasts forever . . .

***

I open my eyes and have to blink a few times to focus them.

I can smell cigarette smoke.

Where am I? I think, feeling thirsty and needing to pee. *Who am I?*

It's as if every memory inside my head has been wiped. I have an awareness of danger, but that's about it.

My wrists, which are on the other side of a metal beam that's supporting my back, have been tied together with a strong cord.

Someone with a Mohawk—*where have I seen him before?*—is sitting on a chair facing away from me, leaning to his right now, stubbing a cigarette out in an ashtray that's on a small wooden table. Beyond him are three other people. There's a tall, slender guy with messy, curly hair standing in front of the far wall, which has been covered with a large sheet of white paper. On it are hand-drawn images, photographs, and scribbled notes. I'm quite far away (it's a large room), so I can't make out any meaningful details, although it looks like something the police or FBI would compile during an investigation.

A wooden desk runs alongside the adjacent wall, which is northeast of me. It's covered with cameras, laptops, and guns. Another man, whom I can only see in profile, is standing over it, loading one of the many firearms. He has dark, short hair, two days worth of stubble, and looks physically powerful, like a child's action figure come to life.

The third person is a light-skinned black girl with short dreadlocks that come down to her defined and prominent cheekbones. She's the strangest of the bunch, petite and elfin, and is staring at me. She's sitting opposite Mohawk, so she's facing my direction, but a little to his right. Her face is expressionless, and her eyes are lifeless and cold.

Is she dead? I wonder, but then I hear, *Hello, Samsara,* in my head. It triggers a rush of memories: Ashkai and the museum, leaving Tammuz behind . . .

Using telepathy, I ask the black girl, *Was that you?* but nothing comes back.

As discreetly as possible, I check left, right, and over my shoulder, taking everything in. I'm in the center of a spacious and beautiful warehouse apartment with dark wood floors and large, arched widows, all of which have been closed and shuttered. I guess they don't want any of their neighbors seeing all those guns, or me, for that matter. An expensive-looking camera on a tripod is next to one of the windows.

A small skylight that's being splattered with rain is directly above. It's daytime still, but night feels just around the corner. Dominating the far end of the room is an elaborate and stylish Edison bulb chandelier. It's switched on, along with a couple of freestanding lamps. The furniture is sparse, clean, and modern. Overall, it feels more like a showplace than a home where people live, although these guys have obviously been here for a while.

There are two questions I want answers to: What are these people planning, and how does it involve me?

Last time I saw the girl with indigo eyes, in the flesh at least, she was at war with Rebus. They say your enemy's enemy is your friend, but the way things are going, I'm not so sure about that.

Moving slowly and quietly, I test the strength of my restraint. It's sturdy and tightly fastened.

How long have I been unconscious? And where am I?

As well as the rain, I can hear car horns and a distant fire engine, so I'm guessing we're still in New York and that it's been a few hours max since I was taken.

The girl with the dreadlocks is still looking at me. I wait for her to say something else, but instead, she raises a hand and smiles. There's something childlike and innocent about her.

Mohawk notices what's going on and turns. Seeing I'm awake, he stands, pulls his phone out, and makes a call.

The two others have stopped what they were doing. The one with scruffy hair over by the far wall, who had his back to me until now, is wearing glasses and has a nerdy, bookish demeanor. What's particularly interesting is they all look about the same age as Rosa and the Latino girl, somewhere between eighteen and twenty-one.

I start paying closer attention to Mohawk, recalling how he barely even flinched when I threatened to shoot him in the car. He's short but has an athletic, toned build and is wearing narrow, fitted jeans, white trainers, and a black T-shirt emblazoned with a large pink skull.

Phone against his ear, he says, "She's awake."

Mohawk, who strikes me as confident but also quirky and smart, hangs up and walks over to the small table. An ashtray, Marlboro cigarettes, and a Zippo lighter are on it.

"Try anything stupid, and I'll have to put you to sleep."

He's standing over me now, holding a syringe with clear liquid in it.

"That how you guys knocked me out in the car?" I ask, thinking Indigo must have jabbed me on the sly.

"No, that was something much stronger."

"Why are you doing this to me?"

"We're trying to keep you safe."

I laugh. "That's a good one."

"Do you want some water?" Mohawk asks, and I nod. He disappears for a moment and returns with a bottle.

He spills some down my chin, but I don't care, using my eyes to tell him to keep going.

"Sorry," he says when I've had enough, putting the bottle down.

The two other guys are still staring, and it's pissing me off. Curiously, I don't feel the same about the girl. Maybe it's because there's something gentle and unthreatening about her.

Looking at Action Man, I say, "Why don't you use one of those guns on yourself?" To the nerd, I say, "You know it's against the law to kidnap young girls and tie them up, right?" And finally, speaking to the whole room: "Who the hell are you people anyway?"

Mohawk, who looks amused, says, "My name is Echo." He gestures toward the girl—"That's Pythia"—then Action Man—"Bythos"—and finally the nerd—"Neith." Looking back at me, he says, "I know it doesn't seem like it, but we're on your side."

"I didn't know I had a side," I say, watching as Bythos and Neith pretend to carry on with what they were doing.

Echo spins his chair and sits. "Well, you do."

I say, "If you're my friends, I hate to think what would happen if my enemies got hold of me."

"We know exactly what would happen, and it's not good, trust me on that."

Instead of responding, I pause to think.

Short of using my mind to do something spectacular, such as manipulating these people or breaking my restraints, both of which would be incredibly difficult—especially as all they'll have to do is stab me with that needle—I've got no idea how to escape. My best bet is to try and talk my way out, but to do that, I need a face to face with the person in charge.

"Who were you speaking to just now?" I ask.

"Who do you think?"

"The bitch who lied to me, kidnapped me, and drugged me?"

Echo smiles. "You've got the wrong idea."

"What happened to my friend, the one you left behind?"

He looks down for a moment. "I'm sorry about that, but I couldn't stop; it was too risky."

"Did they catch him . . . the people who were chasing us?"

"I don't know. But if they did, we'll get him back."

There's a noise at the front door, which is over to my right. Somebody is about to enter, and that somebody is . . .Indigo.

The first thing that hits me is her energy; it's intoxicating and powerful. She's dressed very unassumingly in jeans, boots, and a hoodie, which she has up; large sunglasses cover her eyes. Everything about her makes me think she's trying to keep a low profile.

I feel angry all of a sudden but more at myself than anybody else. Why did I follow this person's lead in the museum? Why didn't I take control of my own destiny?

"Let me go!" I say. You have no right keeping me here."

"It's for your own good," the woman replies, striding toward me, boots connecting loudly with the wood floor. She pulls her hood down, revealing short, tomboyish hair, but leaves her shades on.

"Who do you think you are?" I say. "My mother?"

She grabs another chair and spins it, sitting next to Echo, both of them facing me, Neith and Bythos no longer pretending to be busy. Pythia, who is peering over Indigo's left shoulder, is still waving and smiling in my direction, although it's as if she's looking through me. I'm starting to think she might be simple in the head. My kidnapper says, "In a way, yes." Then she adds, "Tell me what you know."

I take a deep breath and try to calm down. Getting angry isn't going to solve this problem. I need to accept my predicament and work with it.

"About what?"

"Let's start with me."

"First time I saw you was about twenty years ago in New York. I was with Ashkai. We were running . . ."

She interrupts. "Do you remember who from?"

"Of course: Meta, Rebus, and their army of agents, the same idiots who have been chasing us since the beginning."

Echo lets out a snigger, but Indigo ignores him. "What happened?"

"We made some bad decisions and ended up on the roof of that building with nowhere to go. Ashkai was shot. I wanted to help him, but he wouldn't let me. To make sure I wasn't captured, he pushed me and I fell to my death."

"How did you feel about that?"

"Angry, let down, guilty . . . nothing good."

"If it's any consolation, he had no choice."

I roll my eyes. "What's your excuse?"

"Regarding what?"

"Failing to kill him."

She seems momentarily taken aback. "How do you know that? You were dead."

"I drank ayahuasca."

"When?"

"Two nights ago."

She nods. "What else were you shown?"

"Horrible things."

"Such as?"

"I saw Ashkai and Rebus murder a baby. My baby."

"Then the spirits were deceiving you," says Indigo. "Ashkai would never . . ."

"Rebus did the most damage, but my master was helping him."

There's a short pause before I'm hit with another question. "Did this happen inside a cave?"

Tears rise, and it's a struggle to hold them back.

"Yes."

"The episode you speak of occurred a very long time ago."

"So it really happened? Ashkai was really there?"

"Yes, but it's complicated."

"Complicated enough to justify murdering an innocent child?"

"Perhaps. It's a long story, and we don't have time right now."

I motion toward my restraints. "I'm not going anywhere."

"It's not my place to tell you."

"Then whose is it?"

"Your master's."

Despite everything, the thought of seeing Ashkai fills my heart with hope. "Is he here?"

"Rebus has been keeping him captive since the last time you saw him. But we know where he's being held."

"The Long Sleep?"

"Yes."

"Are you going to break him free?" I gesture toward the guns. "Is that what you're getting ready for?"

She nods.

"Then untie me. I'm coming with you."

"We'll see about that."

"But I can help."

"I know you can."

"So let me go," I shout. "I want answers. Who are you anyway, and why are you helping Ashkai?"

Taking her shades off, the girl leans forward and places a hand on my shoulder. I feel instantly calm, sleepy almost, just like I did in the car before everything went blank. I realize now that she's using her mind—*and those eyes!*—to put me to sleep. I drift off while hearing her say, "Your master and I have been friends since the long ago. As for who I am: my name is Meta. It's a pleasure to finally meet you."

THIRTY-TWO

Pythia is sitting opposite with her legs crossed. She's holding Echo's silver metal Zippo in front of her. Its flame is the only source of light.

I peer into the dark corners of the warehouse apartment, my wrists still bound. From what I can tell, we are alone.

You don't remember me, do you? the strange girl says, speaking telepathically, the flame casting shadows across her face.

Talking aloud, I say, "Should I?"

Nothing comes back, so I repeat myself.

Again, no response.

"What's wrong with you?" I ask, looking into those peculiar eyes that can't seem to focus on anything.

Still using telepathy, Pythia says, *Speak with your consciousness, not your tongue.* Her thought voice is full of experience and wisdom, something that contrasts starkly with her childlike demeanor.

I take a moment to focus, communicating on her terms now. *Why?*

I am deaf.

What about your eyes? Can you see?

Those are two different questions.

I don't understand.

My eyes are useless, but I can see very well.

While it's a comment that piques my curiosity, getting out of here is all that matters.

Hoping to manipulate this girl so that she does my bidding, I ask, *Who are you?*

Pythia holds the lighter under her chin and leans forward, her elfin features becoming ghoulish and scary. *Is this not the face of an angel?*

At first, I think she's playing games, but then connections start firing in my mind, pieces of the puzzle coming together until eventually I remember who this girl is! For a brief moment, I'm even back in Thebes with my master tucking her into bed.

Angel Face! I say, remembering Ashkai's nickname for his adopted daughter, the street urchin he took under his wing, the one who couldn't speak, hear, or see.

Pythia starts giggling.

There are so many questions I want to ask, but first I need a favor from an old friend.

Where is everybody? I ask.

They have gone to rescue Ashkai.

Where is he?

Pythia turns and points at the far wall, although it is shrouded in darkness.

Angel Face, I need your help . . .

Pythia shakes her head. *I cannot free you.*

We are friends. Friends help each other.

Even if I wanted to, I couldn't.

What's stopping you?

You are asleep. This is a dream.

Her words ring true.

I look down at the floor between my legs and try to remember how this conversation started.

I was talking to the girl with indigo eyes . . . she was wearing sunglasses but then removed them . . . I felt very sleepy all of a sudden . . . she told me her name was Meta . . . or had this dream already started by then?

I look at Pythia. *If I am asleep, then why are you here?*

I have come to warn you.

About what?

Your friend.

I know instantly to whom she's referring. *Tammuz is in trouble, isn't he?* I don't even need her to answer; I can feel it in the deepest, truest part of myself.

Unless you intervene, he will die. I have seen it.

What do you mean you've seen it? Has it already happened?

In one way yes, in another no.

That doesn't make any sense, I say. *Where is he?*

249

She points again at the wall behind her.

Why are you telling me this?

Because he has an important role to play.

In what?

Everything.

I have no idea what she's talking about, nor, at this moment, do I care.

I need to get free, I say.

Then you must awaken.

I see a flash of those indigo eyes, recalling how they knocked me out in the car when Echo was driving and again right here in this apartment. I realize I'm more than just asleep; I'm deeply unconscious. Waking will not be easy.

Pythia, still holding the cigarette lighter, says, *I have an idea.* She leans forward, pulls the sleeve of my jacket up, and places the flame against my right forearm. The burn is instant and excruciating.

I close my eyes and grit my teeth. I can smell singed hair and hear the crackle of skin. I'm about to scream, tell her to stop, when the pain eases off.

She must have read my mind. But when I open my eyes, Pythia is no longer there, nor is the lighter. That's when I realize I'm awake. I feel elated at first, but then the uselessness of my predicament comes back to me. I'm still tied up. If I don't find a way to change that, Tammuz is going to die.

***

I'm on my feet and leaning away from the thick metal beam, desperately trying to squirm out of the tightly fastened cord binding my wrists.

I pause to catch my breath, realizing I need a different plan because this one isn't going to work.

It's dark in here, and the windows are shuttered except for the skylight directly above. It's still raining and night has fallen, but my eyes have adjusted to the gloom. I've tried to check my watch many times but haven't been able to maneuver an angle that works.

As if things aren't bad enough, I'm desperate for the toilet. I'm also thirsty and hungry.

Feeling useless and beaten, I slide down the metal beam until I'm sitting on the floor. I start sobbing uncontrollably and banging my head. I have an out- of-body experience and gaze down on myself, just for half a second. I look so pathetic, it's funny, which might explain why I've started laughing and behaving like a maniac.

When the hysteria passes, I'm left feeling beaten, dejected, and confused.

Was my encounter with Pythia real? Is she truly Ashkai's daughter? And is Tammuz in trouble?

When it comes to the last question, I have to err on the side of caution and assume the answer is yes. I remember how Tammuz picked me off the floor of that bus and covered me with a blanket, how he helped when Robbie and his gang broke into my hotel room. He even rescued me from the fire in Kaya's basement. When I've needed Tammuz, he's been there, and I desperately want to return the favor.

"Then save his life," a commanding voice says. It's not the imposter or even my ayahuasca guide speaking. This time, the voice belongs to me. I have the same thought I had at LAX last night, remembering how I forced a man to stab himself using only my mind. I even convinced airport security to let me travel with a gun. I had my Flooding just nine days ago, and in that time, I have made incredible progress, rising to the occasion when it matters most.

What else am I capable of?

With confidence and hope rising in my chest, I look around the room for something with a sharp edge. A knife would be ideal, but a glass (that I could break) would also do the trick. I don't spot either of those things, but I'm still elated. That's because through the darkness, I can see the outline of a packet of cigarettes on the small wooden table a few paces ahead. Right next to it is Echo's Zippo, the same one Pythia used to wake me. Was she giving me a sign?

Speaking aloud, I say, "You can do this, Samsara." Then,

channeling every bit of energy I can muster, I visualize the lighter moving toward me. Nothing happens, so I try again. I close my eyes for a third attempt, then a fourth and fifth, but it's utterly useless.

The problem is obvious: I'm trying too hard.

Rather than focusing on what I want to happen, what I need, I think about Tammuz and the danger he's in, imagining what I'd feel like if his life ended prematurely. Yes, he'd be reborn, but that doesn't mean I'd feel okay about a friend being murdered, especially when the experience would likely haunt him for many lives to come. And I would miss him. There is also no guarantee our paths would cross again . . .

I start imagining what might have happened outside the museum after we sped away in Echo's car. The three people who were chasing us must work for Rebus, a man who holds a serious grudge against me, so much so that he killed my child and even sent one of his "soldiers" to condemn my soul and end my story forever.

Rebus has executed Tammuz once before. Maybe he'd like to make it permanent this time? I'm feeling the abject horror of that thought when something incredible happens: the cigarette lighter, seemingly of its own accord, shuffles along the table by half an inch. At first, it was just a sound—the skid of metal against wood—but then I caught movement in the corner of my eye. Knowing this must be my subconscious mind at work, I fix my gaze on the lighter and beckon it toward me. This time, the tactic works, and the Zippo falls to the floor. Before long, it's within reach of my foot. Seconds later, I'm holding it in my hands. I try my best to be careful, but it's a very awkward procedure, and burning myself is inevitable, although it's a small price to pay for freedom.

As soon as the last piece of cord gives way, I jump to my feet.

The first thing I do is turn on the lights, hurrying over to the open-plan kitchen now, thrusting my hands into the freezer and leaving them there until numbness sets in. After checking the time—2:33 a.m., Monday, October 14—I find the toilet, sighing with relief as I empty my bladder, spotting an Airbnb sticker on the back of the door. Returning to the kitchen, I drink two glasses of water and raid the fridge for food, feeling significantly better now, ready to engage with the images and notes covering the far wall, the one Pythia gestured toward when I asked about Ashkai and Tammuz.

This is what I can see: right at the top are two black and white photographs side by side. Both were taken from an elevated position with a telephoto lens, which means the subjects were oblivious to what was going on. I turn to the camera on a tripod over by the middle window, thinking Meta must have rented this apartment because of its proximity to her enemies. I turn to the wall again, looking at Rebus getting out of a car. Kaya talking on her cell is to the right of him.

Below those two images is a large schematic of a huge building with six floors, two of which are underground. Using a pencil, somebody has added the cross streets, which is when I realize the architecture takes up an entire block in New York's East Village. Avenues B and C run south to north, with Third and Fourth streets going east to west.

The address matches the one I looked up for COSMOS, the multinational technology company that is obviously connected to Rebus in some way.

I lean forward and study the schematic inch by inch, looking for clues and reading the numerous annotations that have been added. After about a minute, I spot "House of Fishes" on the first floor, perfectly centered. "House of Phoenix" is directly above, on the top floor. I follow the line down and there it is: "House of Lotus Flower" on the bottom floor, which is underground. Beneath that, so below the building and outside its confines, there's another word. "Prison."

I don't have it with me now, but Cato owned a black card with two phrases on it: "East Village" and "House of Phoenix." Did the card give him access to this building? And if so, could this place be some sort of headquarters for the nation of Flooders? Is that why they were able to find us so easily in the late 1990s? Did we fly right into the hornet's nest? It seems strange that Ashkai wouldn't have been aware of this place.

I continue scanning, looking at offices, toilets, corridors, tech rooms, kitchen areas, canteens, and air vents . . . eventually, I see something that catches my eye: one of the fire escapes on Avenue B has been circled. There's a date and time next to it: 3:00 a.m., Monday, October 14.

I look at my watch.

I've got eight minutes to get there.

THIRTY-THREE

It's pouring rain, and the blustering wind has an icy bite to it. The streets of East Village are deserted and have a threatening, foreboding feel to them. For a moment, I wonder if I've been transported into one of my future lives—the world a broken and lifeless place—but then a passing taxi throws a puddle over my shins, and the spell is broken.

The apartment is only one block from my destination. I guess that's why they rented it. By the time I'm standing a few doors down from the fire exit on Avenue B, taking shelter under an awning, I'm soaked through.

I check my watch: 2:58 a.m.

On the way here, while crossing Avenue C on Third Street, I walked past one of the many entrances to this behemoth of a building. The logo on display was as expected, COSMOS written in white against an illuminated, starry background.

The photograph of Rebus I found in Kaya's shoebox was taken here. One way or another, he is going to pay for everything he has done: killing my child, snatching Ashkai and Tammuz, and attempting to sacrifice my soul. I have never hated a person so intensely, and the feeling is intoxicating, almost enjoyable . . .

Before I left the apartment, I hurried around, looking for the gun I took from Cato, but I couldn't find it anywhere. The weapons that had been on the table by the front door were also gone. Improvising, I grabbed a knife from the kitchen, but the truth is I'm not sure I'll need it. Revenge courses through my veins as I surrender to the awesome power of hate.

In the past, I would have berated myself for having such feelings and thoughts. Ashkai always preached love and compassion, but his character and motives are now under review. I want to ask a few questions before totally writing him off, but until then, I am my own master.

I check my watch again: it's exactly 3:00 a.m. When I look up, a black BMW pulls in, its front end pointing away from me. I duck behind a wall for cover, seeing four people get out now—Echo, Meta, Bythos, and Neith—but nobody from the driver's side. The fire exit door cracks open. Somebody is letting them in. I wait before making my move. The tall, nerdy one is the last person to enter, so I shove him forward, slamming the door behind me.

We are all gathered in an unusually clean and modern stairwell. The only light is coming from two narrow rows of small LEDs on the floor. Everything feels sleek and high-tech.

The others look ready to attack, but when they see who it is, their expressions go from tense to shocked and confused. Only Meta seems unsurprised.

"Hello, Samsara," she says. "Pythia mentioned you might be joining us."

Before I can respond, the woman who opened the door—white, north of forty, with long hair that's been dyed red—looks at my face, her eyes homing in on my left cheek, and mutters, "The mark of fire . . ."

Bythos, who has pulled a flashlight from somewhere, speaks next. "You okay with this, boss?"

Meta nods, and Echo shrugs as if he doesn't care either way. The nerdy one, who looks afraid, says, "Can we just get this over and done with?"

Talking to the redhead, Meta says, "We can take it from here." She gestures toward the fire exit. "Thank you for your service."

The lady, who can't take her eyes off me, puts her hands together and bows before disappearing into the cold, wet night.

My kidnappers, whom I have willingly followed, are wearing dark clothes complete with tactical vests, looking like some sort of SWAT team, guns at their hips.

Addressing Meta, I say, "What's going on?"

Replying on her behalf, Neith says, "We're about to do something very stupid."

"This way," Bythos says, heading down the stairs.

Echo, also carrying a flashlight, follows. So does Neith, but he seems a little reluctant.

It's just Meta and me now. For thousands of years, I have regarded this woman as my sworn enemy. Now we are working together. The situation is so ridiculous it's almost funny.

Meta, in this life at least, is the same age as Rosa, but it's obvious she's been through many more cycles than I have. I can see it in her eyes and feel it in her presence. There's something about her that reminds me of Ashkai, although I have no idea who he is anymore, so I'm not sure what that means.

"What's down there?" I ask.

"People who need our help."

"Ashkai and Tammuz?"

"You ask a lot of questions."

"Can you blame me?"

We go down two flights, stopping outside a huge, locked metal door. There's an electronic pad on the wall. The nerdy one is attaching wires to it and typing something into a small portable laptop that he was carrying in a backpack.

Echo is providing light while Bythos stands with his gun pointed at the door. Bythos, who is all man, says, "What's taking so long?"

Neith looks over a shoulder. "You're kidding, right? We just got here."

"Leave him alone," Echo says.

"Since when did I take orders from you?"

"Enough," Meta says, and they both apologize, Echo even referring to her as "master."

For the next minute or so, Neith is the only person who speaks, muttering incomprehensibly. I'm left wondering why we're going to all this trouble.

"If you really are Meta," I say, "and have been alive since the long ago, why don't you just use your mind to tear that door off its hinges?"

Without looking at me, she says, "I'm saving my energy for something else."

"And besides," Neith says, turning his head, "she's got me."

While maintaining eye contact, he presses a button on his computer. Almost instantly, there's a sound of pressure being released, and the huge metal door slides left, disappearing into the wall.

More stairs greet us, much narrower and steeper. It's dark in there (no more LED lights), and we can hear machinery and electronics, sounds that remind me of a hospital.

Bythos, who is taking the lead, has positioned his flashlight directly above his handgun. He looks like he knows what he's doing when it comes to covert operations. The same can't be said for Neith, who is just behind Echo. A moment ago he seemed fine, but now he's nervous again.

Looking over my shoulder, Meta says, "Neith, your work is done. You can go."

He turns and shakes his head. "It's okay. I can do this."

The stairs go down a long way, and I can sense we're in a very large space, like a warehouse or airport hanger.

Bythos, focused and tough, pauses to scan the area below with his flashlight. Echo, cool and relaxed as usual, like this is no big deal, does the same thing.

"What was that?" I say, talking to Bythos, pointing so he knows where to look. He aims his flashlight, and it finds something strange and disconcerting, downright frightening for Neith.

We're looking at the top of a naked woman's head. She's upright but not because she is standing. Or conscious. Instead, she's suspended inside some sort of mechanical glass capsule that has been filled with a light green, gelatinous liquid. There is more than one capsule and captive . . . a lot more . . .

After a beat, Meta says, "Keep moving."

"What is this place?" I whisper, but I think I know the answer. It's a prison, one populated by souls who have been sentenced to the Long Sleep. Ashkai, who is down there somewhere, has been an inmate for almost twenty years.

Bythos gets to the bottom first. It's clear we are deep underground. Echo is next, followed by Neith. Then it's finally Meta and me. We turn left and fan out, walking down a wide corridor, our flashlights revealing row upon row of vertical glass capsules on either side of us, each one holding a human being: men, women and children, arms by their sides, palms facing outward, skin tinged green by the strange, viscous liquid. The containers, which are making whirring sounds, are obviously designed to keep occupants alive, but only barely . . .

"There are thousands of them," I say.

"Tell me about it," Bythos says, his voice dripping with disgust and anger.

"And this is just one facility of many."

"Who are these people?" I ask. "What did they do wrong?"

"They got caught," Echo says.

"By whom?"

Neith, who's nervous as hell, speaks next. "The one person who deserves to be inside one of those things: Rebus."

"What gives him the right?" I say, raising my voice. Before anybody can respond, floodlights start coming on. It's such a stark contrast that I'm forced to shield my eyes. When they have adjusted, I look up at the distant ceiling and then at the two balconies on either side of us, each one filled with agents armed with guns.

"Mother Earth gives me the right," a booming voice says. "You see, I honor ancient and natural laws your friends have long since abandoned."

Bythos is up on his toes, looking left, right, and behind. "That bitch double- crossed us," he says. He must be referring to the woman with red hair who let us into the building.

Still exuding peace and calm, Meta says, "Everything is at it should be," which is exactly the type of thing Ashkai would say.

Neith, who's gone pale, looks petrified.

"There's no way out," he says, putting a gun to his head, addressing Meta. "I can't end up in one of those things."

He pulls the trigger. The sound is deafening, his body slumping to the floor in a sad, blood-splattered heap. While horrifying, there's no time to have any feelings about it.

I look again at the balconies, counting roughly forty agents in total. The guns they are holding shoot tranquilizer darts instead of bullets, which means Rebus wants to put us to sleep. For a very long time.

"Old friend," Meta says, "must you skulk in the shadows?"

About twenty capsules down on the left, Rebus steps out, but he's not alone. Kaya is with him, her dark, curly hair hanging freely.

I lean to my right, whispering into Echo's ear. "Who is that woman?"

"She's the whole reason we're in this mess."

"What do you mean?" I ask.

Rebus, his eyes on Meta, says, "Last time we saw each other"— he points at Neith's dead body—"you did that."

I prod Echo to continue. "She's one of the seven oracles." He gestures toward the glass capsules. "Five of them are locked up in here somewhere."

I do a quick sum in my head. "What about the seventh?"

"She's in the car outside."

I think for a moment. "Pythia?"

Echo nods. My head explodes into a million thoughts and questions, but they'll all have to wait.

Meta says, "That was then; this is now."

Rebus smiles and turns his gaze on me. "Hello, Samsara."

I stare at him, my eyes beaming hate.

Rebus points toward Meta. "Your friends did a very good job of keeping you hidden." A pause and then: "Do you know what's going on yet?"

"I know you're a psychopath who likes to kill innocent children."

"That was unfortunate," he says. "But that child was not innocent."

Meta interjects, "How do you know? You never gave him a chance."

Hearing someone refer to my baby as a real person—"him"—is enough to make me want to follow in Neith's footsteps, although of course I don't. Instead, I use the sadness as fuel for my hate.

Rebus loses his temper. "I'm not interested in your self-righteous, delusional fictions. I've had enough of those to last me a thousand more lifetimes. The child had to be eliminated, as did everyone else in that cave. You were the one who should have taken responsibility, but you didn't. I had no choice."

"And what about Ashkai? You two were like brothers. Did you have a choice with him?

260

For a brief moment, I see anguish in Rebus's eyes, regret as well, but neither emotion lasts long.

"He wouldn't listen. We consulted the oracles again and again. They all showed us the same future."

"Nothing is certain, not even the prophecies."

"The stakes were too high to take any chances."

"In your opinion."

He nods. "Right now, that's the only one that counts."

I have no idea what they are talking about, and the truth is I don't care.

"I came here to get my friend," I say, remembering Pythia's warning. "Where is he?"

"Which one?" Rebus asks.

"Tammuz."

Rebus looks at me quizzically. "He's more important than your master?"

"I don't have a master."

Rebus nods as if to say, "I'm impressed," and turns to his right, motioning to somebody out of view. Tammuz is shoved from behind one of the glass capsules.

He tries to run, but Rebus, who must be six foot four, reaches out an arm and grabs him.

"Your life for his," Rebus says. He has a gun now and is aiming it at Tammuz's head.

"What does that mean?"

"Give yourself up, or he dies a slow and painful death. One that will haunt him for eons."

I glance at the two balconies. "I'm supposed to believe you'll let him go if I do that?"

"Yes."

"Why?"

"Because he's of no value to me."

"What about the others?"

Rebus looks at Meta, Echo, and Bythos. "They can take care of themselves."

"What if I say no?"

"Then he dies, and we take you anyway."

"Don't listen to him, Samsara," Meta says. "It's a trap."

Rebus starts counting down from ten.

. . . Nine . . . eight . . . seven . . .

"It's okay," Tammuz says, trying to hide his fear from me. "I'm okay."

Six.

I go to step forward, but Meta grabs my arm. "Don't do it, Samsara. We can beat him."

Five.

I turn to her. "I can't let his life end like this."

Four.

"He will be reborn."

Three.

"But the experience will damage him for many lives to come."

Two.

"Enough," I say, stepping forward, grasping the knife in my pocket, walking slowly. "I'm coming."

Meta raises her voice, and for the first time, I sense fear in it. "He doesn't want you, Samsara . . ."

Pause. "He wants your child."

Without stopping, I look over a shoulder. "We can't change the past."

"I'm not talking about then. I'm talking about now. You're pregnant."

I stop in my tracks, utterly thrown and confused, especially as the words, quite unexpectedly, ring true. "What are you talking about?"

One.

I turn away from Meta just as a gun goes off.

I'm expecting to see Tammuz with his brains blown out, but it's Rebus who has taken a bullet to his right shoulder. I turn to look at Bythos. He was the one who fired the shot. He was the one who saved my friend's life.

Seizing the opportunity, Tammuz elbows Rebus in the stomach and sprints to his left, disappearing into the forest of glass capsules.

I look at the men and women occupying the two balconies, but it's too late because their tranquilizer guns have been discharged.

Strangely, I don't seem to care. For so many lives, going back as far as I can remember, I have been infertile. After witnessing what happened in that cave, an ordeal I have tried my hardest to forget, I understand why. But now, if Meta is right, the curse has been lifted.

My first thought was that she had to be mistaken. Then I felt something in my lower stomach, a spark of life, and remembered how Tammuz and I had sex after I killed Sergei in Viktor's home. It was pure animal instinct. A higher force was guiding me then. I can feel its presence now.

Right on cue, a gravelly, male voice whispers in my ear: "Your potential is limitless, Samsara. Never forget that."

I don't turn to see who it is because nobody will be there. I recall the many times this sinister, dark energy has spoken to me in the past. In the beginning, communication only took place in my dreams (via what I perceived to be an imposter), but things have come a long way since then. When I have been at my most vulnerable, as I was in Kaya's basement, this entity has given me the strength—*and fire!*—I needed to survive. And it's a power that has never left me.

I become aware of an ominous sound—the whoosh of tranquilizer darts—and brace myself.

If only I had more time, I think, just as Meta, Bythos, and Echo crowd around me, the three of them clasping hands above my head.

At first, I think they are sacrificing themselves. But no, they are working together to create a protective force field made of pure energy, one that has bought me precious seconds.

"What shall I do?" I shout, speaking to the darkness within.

"You must embrace your true nature."

"How?"

"By turning away from the light."

As well as speaking, the entity is placing images in my mind, compelling me to remember each and every kind of suffering I have had to endure across my many lives: the times I have been abandoned and betrayed, lied to and manipulated, raped and murdered.

My heart is burning like an inferno. If I don't let out some of the heat, I'll be consumed by it.

Harnessing the limitless power within, I stand and scream at the top of my lungs, unleashing a tsunami of hate, anger, and bitterness, emotions that have built up inside me over thousands of years.

Meta, Bythos and Echo are launched into the air spectacularly. It's as if they had been standing on landmines. A small part of me hopes they are okay but not enough to really care. In fact, they are already forgotten as I turn my attention toward the agents on the left balcony.

But what is this?

Instead of seeing people, instead of seeing the familiar *(and solid!)* components of the material world, I'm confronted by a complex and intricate grid of pure, glowing energy. Not only that, I know how to bend it to my will. It's simply a matter of using my imagination. Guided by instinct, I get to work on eradicating anything that stands in my way, crushing hearts, breaking necks, spreading fire, even sucking souls out of bodies and hurling them into other dimensions. Until now, I thought there were just two planes of existence: spirit and material. But it seems the truth is much more nuanced than that.

How naïve I have been!

"Very good, my child," says the voice. It feels wonderful to please him, and I project chaos and pain toward the right balcony, showing absolutely no mercy as I kill, burn, and maim. Some of the capsules are also exploding, sending shards of glass through the air like razor blades, spilling green, syrupy liquid onto the floor, turning it into an ice rink.

The air smells of blood, charred flesh, and urine, but instead of feeling sick or mournful, I feel stronger and more resolved.

I can see the world normally now. Rebus is standing straight ahead, terror in his eyes. Kaya has disappeared. I reach an imaginary hand out to grab him, but out of nowhere, more of his soldiers appear, a group of them running toward me, firing their guns. I brush the darts away as if they are matchsticks, unleashing hell and murder as I go, hearing bones break and men scream and lives end.

It feels good to kill.

It feels right.

I step through the heap of bodies toward where Rebus had been standing, but he is no longer there.

The people who are yet to die at my hands are disappearing into doors and tunnels I hadn't noticed until now. I have to assume Rebus is one of them. Either that or he is hiding. Just in case, I begin to weave between the rows of broken capsules like a deadly predator certain of the kill (taking care not to slip). While doing so, I edge past prisoners of the Long Sleep who have fallen to the ground, their bodies glistening from the liquid they had been suspended in. Some are even starting to emerge from their slumbers by vomiting green mucous onto the floor. They look like they have no idea who or what they are.

I feel a hand on my shoulder and I turn, pulling the knife out of my pocket, ready to plunge it into Rebus's heart when . . .

Is it really you? I think, all of that hate and anger dissolving in an instant, feelings of tenderness and hope poking through like flowers in the cracks of pavements.

Being propped up on either side by Echo and Bythos is my master. He looks like a slimy, green goblin, malnourished, frail, and barely clinging to life.

"Little owl," he says, his voice raspy and thin. "You kept your promise."

THIRTY-FOUR

I exit the cafe and walk over to Tammuz, who's waiting for me on a bench opposite some swings underneath a maple tree. The autumn breeze whispers through leaves of crimson and gold.

As I'm sitting, bracing myself against the cold, bright day, wafts of coffee and honey-roasted nuts sweetening the air, Tammuz says, "And?" He's nervous and fidgety.

"It takes a couple minutes," I say, holding the pregnancy test in front of me.

He leans over to stare at the little screen.

I'm trying to be calm, but on the inside, I'm going crazy. A positive result would be a miracle—after all, I've been infertile for at least four thousand years—but I'm not sure it's what I want. For a start, there's all of that responsibility, not to mention the fact there's a guy out there who wants this child *(if there is one!)* dead.

Pythia, who is deaf, mute, and blind, was driving the car that dropped everyone outside the fire exit last night. After the battle with Rebus, she was waiting to take Meta, Tammuz, Ashkai, and me back to the apartment. I don't know how she was able to do it—let alone infiltrate my subconscious while I was tied up—but then again, nothing makes sense at the moment.

Echo and Bythos stayed behind to deal with the prisoners who had awakened from their Long Sleep. I imagine they'll be there for a while.

A lot of our enemies died last night, but both Kaya and Rebus managed to escape. As soon as we got back to the warehouse apartment, I wanted to speak to Ashkai, but Meta wouldn't let me, saying he needed to rest. Meanwhile, Tammuz was on my case. He wanted to know if I was really pregnant and if so, who the father was. That's how we ended up sitting in this park staring at a pregnancy test, the two of us nervous as hell.

"Maybe it's broken," Tammuz says. "Have you got another

one?" and right on cue, the result appears. There's just one word: PREGNANT.

I'm overwhelmed by the most incredible feelings of joy and happiness mixed with fear, shock, and trepidation. I open my mouth to speak, but nothing comes out.

"Shit," Tammuz mutters. "You sure it's mine?"

"It has to be. You're the only person I've slept with in the last year."

"What are the chances?"

"Don't worry," I say, placing a hand on his lap. "This is my responsibility. Nothing has to change for you."

Tammuz looks at me as if I'm crazy. "What are you talking about? It's my baby as much as yours. We're in this together."

I remove my hand. "I don't want you to feel trapped."

Staring off into space, he says, "I don't know how I feel, to be honest. It's just a lot to take in."

"You're afraid, aren't you?"

He looks at me. "Petrified."

"That makes two of us."

"What if I let the kid down?" Tammuz says.

I reach out to touch him again. "You're not your father."

His eyes fill with tears. He says, "Let's hope not." Then he says, "There's something you should know."

"That sounds ominous."

"I've got a . . . condition . . ."

"Are you sick?" I ask, remembering the pills he tried to hide when we first met and then again when we were having breakfast on Venice Beach.

"Sick in the head," Tammuz says. "I'm schizophrenic, and I have it pretty bad. What if the kid gets it as well?"

"What do you mean pretty bad?"

"I hear voices. They tell me to do stuff. I was hoping ayahuasca would cure me, but if anything, things have been getting worse . . ."

I turn, bringing my right leg up onto the bench so that I'm looking straight at him, everything starting to fall into place. "When we were with Cato in the office at the meditation studio, you heard a voice, didn't you?"

Tammuz nods.

"What did it say?"

Tammuz looks at the floor as if he's embarrassed. "It told me to hurt him." He's looking back at me now. "I'm not crazy, though, I swear. I've never hurt anybody, and I never will. I take medication. It's under control."

I lean forward and give him a kiss. "I don't think you're crazy." Smiling, I add, "Not so long ago, people who could hear voices were celebrated and honored. It meant the person was very spiritual and connected to the other side. Trust me, that is nothing to be ashamed of."

"Are you saying the voices are real?"

I nod. "Problem is, negative entities often attach themselves to gifted people such as you. But there are ways to get rid of them."

"Thank god for that," he says. "Cos there's this one guy who's a real dick."

It gets me thinking about my own predicament, worrying we're being targeted by the same destructive energy. It's a being that has helped me many times now, but I'm under no illusions about what it is. My actions last night were fueled by pure hate. It was an incredible, all-consuming power, but enough is enough. I'm a good soul, and I won't be manipulated anymore.

"Has he said anything about me?"

Tammuz nods.

"Tell me everything."

"When I first saw you in Exeter, he was whispering in my ear, telling me how important you were and how I couldn't let you out of my sight."

"Did he say why?"

"No, but after that, he wouldn't shut up about you no matter how many pills I took. It gets weirder as well."

"Don't worry; nothing surprises me anymore."

Tammuz nods. "Tell me about it. He kept saying I had to have sex with you . . . that we were meant to be together. It's almost as if"—Tammuz points toward the pregnancy test on the bench—"he knew this was going to happen."

I hear laughter and look toward it. A woman is picking a little boy up and putting him on one of the swings. For some reason, it makes me cry.

Tammuz reaches out a hand. "What's wrong? What did I say?"

"Nothing," I reply, standing.

Not for the first time, I feel like a pawn in a game of chess. Something is going on, something bigger than me, and I need to find out what it is.

"Where you going?" Tammuz asks.

"To see Ashkai."

"But he's resting."

I look at the little boy on the swing again, my gaze lingering. "He's been sleeping for twenty years. It's time he woke up."

THIRTY-FIVE

I march into the apartment and head straight for the bedroom.

Meta, who has just come out of there, positions herself in front of the door and raises a hand.

"Not now, Samsara."

There is fire in my eyes. "Move."

Meta looks me up and down. Maybe she's trying to figure out if I'm going to have another one of my meltdowns.

"Okay," she says, stepping aside. "Just go easy on him."

I walk into the bedroom and close the door.

Ashkai is awake and sitting up. Because he has been washed and fed, he looks considerably better than he did last night. Even so, his dark skin is dry and cracked, and his afro hair, which hasn't been cut for twenty years, is thick and matted.

There's a scented candle burning on the bedside table, and the darkened room smells of chocolate and vanilla.

"Little owl," he says, flashing a knowing, kind smile. "I imagine you have some questions."

Ashkai was twenty-one when he was captured and is technically forty now. Even so, and it must be because he's been in a deep coma for all that time, he's only aged seven or eight years, on the outside at least. He's skinny, though, and frail. I feel like I could snap him in half.

I lean forward and kiss him on the forehead. I'm not angry anymore; how could I be? Ashkai has shown me so much kindness, given me so much love, that all I want to do is throw my arms around him. But I resist the urge. Things have changed, and I have a feeling they will never be the same again.

"It's good to see you," I say, suppressing my instinct to be physically affectionate. "More than good."

He raises an eyebrow. "Is that so?"

"Of course."

"I can sense you are upset."

"You lied to me."

"That is true."

"Why?"

He pats the bed.

Sitting next to him, I ask, "What's going on, Master?"

Ashkai smiles. "When are you going to stop calling me that?"

"That depends."

"On what?"

"How this conversation goes."

"I see you haven't lost any of your fire," he says. Then he adds, "I will do my best to answer your questions."

"You better," I say. "Let's start with a simple one: who am I?"

Another smile. "A very special person."

"You need to do better than that."

He starts coughing. There's water on the bedside table, so I help him drink.

"Thank you," he says, taking a moment to catch his breath. "Do you recall what I told you at the museum here in New York? It was a few days before they found us."

I nod, remembering the flashback I had while standing in front of those skeletons. "Yesterday, when I was there, it came back to me."

"So you know that Earth is the last habitable refuge in the universe, as far as we know?"

"How can that be?" I ask. With everything else that's been happening, I haven't had a chance to consider this issue at all. "What about the other six planets?"

"They were destroyed."

"By what?"

"Fear, negativity, suspicion, and hate."

"You mean the Demiurge?"

Ashkai nods. "Our enemy grows more powerful and toxic with every day that passes, smothering all expressions of love and light, which, of course, strengthens it further."

"That's horrible and tragic," I say, doing my best to stay focused on the questions I want answered. "And I'll do anything I can to

271

help, but what has it got to do with me?"

"Before each of the planets fell, a child was born, a child who was said to be the physical manifestation of pure evil."

My hand goes to my stomach. Nausea washes over me.

Ashkai stares at me, his entire being emanating love and compassion but also regret.

"If certain prophecies are to be believed, your child will play a key role in bringing about the apocalypse here on Earth."

"What prophecies?"

"Many thousands of years ago, the seven oracles were consulted. They all had the same prognostication."

"What did they see?"

"They saw a girl, her face burning with a dark fire."

My hand goes to the birthmark on my cheek.

"It was foreseen that she would conceive a child of great power and that the child would be born when the sky serpent returned to the planet of blood and fire."

I think for a moment. "Mars?"

"A great civilization once flourished there, but unfortunately, over time, the Demiurge was able to exert its poisonous influence, corrupting everyone and everything. War ensued on an unprecedented scale and raged for hundreds of years."

"So the people destroyed themselves?"

"In a way, yes, but not exactly; a comet the size of Manhattan struck the planet, after which nothing could survive, but people were too preoccupied with their own fear and hate to see it coming, let alone do anything about it."

"I still don't understand what any of this has to do with me."

"As is often the case with prophecies, there was some confusion about how to interpret it. You see the comet—or sky serpent— that wiped out all life on Mars was just one fragment in a stream of millions, a stream that passes through Mars's orbit every 4320 years. Sometimes there is a collision; sometimes there isn't. As a result, we knew what was going to happen; we just didn't know when."

"So what did you do?" I ask, noting the reoccurrence of *that* number.

"First we had to find the girl. It took a very long time, but that investigation led to you."

I touch my cheek again. "Because of this mark on my face? Is that what you're basing everything on?"

"No, there is something else."

"What?"

"Your soul."

"What about it?"

"It's unique."

"How?"

"In our purest form, each of us is a single flame of consciousness, one that has broken off from the great fire of all creation. But you are different."

"In what way?"

"You carry two flames. One of them is dark."

"That means I'm evil?"

Ashkai shakes his head. "That means you are different."

"Different enough that you wanted to kill my baby. I remember what happened in that cave. I know what you did."

"I'm so sorry, Samsara," Ashkai says. He's on the verge of tears. "I wanted to take you and your child alive, but Rebus felt he had no choice."

"What do you mean?"

"At that time you were being held by The Shadow. As you know, they work for and serve the Demiurge. If Solar and I had been killed, your child would have been raised by them."

"It doesn't make it right," I say, processing this new and disturbing information, remembering the evil I felt in that cave. "Murder is murder."

Ashkai lowers his head. "After that unfortunate incident, the Chamber of Infinites fell apart for a while."

"Because of what Rebus did?"

He looks into my eyes. "Yes, and because others with influence agreed with him."

"What did you want to do?"

"I wanted to meet the problem with love. As did Meta, but our people were afraid. We only had one planet left. If it was destroyed . . . well, nobody knew what that meant."

"I take it you lost the argument?"

"You could say that," Ashkai replies. "I was exiled."

"What did you do next?"

"I found you and kept you hidden."

"Why?"

"Meeting hate with hate can only lead to more hate. History has proven that."

Ashkai pauses to cough, then says, "Meta pretended to change her mind and agreed with Rebus. Because she had friends with power and influence, he had little choice but to let her keep a seat in the Chamber."

"I thought she was the leader of it?"

"She was, but Rebus declared a state of emergency. The Chamber voted, choosing him to carry the fight forward instead. Besides, leadership is traditionally rotated between Chamber elders, although it hasn't been for a very long time."

"Why didn't you just tell me? You didn't have to lie all these years."

"Can you imagine how you would have felt knowing this? That you would give birth to a child who had the potential to destroy all life forever?"

As much as it pains me to admit it, his argument is undeniable. That knowledge would have crushed me.

"Fine, but why didn't you tell me Meta was on our side? I thought she was the enemy."

"By treating her as the enemy, we strengthened her position in the Chamber. The less you knew, the better."

"If Rebus was such a threat," I ask, "why did we meet with him in Amsterdam?"

"Rebus and I were once like brothers. When the time was right, I reached out, and he agreed to a brief truce. I hoped my old friend would come to his senses once he'd met you."

"But he didn't?"

"Unfortunately not."

"Do you know why?"

"There is one oracle he trusts above all others. Her visions about the apocalypse have never changed."

"Kaya?"

"Yes."

"What if she's right?"

"Then the future of this planet is doomed. And so are we."

I can't think about that. I ask, "How does Tammuz fit into all this?"

"When a soul is created, it splits into two parts: male and female. You and he are one and the same."

"Wow," I say, staring off into the distance. I'm totally blown away and overwhelmed. So much so that I'm finding this revelation—one I know in my heart to be true—difficult to process.

"Does he have the dark fire as well?" I ask, trying my best to refocus.

"He does."

While I'm keen to investigate the subject of Tammuz in more detail, there's something else demanding my attention. "Why haven't I been able to get pregnant until now?"

"I'm not sure. I assume it has something to do with what happened in that cave. You were emotionally scarred on a very deep level."

The questions just keep coming. "What about New York? Why didn't Meta warn you about Rebus?"

Ashkai takes a deep breath. "It was meant to happen, so it happened."

There's something about the way he said it, something that makes me think . . .

"You knew he was coming, didn't you?"

Instead of answering my question, Ashkai says, "Do you remember who Pythia is?"

I nod. "She's the street urchin you took under your wing in Egypt but also one of the seven oracles."

Ashkai raises a finger. "She was and is the most gifted of them all. As the years and lives rolled by, I continued to consult her. The more love I gave you, the more her visions changed until eventually, the future became uncertain. The apocalypse was no longer a foregone conclusion."

275

"That doesn't explain why you were captured."

"You needed to be set free. You needed to feel as if you were alone. You needed something to fight for in order to evolve and grow."

I shake my head in disbelief. "So you just let Rebus take you?"

Ashkai reaches a hand out to touch mine. "It wasn't supposed to go that far."

"What do you mean?"

"Meta was there to usher me into the next life."

"But she failed," I say, remembering how hard she tried to kill him before turning the gun on herself.

"She did her best," Ashkai says. "I have answered your questions, little owl; now it's my turn. The Demiurge has been waiting for an opportunity to pounce. Its goal is to turn you away from the better side of yourself." He pauses to look at me in a deep and penetrating way. "Has it succeeded?"

I think for a moment.

"All I know for sure is this: a dark, malevolent energy has been lurking in the shadows of my heart for as long as I can remember. Since you were captured, it has kept me alive and become a more powerful presence. I don't think it has succeeded in turning me, but if it had, would I tell you? I mean, what if it has been using us all, even Pythia? What if this child is still destined to destroy everything?"

"It's a chance I'm willing to take."

"Why?"

"Because it's the right thing to do."

"Rebus is still out there. He's going to come after me, isn't he?"

"Yes, but I have not given up on him. He has just lost his way. I can bring him back."

The mere mention of *that* man awakens something deep inside of me, an instinct to protect . . .

"Are you sure about that?" I say, removing my hand from his.

The voice speaks to me then. It's as if an invisible man is standing to my left, whispering into my ear.

"You must protect our progeny."

I get a rush of blood and stand, turning toward the sound,

feeling the presence of a deep and ancient darkness. "Leave me alone," I shout. "Or my next stop is an abortion clinic."

There's a ripple of movement in the air, the blur of a predator striking.

Something grips my throat, and I am raised from the ground, choking now. I try to fight, but all I'm able to grasp is thin air. The voice says, "You belong to me. You always have. You always will."

It's as if my soul is being siphoned out of me.

Ashkai is on the bed behind me. He says, "Resist, Samsara. You are stronger than you realize."

Meta bursts into the room. Her indigo eyes lock on mine. She raises a hand, and a white, blinding light burns through the air. The grip on my throat releases, and I fall to the ground.

Meta crouches beside me. "What happened?" she asks, lifting my limp and dizzy head.

I gasp for air and try to sit up, but my energy has been completely drained.

Ashkai speaks next. He has clambered out of bed, weak, frail, and unsteady on his feet.

"It's okay, Samsara. Together we can beat this. You have to believe that."

I touch my stomach, worried something might have happened, relieved because I can still feel a spark of life inside of me.

"I hope you're right," I say, readying myself for the battle ahead, promising my unborn child I will do my best.

But will it be enough?

THE END

ABOUT THE AUTHOR

Sean Hancock was born in1977 in Oxford, England. He lived in London and Kenya before his family settled in Devon where Sean spent his formative years. His mother is from Somalia, East Africa, and his father is English.

In 2010, after a decade working as a freelancer in television, Sean joined the BBC as a commissioning editor in entertainment. Among other notable shows, and during his four years with the corporation, Sean commissioned and executive produced *The Revolution Will Be Televised*, which won the BAFTA for Best Comedy Programme in 2013.

In 2011, Sean released a coming-of-age novel, *Trick*. The book was shortlisted for the Crime Writers' Association Debut Dagger Award. It was also a Top-20 Kindle bestseller in the United Kingdom.

The Flooding marks a change of genre for Sean, who now resides in Los Angeles with his wife Simone.